Private Lives of Private School Moms

A NOVEL

Julie Heath

authorHOUSE®

AuthorHouse™
1663 Liberty Drive
Bloomington, IN 47403
www.authorhouse.com
Phone: 1-800-839-8640

First published by AuthorHouse 8/17/2009

ISBN: 978-1-4389-9431-4 (e)
ISBN: 978-1-4389-9430-7 (sc)

Printed in the United States of America
Bloomington, Indiana

This book is printed on acid-free paper.

A portion of the proceeds from the sale of this novel
will be donated to the Arthritis Foundation.

Private Lives of Private School Moms
By Julie Heath

To my family and my son Sam, I am thankful for
your perpetual
encouragement and support.

To my friends who inspired and guided me over
the years, I'm blessed to
know each of you.

To my soul mate, I'm glad we found each other.

To my amazing sister. I miss you.

"Tell me your friends and I'll tell you who you are."
Assyrian proverb

Table of Contents

Prologue:
The First Day of School, Observations from Vic the Maintenance Guy

"I've got my feet in two worlds here at the Archimedes School. I'm a parent of a kid who goes here, and I work in the maintenance department to keep this place ship shape. There are moments I get pretty sick of being treated like shit by some of these overly entitled parents—I'm just as much a parent at this school as they are, but being one of the many parents who work here, especially since I wear blue overalls and construction boots, I'm just a lower life-form to many of these moms. Most of 'em treat me like I'm invisible. On the other hand, *Thank God* I'm not playing their games! If their husbands heard one-tenth of what I hear everyday. In the eleven years I've been here I've overheard hundreds of stories, stuff you think only exists in movies and books. There's wife swapping parties, women who discretely take their "boy toys" with them on $20,000 dollar shopping excursions to New York, and pre-nups that dictate the frequency and type of sexual acts required weekly—these are especially popular with mega rich seventy year olds who marry beautiful young women. I knew about one stunning mom who had a long standing affair with an ancient English rock star—he had more wrinkles than a bull dog, but with all that money and fame, he was still a babe magnet. He'd fly her anywhere on his private jet. Her husband thought she was attending yoga retreats in Arizona, until he found her passport which had been stamped in twenty different countries. Of course, there's the normal stuff about moms having affairs with their ob-gyns or plastic surgeons, dads hitting on underage baby sitters, drug and food addictions where parents have to be discretely sent away, embezzlement, bribery, and in one case, jail time for a mom whose preferences for designer clothing exceeded the size of her wallet. Just another day in the life of the Archimedes School. I'm sure this stuff happens in all private schools. When I get home from work, I put my feet up, crack open a beer and have a good long laugh at the whole damn thing. A very good laugh, everyday. It's never boring for me, *the invisible man.*"

"I can never leave this job. Sure, the school's got its share of bitchy snobs, but there are also some good people here—both parents and staff. When my wife Jeanne died they kept me alive, kept me going. My kid's been here for eleven years now, surviving an education among the over-privileged. Rob's smart and has a much better shot at life with this kind of education at Archimedes, the whole accelerated math thing, maybe even the connections with these people. I could never work anywhere else and raise a son on my own. Nine years now since she's passed, Jeanne liked him being at this school, she would have wanted him here. The guys here kept me going, the good ones did; they gave me a reason to get out of bed when it happened. This place is family for my boy. I don't know how I would have gotten through everything without these people. It probably wouldn't have been my first choice, but now we're lifers at this place."

"No one would last more than a week in this job if it weren't for our maintenance supervisor. Everything we do must be cleared through him. Some of the moms here are so used to snapping their fingers and giving orders to their personal staff, they think they can do the same here at school. I remember a few of their demands from last year.

"Vic, I need you to scrub the carpet in my husband's Hummer—some kid got car sick during the fieldtrip" the surgeon's wife asked me. Shoot, she had enough money to buy the entire damn chain of *Squeaky Clean Car Wash* centers, why'd she need me?

One mom had the nerve to demand that I carry her across the campus one rainy day. "You there," she began, "I just bought these Gucci's and I refuse to ruin them by walking through that shitty wet grass." I just smiled in her direction and used sign language with my hands pretending I couldn't hear her. It worked. She ripped those shoes right off her feet and stormed across the campus barefoot. As an added benefit, half of the moms now think I'm hard of hearing and they avoid me like the plague. My favorite request was when one recently separated hot mom passed me a note asking, *"I have a little project for you at my house. Please come today at noon. I tip big."* I didn't go, but I was certainly tempted. The next day she passed me another note. *"Asshole"* was all it read. I had made an enemy, but at least I didn't cross any boundaries and lose my job."

"These moms don't seem to realize we have enough to do without their suggestions. Every morning our supervisor gives us our action items. We divide them up and get to work. Each of us usually has some sort of long term project –

right now, mine is to figure out why water is seeping into the basement below Mrs. Casper's Kindergarten classroom."

"There's a picnic table outside of the preschool building about fifteen feet from where I began digging on the first day of school this year. Everyday for the last few years, four moms sat and chatted at that table, regardless of the weather. Sometimes for just a few minutes, sometimes for hours, the same moms. These aren't the bad moms; they're actually pretty decent ladies. They don't ask a lot of us, and they have their little routine. Typically, they talk, they get up and walk around the neighborhood for half an hour or so, then they leave. An added benefit, each one of them is a babe. It seems more than a few guys—teachers included, are regularly making detours to walk by that picnic table each morning, "scoping out the MILFs," they say. *You know*, "Moms I'd like to fuck." Four women, as different as could be, yet each one a looker."

"One of them is Jodi McGarvey; my son Rob is all hot and bothered over her older daughter Ashlyn. I would be too if I was 15. Jodi's nice enough, but she can be a bit intense. Since I've known her for years I don't get intimidated by her, but on first impression most people think she's got Junior League written all over her—you know that preppy bitchy look. But the real Jodi is totally different, yes she's smart, confident and she always looks perfect—everything matches and looks fresh from the dry cleaners, if you know what I mean. She's not thin – she's got nice smooth full curves that she knows how to show off and still keep that "look but don't touch" veneer. She also has that whole nurse thing going—that's what she used to be a couple of years ago. She's super-knowledgeable about everything. But, sometimes she can be a real pain in the ass because she's a total takeover and control freak. I betcha if the

Archimedes School were attacked by armed gunmen, Jodi would and *could* disarm them without breaking a sweat. I once read about her delivering a baby in the produce section at Safeway, she even got featured on the local TV news. Cool as a cucumber she helped some lady pop out her third kid. Of course, she's always at school running one thing or another, she even subs for the nurse sometimes."

"Jodi sure does have her hands full with her older daughter Ashlyn. She's probably one of the smartest kids I've ever met; she won some big science award in Middle School. Ashlyn's also a hellion, drinking since Middle School, smoking pot in the school parking lot, putting moves on older guys, wearing next to nothing (unless her mother is at school). Jodi with her control freak, no nonsense style is trying to reel in Ashlyn, keep an eye on her and make sure she doesn't lose her virginity before the end of high school. It's my job to keep Rob and his strange brew of hormones arm's length away from Ashlyn.   Jodi quit her job at the hospital to do the same thing."

"Jodi also has a little preschool girl, too; Faith. I think she's in Kindergarten now—cute little thing and probably scary smart like everyone in that family.   Jodi's a good lady, very easy to talk to, not stuck up or anything. She's always there when you need her. It's funny; I don't think I've met her husband, though they've been at this school for twelve years. He's some kind of hotshot surgeon up at Hopkins."

"Charleigh Brooks is another one of these four hot moms. Late 30's probably, long blonde hair, tall—we could probably see eye to eye if she'd let me get that close. You could charge admission for any event she attends, Charleigh is drop dead gorgeous. She was a news anchorwoman on one of the DC channels. Married to some other news guy, they were in the paper all the time. I don't normally recognize newscasters, but Charleigh is real special, she was one of those ones you remember—absolutely stunning. Confident, powerful, she could intimidate the president during a live interview and also hold her own with any of those top supermodels. She's got brains plus that Playboy bunny build that could stop traffic (and does) and she doesn't hide a thing. I kid you not – she is the real thing, the woman is a National Resource. Back then, when she was at the top of her game, something real bad happened to her, something about a baby, but I'm not sure what. But before you know it, her newsboy husband is yesterday's news and soon after she gets married to Bud Brooks, who pitched in the World Series in the 80's. He's an older guy and now he calls the games for the O's. He's big and very over-protective. Who wouldn't be? His wife's a goddess. Soon after she married Bud, Charleigh had twins; they're both in Kindergarten now. Honey is the little girl, the boy is Wilson or Woodrow or something – one of those president's names. Charleigh's got a toddler in tow with her now, even after three kids, she's still gorgeous. Somehow her picture has ended up in the Archimedes School Admission brochure for the last two years. She's incredibly classy, but man, all of us on the maintenance crew and probably all the male faculty fantasize about what we could do if we just had *one hour* alone with her. I better stop now, before I get myself into trouble."

"Then there's Chrissie Thompson. Chrissie's a sweetheart. She's another one of the MILF's who sit at that picnic table each morning. Chrissie's cute as a button, real tiny, and she's got this perfect little ass—my eyes tend to land there right after I've studied Charleigh's cleavage. Yes, she's fun to look at, but the best thing about Chrissie is that she's real easy to talk to and she's *normal* people. She treats everyone like equals, from us maintenance guys to the head of school.

She's on the PTA and volunteers for everything at school. I got to know her last year when she painted the sets I built for the Lower School music performance – even though she doesn't have a Lower School student, she's only got the one boy in Kindergarten, Harrison, she talks about him all the time. I half think she volunteers just so she's not far away from him when he's at school, they're super-close. Her son is on scholarship, like mine is – we talked about it once. For me, it's not so tricky, obviously the maintenance guys here can't afford the $27,000 tuition it takes to send your kids here so everyone knows I'm on it, but for her it's different. I would never mention her scholarship in front of other moms, some of these bitches need little to no reason to look down on people, why give them any satisfaction? I don't even know if Chrissie is married, she never mentioned it. She's someone I'll seek out if I see her on campus. You always feel good after shooting the breeze with Chrissie. Plus, you can always count on her to wear something to show off that nice ass."

"The last of the four moms is Ayani Jenkins. She's African American and something else, Indian or Native American, I think. She told me once that "Ayani" means something like blossom or flower—I can't remember exactly. She's tall, dark, and striking and has this amazing head of curly hair that falls to her waist. I'm a sucker for long hair. Her parents were famous politicians in Washington and she grew up here in Annapolis. I noticed in the school phone directory she's an alum of the school—there's a Archimedes School nautilus emblem next to her name in the directory—the nautilus emblem is stuck on everything here at school. I also heard a rumor that she's a Harvard grad. Her husband Derrick is smart, too. I know him better than I know Ayani—he used to volunteer as an assistant coach for the Archimedes tennis team. And, recently he became the first Black law partner at this stodgy firm in downtown Annapolis, so he doesn't have as much spare time as he used to. I do know that his wife Ayani teaches yoga, she's got this hippie vibe about her. I have no idea how she deals with all the buttoned-up, Bush loving conservative parents who send their kids to this school. She's very religious or spiritual or something, it's like she's tuned in to some higher power floating above the rest of us. Nice lady with a strange name – yeah, it's Native American or something. The fun part is that she's always running around in Lycra showing off her killer body. Ayani has two kids here at Archimedes. Sara's in Middle School, her son Carver is in Kindergarten. He's a sweet kid with dark skin and big brown eyes. He's always giving me this huge smile, and hoping for a ride in the utility vehicle I use as I work around campus."

"We have a real problem with people bringing their dogs on campus. Officially, you're not allowed to bring dogs here, yet nearly all the dog owners ignore the rules. Half these moms can't control their animals and their beasts end up running wild, tripping people, and pooping all over the campus. Of course, it would be below them to use a plastic bag to scoop it up. I've had several moms look in my direction and point to the ground, expecting me to drop what I'm doing and run to their aide. It's disgusting. Don't get me wrong, I love my own dog, I just don't bring him to work where he's not allowed. I like to follow the rules; the entitled parents here at Archimedes tend to ignore them. Ayani is the only one officially allowed to bring a dog here because she sometimes trains service dogs, you know for handicap or blind people. Her dogs are smarter than half the parents here and never a problem."

"On the first day of school I was assigned to fix the leaky basement problem below the Kindergarten. That day was one to remember; it started out like a National Geographic documentary and ended up creating a memory that leaves me needing a cold shower every time I think about it."

Chapter One:
Clawing Her Way In

On the first day of school one of the Archimedes School maintenance guys was assigned to fix the leaky basement problem below the Kindergarten classroom. That day was one to remember for Vic; it started out like a National Geographic documentary and ended up creating a memory that left him needing a cold shower every time he thought about it:

> *Warily, the lone female circled the pack, occasionally extending her claws or barring her teeth to demonstrate her personal arsenal to the group. Acceptance will be critical to her survival, rejection fatal. She seeks to identify the alpha female and gain her acceptance.*

The close knit bunch of the 'A list' hot moms had just dropped off their offspring for the first day of Kindergarten, as they did nearly every day in previous years when their children were in PS 3 and PS 4. They met at the picnic table positioned just outside of the preschool building. Ayani, Chrissie, Charleigh and Jodi leaned their heads in closer when the gossip got good. Bits and pieces of their conversation floated across the preschool playground.

"You mean he caught her in the act with their lawn guy?" exclaimed one of the four moms in stunned tones, trying unsuccessfully to keep her voice low.

"Yep, her husband walked right in on them doing the 'horizontal tango' in their brand new kitchen," announced the mom telling the story. She continued, "Apparently they tried to deny it, saying she was helping him look for bug spray under the sink." At this, the four moms simultaneously burst into unrestrained laughter, each showing their perfectly white teeth. Parents who had just arrived to drop off their children turned to look in the direction of the laughter.

"Shhhhh, keep it down, we don't want to create a scene," whispered one of the moms at the picnic table.

Just then, an unidentified fifth mother tentatively approached the table looking for a way in. Mom number five was spanking new and dressed for either tennis or cheerleading for the NFL; an obscenely short white skirt had given up its efforts to cover some lacey underwear while a skimpy polo shirt had also failed to cover her firm, tan belly. She had a considerable personal arsenal that nearly burst through the buttons of her tight shirt and looked like she was younger than the others, maybe low thirties. When Vic heard her Texas accent, he thought they would eat her alive, but one of the moms at the table, *Chrissie of course*, welcomed her to the school.

"Hey there, are you one of the new preschool moms?" Chrissie asked.

"Yes ma'am, we moved here in August. I'm Tara Hunter and my son Clinton got the last spot in Mrs. Casper's

Kindergarten class." Chrissie cringed slightly at the "ma'am" reference, self conscious about being the oldest of the group. Each of the four core moms then introduced themselves to Tara and described the names and ages of their respective children.

Tara continued, "We were so desperate to get into Archimedes we hired a consultant to coach little Clinton and prep him for his private school interview. In the end it was a toss up between Clinton and some little Hispanic kid. We were worried that the school needed to fill some quotas. So, our consultant advised us to make a sizable donation to the school and voila, $25,000 dollars later and here we are."

Chrissie quickly glanced over to Ayani to see her reaction to Tara's comment about quotas, but Ayani didn't flinch. It took a lot to raise Ayani's blood pressure.

"*Ouch*, I heard the competition was tough for Kindergarten, but I didn't realize the school had resorted to bribery," said Jodi, who had a knack for cutting to the chase.

"Oh, all the best schools do it down south. Randy and I were ready with our checkbook in hand," said Tara in her sweet southern drawl.

"We love it here, but thank goodness I didn't have to cough up the cash when Harrison started PS 3 two years ago," said Chrissie, referring to the preschool class for three year olds. "We would have been forced to go to public school." Chrissie paused, not willing to reveal too much about her financial status to this new Archimedes mom.

"Tara, we were just about to start our morning walk—we walk nearly everyday around the neighborhood—would you like to join us?" asked Ayani, in her gentle, almost hypnotic voice.

"Sure, I'd love to. I have an appointment for a facial and manicure at ten, will we be done by then?" Tara asked.

"Absolutely, but you may be pretty sweaty when you get to your appointment. We do serious power walking," said Chrissie.

"No problem, I'll just give them a bigger tip," boasted Tara.

Chrissie observed that Charleigh had barely said a word during this introductory conversation, and when Tara agreed to join them on their walk, Charleigh grimaced. It took a long time for Charleigh to warm up to a new woman. She preferred to keep a very small and intimate circle of friends. Then Tara said, "Let's stretch, girls," causing Charleigh to moan slightly, but she begrudgingly complied. She didn't want to offend the brand new mom within minutes of meeting her. She'd save that for later.

Chrissie noticed that Vic the maintenance guy was enjoying an eyeful while the five of them stretched and bent this way and that, clothes slipping, skin showing. Chrissie felt his eyes on her backside, where she knew the top of her black thong was exposed. When Charleigh reached behind her chest to loosen her shoulder muscles, two of her shirt buttons popped open revealing a portion of her perfect breasts in a pink lace bra. Chrissie saw Vic smile from ear to ear; he shook his head, then turned and walked away. She thought she overheard him say, "*God*, I love my job."

———

Returning to the Archimedes School campus after her long walk, Chrissie wanted to discreetly peek in on her son Harrison. In the car that morning he had cried all the way to school. At one point during the short drive, Harrison was sobbing so uncontrollably Chrissie had to pull over to the gravel shoulder and sit in the back seat and hold him reassuringly in her arms. A quick check on her boy would ease her concerns about him settling into the new school year. Rounding the corner of the preschool building, she bumped into Vic, her buddy in the maintenance department.

"Did you enjoy the show this morning?" she asked with a grin. Vic was one of her favorite employees at the school and she enjoyed ribbing him whenever she got the chance.

"What show?" he replied innocently, then continued, "Whose the new girl? She's got quite a body on her."

"She should have an awesome body, she's at least ten years younger than me," said Chrissie. "You should have seen *me* at thirty."

"Oh Chrissie, you know you're my favorite, don't get jealous," Vic replied.

Chrissie and Vic had developed a close friendship when the two of them worked on creating the lower school music set last year. They enjoyed this type of flirty banter with sexual innuendo. After all, they both knew it was innocent fun.

"What are you working on, anyway? You're slimy and disgusting," Chrissie said jokingly. Noticing that he had clearly overexerted in the oppressive Maryland heat of late summer, his face was so red she hoped he wasn't getting heat stroke or something. With a tone of worry in her voice she asked, "Actually, are you feeling okay?"

"Don't fret, I'm fine, just a little sweaty," Vic said as he finished packing up his tools from digging outside the Kindergarten classroom. "That's the way you like it, isn't it?" Vic added with a chuckle.

Slyly ignoring his comment, Chrissie asked, "Vic, do you mind if I peek in on my baby?" Vic willingly stepped aside from his digging to let Chrissie peer into her son's classroom.

Chrissie felt a bit guilty about sneaking back to the Kindergarten but being able to chat with Vic for a little while gave her visit dual purpose. She knew she was giving in to temptation, but she was compelled to wander over to the window of Mrs. Casper's room to check on Harrison. He looked so happy; she was crazy to worry about him. No sign at all of this morning's tears. He was laughing and smiling with his eyes glued on Mrs. Casper. *Now* the classroom looked more normal and cheerful, it had been much too clean and perfect when Chrissie and Harrison arrived early this morning. The classroom walls were already decorated with art the children had completed just that morning. Chrissie noticed that Mrs. Casper had hung a big yellow construction paper caterpillar from the ceiling with the words "WELCOME TO KINDERGARTEN!" printed on the top circle. As Harrison's gaze moved around the room she ducked her head below the window frame to avoid his view. Chrissie turned and moved quickly away from the preschool building. She didn't want to take any chance that she could ruin Harrison's first day if he caught a glimpse of her and switched back to that clingy, crying mommy-boy thing he had done this chaotic morning. Those first few morning transitions were never easy for him, especially after a summer of togetherness. She was sure that Harrison hadn't been alarmed by the prospect of all day Kindergarten—Chrissie had been preparing him for weeks for "big boy" school. But Chrissie was well aware that she was over attached to her only child and was definitely going to suffer his all day absence. She felt half a person already.

After prying herself away from Harrison's Kindergarten classroom, Chrissie headed to the school's parking lot where she saw Charleigh strolling gracefully toward her brand new white Porsche Cayenne. It had become a tradition for her husband Bud to buy Charleigh a new car at the beginning of every school year. No need to start a fresh year with sticky juice covered seats and old Cheerios crunched on the floor mats!

"What are *you* still doing here?" asked Chrissie.

"I couldn't resist sneaking a peek at the twins who were playing on the other side of the preschool building at snack recess. They seemed just fine," said Charleigh.

"I'm glad I wasn't the only one. I just checked on Harrison. We had a tough morning, but he's doing fine now."

"Actually, there are several Kindergarten parents hiding in the bushes near the playground equipment spying on their kids," added Charleigh. "One mom is having a melt down because her daughter's new $1,000 dollar Neiman's outfit is covered in finger paint. What did she expect?"

"Thank goodness for consignment. Why would anyone spend that kind of money on clothing they just grow out of in three months?" asked Chrissie. "I bought Harrison's entire outfit, in his favorite color, shoes included, for $15 dollars from *Second Time Around*." Chrissie prided herself on her thriftiness and ability to dress her child in quality, high end clothes at a fraction of the price. As an added bonus, she liked the fact that using recycled clothes was also considered "*green*" and good for the environment.

"Sweetheart, I didn't spend much more, I live at Target," added Charleigh, pronouncing it *Targeé* with a fake French accent. Chrissie knew Charleigh had the resources to buy all of her children's clothes at Neiman-Marcus, and totally respected her for not—even if she did get a new $80,000 dollar car each year!

Walking to the school's parking lot, Charleigh and Chrissie passed an area everyone called *The Beach* which should probably be renamed *La Playa*, or what was it in Portuguese? *La Praia*. The beach was a small strip of sunlit grass adjacent to the parking lot, out of sight of any buildings, yet full of eye catching *sights* as today two Brazilian nannies were in residence trying to lap up the last few rays of summer as August came to an end. These two twenty-something nubile newbies donned teeny sherbet colored shorts with matching triangle bikini tops that were not much bigger than the palm of your hand. Their tan, firm bodies gleamed in the morning sun and the diamond studs attached to their belly buttons sparkled as they caught the light. They had that irresistible glow of youth which filled Chrissie with pangs of envy as she glanced at her own forty-four year old body reflected in a window of one of the teacher's cars. Charleigh picked up on Chrissie's thoughts.

"Chrissie you have nothing to worry about. You might be forty-four, but you've still got a perky body of someone at least ten years younger. No—better yet, you could still stand in for any upper school cheerleader," said Charleigh. She added, "Everywhere you go men drool over you."

"Thanks, I needed that, especially coming from *you*. I'd like to see what these girls look like in twenty years," Chrissie wondered out loud.

The two nannies were prattling on rapidly; too engrossed in their conversation to notice Chrissie and Charleigh stroll by. With her fluent Spanish, Chrissie could understand bits and pieces of Portuguese.

"*Jonathan era o mais melhor que eu tive sempre,*" said one of the nannies.

"Melhor? Mejor," Chrissie translated to Charleigh. "She said Jonathan is the best lover she's ever had in her short life."

"Go for it, Jonathan," said Charleigh with a slight smile showing at the corners of her mouth.

It was already 10 a.m. and these sun-goddesses would have to re-collect their preschool charges by noon, so why spend that time driving the round trip to the waterfront McMansions south of town when they could soak up the sun for a few more hours? Always friendly and gregarious, Chrissie would know their names by the end of the month, but this was a new crop of nannies and somehow it just seemed wrong and invasive for a middle aged fully clothed mother to walk over to chat with these bronzed beauties babbling on in Portuguese. Maybe next week. From past experience, Chrissie knew these young foreigners were vital in rearing so many of Archimedes' preschoolers, so she often offered helpful advice to nannies in need. By next week they would have Chrissie's phone number programmed into their cells. Still, "*The Beach*" drove Chrissie crazy, but she wasn't sure if it was because she dreaded seeing these glistening bodies up close flaunting their youth in her face or if it was because she was offended that there were half naked women in the school's parking lot. It's not like the Upper School girls wore much more.

Walking toward the parking lot, Chrissie noted that the Archimedes School campus looked wonderful – the maintenance department always did a great job preparing it for the first day of school. Fresh mulch was compacted perfectly into the neatly landscaped and edged beds, the expansive lawn leading down to the water's edge was freshly cut, and the ivy growing up the sides of each building was trimmed to perfection. New and larger engraved signage had been placed on the front of each building, hopefully to avoid last year's debacle of new-to-Archimedes parents wandering aimlessly around the campus looking for the preschool building and mistakenly taking their children to the Upper School classrooms where teenagers spent most of their time sending pheromone signals to each other; the school went to great lengths to keep the newly admitted preschoolers segregated from the Upper School rebels.

The core building that today houses a portion of the Archimedes School was originally a post civil war finishing school for girls, built as a complement to the all male environment of the United States Naval Academy, located just one-half mile away. After all, those bright, young future officers of our Navy needed a bevy of potential dance partners for their cotillions. "The Annapolis Finishing School for Girls" did do an excellent job of preparing Maryland's fine young ladies in mastering the skills of how to engage in enlightened parlor discourse and gave them the tools of proper etiquette when hosting elaborate dinner parties designed to impress the business partners of their future husbands. Chrissie laughed imagining the paragons of virtue of yesteryear fainting at the sight of today's female Upper School students, brilliant, bold, and bearing birth control patches that somehow always managed to peek out from their tiny little outfits.

Times changed with the onset of World War I and the Annapolis Finishing School for Girls closed its doors and remained vacant for nearly a decade. Years of neglect impacted the school in obvious ways; most of the building's windowpanes were cracked or missing, the mortar between the hand hewn bricks was crumbling, and wild grape and kudzu vines had climbed as high as the second story. Then a wealthy and visionary local physician, who had just come into significant sums of money due to a successful patent and subsequent production of a new optical lens, saw great potential in acquiring this historic, yet decrepit mansion and the surrounding twenty acres of land. Dr. Franklin was poised to create a brand new exclusive, private school which had a unique curriculum focusing on math, science and new technology—the foundation of the Archimedes School. Of course, the Greek mathematician, Archimedes, was considered to be the greatest mathematician of antiquity and perhaps the greatest of all time and thus his name was perfectly suited for this newly founded school. The original school building was perched high on a hill overlooking Spa Creek, a scenic tributary off of the Severn River—the main river leading from Annapolis into the Chesapeake Bay. The design of the two story building was in the architectural style of early Victorian "Second Empire." Perfect symmetry was the rule of that day with matching sets of three, six foot high arched windows placed proportionately on both sides and both stories of the front of the building, eight marble stairs led up to the double entry ten foot high front doors, and visitors were sheltered at the entryway by a flat roofed white portico anchored with four white pillars. Red hand hewn bricks were framed in neatly by the white granite cornerstones set on all four sides of the building, which today were graced by perfectly manicured ivy vines kept in check by the maintenance crew. A steep incline slanted grey slate roof topped off the building with four dormer windows peaking through. A square cupola which housed the building's German made clockworks sat staunchly in the center of the innovative roof that lifted open for Friday night astronomy club gatherings.

Since the purchase of the original building in the early 1900's, several additional structures were built on the grounds, all complimenting the original building's architectural style. With the implementation of the unique accelerated mathematics based curriculum in 1965, the nautilus shell was adopted as the school logo. This was also a logical tie in to the mathematical theory of the Archimedian spiral. The chambered nautilus grows so that its shell forms a logarithmic spiral—the perfect symbol of nature and how it relates to geometry. The Archimedes School grounds were designed so that brick pathways connected each of the buildings following the curvature of a nautilus shell, with interconnecting septa separating gardens of varying botanical themes. The entire pattern devolved to an elegant swirling pathway that ended in the middle of the school's expansive lawn. "The whorl" as it was known, formed the school's huge courtyard which served as a lunch gathering spot for the Middle and Upper Schoolers, or an assembly area for the school on warm days. With a student body of just 800 children including preschool through 12th grade, the entire school and faculty could easily gather in this one location.

The Archimedes School's accelerated math curriculum was unique in the nation, *though* carefully reproduced in Japan. Just getting into Archimedes was a significant accomplishment, the admissions process struck fear in everyone's heart.

Chrissie's son Harrison was a clever baby, always doing something surprising like sorting the seven-bean soup into the muffin tins or arranging blocks into fantastic symmetrical patterns.

"Look mommy, I parked all the purple cars together, then the blue cars, then the green cars, then red, orange, yellow. It looks like a car rainbow!" She fondly remembered her very verbal 20 month old proclaiming. Chrissie knew he was smart and wanted the best for him which prompted her to take him in for the admissions testing. Two year old Harrison was still in diapers when he went in for the Archimedes School interview. Chrissie had to admit, the test was tough, but he came through with flying colors.

"Harrison, can you stack the marshmallows in the same pattern that I've made?" asked the Director of Admissions. Little Harrison quickly reproduced the same pattern, and then promptly ate his creation.

"No honey, we'll need those for later," she said. "More marshmallows in here," she announced to her assistant who was sitting at her desk down the hallway. Chrissie wondered if exposing her child to temptation was part of the test.

"If Moses had two animals of every kind on the ark and he had fifty different types of animals, how many total animals did Moses have?" she asked.

"Are you tricking me?" Harrison asked, his eyes sparkling. "Moses didn't have any animals on the ark, it was Noah."

"Nice job, Harrison, yes I was trying to trick you," she said. The testing continued for at least another hour, an impossibly ridiculous amount of time to keep a two year old focused. Harrison held on the best he could, answering the last question with a big yawn, then he fell fast asleep the minute he laid his curly blonde head on the miniature desk.

The accelerated math program at Archimedes was based on the concept that with the proper introduction children could learn higher concepts of math more easily and more thoroughly than their undergraduate counterparts at other schools. The top Archimedes seniors were always scooped up by MIT or Caltech, students got into great colleges, especially if they were going into math or science.

The originators of this unique curriculum had envisioned training the next Newton, Bernoulli or Feynman; the current administration would be content to train the next Bezos, Jobs or Gates instead. The whole program started in the preschool. Simple number concepts and basic math functions were taught to the three and four year olds, but the real curriculum was kicked off in Kindergarten. For the parents it was called "Intro to Pre-Iterative Processes," but for the kids it was called, "The getting tiny unit." The students learned and practiced the fundamentals of math while doing exercises based within calculus.

"Calculus in Kindergarten, *damn*, I never even took it in college," Chrissie worried out loud after the initial interview.

"Plenty of the preschool parents at Archimedes are in the same boat," said the Admissions Director. "We have a long list of tutors you can hire for your son."

Chrissie didn't begin to understand this whole math thing no matter how many Parent Coffees she attended, whatever the school was doing, it seemed to work and lots and lots of people wanted their kids at Archimedes.

The Archimedes School certainly was a beautiful school with an exceptional curriculum and it should be for the *amount of tuition they had to pay.* Compared to the other private schools in the area, The Archimedes School was the most expensive. Parents of Upper Schoolers had to pay nearly $30,000 for their child to attend. The cost of the tuition increased by grade.

By the time Chrissie and Charleigh had completed their first walk of the school year it was now 10:00 am and the Archimedes School parking lot was filled with *teacher cars*: Toyotas, Hondas, Saturns, Volvos ten or more years old, all parked in an orderly manner between the lines of the parking lot. This was a stark contrast to the rush hours of drop off or pick-up when dozens of Mercedes, Jags, Porsches and Hummers parked in random patterns, blocking roads, and pinning in other cars. The parking lot could be half empty yet a dozen idiots would still find a way to double park—most of them being above the mundane rules of etiquette because of their spouse's stratospheric incomes. Chrissie just stayed out of their way – she wanted to live a few years longer. Her rule was to come to school early and depart later after the rush on both ends of the day. There seemed to be a direct correlation between the decrease in driving ability and the miles per gallon rating of these massive SUVs. There was no way Chrissie was walking her little boy through that parking lot until the luxury behemoth automobile crowd had zoomed their vehicles out of sight. Chrissie slipped into her black Volvo and slowly pulled out—another year had officially begun. Another year and here she was—with a miserable marriage, no career, and now no little boy to cherish all day, she felt empty and alone, always alone.

"This is crazy," Chrissie said to herself, quickly switching gears. She had just had a fantastic morning. It was so good to see everyone again. Charleigh, Jodi and Ayani loved her like a sister. Just being with them was like sipping a warm, familiar cup of herbal tea. Jodi was in good form, and not nearly as stand-offish as she could be when meeting new moms. Tara might even fit in, but Lord, she was young, in many ways; thirty-two, husband clearly rolling in the profits of his toilet paper import business or something like that, one child, Clinton in Harrison's Kindergarten class. It was a bit disturbing having a fifth person to throw off the lovely balance that had sustained them through the last few years, but on the flip side, there were enough exclusive mom-cliques at this school, who wanted to be like that? Tara dressed like an Archimedes mom, well manicured and coiffed, firm body, big boobs; Chrissie might even be able to get past the Texas accent. Tara walked the walk and talked the talk. She was sweet; she seemed to be concerned at the right places in the conversation and laughed at the right jokes. But, Tara did seem to have a problem with Ayani. The atmosphere in the air became uncomfortable when Tara focused too much attention on Ayani's ethnicity.

"Tell me about your people," Tara asked Ayani during their walk.

"I grew up here in Annapolis and my parents used to work for the government in D.C.," was the only information Ayani volunteered. There was no need to add that her parents were famous politicians and that she was an Archimedes "lifer," meaning she had gone from preschool through high school graduation—not to mention her degree from Harvard.

"Archimedes must have been happy to have you at the school. They filled two quotas, African American and Native American!" Tara added. This comment made Jodi bristle with irritation. Jodi was frightfully protective whenever she sensed any of her friends to be in danger. Poised and ready to jump down Tara's throat and berate her for racism, Jodi was silenced when Ayani raised her palm slightly in her direction, a gesture designed to indicate she had everything under control.

"Do you and your family miss the wide open spaces?" was Tara's next ridiculous question.

"No, my husband and I travel out west quite often. We have a vacation home in Sedona," said Ayani, completely unflustered by Tara's comments. Sadly, Ayani had to deal with prejudice and ignorance throughout her entire life.

Jodi, Charleigh, and Chrissie exchanged concerned looks as Tara bumbled on, continuing to ask stupid questions. Hopefully her ignorance would be short-lived. They'd cut her some slack this first day, but if this kept up, Jodi would be sure to rip her a new one.

The conversations during these morning walks typically followed this loose agenda: First, the kids, and the most recent incredibly impressive things they did. Then, school events, there's always something brewing.

"Did you hear that Laurel Somerville is chairing the "Welcome Back Picnic" on Friday?" said Jodi.

"This is Laurel's first shot at chairing an event, I hope she doesn't blow it," added Chrissie, who was already an active member of the board for Archimedes' Parent Teachers Association. As far as Chrissie knew, Laurel had yet to round up the usual bunch of volunteers to help coordinate the event.

"Have any of you noticed that Laurel seems so spaced out these days, even physically shaky?" asked Charleigh.

"Sounds like she might be on the verge of a hypoglycemic seizure," interjected Jodi, tapping into years of nursing experience. "Have you noticed if she's sweating or confused?"

"She's always *confused*," said Charleigh with a chuckle. "But no, I haven't seen her sweating," said continued.

"I'm not sure if Laurel's up to the task of coordinating the picnic. It's a huge event and I haven't seen one sign-up sheet yet!" worried Chrissie.

The next topic on their walks was a review of the latest gossip. There were no surprises today as they covered the initial pass.

"Did anyone notice that Astrid had a boob job over the summer?" asked Chrissie. Astrid was another hot, young Kindergarten mom.

"I know the maintenance crew noticed. Your buddy Vic was almost stepping on his tongue," said Jodi to Chrissie.

"Oh my God, they look massive, at least a double D. How does she stand up with those tiny feet?" responded Charleigh.

More gossip was reviewed and discussed about the two math teachers, Berri Franconi and Matt Worthington who were (reportedly) having an affair. These two teachers had been flirting with each other for years and now it may have progressed to the next level.

"Vic told me he saw Berri and Matt sneak into in the physics lab several times over the summer. They always emerged with their hair looking like Einstein's," said Chrissie.

Jodi announced that two other Kindergarten parents, Jonathan and Ellyn Smyth, got a new hot nanny imported from Brazil. Jonathan is now all interested in spending time at home with the kids. Jodi then added another tidbit that over the summer the Weinstein family moved to France and got $4 million for their house. This was great news for Ayani who lived two doors down from them. Ayani's house was actually significantly larger than the Weinstein's and had a better water view.

Tara interjected with her own interesting dirt gathered during the cocktail parties at the Old Bay Yacht Club where she and her husband were members. When Tara mentioned her yacht club membership, Jodi, Charleigh, Ayani and Chrissie exchanged knowing looks. Tara had again shared her financial prowess (the first time was when she mentioned her $25,000 school donation). The Yacht Club had a $10,000 annual membership fee, along with a monthly restaurant and bar tab requirement of at least $1,500, then they had to pass the strict membership screening permitting only the most influential in the community to join—that plus her address in the Murray Hill neighborhood of Annapolis put Tara's husband in the upper-echelon of earning power. Well, clearly the market for importing all those hygienic toilet paper products was lucrative. *I guess someone's got to do it*, Chrissie thought.

"Did you hear they're filming another movie in town this fall? I think George Clooney and Ben Stiller will *both* be in it," said Tara. Annapolis had in recent years become a trendy spot for the movie industry. "Someone said they saw George eating dinner at Pacific Rim with Jennifer Anniston on Thursday."

Tara continued, "They're looking for extras, especially for people of color, Ayani you might check that out. Maybe you could earn some extra money."

Chrissie was used to being surrounded by really wealthy people but sometimes that common subset—the "more money than brains" crowd could be so crass. She cringed at the thought that they might find out Harrison was on partial scholarship. She knew how cruel Harrison's peers could be, especially when they hit those awkward "middle school years" and she didn't want to give anyone ammunition against him. Her friends knew of course, but how would Tara react? Well, if Tara couldn't deal with Chrissie's lack of wealth and Ayani's ethnicity, Tara wouldn't last long.

Chrissie pulled away from school, driving past the four-foot high brick wall that surrounded the campus. Was the purpose of the wall to keep the higher learning *in* or was it to prevent the outside community from knowing the insanity that sometimes went on inside? Like so much of Annapolis, great efforts were taken to prevent the general public from having any glimpse of the Chesapeake Bay. Water views were for the privileged only; if you couldn't afford waterfront property, you were welcome to enjoy the view from the beaches of the state park located just off Highway 50. It was a shame that so many people lived just footsteps from the water, but because they didn't own *waterfront* property they yet rarely got the chance to actually view the beauty of the bay. The "Save the Bay" people campaigned continuously, though their job might have been easier if their constituents actually had a chance to *see the Bay* now and then.

"*This is why I love Eastport*," thought Chrissie as she pulled into the driveway of their Eastport home. With its little waterfront parks at the end of each street, Eastport offered everyone the opportunity to enjoy panoramic views of the Chesapeake Bay. Eastport is a lively and diverse peninsula neighborhood separated from downtown Annapolis by the Spa Creek Bridge. It was settled back in the mid-1600's and was annexed by the city of Annapolis in 1951. Despite the merger, the residents continue to proclaim their separate identity from the stuffy historic district across the creek. Eastport is an eclectic community where million dollar waterfront homes share property lines with quaint cottages, warehouses and boat yards. The neighborhood is populated with a diverse mix of young professionals, blue collar workers, wealthy entrepreneurs, musicians and students. It's where you'll find the majority of Annapolis' marinas, boat yards, yacht designers and brokers, boat builders and sail makers. It is both industrial and residential. Chrissie loved it here. At the corner coffee shop she could chat comfortably with "toothless Dave" a colorful, scruffy, classic Maryland crabber who often smelled like day old fish or she could turn to her other side and talk about marketing strategies with Martin, a handsome Englishman who manufactured rigging for racing yachts.

Chrissie's home in Eastport was an charming Craftsman bungalow originally built in the early 1900's which she and her husband Seth renovated just last year. Now they were in debt up to their eyeballs, but it was worth it. Chrissie relished every moment of the renovation process, from working with the architect on the overall floor plan and great room addition, to selecting the hand painted fish tiles for her bathroom shower. On the other hand, she called Seth the "joy sucker" who never failed to come home to the renovation project every night after work with a scowl on his face and angry words about the inefficiencies of the contractor.

"Why did they spend *four hours* installing this bead board? This was a thirty minute job any moron could do! At that rate, we'll exceed our budget by $100,000!" were the types of things Seth would say every day when he returned home from work. Joy sucker.

Now completed, her home was near perfect. She loved the wide overhanging eaves that sheltered the deep front porch, where she and Harrison spent many humid summer days in the shade playing games, doing crafts, and eating lunch. Chrissie thought about the last day of their summer vacation when they sat on the wood floor of the porch and had a tea party. Yes, she knew Seth would be enraged at the prospect of their son having a tea party, so she always reminded Harrison to "keep this as our little secret." She made special peanut butter and jelly sandwiches cut into heart shapes and created Harrison's favorite "bug juice" by combining ginger ale and fruit juice with gummy worms propped on the side of his plastic cup. They carefully sipped their bug juice with pinky fingers pointed outward, while the gummy worms dangled from their lips. She hoped that Harrison would have at least one childhood memory of the good times they spent together on that porch.

She chose a lively striped red and white pattern for the cushions she placed on the porches' white wicker furniture. Another Archimedes mom, a very talented artist, hand painted a bold floral pattern on a traditional style floor cloth that graced the entryway. Inside the bungalow, the front doors opened directly into an open, sunny space, where the living room flowed to the dining room, separated by a huge arched opening, then to the modernized kitchen upgraded with granite countertops and stainless steel appliances. The interior was warm and featured natural building materials, honey toned woods, a huge stone fireplace, detailed moldings and lots of built in shelving. Chrissie's decorating style was a clean and uncluttered mix of Pottery Barn knock offs and funky inexpensive antiques she acquired at an auction house on the Eastern Shore of Maryland.

She paused in the driveway. She took a deep breath and then walked in through the front door. Inside more bills littered the floor behind the mail slot. *God, I wish I could earn some cash. Now that Harrison's at school all day I've got all this extra time*, she thought. Chrissie was at the crossroads that so many women faced when the last child, in her case, her only child, was off at school full time. She had to redefine her purpose in life. Chrissie hit the answering machine. Seth telling her he would be late tonight, no surprise there. Verizon asking her to change plans and kindly including a long distance number that she could call just to sit on hold for ten minutes to get on their "do not call" list. Well, at least it would be something to do. No other messages. Chrissie looked at the clock—four more long, lonely hours until she could pick up Harrison at Archimedes. "Man, this sucks," she said to herself.

She busied herself tidying the house. As she did the comforting chore of sweeping the floor, Chrissie couldn't help thinking about Harrison. He would be eating his lunch right now...then recess, then quiet time.

Reflecting again on their walk earlier that morning, the moms had talked about the new kids in the class. Lots of unusual virtuous names: in addition to Charleigh's daughter "Honesty" (though we all called her Honey), "Truth" was in Harrison's class and "Justice" was in the other Kindergarten class. All we need is to have "The American Way" join their class next year. One little girl was named "Agape." Chrissie had wondered out loud why anyone would name their child Agape.

"It's pronounced Ah-Gah-Pay, it's Greek and means something like Biblical or Platonic love," Ayani had explained.

Jodi came back, "It looks like Ah-Gāpe, meaning standing there with your mouth wide open. We need to start calling that poor child Aggie soon, or just wait five years from now when those vicious kids in Middle School eat her alive." Poor little thing.

Ayani commented that the first day of school seemed to go smoothly, there were no tearful kids and the teachers seemed excited and so warm and loving.

"They greeted the children with a hug and knew each and every child by name. I was impressed, they had certainly done their homework over the summer," Ayani said.

"Yes, but what about that shit for brains mom who brought her dog into Mrs. Casper's class?" said Jodi. "She was completely oblivious that Mrs. Casper was dying in there—sneezing, eyes watering and itching."

"Who was that idiot? Was it Deborah Brown? She's always bringing that dog everywhere with her. I think she loves her dog more than her kid," added Chrissie.

"It was a shame that Mrs. Casper had to move her greetings to the adjacent classroom until the dog left. Some of these moms are absolutely clueless," said Ayani.

"How about absolutely *entitled*?" said Charleigh. "The greater the donation to the school, the more likely they feel they can do anything they want."

"Remember the parents who demanded that the Upper School play should be the crappy musical their gay son had written—something about ice skaters?" reminded Jodi. "They had just donated their used fifty foot Sea Ray to the school," she added.

Throughout the entire morning walk Tara was rather quiet and listened attentively as if taking notes (*Note to self – do not bring dog in classroom, this behavior is frowned upon. Don't make school do the musical your child writes*). Wanting to learn is a good thing.

At the end of their walk, Jodi entered that oh-so-interesting, yet oh-so-uncomfortable arena of their personal sex lives. Tara seemed uncomfortable and wasn't ready for this round of over-sharing. For Charleigh, Jodi and Ayani, sex was like exercise, food and oxygen—it's healthy and you needed to partake often. For these women, having sex was like eating broccoli, it was good for you. Chrissie's marriage was the least intimate and she always felt like an outsider when this topic came up. How long had it been since she had sex? Years? Well, Harrison was five now, so at least five years. As close as they were, Chrissie had never fully confessed this secret to the other women—they knew Seth was obsessed with work and their sex life was lacking, but they didn't know it was non-existent. Every night after dinner Seth would sign back onto his laptop and start tracking inventory, managing accounts receivable, *or doing something*, until the wee hours. Chrissie could never stay awake long enough to welcome his arrival in their bed. "Oh well, I guess I'll never get my quota of "broccoli" at this rate," she thought.

Tara brought up her invite to Astrid's (yet another!) sex toy party—welcome to Archimedes! Astrid had a lucrative in-home party business that focused on selling sex toys and lingerie—as if she needed anything more to stimulate her nympho-maniacal qualities. Apparently, Astrid had already sought out all the new-to-Archimedes as potential marketing targets for her in-home parties. That's when Charleigh interjected her spirited opinions on the whole sex toy thing.

"Well, I've never had a hard time getting Bud turned on. Sometimes it seems like he's never turned off. I'll just be brushing my teeth or loading the dishwasher and the man goes absolutely crazy," Charleigh said. Well Charleigh is Charleigh, half of the males in Washington, DC used to watch her news broadcasts for reasons other than a burning desire to follow current events, though a burning desire definitely played a part in their interest.

"Rip gets tired sometimes, but we hop in the shower or hot tub and he's *rip*-roarin' again. Something about water usually does the trick," Jodi said with a laugh. *Good god, stop talking, Jodi,* thought Chrissie, no more details, please. She tried to blink away the visuals.

Ayani was in agreement with Charleigh, "A few things turn Derrick off, but most things seem to turn him on—I think some men get that hormone thing in puberty and never turn back."

"So what turns him off?" Chrissie asked.

"Oh, I had the stomach flu one time and kept running to the bathroom to throw up. Thankfully, he gave up and let me be until I felt better," replied Ayani.

They all looked at Chrissie and she shared the current family marketing spin on sex or the absence thereof, old news, she knew her friends would be kind, but would Tara?

"Seth is so consumed with work right now and has been for awhile. It's been awhile—I don't know how long," Chrissie said, and then added after a reflective pause, "I'm starting to think I should go to the party to figure out how to get his attention."

So now it was Tara's turn–with a new person along, this whole conversation felt like Truth-or-Dare, poor Tara, now she was in the spotlight. Tara started by saying she never had any problem turning on her husband, Randy (long pause, tacit implication: "like Chrissie," grrrr). She gave an overly detailed story about hot lingerie, perfume, candles, and champagne, and generally it all *did* sound more like an article in *Cosmo* than the real world. She did everything but quote pages out of the Kama Sutra. She just kept going on and on, and on and on, saying how they did it every day, sometimes several times a day–when Chrissie started to recognize her re-telling of scenes from various recent films, it was clear to everyone, including Tara, that she went a bit too far.

Jodi called her on it, if this was Truth-or-Dare, Tara had blown the first round, "You're full of crap, Tara – you're not getting any more than Chrissie, are you?"

Tara was cool and to Chrissie's surprise, shook her head sheepishly. Tara *totally* looked and dressed the part of the hot mom who was getting it every day in every way. So, now the cat was out of the bag, Tara's sex life was just as mundane as Chrissie's.

"OK—here's the deal. When it comes to turning on men, husbands number one through three have no need for sex toys, Bud goes for me when I'm breathing, Rip gets hot in water, and Derrick gets turned on by Ayani as long as she's not vomiting. Seth and Randy either like boys or need to be reminded of their manly duties. Bring on the sex toys! Why don't you two girls hit Astrid's party and report back to us on the latest technology," said Charleigh, laying down the *Dare* in this game.

So now Chrissie would join Tara at Astrid's orgy-a-thon on Thursday night. Her stomach churned with nervousness at the prospect of bringing kinky sex toys home to try on Seth. Would this finally entice him or was there no hope? Tara may have had the same thought about her husband Randy, because simultaneously they exchanged despairingly looks that expressed complete futility of ever reviving the *physical* aspect to their marriages.

Life Observations from Vic the Maintenance Guy:
"I could always tell if a woman was a keeper if you actually enjoyed talking to her over a cup of coffee in the morning. As long as you're friends, everything else falls into place."

Chapter Two:
The Welcome Back Picnic,
How <u>Not</u> to Volunteer

The Welcome Back Picnic was the first Archimedes School event Laurel Somerville had ever chaired and her nerves were a little rattled and her hands were already shaking. She checked her purse to make sure she had enough Percosets to get her through the evening. Great. She was set, nothing could go wrong now.

━━━━━━━

Ayani Jenkins stepped out of the shower fresh and energized. Her lean, lithe, perfectly toned body glistened with droplets of water that sparkled from the afternoon light streaming through the bathroom windows. She buffed her body gently with a soft Egyptian cotton towel, and dropped the towel delicately to the floor. Naked, she stretched high in anjanaya-asana, the salutation pose, welcoming the next part of the day—the Archimedes School Picnic. Taking a deep breath through her nostrils and exhaling loudly through her mouth, she worked to clear any blocked chakras and open her soul to all positive energy. Yet, despite her careful preparations, her thoughts wandered to concerns about the events that were about to unfold.

Laurel Sommerville had never chaired an event before and Ayani hoped this one wouldn't prove too taxing for her. Laurel seemed so eager to get involved and to, well, to bond with people. Yet, whenever Ayani made an attempt to get to know her, Laurel continued to be so detached and distant—spacey even. She had known Laurel since their children were barely three years old, yet just last week at the morning drop off Laurel seemed to forget ever meeting Ayani.

"Excuse me, um, um, ma'am…" Laurel's voice trailed off as she attempted to retrieve Ayani's name from her memory banks.

"It's *Ayani*, Laurel," Ayani gently reminded her.

"Oh sorry, yeah…okay, sure…Ayani, Ayani," Laurel absently replied, whispering her name over and over silently as if they had never met before.

Ayani hoped that Laurel's involvement in coordinating tonight's event would help her to ultimately connect with some of the Archimedes School parents.

Ayani wandered into her closet looking for something cool, crisp and comfortable to wear. Sadly, she thought to herself, nakedness, her preferred state of attire was not acceptable! The picnic was a long standing tradition that always occurred within the first two weeks of the new school year. In Maryland, these September evenings could be just as brutally hot and humid as those sultry nights during the peak of summer. Charleigh, Ayani, Jodi, and Chrissie always enjoyed these events, not just to eat, socialize and reconnect with friends beyond their little group, but also to have an opportunity to play their *fashion faux pas* game where they would casually and quietly critique the appropriateness of what other parents wore. The game was basically harmless as long as they kept it among themselves, and by now they could convey paragraphs of information to each other with just a glance or smile. The game was simple and tonight's candidates would likely fall into two categories: those showing too much skin—which would undoubtedly be the case on this hot, humid night, and those displaying their wealth on their sleeve; literally. It never failed that some newly divorced middle aged dad would arrive at the event with his latest twenty year old bimbo attached to his arm who apparently didn't get the memo that this was a *picnic* and a *family* event. These women typically sported short body-clinging skirts and low cut frilly blouses that always provided a little extra entertainment when they awkwardly maneuvered to sit on the plaid picnic blankets provided by the school. The added bonus was watching the perky, nubile and oh-so-eager blondes (were they ever anything but blonde?) hop on their tiptoes across the often mushy grounds to the picnic area in the Whorl in an attempt to keep the three inch heels of their Manolo Blaniks from sinking into the soil.

Ayani remembered last year's picnic which was delayed briefly for the afternoon summer thunderstorms that had watered down the already damp school grounds. One of the new-to-Archimedes parents arrived in a chauffeured car wearing cocktail attire: he, in a crisp dark Armani suit, white shirt and tie, and she, just returned from a New York shopping spree to buy that perfect little black dress weighed down with diamonds attached to any part of her body that would support jewelry. Amazing, Ayani had thought, "Was this a premeditated attempt to show off their status or was it truly a genuine mistake?" Ayani had given them the benefit of the doubt and figured they had misread the invitation, though the others hadn't been as compassionate.   Had they ever been to the Archimedes School or even Maryland this time of year? Well, by the time they had left, the combination of tropical heat, 100% humidity, Armani suit, diamonds and mud (the great equalizer) had taken its toll and that primped up mom looked like drowned mouse, and her hubby, not much better. Would they be back this year? Probably, but this time they'll be wearing the latest Ralph Lauren tropical safari collection.

Ayani stood with her hands on her hips as she surveyed the contents of her closet. She wanted to wear her perfectly shredded Lucky Jeans and a faded t-shirt from some rock band that stopped touring fifteen years ago, but knew her twelve year old daughter would be mortified by her mother's attire. Ayani didn't care if the Archimedes School parents raised their eyebrows, but making her daughter uncomfortable or embarrassed was never her goal. Instead, Ayani reached for an exotic print turquoise and brown silk wrap skirt she had purchased several years ago on an excursion to India. She coupled this with a more contemporary Michael Stars scoop neck brown tank. As Ayani completed her clothing selection, the service dog she was training sauntered in purposefully to watch her dress. Ayani was caring for the dog and continuing his training for six months while his primary trainer recovered from a hysterectomy.

Ayani looked over her shoulder to see "Blaze" curl his lip to expose a happy, toothy grin as she stepped into her bra and panties. Just the day before, Ayani told her husband that the dog acted like a reincarnated dirty old man. Blaze always had a sly look on his face that seemed to say, "I'd like some food now, but could you do it naked?" She enjoyed Blaze's company, even in these private moments. But Blaze needed to get out as much as possible to get used to functioning in complicated scenarios like rowdy crowds, so tonight would be a great opportunity for him to show off his self-control. The interesting part would be to see which Archimedes parents had significantly less self-control than this beautiful and clever German shepherd.

"Blaze, just wait, 'ol boy. In just a little while your self control will be surely tested as we witness all the strange humans that show up at these Archimedes picnics," Ayani said to her service dog. She then muttered to herself, "Not to mention all their beastly overly bred $5,000 puppies."

Ayani looked at the clock and realized she only had thirty minutes to get her family out the door if she wanted to arrive by 6:30 to help Laurel with any last minute details. Those final moments before any major event are always the most hectic. Glancing into her daughter's bedroom, Ayani stopped and watched as her pre-teen daughter twirled in front of the mirror admiring her brand new field hockey uniform. *Sara's really starting to bloom now*, thought Ayani, looking at Sara's long lean legs in the short plaid kilt and her tiny budding breasts safely secured in a lycra sports bar. Ayani's twelve year old daughter looked so very different than the young girl who splashed around the pool all summer. Even in her braids, Sara was starting to look like a young woman.

"Honey, we need to hurry, it's almost time to go," said Ayani.

"Whatev...I mean, okay Mom. I don't have to stay with you and Carver all night, do I? I'm supposed to hang out with the team," Sara replied, quickly correcting her attitude.

"That's fine, just be ready to leave when I say, 'we're leaving.' So how do you girls plan on drumming up fans for tomorrow's game?"

"Becky said we look so hot in our uniforms we just need to show them our stuff and no one will be able to keep away from us."

"Well then, let's just bring that big hockey stick along tonight as well. You can use it to beat off the boys," Ayani said as she cringed to herself, hoping Sara was too young to understand the double entendre. Ayani also made a mental note of shifting Becky from the 'sweet girl' side to the 'potential threat' side in the tally sheet of Sara's friends.

Ayani hustled downstairs to the playroom where she found her five year old son Carver playing with little Matchbox cars (what is it with little boys and little cars?).

"Carver, let's hop in the car, it's time to go to the school picnic," Ayani said.

"Mommy, is there food there?   Is Daddy coming? He's gonna miss everything again," said Carver, whining slightly.

"There'll be lots and lots of food and Daddy may join us after his tennis game." At that moment her highly competitive husband was doing his best not to crush his brand new legal client in a game of tennis on the courts adjacent to the neighborhood pool.

Ayani packed up Carver and Sara, and loaded Blaze and his harness into her Prius. They lived within ten minutes of the school in one of the most prestigious neighborhoods in Annapolis called Waterside Villas. Each home built in Waterside was required by their neighborhood architectural committee to be no less than six thousand square feet in size. The community association wanted to insure that no home had a value of less than $4 million. Waterside lived up to its name, with every home situated directly on the Severn River, the main waterway connecting most of Annapolis to the Chesapeake Bay. This was definitely not a cookie-cutter McMansion housing development. Rather, the neighborhood was comprised of a broad spectrum of architectural designs ranging from cedar shake beach style with lots of windows, decks and porches to those traditional staunch brick mansions, anchored by bulky white columns in front. The neighborhood was nearly five years old, which was just enough time to allow the original landscaping to grow and develop into maturity. The common grounds of the neighborhood included a fifty slip deep water marina, club house, two pools, tennis courts, and crabbing pier. The $5,000 annual community dues collected from each of the sixty or so homeowners was just barely enough to cover the expense of upkeep. It almost seemed incongruous that Ayani and Derrick lived in such an ostentatious development; they were so grounded, in touch with nature, and preferred to avoid the five o'clock cocktail scene. But, since they were the first family to buy property and build their home in Waterside, they did not foresee the grandeur that was soon to come.

To Ayani her home was just a pleasant place in which to live with a serene view. She always seemed puzzled when after telling people where she lived, they would always exclaim with a tinge of jealously in their voices "oh, you live *there*." She and Derrick simply liked the fact that their home backed up to the marshes which came alive every morning with the sights and sounds of blue herons, ducks, geese, and the occasional visit from a muskrat. During the summer they had crab traps hanging from their pier and they typically caught enough Maryland blue crabs to enjoy a feast each week.

With the children and dog strapped into her car they headed to the picnic. After their short drive through the historic downtown section of Annapolis, Ayani arrived at Archimedes to discover that basically *nothing* had been readied for this huge all-school event. Laurel just stood there in the Whorl, the main gathering point on campus for all school events, with her hands on her hips, staring at a centerpiece that had been placed on the one and only table set up. Laurel repeatedly "fluffed" the flowers, then stepped back to gaze at her arrangement. Ayani noticed that by this time Jodi had already arrived and was commandeering the early appearing parents to get tables, chairs and ice coolers from the storage room in the gymnasium. Ayani's children Carver and Sara, sensing chores were about to be assigned, disappeared quickly. Carver headed to the preschool sandbox and Sara to the large clump of field hockey girls, giggling and trying to look 'hot' in their plaid uniforms.

"Laurel, shouldn't the caterer be here by now?" asked an exasperated Jodi. "If you used *Instant Cuisine* they're always here on time."

"I used someone else, I just can't remember their name right now...their number is here somewhere, I told them 6:30...I'll try to track them down. I only remember their logo had a *spotted cow* on it," said Laurel, as she juggled her cell and fumbled in her pocket looking for the phone number and the name of the caterer, which she had completely forgotten.

"Laurel, where's your husband?" asked Jodi. "We could put him to work hauling tables."

"I know, I know. Of all the nights, our kids are sick. He's home taking care of them," said Laurel.

Jodi looked over her shoulder to see Ayani arrive with her children and service dog. "Oh good, Ayani, you're here," exclaimed an already irate Jodi. "I have no idea what the *fuck* is going on—Laurel hasn't done a thing to get this picnic going. I just called Charleigh and she and Bud are picking up some powdered lemonade and cups. She'll be here any minute. Could you give Ashlyn a hand filling up those drink dispensers?"

Ayani and Jodi's teenaged daughter Ashlyn found the only available water source and began to fill the containers using a garden hose, after brushing mulch from the spout, of course. Leaving Ashlyn in control, Ayani walked Blaze over to a quiet shady spot overlooking the sandbox. Chaos was growing quickly.

By now, thirty to forty parents had arrived at Archimedes and were milling around the campus, many of whom seemed bewildered by the lack of food and were wondering if they had arrived too early or on the wrong day. Two Upper School moms, Susan Roper and Michelle Baker, both looking very Junior League in their bright pink and lime Lili Pulitzer sundresses and enormous white Chanel sunglasses, came over to Ayani to flaunt Susan's latest designer dog, a "pure bred" Shepadoodle puppy. To most people at Archimedes, Ayani was the resident dog expert because of all her volunteer work at the animal shelter.

"Isn't he just the cutest little booboo? He's the perfect blend of poodle and German shepherd. Look at all these adorable poodle curls—and he'll be able to protect me at night when my husband is off playing poker," said Susan. "I told the breeder it would be great if he could also add a little Portuguese Water dog to the mix—wouldn't it be wonderful if my little "Harvard" could guard children on the beach, too?"

"Sorry Susan, I'm a little confused about *pure bred mixes*. Isn't pure bred just one type of dog? How exactly do they mix three breeds of dogs?" asked Ayani.

Susan clarified, "Ayani darling, I can't believe you've missed the boat on this one. These are not common mutts – where you just breed one dog to another. These dogs are designed and engineered by specialized breeders. They're carefully trained specialists with walls of diplomas. They select very special purebred dogs that are bred to produce these mixes, to keep the mixes pure. To add a third breed, a selected pure mix is bred with a pure bred dog – to produce the pure *mixed-mix*. It's all very scientific. Designer dogs cost thousands and they're worth every penny."

"Barb Abrams' Cockeranian cost $6,000, and Yorkipoo's are almost that much. I saw a Puggle, a pug-beagle designer mix for $3,000 – you've got to pay the big bucks if you're working with the best breeders," said Susan.

The yipping puppy hadn't stopped barking since it had walked over. Blaze looked up as if to say, *"Am I supposed to actually play with this nasty little thing or eat it?"* Ayani smiled back and he returned to his ready-for-your-next-command stance. Ayani wondered if they should start examining the possibility that some of the dogs at the shelter were not merely mutts but 'designer dogs.' Hey, if that could help get them a home why not? This was ludicrous, thought Ayani.

"How do you 'select' for specific characteristics from each breed, especially with just one pairing?" asked Ayani. "Blaze here comes from a line with an 85-90% rate of successful service training. That's very high but comes only after many pairings to select for characteristics leading to success and attempts to avoid medical problems that can accompany specific breeding. I guess I don't understand how you can be so sure your Shep-a-doo-dle has inherited the desirable characteristics and none of the physical or behavioral negatives of these two breeds."

Susan explained, "Oh Ayani, I know you're a brilliant trainer and all, but this is highly technical. Way too technical. It's so much more than 'dog meets dog makes puppies,' it all comes down to how much money you pay to the breeder. You know, I wonder if my breeder could take all of Blaze's training and breed it with something more *adorable*? You know, with fluffy curls and a smaller snout."

You're absolutely gorgeous, Blaze, ignore her, Ayani thought to herself. She decided not to mention the obvious early signs of hip dysplasia she saw in Susan's dog. Meanwhile the adorable little booboo was about as badly behaved as a puppy can be with Susan more interested in its 'design' than its wellbeing. Blaze calmly glanced up at Ayani for instructions on dealing with the out-of-control little mutant, then settled into his royal sphinx pose at the slightest hint of Ayani's hand signal pulling on his harness.

Susan didn't see Ayani's gentle tug. "Isn't that amazing?" exclaimed Susan to Michelle, "You know Ayani is part Native American and she's able to communicate with animals using some sort of magic tribal telepathy stuff!"

Ayani tried to explain that Blaze's behavior had more to do with many years of constant training and hard work but the pair of women preferred the Hollywood version to Ayani's more mundane reason. As the two women left to parade their puppy around the campus, Susan raised her hand in Mr. Spock's pose from Star Trek and said what she thought was a classic Native American blessing, "Ayani, may you live long and prosper."

By seven thirty neither food nor Laurel Somerville was anywhere to be found. Laurel had mysteriously disappeared after being bombarded by parents asking her for instructions, wanting her to call the caterer, begging her to find snacks for the hungry children, and searching for anything but water or lemonade to drink. The only clue Laurel gave to the hungry masses before she disappeared was that the caterer had a large cow attached to the roof of his delivery van.

Ayani, Chrissie, Jodi, Charleigh and Tara took a much needed break to breathe and reconnect after the frenzied pace setting up the "non-picnic." Charleigh's husband Bud hovered nearby to watch their three children, giving Charleigh her space, but also keeping a protective eye out for anyone too interested in his gorgeous wife. Just then a well dressed dad shouted across the Whorl, "Hey Charleigh, what's cookin'? I bet you've got some juicy home cooked meal tucked somewhere." Bud turned in the direction of his voice, locked eyes, and gave him a stare that would boil blood. Consequently, the overly friendly dad cowered away with his "tail" tucked between his legs.

"I need to sit. I think something's seriously wrong with Laurel, this picnic is a complete disaster and she's nowhere to be found," said Ayani, as she subtly signaled Blaze to lie next to her.

"She's history, she'll never chair another school event," said Chrissie sympathetically. "I figured she went home. I saw her head to the parking lot a while ago. Meanwhile, what do we feed the kids? For that matter, what are we going to feed them at school everyday? Did you get the word? 'Archimedes preschool is peanut-free.' Give me a break, my kid lives on peanut butter. Why not just deal with the allergic kid instead of making the whole Division peanut free?"

"Peanut allergies are tricky," Jodi replied with confidence. Years of work as a pediatric nurse always placed Jodi as the authority on any healthcare issues. "Peanut allergic kids can react from just being in the same room as the offending allergen. That said education would be a far better approach than prohibition. That's the way we dealt with it in Ashlyn's time."

Charleigh weighed in, "It looks like prohibitions are going to be a part of our world. I read how private schools everywhere are running scared of lawsuits. Do you know how many times Archimedes was sued last year? It's insane, and explains why they freak and over-react to things like this."

"So who's the allergic kid?" Tara asked.

"Leona Lowe's little girl—Patience."

"Leona, the actress and famous star of community theatre?" asked Charleigh.

"One and the same," continued Chrissie. "She said her daughter's doctor found the allergy on a routine blood test."

"The blood test is notorious for picking up false positives. Johns Hopkins reported 90% are false positives when challenged by the offending allergen in a controlled setting, like a hospital. But most physicians and parents don't want to chance the challenge, so it's welcome to the peanut-free world for all of us, even though she may not even be allergic." Jodi added, feeling very comfortable again in her former nurse role.

"I found some soy based peanut butter at the Health Food store. It has kind of a plaster-like taste but I haven't tried it on Carver yet. I'm planning to load it up with honey before I give it to him," said Ayani.

"My daughter Honey will eat anything with *honey* on it – it's kind of her trademark," added Charleigh with a smile.

"Okay girls, it's time to get down to business, quien ganara el premioesta noche?" asked Chrissie with a smile, changing the topic.

Tara looked confused. "Sorry, who's gonna win the fashion faux pas award tonight?" Chrissie clarified.

"Oh I got it, um...did you see the rocks on that lady over there?" said Tara, wanting to participate. "The necklace, earrings, tennis bracelet – they must have cost a fortune!"

"Dearest, I'm afraid hundreds of cubic zirconia died to make that necklace. She and her husband just refinanced their house to pay for Archimedes, she's just trying to save face," informed Charleigh.

"O.K. but how about that trophy babe on Gil McDonald's arm, the one with the mini skirt spray painted on and Jimmy Choo spikes?" asked Jodi. "His ex is here tonight and she's doing her best to keep some distance away from them. Poor thing, the stress from the trial made her wrinkles deeper than the Grand Canyon. Meanwhile, Gil got a face lift and a barely legal babe. Divorce really sucks."

Chrissie agreed, "Gil is a total jerk to bring out this *"woman"* before the ink dries on their papers. She and the kids are better away from him. I'm betting the babelet loses her stilettos and goes native before 8:30."

"Quiet girls...don't look behind you now, but Astrid's here and I think she'll win the fashion faux pas award today. She's wearing shorts so tiny the bottom half of her butt's hanging out. And she's showing off her tan with that pink silk Pucci top unbuttoned just enough to reveal her brand new belly button piercing. Oh no, look...*no don't look*, she's got matching Pucci platform shoes!" exclaimed Charleigh. Astrid confidently strolled past the five women enjoying the attentive stares from most of the men, and even a few women, at the picnic.

"Speaking about Astrid, guys, tell us about last night. What happened at her sex toy party?" asked Jodi anxious to catch up on the latest news. The group had missed their opportunity to walk that day since morning rain showers drowned out their exercise routine.

Chrissie paused then began, "Actually, it wasn't a sex toy party at all, apparently that's passé. No, we got to experience the latest trend in the at home party circuit—it was a 'training session' on *ten secrets to a happy sex life*. Part one included some tips on how to give your husband the perfect blow job." Chrissie said with a shudder. "Astrid actually hired some lady—some sex therapist lady, to teach us what to do. The goal is to keep your husband happy so he'll be more likely to satisfy your needs."

"Needs like romance, chocolate, music, flowers and champagne? Or other needs?" asked Ayani.

"Yeah, somehow I think some man thought this up. So we work to please him to satisfy *our* needs?" added Charleigh.

"Cool it guys. You can see Chrissie is upset. Was it awful?" interjected Jodi as she leaned in closer to Chrissie to get the gory details.

"What did they do? Did they use a real guy? God, I hope you didn't have to touch him!" exclaimed Charleigh with concern in her voice. Then under her breath, "Astrid and her gang have way too much time on their hands."

"Oh no, it was very sanitary, very hygienic" exclaimed Tara with her southern drawl. "That sex-expert lady reached into the dishwasher where they had been sterilized and started pulling out these rubber...um, you know... *thingies*...all different sizes and colors. They even had veins and doodads."

"Please tell me you didn't put that thing anywhere near you," said Jodi.

"Not me, *no way*, but Tara kinda got into it. Right? I just stood there in shock, claiming I was coming down with something and was feeling a little queasy and couldn't put anything in my mouth, while Astrid passed these *thingies* out and the women got to pick the one they wanted. There were all shapes, sizes and colors, but these women tended to pick the ones they were most used to—you know, the average sized white ones," said Chrissie.

"I needed to have a few cosmos in me before I did anything, said Tara. "But it was fun once you loosened up. Plus I didn't want to offend Astrid—I'm just getting to know the moms at Archimedes. That sex therapist lady was very professional and showed us lots of things we'd never tried before—you know, how to use your hands, twisting your mouth in a special way, and that new trick with your...."

"Oh *please* stop, I can't re-live that scene again," squirmed Chrissie, obviously very uncomfortable with the visuals.

"When we were done, they just gathered up all those little rubber thingies and popped them into the top rack of the dishwasher. I was only worried what her husband might think if he was searching for a tumbler later that night," giggled Tara. She continued, "We finished the evening by checking out Astrid's collection of fifty or so sex toys. She showed us how they all worked, battery operated or no batteries, some were shower safe, some had extra attachments, one glowed in the dark! One even connected to your iPod and played music! It was kind of like a woman's version of Guitar Hero."

"Yeah, I missed that bit. I was already driving back to Eastport, trying to decide if I could induce amnesia by mixing Ativan and bourbon," said Chrissie.

"Try the med Versed, darling, but you need a 'script," suggested Jodi.

"Good Lord, only Astrid and her gang could have a party like that. So what's on the next level, where does she go from here?" asked Charleigh.

"I don't want to even think about it," replied Chrissie with a shudder that seemed to go all the way from her head to her toes. "All I know is Astrid could probably teach it," Chrissie ended with a slight giggle.

Right on cue as if other Archimedes parents had overheard this conversation, whoops of laughter spilled from the parking lot where a huge crowd was gathered around someone's spanking new black Mercedes SUV.

"Girls, let me check it out," Tara said. Tara volunteered to investigate and followed an extension cord leading from a school building to a Mercedes in the parking lot where some Archimedes Upper School parents had two blenders whirring away producing margarita after margarita for the hungry and parched parents. Several Brazilian nannies had already had too many and were being thoughtfully supported around the waist by the strong arms of a couple of helpful dads. Each time one of these girls wobbled and teetered from the combination of alcohol and three inch stilettos, the dad got the opportunity to let his hands slip upward and discreetly cop a feel. Eventually, the nannies figured out the cause and effect of their weaving and appeared to totter all the more. Ayani watched from a distance and saw Tara's lips form the word "thank you" as she reached for a plastic cup. That would be the last time the four core women saw Tara that night.

By 8:30 there was still no food in sight and the tequila was having a huge impact on the empty-bellied parents hanging out in the parking lot. The last remnants of a gorgeous pink sunset glowed over Spa Creek, reminding Ayani of the saying, "Red sky at night, sailor's delight." The weather would be good for tomorrow's field hockey game, she thought. For just a brief moment the campus was veiled in darkness until the outside facility lights blinked on. Mr. Greenspring, the headmaster of Archimedes, took this opportunity to welcome the parents, staff and children to the annual 'Welcome Back' picnic. Since Laurel had forgotten to arrange with the maintenance department to have the P.A. system set up, Mr. Greenspring resorted to raising his hands and holding up two fingers in a sign for silence—it was the signal all teachers had been using since Kindergarten to quiet the children, but it had minimal effect on the adults. The noise from 'Margaritaville' only got louder. Finally, when it was clear that the rowdy cheers from the parking lot would continue, Mr. Greenspring began to shout his greeting.

"WELCOME TO ARCHIMEDES," he screamed. "Welcome to a new year at our very unique institution...." The crowd applauded politely on cue.

"Thank you for your patience, I assure you the food will arrive shortly. First and foremost I would like to thank Laurel Somerv...."

Silently, every light on campus blinked out.

"What the fu...," someone in the crowd started to say.

The crowd buzzed, and several folks muttered the words "timed outage for the Friday night Astronomy Club..." Many people looked up at the sky expectantly and sure enough the stars had begun to pop out one by one. The combination of eyes adjusting and light fading made this phenomenon almost startling and quite beautiful. Even the party animals in the parking lot seemed to settle down slightly.

Teacher Matt Worthington announced, "Somebody must have forgotten to override the timer, it's in the maintenance building. I'll go take care of it." Seizing the moment, Berri Franconi, his *friend* and fellow teacher, stepped away from her husband and volunteered to assist Matt with his task.

"I think I know where the switch is," Berri said with a sweet smile. No one saw as she gently placed her hand on the small of his back.

Jodi edged over to Ayani. "Well, Laurel really screwed this one up. No volunteers, no food, no drinks, no tables or chairs. Clearly she didn't follow the checklist the Events Chairperson handed out. Contacting the maintenance crew is the first step," said Jodi.

"Be nice, Jodi, she probably feels really bad about this," said Ayani.

"Ayani, you're kind to a fault. I don't think Laurel feels a thing right now. Anyway, she's been missing for at least an hour," added Jodi.

"They said the Astronomy Club has the exterior lights timed to go off from 8:30 to 11:00 every Friday night," said Ayani, a statement that would be repeated many times that night. "I've lost Sara in this darkness and I'm really starting to get worried. Could you guys keep an eye on Carver while I start searching for her?"

"No problem," said Jodi who was already busy taking glow-in-the-dark bracelets and necklaces from her purse to attach to each of their kindergartners who were playing nearby.

"What's with the bracelets, Jodi?" Ayani asked, wondering why Jodi was so aptly prepared. Jodi explained that her daughter Faith wore one whenever they went out on the boat at night.

"Don't worry, we'll keep Carver entertained…and safe," said Jodi. By now Chrissie, Charleigh, her husband Bud, and all of their glowing children had gathered close together in the Whorl.

Ayani collected Blaze's collar in her hand and left the comfort of the group to search for her older daughter Sara. Just then her cell phone sang with a Jimi Hendrix tune identifying her husband's call. The tennis game was over (yes, of course he won) and after he took a quick shower he'd be heading to school. He wanted to know if they needed anything for the picnic.

"No dear, just stay home, unless you want to bring hamburgers, hot dogs, salads and drinks for five hundred people," Ayani told her husband. "The caterer never showed, the lights are out, I've lost Sara, and the picnic is a complete disaster!" For the first time that night Ayani who was always so calm and even keeled was visibly shaken by the turn of events.

Ayani sensed a change in the crowd, what was it about darkness that gave people the permission to be mischievous? It was as if all the rules evaporated once everything was shrouded in shadows. Within moments of the lights extinguishing, the mood of the crowd shifted from alarm and surprise to something more chaotic and naughty. "What can we get away with now?" seemed to be the unstated overall theme.

Blaze was jumpy. He, too, sensed a change in the crowd. People were running, children were yelling, dogs were barking, and the hilarity from the bar scene in the parking lot grew even louder as the tequila crowd began to realize the spreading pandemonium that was taking over the campus. The Brazilian nannies had thrown caution to the wind and blatantly flirted with several of the men. Jonathan, a dad of a preschooler, and his newly hired nanny were tete a tete, deep in conversation. Ayani observed Jonathan's nanny subtly brushing the back of her hand against his crotch. Jonathan, in turn, slipped his hand under her shimmering halter top. Ayani then caught sight of Tara as she tossed her hair and leaned closer into another dad—or was it a teacher, in the darkness she wasn't sure. She knew it was Tara at least, her formerly sweet voice had now elevated to an earsplitting level thanks to the influence of the tequila. It might have been fun to join the festivities if she didn't have her kids along, but that was out of the question tonight. *Anyway, this whole scene didn't feel right.* Something bad was right around the corner, she could feel it. Ayani scurried past the flirtations and led Blaze to her Toyota Prius in the parking lot where she popped open the glove box and retrieved a flashlight. She was astonished to see several SUV's with their interiors glowing an eerie blue while little illuminated faces tilted upward and stared raptly at tiny scenes dropping down from the car tops. So this was where the intoxicated grownups stashed their kids for the night, thought Ayani. She cringed when she caught a glimpse of several preschoolers watching one rather gory decapitating scene from *Lord of the Rings*. "Those poor children, I wonder how they'll sleep tonight," worried Ayani. Sadly the still-drunk parents would probably remain oblivious to their children's cries in the night.

As Ayani and Blaze left the parking lot, they walked quickly past a massive Hummer that rocked in a tell tale manner. "Well, at least they're not cramped in there," Ayani muttered out loud to herself in an attempt to cover any errant noises that might have escaped from inside the Hummer.

How was she going to find her daughter? If only she really did have magic Cherokee powers. She imagined putting her ear to the ground, *Blaze, me think Sara come from the west.* Okay, now the frenzied scene had started to play tricks on her sensibilities. Why did the absence of light give everyone license to degenerate? Before you know it, someone would be throwing rocks through classroom windows and looting, walking off with desks and laptops. By now Matt Worthington and Berri Franconi should have found the master light switch for the campus. Even if they did sneak off to have sex in some physics classroom, they should have been done by now. It doesn't take that long! Ayani noticed that Matt's wife was searching frantically for him and Berri's husband had a flashlight in his hand. Whatever Matt and Berri were doing, they should wrap it up soon or *enraged spousal assault* might be another element to add to the bedlam of the night, thought Ayani.

Blaze, find Sara boy, find Sara. Ayani had one of Sara's hair scrunchies in the car, but Blaze was a seeing eye dog and had spent months of training for something other than bloodhound work. Oh well, a good opportunity lost. At least Blaze did a great job keeping Ayani grounded in all this commotion, the dog remained calm and alert, *top marks for Blaze.* Ayani took a deep cleansing breath and wandered back toward the Whorl to continue her search.

Just beyond the parking lot, a large boxwood shrub began to shake. Ayani aimed the flashlight at its base where a woman's body lay on the grass. Ayani felt her skin crawl and feared the worst, when suddenly the woman rolled over, readjusted her blouse, and smiled into the beam of the flashlight. Crystal, mother of first grader Chastity, sat up, clearly unharmed, and greeted Ayani.

"Oh, Hi...um Crystal, have you seen my daughter Sara?"

"No I haven't—I've been …busy," Crystal said as she brushed some leaves from her hair.

"I haven't either –she's not here." Astrid sat up, sharing her smarmy smile as she pulled another leaf from Crystal's blonde locks.

Okay, just get me out of here, thought Ayani. "Thanks guys. Um, pretty stars tonight. See you later, I guess." *Blaze, dear, stick with your own kind—these people are wacko.*

From around the corner of a classroom building teenage girl-giggling was heard. Blaze's ears perked up at the sound. Ayani instinctively headed in that direction. As she approached she saw a small flame briefly illuminate the face of a young girl wearing field hockey plaid as she lit what was hopefully a cigarette. This young girl was also under the decadent influence of what Ayani had begun calling the "Lights Out Effect." Under the protective cover of darkness, Ayani thought she could probably talk to these girls without embarrassing Sara. She approached the group of five shadowy figures; the faces of several were hidden by the darkness.

"Hey, Becky. Have you seen Sara?" asked Ayani. There was a long uncomfortable pause.

"I'm here Mom," said Sara with obvious teenage annoyance in her voice. This was followed by an even bigger pause.

The girls exchanged loaded glances. As if on cue, Sara begged;

"Pleeeease, please, please can I stay? No one else is going home now and it's really fun here tonight. Please."

"She'll be safe with us," shared Becky, now the authority, exhaling a stream of smoke. Ayani was bothered that Becky made no semblance of an effort to actually hide the cigarette. She stood there, on school property, smoking as if it were the most natural thing in the world for a 12 year old to be doing. Ayani paused a moment to think. *Drunken laughter flowed from the parking lot, bushes moved, cars rocked, teachers disappeared, stars shone, and smoke got in her eyes.*

"Are you out of your freaking mind, Sara? Get over here now and help me get Carver and Blaze to the car. We're outta here."

Angrily and reluctantly Sara followed her mother. Ayani swiftly returned to the safety of her friends who were watching her youngest child. She scooped Carver onto her back, piggyback style, and handed Sara the flashlight. Sara quickly kicked into gear with this adult-like responsibility, the "official illuminator of the Jenkins family." With one hand on Blaze's collar they made their way toward the parking lot. Jodi's children Ashlyn and Faith were complaining loudly about "starving to death" so Jodi followed Ayani and her crew to their cars. As they passed Laurel Somerville's car the mystery of her whereabouts was solved—Sara's flashlight momentarily illuminated a figure slumped over the steering wheel in the driver's seat. *Laurel!* Jodi quickly jumped into action. She flung open the car door and began checking Laurel's state of consciousness.

"Pulse is fine, respiratory rate is tanked. Damn. Ayani, look around the car for her purse. See if she's on anything," commandeered Jodi. Seeing a passerby with a cell phone in hand, Jodi shouted, "You there—yes, *you*, call 911, we need an ambulance. We've got a lady trying to die over here."

The older girls Ashlyn and Sara simultaneously picked up the little ones and turned to shelter them from the view. *This can't be happening*, thought Ayani. Blaze dropped to sitting position as she let go of his harness and began tearing apart Laurel's car. Did this woman live in her car? Look at all this crap, and it was 'mom crap' not kid stuff.

Jodi was holding Laurel's head upright to keep her airway open. "If the ambulance isn't here in two minutes we start CPR, she's breathing but not enough." Laurel's face was a bluish grey, the color worsened by the dashboard lights illuminating it. Jodi had the flashlight in her mouth while she timed something with her watch. Ayani found no purse, no tote bag, just lots of papers, bills, empty water bottles, and receipts: crap. Ayani hopped in the passenger seat and opened the glove box to see if there might be anything in there. An empty orange pill container rolled out.

"Grab that, gimme that." Jodi barked. Ayani felt blindly on the floor until she found it and handed it to Jodi.

"Percoset. Shit. That makes sense. Narcosis. Ayani, check the trunk, see if you can find anything else, we're starting CPR."

Ayani quickly climbed across the gearshift to reach the trunk release. Ayani leapt out of the car to the trunk where it appeared Laurel had kept a stash of purses for every occasion. Gucci, Dolce & Gabbana, Coach, Kate Spade—there were clutches, patent leather backpacks, satchels, hobos and totes, a vast collection if sold could easily pay for a year's tuition at the Archimedes School. Hurriedly dumping the contents from each, Ayani found what she was looking for in an oversized crocodile leather Prada bag that was tucked safely from view in the back recesses of the trunk.

"Jodi, another Percoset bottle is in one of her purses, this one's not empty." By now Laurel's body was cool to the touch. She was so still, as if in a deep, deep, deep sleep.

"Damn it Laurel, why do you screw with this stuff?" said Jodi.

Ayani jumped to help Jodi gently lay out Laurel's body on the black parking lot that was still warm from the heat of the day.

"Ayani, you remember how to do CPR? I'll do the respirations; that's all we have to do right now. Ayani, just listen. First, take your own pulse, both sides; then take hers. If her heart stops, and it might, you start with the chest compressions, I'll talk you through it, you can do this, got it?"

Jodi had just begun breathing into Laurel's mouth when they both heard the distant wail of the ambulance begin to grow louder. "Thank God" both women muttered in unison. Ayani felt her own heart racing and tried to calm herself with deep cleansing breaths. Conversely, Jodi seemed controlled and relaxed as she gently exhaled into Laurel's mouth every ten seconds or so. A thin line of drool ran down the side of Laurel's ashen face.

Ayani saw the flashing lights of the ambulance reflected in the side mirror as it drew near. The sirens were turned off as the rescue team silently pulled into the Archimedes School parking lot. Ayani jumped out of Laurel's car to frantically signal the ambulance driver to head her way. As the vehicle gently glided in her direction, the flashing red and blue beams served to illuminate the surreal scene that unfolded in front of everyone's eyes. Just a few cars away, Jonathan's Brazilian nanny was now blatantly grinding up against him (now his rumored affair was no longer just rumor), pressing him into the side of the Mercedes SUV. Lips locked, eyes closed, they were blissfully unaware of the eyes of the spectators glued upon them as their entwined forms eerily alternated in color from blue to red. Another dad with margarita tilted precariously in one hand, had his other arm draped around the bare shoulders of Brazilian nanny "number two" who's tube top (are they still in style?) had slipped to reveal an almost indecent display, held on by just the nipples.

Just beyond the parking lot, another scene was illuminated by the ambulance's rotating beams as the leaves of one section of the ancient boxwoods shuddered, revealing two entangled petite figures who were back at it again. Astrid and Crystal were engrossed so deeply they too were unaware of all eyes pointed in their direction. An astute observer might have also seen Matt Worthington and Berri Franconi as they stealthily scampered hand in hand across the Whorl from the side of the Upper School Library, with their clothes disheveled and hair awry. Apparently they never found that override switch after all.

And finally, all eyes rested on the raison d'etre for the ambulance. The EMT crew jumped swiftly into action, grabbing boxes and a tank with wheels and moving to Jodi's side.

"Narcan, Stat. Percoset OD. Assume Percoset OD," Jodi informed the technicians, she was becoming winded from the CPR. AN EMT quickly slipped a mask over Laurel's mouth and began forcing the gas into her by squeezing a bag attached to the mask.

"Scoop and run or tube her?" asked the EMT.

"Tube her, she's crashing," Jodi panted back as she backed out of the way. She pulled a Ziploc bag out of their equipment box and dropped the two orange pill containers into it as she met the eyes of one of the EMTs. The other EMT inserted an IV into Laurel's arm, then injected a syringe into it, from their expressions this was an important syringe. This must be the Narcan.

"She's crumping big time, we're out of here. Can you follow?" the EMT asked Jodi.

She replied, "Sure. Medical Center? Yeah, I agree, she won't make it to Baltimore." Jodi looked calm as can be, while Ayani's heart was beating so wildly it threatened to explode from her chest. Jodi came over and gave her a quick hug.

"You were a huge help," Jodi said to Ayani, attempting to reassure her.

"Hardly, I'm still shaking like a leaf. Jodi—just go, your girls can spend the night with us," replied Ayani.

"I'm sure Ashlyn won't mind," Jodi laughed as she wandered over to her car.

Blaze stood up and followed Ayani to her car, in all the commotion she had forgotten he existed but was very glad to have him by her side right now. *High marks Blaze, you wonderful dog. You're cooler than I am in the midst of all this madness.* Blaze uncharacteristically brushed the back of his head against her leg, sensing Ayani's need for contact and love right now. She returned his gesture.

As the ambulance drove away, a collective sigh was heard through the crowd of parents and students, who took this as a signal to pack up and head home for the night. Another year, another Archimedes School Welcome Back Picnic was over. As Ayani climbed into her car, her familiar little world, her heart began to resume its normal programming. Jodi's teenaged daughter Ashlyn looked quite shaken and agreed without a hint of resistance that she and her little sister Faith would stay over at Ayani's house. Ayani looked around her car filled with quiet, sweaty, hungry children and one very obedient dog. She took another deep breath before turning the key in the ignition, then drove away, to home, to Derrick, to light, and to sanity.

———

The following day the Middle School girl's field hockey team had their first big game in the field adjacent to the school's parking lot. Fifty Middle School parents smiled and cheered their young plaid-skirted warriors, making significant efforts to keep from laughing when power swings of the sticks missed their mark and the girls did the occasional impression of golfers missing the tee. Ayani looked over at the nearly empty parking lot, the drama and comedy of last night had left no mark, not even a plastic cup littered the ground. There was no evidence that hundreds of people had laughed and cried, loved and almost died here less than twenty four hours ago. There was still no word on Laurel's condition, Jodi remained professional and dodged all questions. There probably would be news circulating on Monday when someone would learn something or at least make up an interesting story to pacify the rumor mill.

Ayani's passing thought about Laurel did seem to have some magical effects, if not just good old fashion intuition (*oh that magic Cherokee telepathy stuff*—she smiled to herself) because just then an aluminum-sided delivery truck decorated with a *huge spotted cow standing on the roof* pulled into the parking lot. Poor Laurel's muddled brain had arranged for the caterer to arrive on the wrong day.

The crowd of fifty Middle School parents and their children enjoyed a fabulous barbeque feast for five hundred after the game.

Life Observations from Vic the Maintenance Guy:
"You know, I like to think that a rich man is nothing but a poor man with money. The problem is the rich man's just got bigger problems and more to lose."

Chapter Three:
The September Preschool Parent Coffee

A cool September pre-dawn breeze wafted gently through the Archimedes School campus. All was quiet, except for the rustling of a handful of crumpled school flyers that were caught up in the current of air, tossing, turning and fluttering across the school grounds. On one flyer were the words, *Reminder: Preschool Parent Coffee This Monday.*

═══════════

Bud Brooks reached for his wife Charleigh as she quietly slipped out of bed. Their two year old son Harding was singing loudly to himself in his bedroom down the hall, attempting to wake everyone in the household well before sunrise.

"Let Miss Elke get him," he mumbled, "come back to bed—just once more before I have to go today." Bud had a late September Yankees game to cover in New York tomorrow and had to catch a plane out of BWI airport around 10:30 that morning. Back in the days when Bud was a carefree bachelor and a successful starting pitcher for the Orioles he loved life on the road, traveling with the team, meeting people in every city—that is to say, *women* in every city, but mostly he loved the adrenaline rush he got every time he stepped on the mound in view of thousands of spectators, to face his first batting opponent of the game. That was the same adrenaline rush he felt now, every day, each and every time he saw his wife Charleigh. *I'm a lucky, lucky man* he thought to himself as he watched Charleigh's perfect figure glide across the floor when she left the bedroom to check on their youngest son. Sure he loved his sportscaster gig—and he was good at it, too, but life on the road was different now. He'd much rather be home with his stunning wife and three beautiful children than living out of a suitcase at a Holiday Inn. Funny how life changes.

Charleigh put her ear to Harding's bedroom door, and chuckled to herself as her toddler repeatedly sang the words "the kids on the bus go round and round" with the word "bus" sounding more like "buth" with his cute little boy lisp.

His bedroom door creaked slightly as she peeked in. Placing her pointer finger to her lips, she whispered to Harding, "Shhhhh, it's too early to wake up yet, baby. Here, little man, look at some picture books for a short while," as she handed him some educational books teaching shapes, letters and colors. "I'll be back in just a couple of minutes." After distracting Harding, Charleigh returned to her spot on the still warm sheets to enjoy the feel of Bud's nakedness as he spooned up closely to her for a few moments. A slight moan escaped from his lips and she realized they were seconds away from the dramatic shift where simple morning cuddling led to full on sweaty morning sex. "Um, Bud, sweetheart," Charleigh muttered as she gently pulled away, "We don't have enough time…we've got to get going." Moaning again, but this time without pleasure, Bud scooted reluctantly to his side of the king sized bed.

While Bud showered, Charleigh remained in bed and did a mental checklist of her plans for the day. Preschool Parent Coffee—9:00 am, the first one this year, *great*, time to face the mélange of parent weirdness once again; Harding—*Mommy and Me for Terrific Twos* music class at 9:30 am, oh well, Miss Elke will have to take him; lunch downtown at Pacific Rim with a former colleague from her television days who was still in the business working as a local news anchorwoman in Baltimore. "Hope we can get that private table in the back," Charleigh thought to herself, knowing that if they didn't their meal would be interrupted a hundred times by the overly friendly locals saying how much they loved both of these talented ladies on television. Charleigh hadn't been on the air for years, but she was still stopped on the street by well-wishers who said they enjoyed that story she did on *such and such*, as if she had just done the piece last week. She didn't miss the business at all, too cutthroat and too much emphasis on youth and beauty, not enough importance placed on talent and brains---even though she met all criterion. The television business was all about the ratings game and creating programs that appealed to the lowest common denominator—Charleigh remembered the research geeks from her station who briefed the news department on the daily Neilsen People Meter overnight ratings, "our morning numbers are down by 15% with 25-54 year olds and early fringe viewership dropped by 18% for all households, we've got to increase recycling from one daypart to another or we'll lose more of our total cumulative audience for certain." *Whatever.*

Charleigh didn't miss the television business, but she did miss some of her former coworkers. Many of her old friends were still reporting the news locally or held anchor jobs in medium and large markets around the region. She tried to keep in touch with a few, but her hectic schedule as a wife and mother limited the opportunities to socialize. She also avoided meeting her friends directly at any of the television stations where they worked—just stepping through the doors brought the horrible memories flooding back. The death of her first newborn was such a public event. The local television audience watched her every day throughout her pregnancy, witnessing her belly slowly growing and changing each week. Many of her fans sent her gifts and cards when the baby was born. At that time, she was married to her first husband who was simply gorgeous—"he's got *a face for TV*," as they said in the business. He had that boyish blond surfer look, well defined dimples, a perpetual tan, and teeth so white they would blind you on a sunny day. He was also smart. He had to be to keep up with Charleigh. He worked with Charleigh at the same television station, covering the news coming out of the White House and Congress. He aspired to landing a national news position on the network—which he eventually got several years later. In Washington, D.C., Charleigh and her first husband Jack were local celebrities, who were often featured in the Washington Post's gossip column; *Jack and Charleigh were invited to the Congressional Women's Luncheon and sat at Hillary Clinton's private table.*

Just one week old, so tiny, my poor little baby girl, she thought, tears again forming in her eyes. It was a pain so deep it always felt sharp and fresh whenever she thought about her loss—as if it happened yesterday. For several months after her daughter's death she cried constantly, staying alone in her bedroom until well past noon. Unfortunately, her loss was so great and her depression so profound, both her marriage to Jack and her career in television took a huge toll. She never returned to her anchor position and she never slept in the same bed with her husband after her loss. One day four months after the death of her child, she wrote a formal resignation letter to the station and then jotted a note to her husband saying the marriage was over.

Today, fast forward, seven years later, Charleigh was a new woman, married to Bud, living happily in Annapolis with their three children; the fraternal five year old twins Wilson and Honesty, and Harding—a sturdy two year old boy, solid and athletic, just like his dad. Funny how life changes.

Charleigh peered into her vast closet to choose an ensemble that she hoped wouldn't offend anyone—nor entice anyone, either. For Charleigh, that wasn't easy. She could look sizzling and sexy even if she donned one of those baggy industrial orange work suits worn by the roadside trash clean up crews. For the preschool parent coffee she needed to be subdued and also comfortable on this 85 degree late September day. Charleigh pushed a button and the mechanized hum of electronics and gears began as her clothes slowly rotated past her like they did on the conveyor racks at the dry cleaners. She chose a pair of Khaki capris she had bought over the summer at Saks, she picked out her favorite Marc Jacobs white shirt—crisp and simple, and her khaki, orange and salmon colored espadrilles, also from Marc Jacobs—lately her favorite designer. Yesterday Bud watched the kids while she immersed herself in a full day of spa treatments at *Zen*, the latest spa of choice amongst her television friends. Last year the trendy spa was *Naked* in Chevy Chase, Maryland. That was also the last time she indulged in such a treat. People who didn't know Charleigh thought she spent hours every day pampering herself, but actually such indulgences were a rare and special luxury. Today, her skin glowed from the micro-dermabrasion treatment and avocado facial, her nails were polished to perfection, and her hair was freshly coiffed and colored. At thirty-eight she was just beginning to sprout a few unwanted grey strands, front and center along her part. She vowed to fight every last one.

Miss Elke, their faithful live-in German nanny, was downstairs preparing a heart healthy breakfast for the entire family. Charleigh anticipated the typical fare for Mondays; oatmeal with skim milk and raisins, orange juice, and Elke's famous homemade bran muffins. Miss Elke was a wonderful, but predictable cook. Monday, oatmeal, Tuesday, egg white omelets, Wednesday, buttermilk pancakes, Thursday, waffles, and so on. She had been Charleigh's nanny since the twins were born and now after five years of steadfast service she was an integral and trusted part of their family. Miss Elke had her own cozy apartment over the three car garage—in Annapolis many of the larger homes and estates were built with garages that could accommodate two cars *plus a runabout boat.* After her workday was complete, Miss Elke would retire quietly to her quarters where she would occasionally entertain some of her lady friends, many of whom were also the older, rather, *more mature* nannies like herself, and play card games, drink sherry, and gossip about the younger nannies in town and their latest escapades.

"Charleigh, Bud, children, breakfast is ready," said Miss Elke with her heavy German accent, which had yet to diminish even after twenty years in the states.

"Coming," said Charleigh as she took one last look in the mirror before she scooped up the twins and headed downstairs. She nodded approvingly at her image, checked her diamond studs to make doubly sure they were well attached, grabbed her Coach bag, *khaki of course*, and went to the twins' room where they were already dressed and were working cooperatively on a puzzle. *I just love Miss Elke*, Charleigh thought to herself.

During breakfast Charleigh briefed her family on the plans for the day.

"Daddy's going to New York and will be home in two days—we'll get to watch him on TV tomorrow night, Harding—you get to go to music class with Miss Elke today ("Yeah!" from Harding), and kids, I'll be at Archimedes today for a coffee meeting, so I can peek in on you at preschool (another simultaneous "Yeah!" from the twins)."

"In the meantime, we need to hurry and finish breakfast if we're going to get to school on time," Charleigh continued. "Bud, I *have* to go now, we're already running late. Kids, give Daddy a big kiss."

Bud gathered all three of his children encircling them in one huge embrace, kissed each child on the cheek, and then stood to give Charleigh a long, lingering kiss goodbye.

"I'll call tonight," he said. Then he whispered in her ear, "I miss you already."

Miss Elke packed lunches for Honey and Wilson, carefully checking every food label to insure that *those offensive and life threatening nuts* weren't being clandestinely sent in the happy Thomas the Tank Engine and Barbie lunch boxes. *We didn't have all these food allergies in my day*, Miss Elke thought to herself. Charleigh grabbed the twins' Archimedes School Kindergarten book bags, imprinted with the nautilus logo, which were heavy with workbooks, folders, and assorted pieces of projects they had already completed this school year.

"Ooof, I hate to see how heavy these backpacks will be in high school," Charleigh exclaimed. "No wonder they all use those wheel-along bags."

Miss Elke strapped the twins into Charleigh's Porsche while Charleigh gave Harding a big hug and a kiss with the reassuring words "I know you'll have fun at music--love you little man!" Slipping in a Donna Summer disco CD, the music of choice these days for the twins, the happy trio headed off to another fun filled day at Archimedes. Charleigh never really learned anything at these preschool parent coffees, but she felt obligated to go, plus there was always *parental entertainment* that would provide fodder for future conversations on the morning walks with Jodi, Chrissie, and Ayani—and now Tara, too. These coffees were designed to inform parents about the preschool curriculum, answer any questions they may have, provide homework guidance, and discuss any playground issues that have arisen. Inevitably some parent would burst into tears claiming her child was being bullied on the playground climber and would demand to have the offending child removed from the school. Other parents would often pipe in with their complaints about the same child, saying things like, "my little Patience woke up last night screaming—stop Johnny, stop," and another parent would add, "I pay huge money to have my child go to this school just so we can avoid these disruptive, *public school* kids. We should have a say in who goes here or not." *I wonder what crisis will materialize today*, thought Charleigh.

As Charleigh turned her car onto Rowe Boulevard, the main road that led directly into downtown Annapolis, she braked hard to avoid hitting a burgundy Chevy pick-up truck that sped out of a convenience store parking lot. Charleigh laid on the horn as the twins in the back seat shouted encouraging words, "Go Mommy, catch up to that truck, get him!" Charleigh instinctively wanted to give the driver a piece of her mind, but didn't want to create the potential for inciting road rage, so common these days. Instead, she calmly pulled up to the next light, side by side with the offending vehicle. Inside were two scruffy young men wearing dingy brown coveralls, 7-Eleven coffee cups in hand, cigarettes dangled from their mouths.

"Hey Mommy, the bad guys are right next to us!" exclaimed Wilson.

"Shhhh sweetie, they can probably hear you," Charleigh nervously replied.

Just then the driver looked directly at Charleigh, caught sight of her knock-out good looks, and proceeded to make obscene gestures with his tongue, completely ignoring the fact that there were two young children were in the back seat.

The passenger of the truck then shouted, "Hey baby, what 'ya doing today? Wanna try some of my hot sausage?" he said while waving a half eaten *breakfast* hot dog in her direction.

Charleigh quickly closed the Porsche's sun roof in an attempt to block their obscenities. No matter, the passenger joined the driver in making licking motions and then pointed to his crotch. Charleigh floored the gas pedal as the light turned green, leaving the two men laughing and smacking each other, thoroughly enjoying their rude performance.

I won't tell Bud about this, Charleigh thought, shaken to the core. She knew Bud would use every contact and resource he had to track down these two men and then string them up by their toes. Bud's protective streak had the potential to turn violent if he thought that Charleigh's safety was ever in jeopardy. "Why does this always happen to me?" Charleigh said out loud to herself, remembering several similar incidents from her past. Yes, Charleigh was smart, but she sure was oblivious to the influence her beauty had over men.

Unfortunately, just as she pulled into a parking spot at Archimedes, Wilson started to imitate with great accuracy the hideous mouth gestures he had just witnessed.

"*No*, no, Wilson, don't do that, it's nasty!" exclaimed Charleigh.

Wilson listened and obeyed his mother just until he walked into the Kindergarten classroom, when he started recounting the morning's excitement to another classmate. Overhearing the boys' conversation and watching Charleigh's inability to quiet the children, Mrs. Casper, the Kindergarten teacher, intervened. However, it wasn't soon enough. Within seconds all of the Kindergarten boys began to make that same obscene motion with their tongues. Charleigh recoiled in horror and quickly left the room.

Within the preschool building there was a center atrium set aside as a gathering space for large meetings, children's performance, and holiday parties. Charleigh left the chaos of the Kindergarten classroom and sat down in one of the folding chairs that had been set up in a semi-circle in preparation for the coffee discussion. She was the first one to arrive, which allowed her a moment to calm down and regain composure—cool, calm and collected was her trademark appearance. Others who didn't know her interpreted it as—aloof, snobbish, and bitchy. Add in her looks and you got the explanation as to why most of the other moms at Archimedes spent a lot of energy gossiping about Charleigh's so-called affairs and wild parent parties. Charleigh's very existence often put her in the center of most scandals. Truth be told, none of it was true.

Charleigh welcomed the early arrival of Jodi, Ayani and Chrissie who had volunteered to be the set-up team for the preschool coffee. Chrissie had also enlisted Vic to help carry the eight foot tables from the maintenance shed. Vic, who was slightly intimidated by Charleigh's presence, coyly smiled at her, but stayed well beyond her personal bubble of space. He knew Charleigh was one of the *good moms*, at least that was what Chrissie said, but she was such a turn on he needed to keep his distance.

Once the set-up was completed, Charleigh, Jodi, Chrissie, and Ayani had a few moments to rest and catch up, using this brief time as a replacement for their missed walk this morning.

"Charleigh, what's up, you seem to be a little stressed?" inquired Ayani, always intuitive when it came to her friends.

"Nothing, I really don't want to talk about it. Just a rough morning. I'm fine," Charleigh tersely replied. Her friends recognized that tone in her voice and knew not to delve deeper.

Changing the subject, Jodi announced, "I've been meaning to tell you guys that I volunteered to host the Kindergarten parent pot luck dinner this year at my house."

"*Are you crazy*, remember what happened at last year's PS 4 pot luck? You can blame Ted and Becky's divorce on that night," said Charleigh.

"Yes, precisely, that's why I wanted to host it this year. I thought I could have more control over the events of the night if it was at my house," said Jodi with determination in her voice.

"You're brave Jodi…but you know you can count on us to help," said Charleigh.

"Hey, by the way, where's Tara? I asked her to help this morning, too." said Chrissie.

"She called me to say little Clinton's sick, you know, that stomach thing's going around. Neither one of them will be here today," said Jodi.

"Well, based on past coffees, she's certain to miss some drama for sure," added Charleigh.

Right on cue, the drama began as the two moms known as the "botox blondes" arrived. It was rumored that these two moms of preschoolers were nearly fifty, although with their plastic, seamless facades it was hard to tell. They frequently hosted "botox parties" where invited guests would be served smoked salmon, drink white wine, then pay up to $1,000 each to have a doctor inject their wrinkles with *botulinum toxin*, aka the elixir of youth, giving new meaning to the phrase "doing shots at happy hour." The botox blondes entered the room, revealed their true age by being encased in conservative, boxy, jewel tone St. John knit suits. They walked directly to the coffee maker, poured their cups of brew, and proceeded to chat casually about nothing in particular wearing a *frozen look of astonishment on their faces.*

"Looks like they got a touch up recently," whispered Charleigh. Chrissie could hardly contain her giggling. *By the time their children were in middle school, they could have probably bought a vacation condo in Ocean City with the amount of money they'll spend on "work,"* thought Chrissie.

Next to arrive was the recovering Laurel Somerville, fresh from immersion in a two week Narconon detox program where she was an inpatient at an addiction treatment center somewhere in Connecticut. Apparently she opted out of the recommended thirty day program and hired a "professional" personal sponsor and life coach instead, who's primary responsibility was to help Laurel face normal, everyday situations, like the preschool parent coffee—and, also to feed her a steady supply of vitamin supplements at each designated hour—part of her Laurel's detox program. The young Jamaican woman who escorted Laurel into the atrium carried a gallon sized plastic bag filled with vitamin supplements of every shape and size. As she helped Laurel to her chair, she handed her a green pill the size of a dime, and said with a thick accent, "it's for your liver, Laurel gal, take it."

Astrid and Crystal followed shortly and arrived together, wearing outfits so similar they must have called each other to say, "I'm wearing my True Religion jeans and Juicy shirt, how 'bout you?" Charleigh had to admit, these two women did look good, and she even inquired, "Love your shoes, are they Jimmy Choos?" Chrissie cringed at Charleigh's question, making a mental note to tell her that it was stuff like this that made people think Charleigh was so superficial. Despite Charleigh's high IQ, *or maybe because of it*, she did appreciate good style.

Leona Lowe, the woman well known for performances in local theater, appeared carrying one of those folding three part boards, typically used for science fair presentations. Avoiding eye contact with the other women in the room, she cautiously placed the board behind her chair, taking care not to let it open to reveal the contents.

The room began to buzz with conversation as thirty or so parents arrived. Apparently several parents were too busy to attend the "preschool *parent* coffee" so they sent their nannies as their stand-in. No problem for these eighteen year old girls, they got free coffee, donuts, and a chance to flirt with the handful of dads who attended.

Finally, the last person to arrive was Deborah Brown. Slung over her shoulder was an oversized Gucci bag, easily large enough to qualify as carry-on luggage, which she carefully set at her feet. Mrs. Casper and the other two Kindergarten teachers walked to the front of the semi-circle to welcome the gathering of parents.

Precisely as Mrs. Casper started, "Welcome par....par.... par...." she began to sneeze. Tears formed in her eyes, then poured in streams down her checks. Her nose turned the color of a beet. "Does...*sniff*...someone...*sniff*...have a dog in here?" she managed to ask. "It's the only thing that does this...*sniff*...to me."

Chrissie and Jodi turned simultaneously to stare hard at Deborah. "What's in the bag, Deborah?" asked Chrissie.

"Nothing...really," Deborah mumbled her reply.

The room was silent, except for the occasional sniffle from Mrs. Casper. All eyes were now on Deborah and her huge Gucci bag.

"Open the bag, Deborah," demanded Jodi, sounding like a police officer on one of those reality chase shows on television.

A little wet black nose poked out from the bag. Deborah quickly pushed the puppy's nose back into the purse.

"Look, we can't start this meeting until that dog's out of here," said one of the other Kindergarten teachers. "Can't you see that Mrs. Casper's in distress?"

"Hey, I pay tuition here, too. I have a right to be here at this meeting," complained Deborah, who now qualified as one of the biggest bonehead parents at Archimedes.

Several other parents chimed in, demanding that the furry creature be removed from the premises. Finally, sensing defeat, Deborah Brown stood up, grabbed her Gucci bag, and stormed out of the room in a huff. "Mr. Greenspring's gonna hear about this," she proclaimed. "Especially since I donated $30,000 to the scholarship fund last year."

After a few moments of heated follow-up commentary from the fuming parents in the room about Deborah and her dog, calm was restored and the coffee meeting resumed.

Mrs. Casper, now visibly improved, continued, "This morning we wanted to review our K-Calculus program we've introduced to the Kindergartners. I understand some of you are having problems with the homework—I've received several emails with your questions." Mrs. Casper then proceeded to describe the Archimedes preschool math curriculum. "The basic objective of our K-Calculus program is to introduce the students to the concepts of functions, rates of change and accumulation. Our K-Calculus program attempts to show students that each of these ideas can serve as a mathematical model for understanding phenomena in our everyday lives."

"We represent functions in four modes; symbolic, numerical, graphical and verbal," she said. Mrs. Casper continued to drone on and on, speaking for another fifteen minutes or so about the specifics of the math program, provided examples of problems they've solved, and suggested websites the parents could peruse for homework help.

All eyes in the room glazed over in a state of confusion, except for those of the botox blondes who continued to express great astonishment at everything.

Chrissie whispered to Charleigh, "We're doomed when they get to middle school."

"Questions, anyone?" asked Mrs. Casper.

One hand shot up. The rest of the parents were still numb. "My son's tutor went to Stanford. He's great. I'd highly recommend him to anyone in the room," said one of the moms. Tutor? *This is Kindergarten, my God, what are these people thinking*, wondered Charleigh. The mom passed the tutor's business cards to a handful of interested parents.

"The next topic this morning was requested by another parent, Leona Lowe, who would like to discuss the very serious problem of food allergies," said Mrs. Casper. "Leona, do you want to come up here?"

Leona carried the science fair presentation board to the front of the room. Inside was a graphic representation of what happens to a child during an allergic reaction to food products. Actual photos of children experiencing anaphylactic shock were posted on the board. Leona went on to explain that death could occur within minutes of *her* child being exposed to peanuts or nuts of any kind. She added that any birthday party *her* child was invited to must be nut free and Leona volunteered to come and inspect the party-givers home prior to the event. Just then Mrs. Casper interrupted briefly to add, "I hope everyone has seen the happy caterpillar sign hanging in my room that says we are a nut-free, dairy-free, and now *wheat-free* classroom."

Many of the parents in the room went ballistic with anger. "What…wheat-free, too!" "What are we gonna feed our kids now?" "Can't we just put the allergic kids in a special room?" "Why do we have to cater to these allergies?" "My son only eats peanut butter." "My daughter only eats cheese." Everyone was talking at once, the volume in the room raised to a crescendo.

Mrs. Casper tried to restore order in the room by making the "bunny ears" sign with her two fingers, then calmly responded, "This is a serious problem which we are trying to address. Right now we think that prohibiting these dangerous foods in the preschool building is the best answer."

Leona began again, this time shouting to be heard above the enraged mob.

"I would like to demonstrate the symptoms of anaphylactic shock so that everyone in the preschool building is aware of what to look for if my child, I mean, *any child* is in danger," Leona said.

Parents in the room became quiet in anticipation of her presentation.

Leona held her breath until her face turned blue, she puffed out her lips to illustrate the swelling that would occur, grabbed her chest as if it was constricting, pretended to vomit, then began wheezing, choking, drooling, and finally, fell to the floor in a mock seizure. After flopping around for a few moments like a dying fish, she came to a stop in a position that was just begging for a chalk outline drawn by an investigating officer. It was truly an excellent performance. No wonder she won that award last year from the local newspaper for "Best Actress." When her performance was finished, no one in the room moved. No one spoke. All you could hear was the collective sigh from the parents as they gazed at the crumpled figure lying on the rug.

"Well, um, thank you Leona for that, um, demonstration," said Mrs. Casper, clearly astounded by the performance. Leona pulled herself up from the rug, gathered her presentation board in her arms, and quietly returned to her seat. This time the expression on the faces of the botox blondes accurately reflected their astonishment of the situation. Parents in the room remained silent, too stunned to move, breathe or talk.

Mrs. Casper took a deep breath, looked around the room at the astonished expressions on *everyone's* face and began, "Well…um….Thank you for coming this morning. Please remember to mark your calendars for the next preschool Parent Coffee which will be in eight weeks. The topic will be "How to Avoid Raising Over-Stressed Children."

Charleigh, Jodi, Ayani and Chrissie stood up in unison, still numb from what they had just witnessed and silently left the building.

Life Observations from Vic the Maintenance Guy:
"Where were all the allergy ridden kids when we were growing up? Is this something new, or was it just survival of the fittest? Maybe it's just that all those darn chemicals we're eating everyday have screwed up our immune systems."

Chapter Four:
Archimedes Parents Gone Wild—The Kindergarten Parent Potluck

Chrissie was right. It was insane to volunteer to host the pot luck, thought Jodi, as she pushed the button on her answering machine to check for "yes" or "no" responses. Thus far, the Archimedes Kindergarten pot luck was shaping up to be *the* primo "A-List" event of the fall. Taking the notepad next to her phone, she jotted down the names of five additional couples who thanked her profusely for the invitation and were thrilled to attend.

"This is Sheryl Waters, Agape's mom," one message began. "Mike and I would love to come to the potluck. I just wanted to know what caterer you'll be using?" she asked.

"It's a POT LUCK," Jodi yelled out loud to the answering machine. Exasperated, Jodi decided that she would not clarify this point to Sheryl. Why bother? One less dish wouldn't be missed and she could avoid additional one-on-one personal contact with another clueless parent.

There were sixteen children in each of the three kindergarten classes. Forty-eight kids total, and you would think that would equate ninety-six parents. But, with the divorces, remarriages, one lesbian couple and the natural dad, there was the potential for over 120 attendees. Thus far, Jodi counted a whopping ninety "Yes" responses.

"I need the girls, this is going to be huge," said Jodi.

━━━━━━━━━

The next morning proved to be the coldest day yet of the fall season. Jodi prepared for the ritualistic female bonding experience of power walking around the neighborhood surrounding the Archimedes School's campus. She selected an LL Bean fleece pullover and her brand new black lycra yoga pants she had just bought on a day long shopping excursion she took with Charleigh. Jodi was in a habit of never shopping for herself, her daughters Ashlyn and Faith came first, so Charleigh decided it was a long overdue indulgence for the ever-practical Jodi—plus Charleigh convinced her to go by positioning it as "Jodi's birthday treat." Jodi turned forty-three last week. The process of becoming another year older was not a concern for Jodi, like it is for so many other women. It was natural and expected. No big deal. It also helped that Jodi looked at least five years younger than her actual age.

On the other hand, Jodi did fight the perpetual struggle of trying to maintain an ideal weight. Compared to her friends, who were either petite and perfect or long and lithe, Jodi was a more substantial woman. Big boned, tall at five foot nine, frequently tipping the scale at 150 pounds or more, Jodi was the only one who wore something larger than a size two.

She braved a glance in the full length mirror. Standing there naked and fully exposed she noted that, yes, she had lost a few pounds on her new diet. She took the tape measure and clip board out from a dresser drawer and scientifically began documenting her measurements. Thighs, one inch smaller, waist, also an inch smaller, but her upper arms were about the same as last week. Just as she had done in her past life as a nurse, Jodi meticulously recorded the data on the progress report. Jodi scribbled in the comments section, "Do more upper body work."

Once she got dressed, the yoga pants came a little low on her belly. But, with her diamond belly jewel, she could wear tight pants only if they fell about an inch below her belly button. Jodi was the most outwardly conservative woman of her group, yet inside there was a part of her that was still being developed—a sexy, simmering side, that she was just beginning to realize. The belly button piercing that she got on her fortieth birthday, much to her husband Rip's chagrin, symbolized an awakening of her new sexuality, anyway, didn't women reach their sexual peak in their forties? After creating two lovely daughters, and being married to a wonderful, but frequently absent husband who spent most of his time at the hospital saving lives and mending wounds as an orthopedic surgeon, Jodi felt that every waking moment of her life was spent caring for and supporting her family's needs. Make sure Rip's suits and white shirts are picked up from the dry cleaners, get the oil changed on his Mercedes, order his new cell phone, make travel plans for that upcoming conference, arrange dinner plans, and so on. For her daughters it was always; set up play dates, schlep them to gymnastics, music and art camp, violin lessons, purchase school supplies, help with homework, set boundaries and discipline them when needed, feed them, shop for them, and more. Not that Jodi would ever shirk her duties, she wasn't one of those women who suddenly said, "see ya, it's time for me now." Instead, Jodi opted for finding subtle, secretive ways to express her independence and stirring rebirth of sexuality, like the diamond belly button stud, and her new passion for Italian lace panties and silky sleepwear—her one and only extravagant indulgence. Rip didn't seem to raise an objection about that!

"Ninety parents coming this Saturday night," she said to herself. "What have I gotten myself into?" she worried aloud as she drove the children to school.

"Hey Mom, no problem, it'll be fun, plus I can help bartend," said her teenaged daughter Ashlyn.

"Over my dead body!" Jodi exclaimed. "But I may put you to work on the clean-up crew."

"*Ohhh* Mom," she whined. "If I do, can you at least buy me a new outfit from Abercrombie?"

"You get enough allowance now, but we can talk about it later," said Jodi, not closing the door on the option. Jodi was opposed to rewarding children for what she considered to be "life responsibilities" like making your bed or putting dinner dishes away. In her opinion, allowances shouldn't be used as incentive for simply being a responsible family member. Instead, Ashlyn's weekly allowance of 15 dollars, one dollar for every year of her age, was meant to teach her fiscal responsibility—like saving money, budgeting, and planning for major purchases.

In the Archimedes School parking lot, Jodi carefully glided her five year old hunter green Range Rover next to a brand new sleek, white Lexus SC 430 convertible, with temporary tags still in place. Expecting to see one of the hot, young lawyer-type dads emerge from the vehicle, Jodi was surprised to observe two 11th grade girls materialize, who were immediately descended upon by a swarm of Upper School girls, who jumped, squealed, and screamed their excitement about "Kerry's" new sweet sixteen birthday gift. *I hope Ashlyn's happy with my ancient Range Rover she's getting next year*, thought Jodi. Jodi loved and respected the education her children received at Archimedes, but it was a daily struggle to keep her children balanced and grounded with strong morals and values when $70,000+ birthday gifts for teenagers were commonplace.

Jodi's attempt to kiss Ashlyn's forehead was thwarted by a skillfully executed evasive move when Ashlyn stepped sideways and held up her hand in protest, "Mom, not in front of my friends!" Never mind. Her kisses and hugs were still well received by five year old Faith.

"Love you, have a great day," Jodi said as she handed Faith over to Mrs. Casper. Glancing inside the classroom, Jodi noticed that the happy caterpillar sign had a new item added to the list of offending allergens....*no dogs*. Chalk one up to those clueless parents. They'd probably ignore the sign anyway.

Passing Vic the maintenance guy, who after two months continued to work on the drainage problem outside of the Kindergarten classroom—he had uncovered a crumbling foundation and some termite damage, a familiar occurrence with waterfront structures, Jodi caught up to her companions who were already waiting for her at the familiar picnic table. Ayani looked fresh and alert as she performed a subtle version of some yoga pose designed to stretch her calf muscles. Tara was there, too, her face lit up in a huge smile when she saw Jodi. Good old Chrissie was busy chatting away with Vic, telling him that all the exercise he was doing was making him look so buff. Vic smiled at the complement. She had probably just made his day, maybe his entire week. Chrissie always went out of her way to say a few kind words to friends, acquaintances and even occasionally to strangers. Charleigh was bent over the jogging stroller, trying to keep little Harding entertained before embarking on their walk, while simultaneously giving Vic an eyeful of her perfect rear end. A couple of the Archimedes math teachers were stopped dead in their tracks as they also caught sight of this exquisite vision. Charleigh turned her head in their direction and smiled slightly, causing the two geeky male teachers to pull up their plaid trousers and puff out their chests, feeling more manly than ever before.

"Girls, let's hit the road, I'm on a mission today," said Jodi, already strolling deliberately in the direction of the Whorl. Ayani, Charleigh, Chrissie and Tara hastily ran to catch up with Jodi who was now fifty paces ahead.

"I'm stressin' out over the potluck," she began. "Ninety Yes's as of last night, I'm worried that everyone's gonna bring dessert, there won't be enough wine and beer, I don't have the party "signature drink" set, I need tables, chairs, glasses and dishes for everyone…do we need stupid nametags, should I set up a valet service for the cars, parking is gonna be a nightmare…." Jodi rambled on nervously.

"Whoa…Jodi, chill. Let me help—let *us* help," said Chrissie. She continued, "I'll call the caterer and request tables, chairs, dishes and silverware to take care of at least 100 people. We'll all come early to set up the bar and the buffet table, get the music going, prepare cocktails in advance, light candles, and do whatever else needs to be done."

"I'll buy flowers," said Ayani.

"My girlfriend in Texas said the latest drink craze are these *Panty Rippers*—I can get the ingredients and prep them in advance," volunteered Tara.

"Panty Rippers? Can't we do something more sophisticated like Champagne and Chambord?" asked Jodi.

"No, honey, these'll be fun, they're all the rage down South," replied Tara.

"All you need to do Jodi is make sure your house is ready—we know it's always *clean*, and buy the wine and beer, we'll take care of the rest," added Chrissie.

"Thanks guys, I feel better already," said Jodi, now visibly more relaxed and composed. The five women completed their brisk walk for another thirty minutes then returned to the warmth of their parked cars, the interiors toasty from the rays of morning sun that poured through the windshields.

By Saturday afternoon all Jodi had to do was open the wine bottles, light the candles, and then choose the outfit she would wear for the pot luck dinner. The cleaning ladies had made a final visit to her home that morning, leaving the house smelling fresh from lemon oil, and the caterer had delivered tables, chairs, dinnerware and silverware for one hundred people, plus wine and cocktail glasses for at least 300 people—to handle those parents who typically filled a drink, then misplaced it five minutes later. Ayani ordered huge bouquets of organically grown flowers that were delivered fresh from Harbour Florists at noon. Jodi decided earlier that week that she would hire several of the Upper School children from the Archimedes School to help with serving the food and manage the ongoing clean-up throughout the evening. Ashlyn was thrilled to be joined by her friends. Little Faith was sent to Charleigh's house where Charleigh's nanny Miss Elke was supervising a huge sleepover with Harrison, Wilson, Honey, Carver, and Clinton—the five year old offspring of the core moms.

Everything was set. Nothing could go wrong now. Jodi's husband Rip was already downstairs programming the music for the evening, dressed in a sport coat and tie—he never attended any function without the obligatory tie. The sport coat was his concession to dressing casually, as the head of surgery he much preferred his standard uniform of wearing fine, Dolce and Gabbana pinstriped wool suits. After all he had to keep his image with the CEO of the hospital. Not bothering to ring the doorbell, Ayani, Charleigh, Chrissie, Tara and their husbands burst through the door arriving en masse, they had rented a huge black stretch limo for the evening hoping to alleviate some of parking problems, and anticipating a late, perhaps raucous evening of fun. Tara was already slightly tipsy from sampling the Panty Rippers she had prepared in advance which she brought in three huge coolers. "I'm worried we won't have enough," she said as she plopped them down on the kitchen counter.

Hearing the commotion downstairs, Jodi made her grand entrance by descending gracefully down the spiral staircase that led from her master suite to the impressive marble tiled entry foyer, illuminated by a custom made sparkling $20,000 hand blown glass chandelier created by a local Annapolis artisan. In unison, the husbands who had gathered below, whistled appreciatively at Jodi, who was dressed in the most cleavage revealing and sexiest outfit she had ever worn, at *least in public*. The satin gold halter top shimmered as she moved, revealing perfectly shaped and toned shoulders, creamy in color from years of carefully avoiding sun exposure. Her form fitting jeans accentuated her womanly curves. The gold bejeweled Prada pumps added to Jodi's statuesque presence by increasing her height to nearly six feet tall. Last week on their shopping spree

Charleigh had helped Jodi select this dynamite ensemble. Jodi would certainly turn every head in the room in her direction. Inwardly Jodi beamed, this was sexiest she had felt in years. Buoyed by the enthusiastic whistles and approving applause from her best friends' husbands, Jodi felt her confidence build, *this will be the best potluck of the year*, she thought to herself.

Tara handed Jodi one of the premixed Panty Rippers, served in a martini glass garnished with a fresh strawberry perched on the side. Jodi noticed that everyone else in the room already had a beverage in hand waiting to toast the hostess and host.

"Here's to a great evening!" said Chrissie, touching the glass to her lips. "Cheers," echoed her friends.

Just then, the doorbell rang, announcing the arrival of the first set of Archimedes parent partygoers. The festivities were about to begin.

Astrid and her husband Bill, arriving unusually early for these typically late night party hoppers, walked through the double entry doors into the foyer, the smoky herbal scent of something, marijuana or patchouli still clinging to Astrid's full length sheared beaver coat.

Handing the coat to Jodi, Astrid asked, "Where's the basket for our car keys?"

Bewildered by her question Jodi said, "Well, there's a basket in the kitchen we use for our mail, I guess that would do."

Jodi thought that maybe this was Astrid's method of insuring that neither she nor her husband drove away overly intoxicated. The next parents immediately followed Astrid and her husband through the door. The woman was completely overdressed for the "casual" event, wearing a short black chiffon cocktail dress, diamonds dripping from her ears, fingers, and dangling between her breasts, sexy cocktail shoes with ankle wraps accentuated her long sleek legs. He wore dark denim Italian jeans, black silk t-shirt and sport coat and looked more apropos for the evening.

Taking her wrap, Jodi was again asked, "Where is the basket for the keys?" Repeating the comment she made to Astrid, the woman in black marched directly to the kitchen and deposited her husband's set of jaguar keys into the mail basket. *Interesting*, thought Jodi, *these parents are much more responsible than I thought,* assuming nearly everyone was concerned about their future levels of intoxication. This question was repeated many times throughout the evening. At night's end, there were at least twenty sets of car keys in the basket.

By nine o'clock the Archimedes Kindergarten parent pot luck was in full swing. At last count, Jodi estimated that more than eighty parents were there, just slightly shy of the originally expected guest total. Parked outside Jodi and Rip's home was such an impressive array of high end luxury cars, the editors of *Car and Driver* magazine would wet their pants if they could do a pictorial spread on the event. The BMW 7-series sedan was parked next to a classic Bentley which was parked side by side with a Ferrari that sat carefully next to a vintage cherry red 'vette and so on. The combined value of the vehicles outside their home was probably close to the gross national product of some third world counties.

Everyone appeared to be thoroughly enjoying the party. The cheerful sound of laughter flowed from every room, glasses clinked, dishes clattered, while Ashlyn and her high school friends busily gathered any half finished glass of wine or plate left unattended, removing them to the kitchen for cleaning. By ten o'clock, the Panty Rippers were starting to have a major impact. Women removed their heels, men took off their sports jackets, several parents leaned on the kitchen countertops for support, and two people simultaneously dropped wine glasses, crashing to the floor. Chairs and a sofa were removed from the center of the media room making way for a night of dancing to disco tunes from the 70's. Gloria Gaynor's *I Will Survive* blasted from the surround sound Bose speakers discretely hidden in the walls and ceiling of the room. The adults began bumping and grinding recalling dance steps they knew from high school or if they were too young to remember, using much more suggestive moves they'd seen recently on VH1. The threesome of Astrid, her husband Bill and Crystal were dancing seductively together. Charleigh's husband Bud got pulled into the mix by the woman in the black cocktail dress, who attempted to teach him the steps of the *hustle*. One of the hot, young dads had cornered Jodi who tried in vain to pull away—*where's Rip when I really need him?* Her eyes anxiously searched the room for her husband, not knowing that Rip, Chrissie's husband Seth and Tara's husband Randy were taking another Archimedes School dad's Lamborghini out for a spin. They had slipped out the front door ten minutes ago, completely missing the Annapolis version of Saturday Night Fever. One new to Archimedes father had pulled fifteen year old Ashlyn onto the dance floor, shouting, "Show us your stuff, girlie." The lesbian moms looked wistfully at Charleigh as she skirted quickly through the maze of dancers, trying to avoid any bodily contact with the sweaty crowd.   Overall, twenty or so couples were on the dance floor, moving suggestively with anyone other than their chosen life partners.

Someone dimmed the lights and with the cover of darkness the sexual tension in the room began to build.

Chrissie could feel it, so could Ayani and Jodi. Charleigh had stepped out of the house for a few moments to use her cell phone to call Miss Elke to check on the children so she was oblivious to the sexual heat emanating from the dance floor. Jonathan had somehow snuck in his Brazilian nanny, unbeknownst to Jodi. She did remember when Jonathan arrived *alone* he said his wife was home sick with a nasty cold and sent her regrets. Jonathan and Violeta, now the nanny had a name, were dancing so close one of her legs was slipped in between his, she had her firm twenty-one year old buxom pressed tight against his chest. By now, most of the parents in the room were so overwhelmed by the Panty Rippers and bleary eyed from the affect of alcohol they were completely unaware of this blatant affair unfolding in front of their eyes.

"This has got to stop," said the panicked Jodi as she finally broke away from her dance partner, yet no one heard her above the volume of music.

Tara, who had also been dancing and not knowing she was about to save the day, and perhaps save several marriages, shouted in Jodi's ear, "When do we start the party tricks?"

"Party tricks? What are party tricks?" asked Jodi, excited about any opportunity to cool off the parents who had completely lost their senses.

"It's what we do in Texas. Everyone's got some special trick they can perform," said Tara.

"Okay, Tara, I'll stop the music and I'm putting you in charge for a few minutes," said Jodi.

Jodi walked over to the vast array of electronic equipment carefully secreted from view behind custom built cabinetry, pushed what she thought was the "off" button and hoped for the best. The music stopped just as the dancers were forming letters with their arms, Y...M...C.... Then a moment of silence followed by moans and groans in complaint. Bud was the only one grateful for the reprieve, and mouthed the words "thank you" to Jodi.

"Tara, I need to check on the teens in the kitchen—it's been a little too quiet in there. I'll be back in just a moment. The floor is yours," said Jodi.

"Okay everyone," Tara began in her sweet accent, "It's time for *party tricks*." All men in the room had their eyes glued to the scantily clad Tara, not caring about any particular party trick, just wondering how much skin she might reveal when she did her special feat. "Girls, guys, think about somethin' special y'all can do. Here's mine, wait a second, I need to loosen up."

Tara turned her back on the crowd, yawned wide, stretched her mouth this way and that, then spun on her heels to face her friends and fellow parents. "Here's my trick...I can put my *whole fist* right in my mouth," she said.

Tara proceeded to open her mouth wide enough to allow her entire fist to fit right in. The crowd gasped. Men nodded appreciatively. One man exclaimed, "That must come in handy, I bet I know another huge thing you could put in your mouth." The parents roared with laughter. Another parent chimed in, "I doubt it's that huge, after all don't you have a 50 foot yacht?" The room exploded in hysterics, all sharing the common knowledge that the larger the boat the smaller the male appendage.

After delicately removing her hand, which appeared to be the most complicated aspect of the trick, Tara asked, "Who's next?"

Astrid immediately leapt to the center of the room.

"I can put my both of my legs behind my head," Astrid announced.

Chrissie quickly interrupted, "Um...Astrid, *not here*, you're wearing a dress, wouldn't you rather be wearing workout clothes?"

"Doesn't bother me, how 'bout you guys?" she said. The men in the room cheered her on enthusiastically; several women were also shouting words of encouragement. "Do it...do it...do it" became the chant from the parents congregated in the media room.

Astrid took a seat on the antique Oriental rug, bunched her dress up to her thighs, then methodically placed one leg, then another behind her head. Her black lace thong left nothing to the imagination, giving everyone a full view. Several women nudged each other and said, "Look, she's got a Brazilian wax job, too." The intoxicated parents in the room erupted in hoots, whistles, and clapping. Astrid was now the most popular girl at the party. Two fine looking dads helped her stand upright and promptly handed her another glass of the Panty Ripper concoction.

Chrissie's eyes searched the room frantically for Jodi, not realizing Jodi had stepped away to check on the teen helpers, *where could she be?* Chrissie wondered. Sensing that the next party trick might trigger a possible group orgy, Chrissie jumped swiftly into action.

"Well thank you ladies for sharing your...um... special talents, I doubt that anyone could beat that," she began, then hesitated briefly before stumbling on the next idea. "Dessert and coffee are being served in the dining room." The parents, Tara included, began to filter into the kitchen en route to the adjacent dining room, calm was momentarily restored.

"Great job, Chrissie," said Ayani, her husband Derrick was by her side and nodded in agreement. "Something had to be done to cool off this primal mating ritual."

"Charleigh and Jodi missed the whole thing. Charleigh's still outside making a call to check on the kids and I can't find Jodi anywhere," said Chrissie.

Suddenly Jodi burst into the media room, mouth tight, face flushed with anger. "You won't believe what just happened. I was looking for Ashlyn and her friends, who I've yet to find. I checked upstairs in my room and standing there...right smack in my *bedroom*, was Mike Murray, his face buried in a handful of my underwear. *He was sniffing it!*" Jodi exclaimed. "It was so disgusting, I'm burning those, and they were brand new, too!"

"*No!*" said Chrissie and Ayani in unison.

"Actually, I heard he's a total creep. This isn't the first time he's done something like this," added Chrissie. "He copped a feel on some middle school mom when the boat keeled hard to one side as they were sailing last summer. Her husband almost decked him."

"Gross, I feel so violated," said Jodi. "Does his wife know he's a pervert?"

"Nope. She's pretty clueless, she's so busy selling real estate to the rich and famous, she's never home to satisfy his needs," said Chrissie.

"If I ever host another Archimedes School party, I'll just lay some cheap underwear on the bed, with a sign that says—*please sniff.* That way he won't ruin my good stuff," added Jodi. Looking around the room, she asked, "Hey, where'd everyone go? Tara must have done a great job with crowd control."

"If you could call it that. The party tricks were a huge hit, especially with the men. They'll be talking about them for years in the locker room at the yacht club!" said Ayani.

Charleigh completed her phone call to Miss Elke and came in from the outside to rejoin Jodi, Chrissie and Ayani who were now taking a brief moment to relax on one of the sofas in the media room, anxious for any opportunity to sit down and slip off their high heels.

"The kids are all fine, Harding's got a little stomach ache, nothing major." Charleigh reported. "Hey, where'd everyone go?" she inquired.

"They were sent to the dining room for dessert," said Ayani.

"Sorry to break the news to you, but no one is in the dining room, I just passed the dessert table on the way in and nothing's been touched," said Charleigh.

Jumping to her feet, leaving her shoes behind, Jodi exclaimed, "Oh no, *now what?*"

The four core women began their search for the missing adults by heading to the kitchen, the perennial gathering spot for any party, it's where everyone eventually lands no matter how large the home. The wicker mail basket where twenty or so couples had placed their keys was now sitting prominently on the kitchen table. The basket was empty. All the keys were gone. "They all left!" exclaimed Jodi. A quick peek outside Jodi's kitchen window revealed that all of the cars remained. "They're still here...in the house....*somewhere*, we've got to find them," said Jodi. "I'll go upstairs. Ayani, you and Derrick check outside by the pool. Chrissie, check the basement. Charleigh, *please, please* come with me. I've got a feeling I'm not gonna like this."

Bud protectively came to Charleigh's side and volunteered to escort the two women upstairs. "Bud, we're okay," Charleigh said. "Why don't you check the parking area outside?"

Jodi and Rip's home was a vast 6,000 plus square foot mansion with several wings, many decks, two hot tubs, a heated pool that even in October remained warm enough to use. There were lots of nooks and crannies where people could hide. Jodi and Charleigh wordlessly climbed the spiral staircase that led to the second story where the master suite and four other bedrooms were located. As they drew near, the muffled sound of laughter was heard from behind several closed bedroom doors. The recessed lights in the hallway had been turned off, and no light spilled out from under any of the bedroom doors. Upstairs it was nearly pitch black, except for the tiny glow of a small night light plugged into an outlet in one of the hallway bathrooms. Jodi reached for the doorknob leading to the master suite. She felt behind her and grabbed Charleigh's arm for security. She turned the knob, pushed open the master bedroom door, and she and Charleigh witnessed a scene right out of the Playboy mansion. Hugh Hefner would have been proud. Wearing nothing but one of Rip's velour robes, Astrid's husband Bill was on the carpet perched on all fours, another mom, *not Astrid*, wearing just panties and a bra sat astride Bill riding him like a pony, saying "go little doggie, go little doggie," and proceeded to whip his rear end with the cloth sash from the robe.

"What the *fuck* is going on?" asked Jodi, furious at the invasion of her personal space and lewd display taking place on her brand new wool carpet. "If you get any bodily fluids on my new carpet, I'll kill you both!"

"We're just doing the *key party*. You collected the keys downstairs, we figured you approved," said the nearly naked woman, who Jodi now recognized as Sheryl Waters, Agape's mom.

Taking a breath to regain composure, Jodi asked, "What the hell's a *key party*?"

"It's where the woman picks out a set of keys and she's goes off with the owner of that car—whoever owns those keys," said Sheryl grinning ear to ear, obviously enjoying sharing information along with sharing *other things*.

"This started two years ago with some of the Upper School parents. We thought we'd try it with the preschool parents," she continued. "Come on. Join us—it's just innocent fun!"

"Charleigh, I don't know about you, but I'm sure neither Rip nor Bud would think this was so innocent," said Jodi to her friend, who she continued to hold by the forearm. Searching for some way to boot these two semi-clad parents from the premises, Jodi continued "Oh my gosh! I just heard a car door—that must be my husband now. Rip's a surgeon and he knows how to use a scalpel. Bill, he'll turn you into a soprano in about two seconds flat, so you better get your ass out of here, *stat*!" Charleigh and Jodi turned on their heels, leaving the two rodeo partners scrambling for their clothes.

In each of the remaining four bedrooms, couples who had not originally arrived together were now becoming very intimately acquainted. Chrissie and Charleigh took it on themselves to interrupt the special adult bonding by throwing open each bedroom door, flipping the light switch and shouting "Party's over, Rip's coming with his scalpel." Within seconds, twelve couples emerged from the five bedrooms, pulled clothes over their heads, and ran barefoot down the stairway with shoes in hand, shirts unbuttoned, zippers undone, and scrambled for their cars.

"That accounts for about half of the adults at this party, where are the rest?" asked Charleigh. Outside several cars started their engines simultaneously, tires screeched as they pulled away at full speed.

"They must be outside by the pool," said Jodi as she and Charleigh rushed down the spiral staircase en route to the sliding glass door that led to the lushly landscaped back yard. Here they encountered another party in full swing. Astrid and Tara were holding court with four men in the hot tub. The women had stripped down to their panties and bras, the men wore only their boxers or tighty whities. Next to Astrid's clothes on the hot tub deck was a set of Mercedes car keys, presumably belonging to one of the men she was busy 'entertaining.' Tara was enjoying herself immensely. She was giddy as a schoolgirl, loving the personal attention she received from these four handsome men—it might have been the closest contact she had with the opposite sex in years. Her husband Randy made it a point to travel for business every week.

At the edge of Jodi's property, near the tall sea grasses that framed the small sandy beach, Jodi saw the flicker of a lighter illuminate the faces of several partygoers. Whatever they were smoking was passed from one person to the next. Jodi knew that many of these parents grew up in the 70's but she was still surprised to see them smoking weed. *Where do they get this stuff? I sure could use a hit right now,* she thought to herself recalling her old college days. *If Ashlyn wasn't here, I'd be back there, too,* as she jealously watched Ayani casually saunter over in their direction. Ayani looked at Jodi with an expression on her face and a shrug of her shoulders that said "if you can't beat them, join them."

"Ashlyn! Oh my gosh. Where the hell did she go?" Jodi suddenly remembered one of her searches from earlier that night. The answer came quickly as giggling spilled over the deck off of her second story master suite where hot tub number two was located. This time Ashlyn was holding court with her teenage male friends who had been hired as clean-up crew for the evening. Instead of cleaning dishes, the two boys were now scrubbing Ashlyn's back with a loofa sponge they must have removed from the bathroom. Bubbles were spewing from the hot tub, trickling over the side of the deck and dripping into the swimming pool below. The teens had emptied an entire bottle of bubble bath and turn the hot tub jets on full force, creating a scene reminiscent of the Lawrence Welk show. Jodi was nearly overwhelmed with anger at these adults who had lost their minds, and at her daughter who was doing a fifteen year old version of the same. Jodi stood there briefly, composing her thoughts and her plan of action.

Finally after being gone for nearly an hour, Rip, Randy and Seth returned just in time to see Tara leap from the hot tub into the pool, followed without delay by two of the men, bodies steaming as their skin hit the chilly October air. There were at least thirty other adults stripped down to nearly nothing who were swimming in the 80 degree pool water. Astrid lingered in the hot tub and was well beyond the flirting stage with the two remaining men. The folks from the smoking section of the yard, Ayani included, dashed toward the house saying "dessert time!" "hope there are still brownies left" "I've got dibs on that pecan pie." Obviously the munchies had hit. Thousands of bubbles from the hot tub floated everywhere adding a surreal underwater feel to the insanity.

Rip, Randy, and Seth just stood there in shock. Jodi abruptly asked them "Where the hell have you been?" Knowing any response would be self incriminating the men remained silent as statues.

"Get these people of here, *now!*" demanded Jodi, a command she directed at her husband Rip. "I'll take care of our daughter." Jodi stormed into the house, fully intending to mortify her daughter in front of her two male friends. *When she's forty I hope she tells her therapist how her mom scarred her for life*, thought Jodi as she swiftly climbed two steps at a time up the spiral staircase to the master suite. Then a horrible thought crossed her mind and almost stopped Jodi in her tracks, *"Ashlyn was on the deck right outside my bedroom when those two rodeo clowns performed their show. What if she saw something?"*

Grabbing a terry robe from a hook in the bathroom, Jodi barged onto the deck and ordered the teenagers out of the hot tub. She wrapped the robe around her daughter, sent her to her room, handed towels to the two boys, and told them to leave the premises immediately. Glancing below she saw a steady stream of wet bodies exit the pool and scurry through the house to their cars, clothes in hand, not bothering to dress. Whatever Rip said certainly persuaded them to move in a hurry. Maybe he did actually threaten to use his scalpel.

There were still several parents remaining, specifically those who had chosen to be innocent bystanders throughout the course of the evening. Their most scandalous act that night was to bum a cigarette or two—something they would do only at parties. They sat on the chaise lounges placed around the pool deck, cocktail glasses in hand,

and enjoyed the show that unfolded in front of their eyes. Bemused by the events of the evening, they thanked Jodi and Rip profusely for *hosting a wonderful party, the best pot luck ever*! Gathering their coats, these well-behaved adults quietly exited the pot luck.

After the last guest left the premises and the last Mercedes drove away, Jodi, Charleigh, Ayani, and Chrissie silently collected wine glasses, plates, paper napkins, and cigarette butts that had been carelessly discarded around the manicured lawn and throughout the formerly pristine home. A full glass of Merlot had spilled onto one of Jodi's white chairs in the media room. Someone had made a feeble attempt to clean it with seltzer water.

"Give it to me, I've got an idea how to fix this," said Chrissie, the creative gears churning in her head. She was already anticipating a quick stop to the local craft store to buy paint and supplies and was visualizing a hand painted floral explosion across the merlot stain.

The husbands, Randy excluded, were back in the kitchen stacking wine and cocktail glasses into the bins provided by the caterer.

Tara and Randy were having a heated discussion by the water's edge, trying to avoid being overheard, yet Jodi caught the occasional phrase or word and knew serious trouble brewed.

"That does it, I'm outta here," said Randy in disgust.

"You're never home," replied Tara, "You never, ever touch me."

"That's because you're a filthy little slut," said Randy. Tara ran past the pool toward Jodi's house, mascara streaming down her face. Moments later, a door from the rented limousine slammed shut.

Jodi, sensing it was time to send her best friends home, said, "Girls, thanks, you've done enough for tonight."

"We can come back tomorrow to help with the rest of the clean-up," volunteered the perpetually kind Ayani.

"Thanks, but no thanks, I think Ashlyn will be *very, very* busy for the next couple of days," said Jodi, already formulating her punishment.

Jodi flipped the master switch that controlled the pool and hot tub lights. Gathering the shoes she had discarded in the media room, she and Rip walked slowly up the stairs, hand in hand to the serenity of their bedroom. Another Archimedes School parent pot luck was finally over.

———————————

Early the next day in the cool, still air of morning, the river behind Jodi and Rip's home was smooth as glass, the water reflected the color of the leaves just beginning to change. A flock of ducks took restlessly to the sky, startled by something moving in the tall sea grasses along the shore. Jodi stood on the balcony off her bedroom and breathed in the fresh sights and sounds of dawn, the memories of the surreal insanity from the previous night were already beginning to soften and fade. Suddenly, the sea grasses rustled and parted to reveal a disheveled dad who emerged from the reeds. As he staggered to his feet, Jodi noticed that his khaki pants were muddied from sleeping on the marshy banks, and his formerly crisp blue Oxford shirt was dirtied beyond the capabilities of the local dry cleaners. Unbuttoned, it flapped slightly as he swayed, to reveal a Grateful Dead logo on the t-shirt underneath.

"Wow, dude that was an awesome party," he said to Jodi as she watched him from the safety of her bedroom deck. "Let's do it again next week!" He flashed her the peace sign with two fingers.

Undaunted, Jodi flashed back her own special finger sign and returned to the warmth of her master suite and quietly closed the sliding glass door behind her.

Life Observations from Vic the Maintenance Guy:
"I loved my wife dearly and never cheated on her when she was alive—never even thought about it. But, she understood that I would always *look* at other women and especially appreciate them from behind. I told her the day I stop looking, is gonna be the day I die."

Chapter Five:
Designer Ghouls and Goblins

This time of year was always hardest for Chrissie—she dreaded the beginning of the late fall season when the amount of daylight decreased and the night time temperatures dropped to near freezing at night. And for some reason, this particular October morning was especially difficult—earlier she awoke with a familiar knot in her belly, sensing something, perhaps everything, was wrong, but nothing concrete came to mind that would trigger her anxiety. Moments before climbing out of bed, a thousand-and-one partially formed thoughts swirled through her head, mostly they just left her with an overall sensation that something in her world was awry. Usually though, a few solid thoughts would materialize and rise to the surface from this mass of angst that churned within her. Typically these thoughts had the same old repetitive theme: "What can I do to make Seth love me? "How can I help him get rid of his anger? Is there any hope for our marriage? And conversely, "*How the hell* can I get out of here and survive on my own with just me and my child?"

She figured she suffered from some degree of Seasonal Affected Disorder, the mood disorder associated with bouts of depression related to seasonal variations of light. She hated the cold, despised the shorter days of winter, and got hives whenever she wore her wool sweaters. Several years back there was a kooky television series set in Alaska where one of the main characters wore a head visor fitted with a full spectrum light designed to ward off seasonal depression. Chrissie wished she had one of those. But then, she'd have to elevate herself to the top of her very own fashion faux pas list. At least she wouldn't wear it in public. She would only strap on the full spectrum light visor at night when she was home alone with her husband Seth. *Ooh*, so sexy. What the heck, Seth always wore that disgusting plastic mouth guard every night to prevent him from grinding his teeth down to a nub. Seth's anger at life was so deeply entrenched he took it to bed with him. Without that mouth guard the grinding noises emanating from his side of the bed sounded like an angry beaver gnawing ferociously on a beech tree.

Chrissie had just returned home from school after an invigorating, but chilly morning walk with her *four* friends, Tara was now well integrated as one of the regular daily walkers. Since the night of the Kindergarten parent pot luck, Chrissie and Tara had developed a deeper friendship based on the common bond of marital discontent. Chrissie realized that Tara's marriage to Randy was just as miserable as her own marriage to Seth. People who suffered together bonded together. The unique difference between the two women was that Tara manifested her marital disgruntlement with a different approach than Chrissie—Tara tended to release her stress by exhibiting a wilder, untamed side. She was easily swayed by Astrid and her posse of voluptuous women to join them on their late night forays to the exclusive night clubs in

Baltimore and D.C. where local affluent businessmen would "buy" a private table for $2,500 in order to be surrounded by a bevy of beautiful women. These were the irresponsible and "undomesticated" women who never had any qualms about leaving their kids under a nanny's supervision for days at a time. That didn't jive with Chrissie's core personality in the least, but she was human after all—and on several occasions when Tara invited Chrissie to join them she was tempted. "Come on, Chrissie, you get a free steak dinner, all the cosmos you can drink, and men fawning all over you," begged Tara. In her mind's eye, Chrissie's could visualize the scene; a good looking man in a business suit actually paying attention to her, subtly letting his leg lean into hers, steeling glances at her A cup size breasts plumped up with that best-purchase-she-ever-made silicon gel infused bra. A slight quiver ran through her, which she quickly brushed aside when the reality of her maternal responsibilities came flooding back. For Chrissie, her son Harrison came first and foremost in her life.

On the other hand, Chrissie tended to distract herself from her personal troubles by helping others so much she neglected her own needs. Any diversion, any cause, any special event, Chrissie was sure to lend a hand; preschool class mom, painting sets for the Lower School and Upper School performances (even though she didn't have a child in either division), reading the biography of Albert Einstein to the kindergarten kids in the classroom (required reading for the accelerated math program), making peanut free wild bird food mix for the outdoor education department, selling everything from pine bark mulch to cheese pizzas (that tasted like mulch) for fundraisers, and organizing the parents to bring allergy safe foods to class parties (wheat free crackers, dairy free dips, carrots, celery, and fruit juices with no sugar added), then patrolling the party for illegal contraband that might slip through the cracks like those "dangerous" smiley face cookies or "deadly" cupcakes.

Chrissie would do anything to avoid confronting her marital problems at home. How many years had it been since she had sex? Four? Five? She had lost track. Last year she went to a sexual dysfunction clinic in Annapolis, seeking the advice from one of the leading professionals in the field. After he completed his physical exam—all of her parts were functioning normally—that was good, the doctor ran through a list of thirty or so questions to evaluate her emotional and mental state. Chrissie remembered one of the questions was "are you having any marital difficulties?" Chrissie quickly responded, "No, everything is fine. Seth's a great guy." Even in the protected, unbiased presence of a professional, Chrissie continued to be in complete denial—at least publicly. Seth was intelligent, hard working, and dedicated to his profession, regularly clocking sixty hours or more each week. He contributed a portion of his hard earned money to support several Save the Bay causes and even sacrificed three or four Saturdays a year to labor knee deep in muck and slime to remove debris from precious watersheds. On the surface, he appeared to be a decent guy. Chrissie truly wanted her marriage to be strong and satisfying and it probably would have been had Seth not been such an *asshole*. Behind closed doors Seth was condescending, critical, and judgmental. Chrissie felt like she was on the witness stand the minute he walked through their front door. It was ridiculous—everything she did was questioned, "Why did you drive from the dry cleaners to the post office *then* to the paint store? It would have made more sense to reverse that order so that all of your stops were on the *right side* of the street—so you'd save gas by having fewer left hand turns." According to Seth, Chrissie couldn't even do her errands and chores properly. Typically, upon returning home from work each day, Seth would grill her with such a fierce interrogation even the most innocent witness would break down on the stand and confess. He challenged her with ridiculous questions like, "Why did you buy six light bulbs? We only needed four!" or "Did you check the cost per ounce on those cleaning products? You should've bought store brands!" or "What did you do between 1:30 pm and 2:30 pm today? That's your house cleaning time and there's dust everywhere!" *Whatever.*

Despite Chrissie and Tara's lifestyle differences, they shared many similarities—both were mothers to a single son, both had abysmal marriages, both were searching for an answer to their misery, and both were uncertain about their futures. Should they stay in their marriages, should they split, or maybe they both just needed a wild fling to sow a few oats?

Recently, on a whim, Chrissie went to a local, eccentric psychic who met her clientele once a week on Tuesdays in a classic chrome and neon diner located on the outskirts of Annapolis. "Dolly" was a 300 pound, four foot eleven psychic with a beehive hairdo who sat like a huge bull frog in a cracked and crinkled red leather booth in the back of the restaurant. Over the past ten years she felt the psychic vibes from several hundred people while parking herself at this exact booth. Dolly didn't use Tarot cards and she didn't use astrology charts. Instead she looked deeply into her customer's eyes once, just once, reading into the depths of their souls. Then, in order to focus her psychic communication with the other world, she turned her attention to an ancient silver dollar placed in front of her on the formica table. This silver dollar belonged to a long succession of Dolly's ancestors who also had impressive psychic abilities. Dolly called it her portal to the other side.

Chrissie's psychic reading was shocking. Dolly hit everything on the head. She told Chrissie that her marriage was in turmoil, *this man is surrounded by blackness—that means anger*, and soon it would be time to move on, in the next few months she would meet another man, *your long lost soul mate*, they would become close friends, creating a flurry of rumors and speculation about Chrissie's fidelity to Seth. The most important advice Dolly offered was to *be very careful about your timing.*

"This person must remain just a friend, not a lover, until the time is right. Otherwise it will fall apart. Your women friends may turn on you. People will talk," said Dolly using her succinct and precise manner of talking.

Then Dolly added, "Is there a new woman friend in your life?" Chrissie thought for a moment, then replied, "Yes," thinking about Tara.

Dolly continued, "Beware. There is trouble around her. Don't let her pull you into the whorl."

When Dolly said the word *whorl* Chrissie jumped. "You mean whorl as in chaos, craziness, right?" Dolly nodded in agreement.

Dolly's psychic reading was overwhelming to Chrissie. Every new man she encountered was her possible future lover and soul mate. On the Archimedes campus while waiting to pick up Harrison, she casually struck up a conversation with a charming, mature (a.k.a., *old*), and disheveled gentleman whom she soon discovered to be an Archimedes astronomy teacher. He had just completed his "Introduction to Astronomy" class for the little tykes in PS 4. He obviously cared more about quarks, globular clusters and black holes than he did about his appearance. Astronomy aficionados are always so pale because most of their work is done late at night, he was no exception. Fair skinned, grey stringy hair, crumpled white shirt, khaki pants frayed at the hem—he was so pale he would disappear entirely if he stood against a blank white wall. After their brief, yet very pleasant conversation, he invited her to the astronomy lab on Friday at eight p.m. to observe the night sky.

"There's a new comet, the 59Z Googleman/Hectar that we might be able to see. It's got eight separate nuclei due to the effect of tidal forces of the sun," he said, quivering slightly with excitement.

At first Chrissie was intrigued—she'd never seen the night sky with such a powerful telescope. Then she panicked. *What if this sweet, little old Jewish man was my future soul mate and lover?*

Regretfully she had to decline his offer, especially after envisioning their barefoot, beachfront wedding, she in a flowing white gown embellished with embroidered and beaded comets and stars cascading down and around the train, he in a crumpled seersucker blue suit and a bow tie. That vision didn't work for her. *Okay*, she thought, on *to the next future soul mate.* He would probably appear when she least expected it.

In the meantime, Chrissie went about her normal chores and activities; clean the house, grocery shop, run errands for Seth, buy green felt, a glue gun and Styrofoam balls to make a monster costume for Harrison. Chrissie couldn't sew, but she was dangerous with a glue gun. Of course, none of the ready made Halloween costumes at the toy store appealed to her son. He didn't like the typical array of costumes available for boys. He hated ninjas, sports or action figures, characters from movies or television, cowboys, Indians, ghosts or bloody vampires. After brainstorming several ideas, "Mommy, I'd like to be a plate of spaghetti for Halloween." Chrissie somehow convinced him to be his second choice--a *giant green alien with thousands of eyes.* Even at age five Harrison was already thinking out of the box for his Halloween get-up. It only took her a day of glue gun trial and error to get the costume just right for her little boy. From three yards of green felt fabric, she cut out a circular tunic with a hole for his head, and attached at least one hundred Styrofoam balls sliced in half, painted with black pupils, and decorated with hand curled construction paper eyelashes. Then, she attached eye stalks made from a coat hanger and two more foam balls to one of her old head bands.

When Chrissie returned home that October day after dropping off Harrison at school, she opened the daily mail to discover a professionally printed orange and black invitation with the name and address beautifully written in calligraphy. *"Awww, so cute,"* she thought to herself, *"Harrison's first Halloween party."* She set it aside to give Harrison a special treat when he returned home. She briefly perused a glossy, high end lingerie catalog, wondering how she got on *that* mailing list. "Oh yeah, I'm wearing that pink thong and cami for that wonderful man I married," said Chrissie out loud, oozing with sarcasm. Then her eyes landed on the monthly Archimedes School newsletter called the *Sine of the Times* cleverly named after some trigonometry function. The leading article featured the Archimedes Chess Club which had just won the state championship. A bake sale was scheduled to raise funds to purchase new uniforms—*chess uniforms*? Each month the *Sine of the Times* spotlighted one of the faculty members with a short bio and their recent accomplishments at the school. This month Matt Worthington's handsome, grinning face peered out at Chrissie from the pages of the newsletter. Buried deep in the article was a glowing quote from his colleague Berri Franconi, "Matt's the most gifted math teacher I've ever worked with, he's so sensitive to his student's needs, he can gently guide them to achieving the fullest and most overwhelming breakthrough of understanding. He's so patient and attentive, very hands on."

"I'm glad our tuition money is being spent on such talented teachers," Chrissie said out loud. Remembering Matt and Berri's rumored affair brought a smile to her face. *It's good to see people happy, even if it isn't with their own spouses*, she thought.

Matt in turn complemented his coworkers and was quoted in the article as saying "We all work so closely as a team, often into the wee hours of the night, everyone is so passionate about our experience here at Archimedes. My colleagues, especially teachers like Berri, make it so special to come to work every day."

Chrissie's thoughts of Matt and Berri's romance were interrupted by a telephone call. Her pulse rate quickened when she saw *The Archimedes School* appear on caller ID. Hoping it wasn't from the nurse office at school, she answered the phone.

"May I speak with Chrissie Thompson?" asked the caller.

"Speaking," said Chrissie, with worry in her voice.

"This is Mrs. Casper. Harrison seems to be having some sort of allergic reaction."

Chrissie caught her breath, remembering Leona Lowe's dramatization of anaphylactic shock during the preschool coffee meeting. *"Thank God I don't work outside the home,"* Chrissie immediately thought to herself, "How could I be there for my son?"

"Is…is he in the hospital?" Chrissie stammered.

"Oh *no*, no, it's not that bad, he's just covered from the waist up in hives and a severe rash. We wanted to know if he can take Benadryl," said Mrs. Casper.

"It'll make him sleepy, but he's okay with it," responded Chrissie.

"We think he's having some sort of severe reaction to his wool sweater."

Like mother, like son, Chrissie thought. "I'll come to school and get him right away," said Chrissie.

"Great, we'll see you shortly," said Mrs. Casper.

It only took Chrissie about ten minutes to rush from her home in Eastport to the Archimedes School parking lot. She pulled into an empty parking space between one music teacher's prehistoric Volkswagon van, which still had the hand painted words "flower power" and "make love not war" on it and another teacher's Honda Civic held together with duct tape. Walking to the Kindergarten classroom, she was stopped by Vic, the maintenance man.

"Chrissie, so good to see you. The guys in maintenance were just talking about you and your friends," said Vic, grinning from ear to ear.

"Hi Vic, I'm kind of in a hurry, Harrison's having some freaky allergic reaction to wool," she said, slightly breathless from her jog from the parking lot. Now that Chrissie was only a few feet away, Victor could see the panic in her eyes and the sweat on her forehead.

"No problem, run to your boy, I'll catch up with you later. It's just about painting the set for the Thanksgiving performance," said Vic.

"Sorry I'm in such a hurry, I'd love to talk about it on another day," said Chrissie over her shoulder, now speed walking toward the classroom. She had already filed away the fact that soon she would volunteer for yet another school project. Maybe this time she could enlist the help of her four close buddies.

Chrissie burst into the Kindergarten classroom expecting to see Harrison's face beet red and swollen like a puffer fish. Instead, he was sitting calmly at his diminutive desk, busily drawing something that looked like one of those striped, wooly caterpillars.

"Hi Mom, see I'm all better. The medicine worked," said the smiling little boy. "But, look, Mrs. Casper had to add something to the classroom bug sign." Harrison pointed to the happy caterpillar sign that still hung from the ceiling of the classroom. Under the words, *Nut Free, Dairy Free, Wheat Free, Dog Free*, Mrs. Casper had written the words in permanent marker, *Wool Free*. "*Great, that one's my fault*," thought Chrissie.

"Sorry to trouble you Chrissie," said Mrs. Casper. "He responded so quickly to the medicine. Do you still want to take him home?"

"Might as well, we only have one hour left in the school day," said Chrissie. "Let's grab a pretzel at the mall and buy you some safe *polyester* sweaters." She helped Mrs. Casper gather his jacket and homework, and pack everything into his book bag. Happy to be leaving school early, Harrison skipped all the way to Chrissie's car.

———

The next weekend Harrison was so thrilled to be going to his very first Halloween party that he donned his costume the minute he popped out of bed and wore it throughout the entire day. Several of the Styrofoam eyeballs on the homemade green alien required periodic touch ups with the glue gun. They were the eyeballs strategically placed on Harrison's little rear end which were now squished and battered from being sat upon all day. Unfortunately, the party was scheduled for 6 p.m. that Saturday evening, which meant every fifteen minutes from the moment he woke up until it was time to depart, Harrison would repeatedly ask his mom, "Is it time to go yet?"

Chrissie had heard about Sheryl Waters' home. She had even seen the pictorial display in an issue of Architectural Digest while waiting at the dentist's office. But, she had never actually seen their spectacular home in person. Their massive Tudor style mansion was perched high on a bluff that jutted prominently into the South River—one of the two major rivers considered to be part of the Annapolis area. Sheryl and her husband Dave owned this entire five acre peninsula, considered by many local realtors to be the most desirable piece of real estate in all of Annapolis. Chrissie's Volvo, desperately in need of a tune-up, pinged and sputtered the entire way up the steep quarter-mile long driveway. She was always anticipating the inevitable highway breakdown of her 140,000 mile car so Chrissie kept a stash of emergency water, snacks, coloring and activity books that would occupy Harrison until the AAA road crew could arrive on the scene and save them. Now, rounding the bend, she breathed a sigh once her Volvo miraculously arrived at their destination (yet, once again!). Chrissie saw nearly fifty cars already parked along the side of the road.

"Honey, it looks like the party's already in full swing," Chrissie said to her son. Chrissie noted that thankfully Ayani, Jodi and Charleigh had also recently arrived, judging by each of their car's positions near the end of the long line of parked vehicles.

"Mommy, I hope we didn't miss anything," complained Harrison.

Chrissie nearly creamed the parking attendant who stepped into the driveway to wave her down. Handing over her keys, she was slightly embarrassed that this young man was about to drive off in her ancient vehicle, especially after he had just finished parking another partygoers gleaming silver Ferrari. As he drove away, Chrissie shouted to the attendant, "Hey, there are snacks in there, help yourself," hoping this would compensate for requiring him to drive something that didn't have Corinthian leather seats. Chrissie and her son were greeted at the front door by the hired help, a petite Hispanic woman wearing a black and white maid's uniform topped off with devil horns on her head.

"Welcome to Waters' residence," the maid said with a heavy accent. "Adults go to dining room. Kids to living room," she added. Another hired helper, dressed like Lurch from the Addam's family, appeared out of nowhere to escort little Harrison to the festivities taking place in the living room. Grabbing hold of his mom's arm with an iron grip, Harrison was reluctant to be led away by this monstrous stranger.

"It's okay honey, don't worry, he's wearing a costume. I'll join you in just a few minutes," Chrissie reassured her clinging son. Harrison shot a worried glance at his mom as he disappeared down the hallway.

"Oh, I didn't realize that grown-ups were invited to stay," Chrissie responded, fully intending to greet the hostess and leave while Harrison enjoyed the party without her.

"Yes, cocktails are served, but you didn't wear a costume, Mrs. Waters rented many for friends to use," said the maid. "Follow me."

Chrissie reluctantly but obediently followed the diminutive woman who led her to an upstairs dressing room the size of most people's entire homes. Displayed on a movable coat rack were about fifty or so rented costumes of every shape, size and color. Chrissie could choose from the exotic belly dancer costume, which would expose nearly 90% of the surface area of her skin, or the wild, wild west can-can girl outfit (a.k.a. call girl), or the incredibly short cave woman costume made from life-like fuzzy animal prints, complete with a bone to put in her hair. Instead Chrissie selected the 1970's psychedelic hippie get-up, with fringed moccasin boots, paisley dress, pink John Lennon style sunglasses, and a frizzy blonde wig that cascaded down to her waist. She was certain no true Janis Joplin loving hippie from the early 70's would be caught dead wearing so much polyester, but she thought this costume was the least offensive in the presence of fifty or so preschool aged kids running about.

Chrissie emerged from the dressing room and headed downstairs to find Sheryl Waters outside the kitchen berating the chef because there was too much garlic in the marinated mussel tapas.

"My guests are stinking up the entire house with their breath," Sheryl complained. "Back off on that garlic or I'll take the cost of deodorizing the furniture out of your pay."

"Si senora," the chef replied, then under his breath, "usted ramera gorda."

Chrissie knowingly smiled and winked at the chef, *yes, she can be a fat bitch,* she thought to herself. She caught Sheryl's attention by gently touching her on the forearm.

"Sheryl, thanks so much for including us, the turn out today is phenomenal," said Chrissie.

"Oh *Chrissie*, you're here. Love that outfit, you look scorchin' in that mini-dress," said Sheryl. Chrissie self consciously tugged downward at the hem, then replied, "Thanks, it was so nice of you to provide all those costumes. I didn't realize this was an adult party, too."

"It was Agape's idea actually. She said her friends would stay longer if their parents were too drunk to drive! Isn't that hilarious? She's so precocious," said Sheryl.

"Where are the kids anyway?" inquired Chrissie, "I haven't seen a sign of any of them since Harrison and I arrived."

"Your friends Jodi, Ayani and Charleigh are out back with them now. They volunteered to supervise the pumpkin carving contest."

Chrissie's mind quickly flashed to a scary image of fifty or so five year old kids wielding sharp cutting utensils and stabbing everything in sight except for the pumpkins. Thankful that her trusted friends were supervising, she still wondered if they had enough adult support.

"Don't you think I should be out there, too? I feel guilty if I'm not doing something!" Chrissie asked, never one to shirk her responsibilities.

"No, my dear, they've got it under control. You should hit the bar. We've created two special drinks just for today—the Bloody Eyeball martini and the Brain Hemorrhage. Take your pick."

Sheryl held out two martini glasses to Chrissie, one contained a traditional dry martini garnished with a radish stuffed with an olive to resemble a bloody eye, the other had a concoction of Peach Schnapps, floated gently over Baileys Irish Cream, garnished with a few drops of Grenadine dripping in rivulets to represent blood.

"Oooh, yummy," Chrissie said sarcastically, "What the heck, it won't do any harm if I have just one drink, it'll be at least two hours before I have to drive home. Sure, I think I'll have that Brain Hemorrhage."

Before meeting up with her friends, Chrissie wandered about the main floor to absorb the sights and sounds of the party. Getting into character, Chrissie began greeting the assortment of ghostly humans, aliens, critters and inanimate objects (someone was dressed as a blue Tiffany box with a white bow on her head), she strolled around the room saying things like, "Groovy costume, man," and "peace," or "wow, this is an awesome trip." The Brain Hemorrhage was quite effective at eliminating her initial shyness. The main floor was crowded with women and a handful of men congregated around the bar area. Bumping into a vampire who was talking loudly to the mermaid, who had her arm wrapped around the waist of the French maid who was trying to impress the mummy, Chrissie thought to herself, *this really could be an acid trip.* Astrid and Crystal were dressed as erotic belly dancers in jingly coin bras and layers of sheer fabric wrapped around their hips, and were demonstrating the art of forward shimmys they had learned from a DVD on aerobic belly dancing. They were actually very good and had captivated the attention of many guests with the tiny, delicate muscle vibrations of their bellies. Meanwhile, on the other side of the living room, two of the Brazilian nannies were dressed in full Carnival costumes, complete with huge feathered headdresses, beaded and sequined bikini bottoms and tops, and five inch open toe heels, with silk laces wrapped nearly to their knees. They were leading twenty or so women and tongue dragging men in a hip wiggling conga line around the perimeter of the room. It might have been her imagination, or the influence of the alcohol, but Chrissie thought that Jonathan's nanny Violeta was putting on a little weight around her waist. *"I hope that's not what I think it is,"* worried Chrissie thinking about the ramifications to his family if there was an additional future child in the mix. But, then again, based on the fact that it was *Saturday*, and once again, the parents weren't around to be with their children, perhaps Jonathan and his wife wouldn't notice the new infant in their household.

Where's Tara? Chrissie suddenly thought. *Surely she was invited.* Right on cue, Tara burst through the front doors, tears streaming down her cheeks, her mascara threatening to spill onto her pristine white angel costume. Chrissie ran to her side, prepared to hear the worst.

"What's wrong, Tara, are you okay?" Chrissie asked.

"Yes, I'm fine. Randy and I had another fight. He said I couldn't come to another party where there was alcohol involved and he wouldn't let me bring Clinton, fearing I might do something embarrassing," she said.

"What the hell, I'm wearing this damn *angel* costume just to prove him wrong," she added. "Where's the bar, I need a drink." Chrissie escorted Tara to the bartender who promptly served her a double martini. Astrid, Crystal, and several of the most popular women descended on Tara like flies on poop.

Seeing that Tara had company and sensing it was time to check on the rest of her friends, Chrissie walked through the Florida room filled with an array of twenty foot tall banana trees and an impressive assortment of palms and ferns, to the outside deck and pool area where several tables were set up under heated lanterns for the pumpkin carving contest. Jodi was dressed in a pregnant nun costume, Charleigh had chosen rugged khaki safari gear, which on her looked impossibly sexy, and Ayani was decked out in a gorgeous Native American priestess costume.

"Hey girls! Are you wearing your own costumes or did you use the rented ones?" asked Chrissie.

"Rented," the three women replied in unison.

"This must have cost Sheryl a fortune. Did you know she had these costumes shipped from a New York theater company to the tune of about $200 per outfit?" said Jodi. A quick calculation in Chrissie's head brought the total rental amount to nearly $10,000 for fifty or so costumes. She whistled low under her breath.

"I could certainly put that money toward Harrison's tuition," she said. Then she thought how beneficial $10,000 dollars would be if it was instead donated to spay and neuter homeless animals (Bob Barker would be tickled pink) or help get books, toys and supplies for the local boys and girls club. "What a waste," she mumbled to herself.

"Yeah, not to mention the cost of the chef, maids, parking attendant, tapas, alcohol, magician, and that huge inflated tent on the other side of the garage," said Charleigh.

"What's in the tent?" asked Chrissie.

"Don't know—it's a secret, Sheryl's saving it for the big climax of the evening," explained Ayani.

"By the way, you missed all the excitement earlier in the party," said Jodi.

"What do you mean?"

"When we arrived there were about twenty preschoolers playing on the pier—in the dark with no adults anywhere in sight," began Jodi. "One child tripped over his costume and flopped head first into the water. We got there just in the nick of time."

"Jodi rescued the child, I think it was little Lincoln—but I couldn't tell because he was covered head to toe in river mud," said Ayani. Chrissie's mind wandered to the list of Kindergarten boys who were named after assorted presidents. There was her child Harrison, Tara's son Clinton, another child named Cleveland, Charleigh's son was Wilson, a red headed, rotund boy was named after Garfield—the president, not the cat, and one boy was given the unfortunate name of Truman, possibly classifying him as a geek for the rest of his school years.

"Those idiotic adults were so busy consuming their martinis and brain drinks they forgot all about the kids. These five year olds were roaming wild just like in that book Lord of the Flies," added Charleigh.

"I see you've modified the pumpkin *carving* contest," said Chrissie, noting that the children were now using colored markers and stickers to decorate the pumpkins. "What lame brain came up with that idea?"

Before any one could reply, suddenly a Chihuahua dressed in a miniature superman costume bounded like a bullet across the expansive back yard, headed straight for the pier. Following several seconds behind the pooch was one of the botox blondes, half running and half tripping over her vampire costume, all the while wearing a frozen look of astonishment on her face.

"Stop Taco! Stop!" she yelled.

Laurel Somerville frantically ran out of the house, handed Chrissie her Yorkie-Poo, which was dressed as a fireman, then galloped across the yard to save the Chihuahua from leaping into the water. Deborah Brown, the owner of the dog that put Mrs. Casper's allergies into a frenzy, handed her infamous Pekepoo over to Ayani for safe keeping as she joined in the rescue.

"Watch him for a minute, won't you?" Deborah demanded. The dog was dressed in a little black leather Harley Davison biker outfit.

"What's with the dogs?" asked Chrissie.

"In about ten minutes Sheryl will be judging the Halloween costume contest for the dogs. The kids will have their turn at seven o'clock," Charleigh quickly explained.

"Don't do it Taco!" screamed botox blonde number one. "I give you a good life, good food, play dates—come home to mama."

By now the Chihuahua was perched on the precipice of the pier, glancing nervously over his shoulder at the frenetic women heading his way.

"Ayani, *do something*, use those Native American powers you have to communicate with animals. *Please*," begged Laurel Somerville, who had heard about Ayani's special skills with dogs.

Reluctantly, Ayani walked slowly to the first board of the pier, held up her hand for silence, took off her shoes and silently crept closer to the trembling little animal. By now a crowd of adults and children had gathered near the pool waiting, watching expectantly for the outcome. Would the tiny beast leap to his death, certain to have a doggie heart attack once it hit the freezing water? Ayani continued to slowly approach Taco, whispering soft, reassuring words along the way.

"Hey little boy, it's okay now. Gentle, gentle, come to me," Ayani said in a barely audible voice. Miraculously Taco turned away from the edge and walked cautiously in Ayani's direction. Ayani's warm and nurturing hands enveloped the petite dog, cradling him in her arms. Simultaneously, the assembled crowd erupted in loud applause and cheers, startling the dog once again. Ayani hugged the dog closer to her chest and shielded his tiny black eyes from the scary scene of costumed adults and children standing by the pool.

"Poor little thing, you don't need to be here wearing that silly costume," whispered Ayani.

"Do you have a quiet room where we can put this little guy for a while?" Ayani asked Sheryl. "He needs to calm down." Ayani then turned to the botox blonde, "Actually, it would be best if you took him home now."

"Oh, I'm not in any shape to drive right away," she said, slurring her speech.

Astrid appeared and interjected, "Yes, she's had nearly four martinis. I'll call a cab." Chrissie silently hoped that botox blonde number one wouldn't forget about her child and leave her behind once the cab arrived.

Sheryl Waters then said the first intelligent words that would come out of her mouth all evening, "Let's hold off on the dog costume contest. It wouldn't be fair to do it without little Taco." A few parents grumbled in protest, but their complaints were drowned out by the excited cheers from the children when Sheryl announced it was time to bob for apples. Based on the poorly conceived idea of a pumpkin carving contest, Chrissie envisioned five year olds teetering over the edge of the pool trying to capture apples with their teeth. Jodi must have shared the same thought and quickly intervened just as Sheryl walked in the direction of the pool carrying a basket of red delicious apples.

"Why don't we tie those miniature donuts to strings and get the kids to "bob" for them instead?" Jodi interjected.

"Great idea!" exclaimed many in the crowd, several kids included. At the snap of her fingers, Sheryl's housekeeper began tying donuts on strings to a broom handle. Ayani held one end of the pole horizontal, Charleigh held the bristle end. When the last child had eaten their donut and was covered in powdered sugar, Sheryl announced it was time for the costume judging contest—this time for the children.

"Leona Lowe has offered to judge the contest since she has extensive local theater experience and has personal know-how with costume design," said Sheryl.

Leona took center stage and bowed slightly to the parents who were now congregated in a semi-circle around her. She looked so official with her clipboard, Mont Blanc pen, and bifocals balanced on her nose. Several women were whispering to each other as the children paraded in front of Leona.

"I paid $550 dollars for that Lion costume—it was custom made just for Truman," said one mom. "I sent his measurements and a photo of him to a seamstress I found on the internet, and viola, his costume arrived a week later by Fedex."

"Yes, we were about to do the same, but Justice is growing so fast we figured she wouldn't fit into the costume by the time it was done," said another mom. Chrissie noted that "little Justice" wasn't so little anymore and would probably weigh nearly eighty pounds by first grade. "We rented a costume from the same theatrical company in New York that Sheryl used," the mom added. "It only cost $150 bucks to get that one-of-a-kind fairy costume."

"You can really tell the difference between those willing to cough up the big bucks for quality costumes and those pitiful homemade disasters—check out that hideous green thing with lots of eyes," one mom whispered cattily to another. Chrissie cringed. *Harrison is just adorable,* she thought to herself.

Charleigh had dressed each of her twins in large cardboard boxes painted white, with holes for their head and arms. One box was labeled "salt" the other "pepper." They both wore chef hats with black dots drawn in marker on the top to resemble the shaker lids. These homemade costumes were simple, sweet and perfectly acceptable.

Jodi's daughter Faith had chosen one of the mass produced Princess costumes which she bought at the toy store for $19.99. She looked charming and innocent in her sparking, pink dress. It, too, was perfect for the occasion. And finally, Ayani used a hair pick to fluff Carver's naturally curly black hair into an Afro, put a tie-dyed shirt on him, wrapped a sash around his waist, and gave him a dilapidated pint sized guitar, spray painted purple. Ayani's husband Derrick was a huge Jimi Hendrix fan and Carver wanted to please his dad. There was really no need to spend more than twenty bucks per costume for this event.

When the last child strolled past Leona, she quickly scribbled a few notes, then boldly announced, "I have made my final decision. Silence, please, everyone." No drama there.

"For best animal costume the award goes to Truman," she announced to a spattering of applause. "For best costume for a girl, the award goes to Agape and her fabulous Sea Nymph costume." More applause, this time with greater generosity to recognize the hostess' daughter. "Finally, the best costume award for a boy goes to Harrison and his green multi-eyed alien creation." Cheers were mixed with grumbles of protest from the moms who had spent huge sums of money on designer costumes. Ayani, Charleigh and Jodi gave Chrissie a gentle squeeze. Harrison beamed with pride.

Each of the winners received a $200 gift certificate for dinner at the most popular sushi restaurant in town. Somehow Chrissie didn't think Harrison would love raw tuna and barbequed eel for his meal. Hopefully they also had buttered noodles on the menu.

"Now, for the final event," announced Sheryl. "Children, follow me to the tent, where we have created a special haunted house, *just for you.*"

Squealing with excitement, the children bolted toward the hand painted wooden sign that marked the entrance to the tent with the words "Welcome, enter at your own risk." From inside the tent, a remote sound system broadcast eerie music and ghostly noises that sent shivers down the spines of those waiting in line. Children nervously grabbed the hand of their nearest friend as they cautiously entered the pitch black world and followed the winding path, illuminated just slightly by strings of tiny pin lights along the floor. Within seconds the squeals of excitement turned into screams of raw terror as a torrent of children rushed from the tent, crying, grabbing their parents and begging to go home. Harrison grabbed Chrissie with such an intensity she was knocked to the ground.

"Sweetheart, Oh my God! What happened in there?" Chrissie anxiously asked.

"Mommy is was horrible, a bloody mummy grabbed me and tried to take me away, there was a headless man with goo dripping down his chest, there was some creepy lady who had snakes in her hair," sobbed Harrison. Similar horror stories poured from all of the children. Scattered all around the Waters' backyard, children held tightly onto their parents, crying, screaming, shaking in fear, while describing the nightmare they had just witnessed inside the haunted tent.

"Ayani, Charleigh, what was Sheryl thinking?" complained Chrissie. "These are just five year old kids. They're not gonna sleep alone in their beds for weeks!"

"Sheryl's over there comforting Agape, who peed her pants, oh sorry, her sea nymph tail," said Jodi. "Sheryl hired a troupe of actors who thought they were putting on a show for the adults—not the kids. She feels horrible about this."

"If she really feels so horrible, I'll just send her Harrison's therapy bill," complained Chrissie. "It's only been a week that he's been sleeping alone without me. And that took years of work!"

"Girls, let's get out of here and take these petrified children home. Would you like to come to my house and make popcorn and watch a DVD, something safe like Bambi?" asked Jodi.

"Doesn't Bambi's mother die in the fire?" asked Ayani. "How about Dora the Explorer or SpongeBob, instead?"

"We'll meet you there," said Chrissie, grabbing her Volvo keys from the parking attendant. Carrying Harrison in her arms, she walked nearly a quarter-mile to the end of the long line of parked cars. Hoping to distract Harrison and to help ease his distress, she inserted his favorite sing-a-long children's CD into the player, cranked up the volume, and quickly drove away.

Life Observations from Vic the Maintenance Guy:
"Halloween gives these people around here an excuse to dress up and act insane. I wonder what's their excuse the rest of the year?"

Chapter Six:
The Giving Season

There was something about those old Yes songs that still gave Ayani chills every time she heard them. Driving through downtown Annapolis, Ayani inserted *Fragile* into the CD player of her Prius hybrid, cranked it up to nearly full volume, and sang at the top of her lungs the opening lines from Roundabout. It was almost a religious moment for her and brought memories flooding back to the first time she ever heard anything by Yes—it was at Rehoboth Beach, Delaware in her high school boyfriend's Chevy van, which was outfitted with six massive 20 inch speakers, basically an early form of surround sound. Even back then they were already considered a *classic* rock band from the 70's. That didn't matter. She loved their music the first time she heard them. Passing the city dock, Ayani rolled down the windows and let the music and her voice flow into the street. She didn't care if anyone heard her. On this Indian summer November day, the temperature had risen to nearly seventy degrees and downtown Annapolis was bustling with herds of tourists and locals strolling along Main Street.

At this moment, on this day, in this place, Ayani felt very connected to planet earth. That very morning she had begun the practice of sun gazing, or in her case, solar yoga, a modified version of the ancient practice of achieving a higher consciousness by absorbing the healing and energy benefits of the sun. Ayani knew that many believers actually stared at the sun each day at the prescribed times which were either within the first half hour after sunrise or the last half hour before sunset. She wasn't ready for that, not to mention the concern for her corneas, but she did want to try something new, something grounding, perhaps something that could help to counter the shallow chaos that she so often witnessed and experienced by living amongst the rich. Last week one of the multi-pierced, spiky haired managers of the natural food store Ayani frequented handed her a new paperback book that was featured on the end of aisle display. It was entitled "Leaving the Whorl Behind, Five Easy Steps to Perfection."

"Well, who wouldn't want *that*? Perfection in just *five steps*!" exclaimed Ayani with a hint of sarcasm in her voice.

Of course the title wasn't a reference to the common grounds at the Archimedes School, which everyone called the "whorl" because of the nautilus spiral shape of the sidewalk. Ayani was skeptical because of the impressive claims of the title, but perused the book nevertheless. Actually, there was some merit to the advice it offered, so she decided to give it a shot, plus, she couldn't wait to tell her friends she would be *perfect* in about one week.

"Dude, you just purge your body of any impurities and then get in tune with the sun's healing energies," said the pincushion from the health food store.

Ayani began the ritualistic path to perfection by drinking only organic fruit juice for dinner, she was in bed by nine, and she awoke one hour before dawn—just as the book instructed. She was required to wear only brand new, snowy white, freshly washed, 100% cotton clothes. The author suggested something like a karate outfit. Before dressing, she had to shower using a pure, organic soap, hopefully one that contained olive oil, coconut oil, almond oil, grapeseed, kukui, apricot pits, cocoa beans, kokum, lavender, soy, honey, mango, wild castor bean, celery seed, and hemp oil. After two days of intense internet research she found the exact soap at the Free Range Organic Lavender and Sheep Farm in New Hampshire.

Fifteen minutes before sunrise, Ayani sat in her backyard in a full lotus position facing the river, with her lower body connected directly with the cold November soil. Upon the arrival of the sun, Ayani meditated for thirty minutes. She was required to visualize a new mantra during this first solar yoga experience. Despite numerous attempts to "shake it off" one word continued to float behind her eyelids. *Penetration.* "Great, why couldn't my mind land on a mantra like "heal" or "breathe" or "peace."

Surprisingly, she didn't get cold, despite the fact that she was barefoot, wearing only a karate outfit, and the temperature was barely forty degrees. Just as the book indicated, she would be warmed internally by the sun meditations.

"Now, I'm one step closer to perfection," she said jokingly. Ayani stood slowly unfurling each limb, took a deep cleansing breath and walked to her kitchen, where she began her other daily ritual of packing healthy vegetarian lunches for her children Sara and Carver.

When the phone rang at 7:15 a.m., Ayani instinctively thought one of her friends was having an emergency or needed something from her—Chrissie had been having car problems, perhaps she needed a ride for Harrison, Charleigh's nanny Miss Elke had the flu, so maybe Ayani was needed to help baby sit—why else would someone call that early?

"Ayani, it's Chrissie, I *need* to talk to you, bad."

"What's up? Are you okay?" Ayani asked with concern in her voice.

"I've been up all night long, I couldn't sleep because of something that happened at school," said Chrissie.

"Don't tell me Harrison failed his pre-calc test, too!" said Ayani. "Carver's test scores are miserable."

"No, it's not that." Chrissie paused for a long moment, and began again, "You know I've been painting the set for the Thanksgiving play, right? Well, there's this middle school English teacher who's on board as a drama consultant to Mrs. Casper. His name is Nathaniel Anderson—he's forty-something, he's that widower who lost his wife to cancer two years back."

"Is he being a pain? I know drama teachers can be so moody," Ayani said in her melodic, comforting tones.

"No, he's wonderful, kind, cute, he's a good dad—he's got a three year old, he's just great." Chrissie sighed and gathered her courage to continue. "Alright, now I have a confession to make," said Chrissie. "I can't stop thinking about him, there's this energy between us, something absolutely electric. I'm totally blown away."

"Chrissie, are you having sex with him?" Ayani asked with no hint of disapproval in her voice, it was just a simple question.

"Oh God *NO*! I forgot how to do that. It's been years— I'm sorry, *over sharing*. I'd be too scared. But, remember that psychic I saw last month. She told me I would meet my long lost soul mate soon. I think I've found him…Oh Ayani, I know I can't do anything about it—the psychic said I must wait until the timing is just right. *What the hell* does that mean?" said Chrissie, rambling on clearly in distress.

"Calm down, dear. You haven't done anything wrong, you've just picked up on an amazing physical vibe between the two of you—I assume he must feel the same way?" inquired Ayani.

"Yeah, it was totally electric, as I said. He accidentally touched my arm when he reached for a paint brush and that one little innocent touch sent such a shockwave through me—I think through him, too. We both stopped dead in our tracks and turned to look into each other's eyes. I have never, *ever* felt anything like this," concluded Chrissie.

"Chrissie, my advice to you is to simply enjoy the fantasy right now. Dream about him at night, think about him during the day, you've needed to jump start the sexual side of you for quite some time. Get in touch with your hormones, they've been on hold for years."

"You're right, I feel like a teenager right now. I *am* going to enjoy this...nothing will come of it—I promise. But while I'm in the confessional, can I tell you something else?" Chrissie asked.

"Your secrets are safe with me, you know that."

"Ever since Harrison was an infant, I've been driving around Annapolis looking for a place that Seth and I could buy under the pretenses of renovating and renting, but my real intentions were different. I wanted it to be my home to move into when we separated," confessed Chrissie.

"You've been *that* miserable for nearly five years?" asked Ayani.

"Yep. I've been living a huge, freaking lie. But you know what's funny? I'm just now realizing how many sexless marriages are out there. After I went to the sex therapist, he told me the problem was rampant. Probably one out of every six 'happily' married couples completely ignore each other and many of them sleep in separate rooms," added Chrissie.

"Chrissie, my advice to you is to be very careful, don't do anything that would hurt your stellar reputation at school, and enjoy the moment—feel the energy, feel the connection. You'll know when the time is right." Ayani's words were gentle and authoritative.

"You sound just like the psychic. Thanks for listening Ayani. I better hurry and get ready to take Harrison to school. Plus, I need to find something sexy to paint in," said Chrissie with a giggle. "Oh, yeah, if only I had some of Charleigh's Gucci pumps, I love the ones with the six inch clear plastic heels—I think Nathaniel's got a shoe fetish."

"That's great Chrissie! You're already becoming such a slut puppy. I love it! Show off that cute little ass of yours— you don't realize half the men at Archimedes have been staring at it for years. And *you should* call Charleigh to borrow her shoes," said Ayani, "though I'm not sure how you're going to paint the set wearing six inch heels!" Just before hanging up the phone, Ayani added, "Chrissie, no matter what happens, remember that sex is natural and healthy."

"Oh yeah, I remember, just like eating broccoli and cauliflower," replied Chrissie with a tiny giggle.

On the way to Archimedes, Ayani reflected on Chrissie's sexless marriage to Seth, realizing for the first time that it had been five years since they had been intimate. *Poor thing*, Ayani thought to herself, *they'll be separated by next year, for sure.* A marriage without sex, at least once a week, just doesn't withstand the stresses of hectic daily life. Ayani remembered an article she read in *Vegetarian Times* that discussed what she now calls "old people sex" where happily married seniors in their 80's and 90's considered a sexual act to include simple naked skin to skin touch. Ayani smiled to herself thinking that some day in the distant future she and Derrick would be satisfied and sexually content to "just get naked" and cuddle.

Parking her socially conscious, environmentally safe Prius next to a brand new massive gas guzzling Cadillac Escalade, Ayani nearly creamed Laurel Somerville who scurried across the black top to greet her. Clipboard in hand, pen poised, Laurel asked Ayani if she could volunteer for this year's Archimedes School community outreach project to provide Thanksgiving meals for needy families in the area.

"Ayani, Thanksgiving is a big holiday for *your* people, right?" asked Laurel, alluding to Ayani's Cherokee heritage. "Could you help solicit food donations from preschool families?"

"Yes, we love to celebrate the coming of the white people and the downfall of our culture. Derrick and I always enjoy our tofu Turkeys," said Ayani, attempting but failing to ignore Laurel's comment about Native Peoples. "And, yes, put me down to help out with preschool families."

Laurel quickly scribbled Ayani's name on the sign-up sheet, then handed her a peacock feather as a thank you for her help. "It will remind you that you volunteered—I don't want to mess up this one like I did the Welcome Back Picnic." Ayani was impressed that Laurel admitted to her earlier mistakes and appeared to be rising to the occasion to properly chair this particular school event. Ayani was just about to inform the other four women that Laurel was successfully rounding up volunteers, when she saw that each of them were standing by the preschool building holding iridescent peacock feathers in their hands.

"I guess Laurel got to you, too!" Ayani said, waving her feather in their direction.

"Her drug detox program appears to be working, at least for now. Laurel's showing some sense of responsibility," said Jodi, always skeptical about the long term success of kicking a narcotic addiction.

"I'm going to start asking for contributions right now while the parents are arriving," said Ayani, anxious to be helpful. Ayani wandered off to chat with several of the moms and dads who were dropping off their preschool and Kindergarten children. Most of them willingly agreed to contribute something to the food baskets. A few were offended that anyone wanted to help families who couldn't help themselves.

"Why don't they just get a job?" said one young mother of a four year old, toasty and warm in her full length beaver coat. "My husband is hiring laborers right now to work at each of his car wash companies."

Somehow Ayani didn't think the minimum wage job she offered was enough to feed a family of four or more, but this wasn't the time to educate the over-privileged.

"I give enough money to the Archimedes School, I'm not giving another dime to any other charities," said another dad, in a huff. Win some, lose some, thought Ayani. Fortunately, the overall response was very positive, helping to overshadow the shallowness of a few.

By the next morning, contributions to the Thanksgiving baskets had begun pouring in. Ayani gladly accepted any and all donations, whether or not they were appropriate for the occasion. *At least they meant well*, Ayani thought, while tallying the results from her request. A set of crystal napkin rings, imported white tapers from France, a gift certificate for $300 dollars to a proper attire only restaurant in Washington, DC, a saki serving set, some smoked oysters, olive tapenade, duck liver pate, and a dozen bagels were some of the contributions Ayani compiled. She and her family ate the sushi assortment that Leona Lowe donated. There was no way raw fish would last more than a week until Thanksgiving. Sheryl Waters and her husband offered to loan out their maid and butler to any needy family for a day. And Astrid volunteered to donate five percent of the profits from all of her sex toy parties held during the month of November. Very generous, indeed. Sadly, as of yet, no turkeys, gravy, potatoes, stuffing, or cranberry sauce had arrived. *I guess I need to be more specific with this crowd*, thought Ayani.

Chrissie strolled by the picnic table outside the Kindergarten classroom which Ayani was using as a donation drop off point. Jodi and Charleigh were assisting Ayani with the tally.

"Can I have a bagel?" Chrissie asked, tipping forward slightly in the five inch ruby red heels she was wearing.

"Looks like the *painting* is going well," said Ayani with a sly grin on her face.

"What's with the fuck-me-pumps?" asked Jodi who could sometimes be so abrupt it could knock the wind out of you.

"I thought they looked good with these jeans," said Chrissie, trying to be nonchalant.

"I thought you were painting the set for the Thanksgiving play. But those jeans are so tight it looks like you *painted* them on your body," said Charleigh.

"Chrissie, what's up these days? You haven't been around much, and you're wearing clothes so tight they make you look like a working girl," asked Jodi. "You look like you belong on a street corner."

"I'm just trying to get rid of the seasonal blues I get. I needed something to lift my spirits," Chrissie replied, not willing to reveal the truth about her crush on her teacher friend yet to anyone except Ayani.

"I guess you're not power walking around the neighborhood in those pumps today, unless you're looking for some extra cash," joked Charleigh.

"Nope, the Kindergarten play's tomorrow night, and there's tons of work left," Chrissie said. "Hopefully I can join you later this week. Promise."

As Chrissie sauntered toward the Archimedes School auditorium, Jodi said, "She must be getting some action at home these days. There's this glow about her I haven't seen in a while." Ayani smiled inwardly and remained silent.

―――――――――

The air was filled with tension coupled with excitement on opening night of the Archimedes School Kindergarten extravaganza. The children's happy vegetable costumes had been sent home earlier that day with the explicit instructions from Mrs. Casper to avoid contaminating the costumes with dog hair, wool sweaters, and exposure to any types of food particles that were on the list of banned items. Ayani took Carver's corn cob costume, still sealed in a large dry cleaner plastic bag, and hid it upstairs in her expansive closet. The service dog Ayani was training was wonderfully behaved, but Blaze shed gobs of hair everyday. So much hair it looked like tumble weeds were rolling across her hardwood floors.

Ayani was uncertain about the exact plot of the play, but knew there would be a huge cornucopia filled with dancing vegetables that welcomed the Native Americans and Pilgrims to the feast. Carver had been singing one of the catchy tunes for weeks and the melody and words were now memorized by everyone in her family. While rinsing off the sweat from that afternoon's tennis match, Derrick boldly sang one of the songs in the shower.

"Broccoli, turnips, and carrots we sow.
Eat them, eat them, they make you grow.
Corn and pumpkins and lettuce, too.
Eat them, eat them, yes, you know who!"

Derrick also replicated the same butt wiggle that Carver did at the end of the song.

"That's attractive," Ayani said, watching Derrick jiggle his parts while dancing naked in the shower stall. Ayani loved her husband's solid as a rock body, his thigh and bicep muscles firm and well defined from years of playing sports and excelling in tennis. She couldn't wait to get hold of the dimples in his butt cheeks—her favorite turn on.

"Bet you want me now, baby," said Derrick with a chuckle.

"Save it for later, dear," Ayani said, wishing she had more time to enjoy her husband's company. "Right now I've got to get Carver dressed for the play and try to convince Sara to go. She's embarrassed that her friends will see her attend this *baby* event."

"*Tough*, she's going, no if's, and's or but's," said Derrick.

Forty minutes later Ayani and her family arrived at the Archimedes School parking lot just in time to witness a sleek white stretch limo pull up to the back stage entrance of the school's theater. Out popped ten adorable Kindergarten children dressed in an assortment of happy vegetable costumes, including the stalk of broccoli, the carrot, the two children dressed in matching lima bean outfits, and some pitiful child dressed in a large brown potato costume, that more closely resembled something that came out of the rear end of a dog than something that grew in the ground. Sheryl Waters emerged last and waived in Ayani's direction.

"We didn't want their costumes to wrinkle," she explained. Her butler followed behind, carrying a small cooler into the theater.

A steady stream of families arrived, with one out of every four parents toting a small cooler. Ayani wondered if she, too, should have brought drinks for her thirsty family, she naturally assumed lemonade or iced tea would be provided by the Parent Teachers Association at the conclusion of the play.

The air of the dimly lit auditorium was thick with the overwhelming smell, and to Ayani, *nauseating* aroma of expensive perfumes. Ayani sensed that the fashion show of the latest fall line of designer clothes was about to begin. Typically these huge school events were not about the children, but more about the parents and who's sitting with whom, who's wearing what, who's recently separated, and who's doing it with their best friend's husband. It's a chance to catch up on the latest buzz, air kiss a few cheeks, and then be catty behind someone's back.

"Did you see how much weight Candy's gained? Thank God she didn't wear corduroy, she'd be making *woosh woosh* noises everywhere she walked." Ayani overheard one woman say.

"I heard Mary Beth got a boob lift," began another mom. "She should have saved the money for her turkey neck. Look at all that flesh flapping there!"

"Can you believe that the Vandervine's are in a legal battle with the Dooney's? They're suing them because their

Golden Doodle ate their son's guinea pig. They're claiming their son's been traumatized and has required therapy ever since," proclaimed another parent.

Ayani noted with alarm that the first four rows of the theater had been cordoned off with red ropes and tassels, reserved for parents and grandparents who were in the exclusive Platinum Club at Archimedes—they had donated $25,000 or more to the school that year. *That's great for morale—keep the have's separated from the have not's,* she thought. Tara and her husband Randy were proudly sitting in the front row thanks to their $25,000 bribe to admit their child to Kindergarten. Similar to other parents on this night, a soft sided cooler sat at Tara's feet. Flanking Tara to her left was Astrid, dressed provocatively in a black body clinging Missoni lace dress, leaving nothing to the imagination and Jimmy Choo black patent leather boots with four inch spiked heels. Ayani and her husband Derrick also had the privilege of sitting in this section, since they contributed $30,000 every year to the annual fund, but they chose not to and were appalled by this explicit demonstration of segregation by social class. Ayani decided instead to sit several rows back with her friends Jodi, Charleigh and Chrissie. Conveniently sitting directly behind Chrissie was Nathaniel Anderson, looking sexy and dapper in a sports coat and tie, his curly brown hair brushing the top of his collar. Ayani caught sight of the subtle wink he gave Chrissie when she turned around to say hi. Smiling, blushing, Chrissie crossed her legs to reveal an amazing pair of peach and light brown two-tone boots sneaking from the bottom of her jeans. Ayani worried that Chrissie's entire grocery budget was being spent on footwear to impress her fantasy beau.

"Ayani, is it my imagination or is Jonathan's nanny looking really pregnant?" whispered Chrissie. "I thought a saw a slight bulge at Sheryl's Halloween party, but now it's much more prominent."

"Chrissie, sorry to say, but I think you're right," responded Ayani thinking about the fireworks soon to be launched at Jonathan and Ellyn's home upon this discovery.

"Ellyn hasn't been to any Archimedes School functions lately, and I hear she's traveling to New York every week on business. She's probably oblivious. I bet she doesn't even know her child's in this play," said Chrissie.

Leona Lowe, always looking for an opportunity to immerse in the limelight, entered the auditorium dressed head to toe in a full length Native American Priestess costume, complete with fringe, feathers, beads, animal skins, and headband—it was a perfect carbon copy of the TV version of native people attire. Charleigh elbowed Ayani in the ribs.

"What the hell is she doing? Has Leona lost her mind?" Charleigh exclaimed.

"Oh my God, she's climbing the stairs to the stage," said Chrissie. Leona ascended the five stairs that led to up to the stage, turned, and stood boldly in front of the velvet burgundy curtains, which would remain closed until the play began. Facing the audience, Leona took it upon herself to welcome the assembled parents, grandparents, and siblings, by attempting to use Native American sign language.

"In recognition of the original people that roamed this land, I welcome you to the Archimedes School Kindergarten play," Leona began.

The crowd began to murmur with confusion. *Was this part of the play? Why weren't other parents asked to participate? Why is Leona always chosen? She's just a second rate local actress*, one parent whispered.

Leona Lowe proceeded to place one hand dramatically over her mouth which was opened wide, then moved both of her hands to the side of her head, palms against her ears, fingers spread wide and stretched high, and finally waived her right hand in front of her forehead, moving her index finger and second finger upward toward the ceiling.

"This is how we say 'Greetings and Bless You' using traditional sign language."

Ayani caught her breath, stunned at Leona's completely inaccurate interpretation. The two botox blondes sitting in the second row stared at Leona with a frozen look of astonishment plastered on their faces. Uncharacteristically, Ayani rose from her seat and shouted above the spattering of applause, silencing the crowd.

"Leona, I hate to break the news to you, but instead of welcoming us to tonight's wonderful event for our children, you just told everyone that *the surprised antelope needs medicine*. After a millisecond pause to process this data, the audience then burst into uncontained laughter which continued for several minutes. Leona slinked behind the velvet curtain never to be seen again that evening.

"Sorry, but I had to do it," said Ayani to her friends. "I didn't want to hurt her feelings or embarrass her, but I'm tired of all the misrepresentation."

"It's about time you showed some chutzpah," said Jodi, tears from laughter spilling down her checks.

Charleigh and Chrissie patted Ayani on the back. Derrick gave her a little hug. Ayani's daughter Sara slid down in her chair, mortified that all eyes in the auditorium were now focused in their direction.

Mrs. Casper the Kindergarten teacher moved swiftly from behind the curtain, thanked Leona for her voluntary yet unnecessary performance, and said a few introductory words to welcome family and friends to the event. With a wave of her hand, the curtains opened to reveal a glorious hand painted set depicting the unspoiled Massachusetts coastline from times gone by. A chorus of 'oohs' and 'aahs' trickled from the crowd. Nathaniel Anderson reached forward and gave Chrissie's shoulder a cautious squeeze, sending shockwaves of emotion through her, causing Seth to look back and give him the evil eye. Watching this unfold, inquisitively Charleigh and Jodi simultaneously glimpsed over at Ayani, who simply shrugged her shoulders.

The vegetables danced and sang, Native Americans and Pilgrims broke bread, and overall the play was simply charming. Nearly all of the children remembered their lines, only one little girl refused to appear in public, her shouts of "I hate lima beans" could be heard from back stage.

Just as the play began, Tara retrieved a plastic Gatorade bottle from the cooler placed on the floor by her feet and told the people behind her to pass it backward to Chrissie. Despite Tara's budding friendship with Astrid, she still felt a strong bond with Chrissie. Chrissie nodded thanks then took a sip. Sputtering in surprise from the burn of Jamaican rum searing her throat, Tara mouthed the words in her direction "Panty Ripper." Her Gatorade bottle had enough rum to inebriate the entire auditorium so Chrissie passed it to each of her friends who took a swig.

"So that's what the coolers are for," said a newly enlightened Ayani. "Sure, what the heck." By the time the curtains fell, Ayani, Jodi, Charleigh and Chrissie were feeling no pain.

Getting to their feet, Chrissie said, "That was the best performance I've *ever* seen in my life," slurring her words. "Ayani, isn't Nathaniel so *sexy* tonight?"

"Shhhhh, your husband is right over there, he can hear you." Seth was already standing by the double doors impatiently waiting to retrieve their child and leave.

"Never mind him, I heard you," said Charleigh. "Hey, I saw that look he gave you…guess you're the teacher's pet."

"It doesn't hurt to flirt…I'm not doing anything. Really. Just having innocent fun. Really, I mean it. He's just my friend," said Chrissie babbling on.

"Stop worrying and making excuses, dear. Good for you, Chrissie, you've needed some attention for years," said Charleigh, then changing the subject before Chrissie's husband overheard this conversation. "Let's hit the road, girls, we've got an early start tomorrow helping Laurel Somerville with those Thanksgiving food baskets," announced Ayani.

Children, who were bundled against the cold, grey November morning, arrived at school the next morning bleary eyed and exhausted from the previous night of festivities. Snowflakes fluttered in the air, creating speculation about an early dismissal due to inclement weather. It only took a dusting of snow to close schools in Maryland. Standing by the picnic table outside of the Kindergarten classroom were nearly one hundred eager parents who had been enlisted as volunteers by Laurel Somerville. There was no way she would fail the Archimedes School this time.

Laurel arrived with megaphone in hand, "Thank you for helping on this cold, wintry day," she began, her voice distorted by the megaphone. "We will prepare twenty Thanksgiving food baskets and deliver them in the refrigerator truck I rented." Pointing to the caterer's truck with the plastic cow bolted to the roof, she asked, "Can I get one volunteer to ride with me in the truck?" Deborah Brown's hand immediately shot up.

"Deborah's only here to redeem herself after the Head of School berated her for bringing that dog to class *once* again," whispered Chrissie.

"Thanks for volunteering, Deborah! You can put your purse and things in the truck now so you won't forget it later when we head out," Laurel said to Deborah. Deborah willingly obliged, carrying her huge Gucci bag over one shoulder and opted to wait inside the warmth of the truck while other parents scurried outside in the freezing cold loading the baskets. Chrissie thought she heard a muffled bark coming from inside the purse.

"She wouldn't dare bring that mutt to school again," Chrissie mumbled quietly to herself.

"Do we really need one hundred people to prep and load twenty baskets?" Ayani asked Chrissie.

"Nope, for once let's not volunteer! We do enough around here already. Let's sneak away and get some coffee," said Chrissie.

Tara piped in, "Yes, I'm hurting mighty bad from those *Panty Rippers* from last night. I could use some caffeine. Did you hear Sheryl Waters' limo driver got a DUI on the way home? He had a few of those doctored Gatorades while he waited in the limo. They hauled his ass to jail."

"With all those kids in the limo?" Ayani asked. She was dumbfounded at his stupidity.

"Yep. He'll never drive a limo again, for sure. One of the policemen had to drive the limo back to Sheryl's house. The kids were freaking."

"Do you think it's safe to leave Laurel alone with this huge responsibility?" asked Ayani, hesitant to leave.

"Sure, with all these helpers, what could possibly go wrong?" Chrissie said over her shoulder as she walked toward the parking lot. "Come on, guys, let's go!"

Within minutes the remaining hoard of parent volunteers had loaded baked turkeys, potatoes, stuffing, cans of green beans, sauce, gravy, canned cranberries, pumpkin pies and bags of rolls into each basket, along with a handful of odd items such as smoked oysters and chicken liver pate divided randomly around. The sliding back door of the delivery truck slammed shut and Laurel and Deborah were on their way.

Unbeknownst to Deborah Brown, her sweet little Pekepoo who was always in tow, safely tucked inside her Gucci bag, was tempted by the overwhelming smell of cooked turkey wafting through the truck. The miniature dog leapt from the security of the purse and jumped into the gaping cavity of one of the birds. After spending most of his life hidden in purses, the dog obviously felt at home in small, tight places. Plus the turkey cavity had the added benefit of providing a snack of juicy turkey drippings. When Deborah and Laurel arrived at the home of the Gonzales family, they unknowingly delivered a special bonus 'gift' along with the Thanksgiving bird. That particular Thanksgiving basket containing the bird stuffed with a 'puppy surprise' was delivered to a lovely, nurturing, hard working Hispanic family who had recently moved to the area with their two young children. Laurel and Deborah quickly deposited the food basket and hurried on to the next delivery. Nearly twenty more families were awaiting their meals.

Setting the bird on the table, little Ramon and his sister Josephina, squealed in delight as the friendly Pekepoo emerged from the cavity.

"La mama, miro lo que las personas agradables nos trajeron!" Ramon exclaimed. *Look what those nice people brought us.*

Back at the Archimedes School, upon discovering the absence of her cherished dog, Deborah Brown's hysterical scream could be heard clearly from the center of the campus whorl all the way to the shore of the Chesapeake Bay.

Meanwhile, the happy family of four sat down to their lovely meal, held hands, said grace, and thanked the good Lord for bringing them to America where gifts of puppies were given on Thanksgiving.

Life Observations from Vic the Maintenance Guy:
"My mom used to say that caring should be like a reflex. If you're able to breathe, you're able to give to others. It's that simple."

Chapter Seven:
A Quickie

Once a month, Jodi, Charleigh, Chrissie and Ayani met for a ladies' lunch at one of the local restaurants on Main Street in Annapolis. This month Chrissie decided to extend the invitation to Tara, who as yet had not totally endeared herself to the other three women. But, they figured if Chrissie liked her, they might as well attempt to do the same. As usual, Tara was running late. Knowing how difficult it would be to parallel park her brand new massive Chevy Suburban on a busy street, she opted instead to park several blocks away from the restaurant in the metered lot near the town's dock.

"Dang!" Tara exclaimed as the heel of her boot caught between the boards of the Annapolis city dock pier. Stuck just briefly, yet long enough to catch the attention of an exceptionally handsome man perched on the bow of a gleaming 105 foot yacht anchored at the far end of the dock, he yelled down to Tara, "Do you need a hand?"

"Thanks, but no thanks. I'm pissed that I've ruined the heel on these brand new, damn Manolo's. I just bought them two hours ago!" Somehow with her southern twang even the words *pissed and damn* came out sweetly.

"Love your accent, I haven't heard *dang* since I left Texas," said the man. Tara looked up at him with greater interest, noticing his rugged good looks, skin still tanned even in November, and his curly blond hair was wind blown and tousled.

"Whereabouts are you from?" she asked, curious about *his* accent.

"South Padre Island, how 'bout you?"

"Corpus Christi," Tara replied, "But you sure don't sound like a Texan."

"Originally, I'm a New Zealand Kiwi, but I've lived in Texas for years. I just sold the boat dealership I owned down there and got the bug to do some traveling. Don't ask me why I came to Maryland in the middle of the winter," he said with a laugh. "By the way, I'm Ethan McKnight."

"I'm Tara Hunter, pleased to meet you," she said shivering slightly from the cold despite being wrapped snugly in her new Cavalli shearling and suede military styled coat, an early Christmas present she just bought for herself. Underneath she was wearing a gorgeous black Donna Karan wrap dress, that left nothing to the imagination about her size 2 figure, not to mention she was recently in the habit of not wearing any underwear at all—thanks to a suggestion from Astrid that the constant flow of air was "stimulating and good for you." Right now, the combination of cold air and the handsome man hovering over her was providing a bit too much stimulation.

"You're shivering—darlin.' Would you like to come aboard for a minute? I've got some tools and I bet I can fix your heel well enough to hold for a while."

Tara sized Ethan up from head to toe. *I bet you've got an awesome tool or two.* Then looking at the huge length of the yacht, she remembered the old saying, 'the larger the boat, the smaller the penis.' Oh well.

"I was supposed to meet some girlfriends for sushi, but I really can't walk there like this." Tara hesitated for a moment, and then said, "Sure, I'll pop up for a few minutes. Would you mind giving me a hand? I know boots aren't exactly boat shoes."

Ethan walked back to the stern to help Tara board. Lifting her gently across the transom, Tara could feel the ripple of the muscles in his forearms.

"Come inside, I'll make something warm for you while I work on this heel. Coffee, tea? I've also got some crisps and dip in the galley, if you're hungry." Tara looked at him quizzically. "Oh, sorry, crisps are potato chips."

The interior of the expansive main salon was expertly decorated in warm tones, plush cream colored carpeting, sculpted beige brocade sofas, and a dining area that could seat twelve comfortably. Tiny speakers dropped from the ceiling, and the audio-visual custom built cabinetry housed a high tech German sound system along with a 63 inch plasma TV. The ten foot granite top bar sparkled from the reflection of the mirrored tiles placed along one wall. Rope lighting was attached and rimmed under the length of the granite bar. Tara recognized the Baccarat stemware lining the shelves as being the same pattern from her wedding china. Plush, lush and huge, this was the perfect boat for entertaining.

"I was looking forward to some hot saki, but that's not something most people would stock. You wouldn't happen to have any whiskey and Baileys? I can make a mean Irish Coffee," said Tara.

"Guess what? You're in luck. I'll get you set up and you can make yourself at home." Ethan puttered about the bar gathering supplies, put fresh beans in the coffee machine, pressed the "on" button and then excused himself momentarily to go below the main deck to find his tool kit.

"Please take off your boots, it must feel weird to be hobbling with that one loose heel." Tara willingly obliged, crossing her legs, and slowly unzipped each boot. She had taken off her jacket to reveal the low cut form fitting black dress exposing the luscious curves of her breasts. Tara subtly and unnoticeably squeezed her arms a little closer to her chest to enhance her already pronounced cleavage. She enjoyed the tease; her newly acquired sexual confidence worked to turn both him *and* her on. Remembering she wasn't wearing panties, she was careful not to replicate that Sharon Stone scene from one of her old movies—that would be too forward! Ethan tried to appear indifferent, but Tara knew otherwise. Over the last few months, Astrid and Crystal had done an excellent job educating Tara on how to entice your man. Tara was hoping some of these tricks would work on her husband Randy, but thus far to no avail, except for one night when they did enjoy fine champagne while soaking in a hot tub—until Randy proceeded to fall asleep from the effects of heat and alcohol.

In one of the many mirrors on the boat, she caught a glance of Ethan discreetly adjusting his crotch as he stepped away to find his tools. "Wow, I have to tell Astrid her tricks really work," thought Tara.

"I almost forgot. I need to call the girls and tell them I can't make it," she said.

Searching through her enormous purse she finally grasped her iPhone then Tara quickly called Charleigh to explain her absence.

"Charleigh, I can't make it to lunch, I've run into a little, uh, snag. Tell Jodi, Chrissie and Ayani I'm sorry. But, please keep me in mind for next month's luncheon!"

"Oh, Chrissie couldn't make it either. She's got another project at Archimedes—something about taking apart the set from the play last week."

"She's certainly a sucker for volunteering. She's gotta learn how to say 'no' sometime," said Tara, pressing a button to complete her call.

Tara busied herself pouring the coffee and mixing the ingredients for the two Irish Whiskeys. Ethan bounded up the stairs to the main salon and proclaimed, "I'll have you on your way in no time." Tara silently wished he wasn't so confident.

"Here's to Manolo's," Tara toasted Ethan with the coffee mug. "Without them I wouldn't have stumbled onto your boat." Her bare foot gently (but accidentally) brushed against Ethan's boat shoe.

"To Manolo's," he said with a wide, beautiful grin that made Tara's whole body tingle.

Ethan set to work repairing Tara's heel. "Feel free to find some tunes. I've got Sirius radio hooked up to the boat," he said.

Not sure what Ethan would like, Tara scrolled through the programming line-up and decided against Country Hits—her favorite, and picked Smooth Jazz instead, something more generically appealing. Tara curled up catlike on the sofa and sipped the Irish brew all the while intently watching Ethan's every move.

After a few moments of tinkering with the boot, Ethan announced, "There, it's a temporary fix, but it should hold just long enough to get you back to the shoe store."

"Thanks so much, Ethan, how can I repay you? How about lunch sometime?" Tara asked.

"Can I take a rain check on that? I'm headed south tomorrow. There's a boat in Florida I'd like to buy—a little bigger than this. I'll be back in Annapolis in the early spring."

"Damn. I was truly hoping to repay that debt a little sooner," said Tara smiling as she coyly reached out to touch his forearm.

"Darlin' I'm no fool, I never forget debts owed me by beautiful women. Let's keep in touch while I'm gone—*I mean it*," were his reassuring words. Tara entered his number into her iPhone while Ethan wrote down all of Tara's contact information.

"I just bought a new cell phone and I haven't figured out how to update any of the numbers!" Ethan apologized. "I promise yours will be the first one I enter." Ethan stopped what he was doing and looked directly into Tara's face, their eyes locked together for just a brief moment—but long enough to communicate a thousand thoughts. Tara felt shockwaves of emotion and confusion reverberate throughout her body. In that one tiny moment, Tara's thoughts shifted at lighting speed from her husband Randy, and how frustrated she was that he's ignored her for so long, to this charming, attentive and gorgeous New Zealand man she had just met, to the fleeting thought of *what the heck*, I'd give anything to be with Ethan just once—it wouldn't be an 'affair' if it happened only one time. Anyway, Randy will never find out!

"I, um, think I have to go now," Tara said, almost dreamily. "I have to pick up my son at the Archimedes

School." She was still absorbed in her final thoughts which had now progressed to seeing images of Ethan naked. Tara took a deep breath and composed herself before reaching to open the cabin door to step outside into the icy wind.

Ethan sensed the opportunity to make a move.

"Wait! One more thing," he said. He took her hand from the door, and pulled her gently toward him. Again, their gaze connected and Tara saw his sparkling blue eyes crinkle at the corners when he smiled. Wearing the boots with four inch heels, Tara was almost eye to eye with Ethan. He didn't need to lean down far when he kissed her firmly and passionately on the lips. At first, Tara resisted. *"I'm married, I'm not supposed to do this."* Then, pushing that thought aside, she fully immersed herself in the kiss. It had been so long since anyone had embraced her with such intensity she was overwhelmed with emotion, then desire. Ethan was the first to reluctantly pull away.

"Tara—It's not often a beautiful Sheila stumbles into my life. I'm so glad you broke that 'dang' boot," he said with a warm smile.

"I wish I could stay, but, um...I really have to go, Clinton's probably waiting outside the Kindergarten classroom already," Tara's voice trailed off.

"I wish you could stay, too." He touched the piece of paper scribbled with her phone numbers.

"I *will* be calling you," was Ethan's final promise.

Tara was confident he would.

═══════

Meanwhile, back at the Archimedes School, Chrissie was caught totally off guard. Humming a catchy reggae tune to herself while she dismantled the set from the Thanksgiving play, he approached her silently from behind and put his two warm hands on her shoulders. Gently, he turned her to face him. Nathaniel touched her chin, coaxing her to peer directly into his eyes. Now just inches apart, he pulled her toward him and kissed her softly on the lips. One simple kiss and Chrissie's world was turned upside down. Breathless, she tried to compose herself and said, "Nathaniel, um, we...."

"Don't say anything, not now," he replied. "We'll talk soon." He turned and left the stage.

Life Observations from Vic the Maintenance Guy: "Money doesn't make you happier. Money doesn't make you happier. Money doesn't make you happier. Maybe if I keep saying this enough, I'll actually believe it."

Chapter Eight:
Thank You, Teachers

Many of the shops and buildings in historic downtown Annapolis were decorated for the Christmas season in the 18th century traditional style using only natural materials such as fresh pine boughs, apples and pears tucked into wreaths, and red and green plaid ribbons tied to light posts. Electric candles flickered from every window.   Flurries fluttering down on historic Annapolis made it look like a winter scene from inside one of the snow globes you could buy in a souvenir shop along Main Street. This particular December threatened to become one of the coldest on record, especially in Maryland near the Chesapeake Bay, where the average daily temperatures barely rose above freezing.

At the Archimedes School morning drop off, Kindergarten children scurried from the warmth of their parent's Mercedes, BMW's, or chauffeured driven Lincoln Town Cars, and ran solo to the classrooms. Neither the parents nor the hired help were willing to leave the cushy comfort of the warm interior of their vehicles and expose themselves to the bitter cold.

Chrissie, Ayani, Charleigh, Jodi and Tara had also not ventured around the neighborhood on their morning walks in weeks. The icy wind blowing from the bay was too much of a deterrent. Sadly, Jodi already felt her thighs begin to expand from the lack of exercise, she had bumped up one size in jeans, and several of her lycra walking outfits were so tight they cut off the circulation. It didn't take much for Jodi to gain a few pounds, contrary to her perpetually lithe friends. Always needing to remain connected, the women still took the time to meet each morning at a local funky coffee house just a few blocks from the Archimedes School. It was a friendly spot decorated with a Caribbean vibe where the owners greeted you by name and knew in advance what you planned to order. A crayon box assortment of colored paint was splattered intentionally on the floor, stuffed parrots sat on perches which hung from the ceiling, and the walls were covered with funky posters of resorts in the islands where you'd rather be on these wintry days. The owners even knew many of the menu items their guests would typically order, and they always remembered that Jodi was not a huge fan of anything fruity, so each morning they bantered with her, "We've got fresh blueberries today, they'd be great on your pancakes," said one of the owners while barely containing a sly grin. Or, "How about a fruit cup on the side to go with your bagel?" Hanging on a wall of the restaurant was a wooden sign that read, *Raising teenagers is like trying to nail Jello to the wall.* Jodi knew all about that first hand. Just last week she caught her fifteen year old daughter Ashlyn in her bedroom with one of her male classmates. Of all people, it was Rob, Vic the maintenance guy's son. Jodi had always trusted Rob to be a good, responsible, ethical kid—but not any more. Had she arrived a few minutes later, Jodi might be on the evening news by now. *Surgeon's wife attacks daughter's boyfriend with scalpel. The boy now speaks several octaves higher. Tries out for female lead in school play.* Jodi threw open Ashlyn's door when she overheard the boy saying, "Come on, everyone's doing it. We can be *friends with benefits* and it's not really sex." *Thanks Bill Clinton*, Jodi thought. Now all teenagers think a blow job doesn't qualify as sex. *"I didn't have sex with that woman, Miss Monica Lewinsky," replied the former President.*

Charleigh chose a booth positioned right under the sign about the Jello, making Jodi cringe when she remembered the Ashlyn and Rob incident from last week.

"I think I'm joining a gym, my thighs are getting so huge only one of us can sit on this side of the booth," Jodi announced to Charleigh, as she squeezed next to Chrissie on the vinyl seat.

"Don't bother, just come over and work out on the equipment at my house," said Charleigh. "I'd love the company. I just bought this amazing ab machine. Plus I have a bunch of new exercise DVD's—one's called *How To Get Your Parts Hard in Thirty Days.*

"Sounds painful to me," replied Jodi.

"Hey y'all, let's hire our own personal trainer," added Tara enthusiastically. "I know a woman, who knows another woman, who knows this guy, who knows another guy who'll come to your house and do all the women."

"What?" asked Jodi, slightly confused. "How many women can he do at a time?" At that precise moment, Ayani entered the coffee house and joined the conversation.

"Whoa! I'm pretty happy just doing it with Derrick. I'm not into the group sex thing," replied Ayani. "What are you guys talking about?"

"Jodi's complaining about gaining weight. So, Tara wants to hire some personal trainer stud and share him amongst the five of us," explained Chrissie, worried slightly about the cost. "But I would *love* to look firm for all the holiday parties coming up."

"You've got a lot of parties this year, Chrissie?" Jodi asked with curiosity.

"A few. One for Seth's office, another one with neighbors, a couple of family things, and, um…this." Chrissie reached into her purse and retrieved a formal invitation imprinted with an embossed nautilus shell. "It's for the Archimedes School teacher holiday party. I guess I got this because I'm on the PTA."

"That, or your hot buddy from the English department invited you," said Jodi, with a concerned tone in her voice. "Better be careful there, he's mighty cute." Chrissie had not shared her secret kiss with anyone, not even Ayani. Why bother? It would never happen again, she had to make sure of that.

"Nathaniel? Naa. He doesn't know I exist." Chrissie said, still in denial that anyone would be interested in her.

"Chrissie, don't sell yourself short. He wants to get in your pants just as much as half of the men at school," said Jodi, cutting to the chase. "You don't realize how unbelievably sexy you are."

"*SHHHHH*," Chrissie said, putting a finger to her lips to quiet Jodi's voice, pointing to the clutch of women sitting nearby.

Sitting in the adjacent booth was a group of former Archimedes School moms whose children were now in college. Jodi closely observed these women, thinking that in a few years, her small group of women might end up looking like these chicks, with their perfectly coiffed helmet hair, wearing conservative business suits, practical pumps, and handing out their realtor cards to anyone who passed by. After the six women at the next table squabbled over the minutia of the tab, *I had the diet coke, you had the coffee—you owe a dollar more,* she was stunned to witness one of the realtors return to the table to slyly retrieve half of the tip. *Real estate sales must be slow this time of year,* was Jodi's thought.

"I've been meaning to ask you girls, does anyone want to join me on a shopping spree to New York? I'm going next weekend with Astrid. She's taking her husband's private jet," announced Tara. "I need to buy a few party dresses." To Jodi the words party dresses evoked an image of little girl's pink chiffon dress shaped like a little lamp shade. Somehow she didn't think that's what Tara meant.

"Tara, how the hell have you been sitting on that juicy tidbit? He owns a private jet? Is Crystal going, too?" asked Jodi.

"Nope, they're not speaking to each other. Last week Astrid accused Crystal of stealing cash from her bedroom. Apparently she keeps about $10,000 in her underwear drawer. Astrid said she discovered half of the money missing right after Crystal left her house—they had a psychic reading party to identify past sex partners. There were other Archimedes moms there, so Crystal denies it—said it must have been someone else. Oh, by the way, this is Astrid's first incarnation as a female. In her past lives she was always a male—she's been a warrior, a sheep farmer, a feudal lord, a plantation owner...." Jodi cut her off with a raise of her hand.

"Yeah, yeah...she was probably some sultan who had her own harem, too, the hussy," said Jodi while grimacing.

"Back to the private jet...her husband's a pilot?" asked Chrissie.

"No...well, sort of. It's the plane he leases for his company. He travels all over North and South America so much that with the cost of airline tickets these days, he said it was cheaper to lease a plane and hire a pilot. Astrid said I could invite all of you—it seats up to twelve people. She gets to use the plane at least once a week—she said that was her deal as long as she gave her husband a weekly morning blow job. No blow job, no plane," giggled Tara.

"I guess that's the married version of *friends with benefits*," muttered Jodi to herself. Her friend didn't hear her, nor did they remark negatively about the blow job for airplane ride deal. Astrid lived for sex, so this wasn't any effort on her part. But, there were loads of women out there, especially the most affluent women in town, who maintained the illusion of appearing happily married, but, actually were just faking it, big time. Basically, they got their stuff if they accepted their package deal. Their "stuff" included enormous custom built mansions with all the high end extras plopped down on two acre beautifully landscaped lots on the water, a new Mercedes SUV every year, a constant supply of diamond trinkets, and a $15,000 dollar monthly American Express allowance for anything they wanted. The trade off was that they had to look the other way when their husbands came home with a size zero pink lace thong tucked into the pocket of their Armani pants, or when $250,000 dollars mysteriously disappeared from their checking account after he set up his paramour in a new condo or townhouse. So, in comparison, a blow job for a free airplane ride wasn't a bad deal.

"Oh, let's go, girls. That would be so much fun!" said Chrissie, excited at the chance to get away from Seth and be with her friends, even if it did include Astrid.

They each agreed to check in with their husbands for approval and get back to Tara tomorrow. It was wishful thinking because Chrissie knew Seth would never let her go. Since he always worked, even on the weekends, he needed her home to take care of Harrison. And, beyond that, she just didn't have the extra spending money cash. What was she going to do, simply watch the others while they swarmed over the latest fashions and cleaned out the women's department at Barneys, or just order an appetizer when they went to the latest up and coming sushi restaurant in Greenwich Village? Likewise, a weekend trip was out of the question for the others, too. Jodi was afraid to leave her teenage daughter alone for more than one hour, Charleigh figured one of her children was certain to get sick again—it had been a rough flu season for her family, and Ayani remembered later that she had signed up for a seminar on how to improve your orgasms with solar yoga. A trip to New York City was a wonderful fantasy for these four women.

Suddenly, Tara's iPhone rang with the happy tune "Waltzing Matilda" causing her to leap from the booth and announce, "My cell reception's bad in here, I'm stepping outside." She nearly skipped to the door, almost knocking down an elderly patron creeping along using a walker. From the window, Jodi could see Tara smiling, giggling, and twirling her hair around a finger while talking on the phone. *Wonder what that's all about?* Jodi thought.

"Hey girls...not to change the topic, but...," said Chrissie switching gears and putting on her PTA hat. "I need to assign someone to be in charge of the Kindergarten teacher holiday gifts. Do you think Laurel Somerville can pull it off?"

"She certainly got enough volunteers for the Thanksgiving baskets," said Ayani, remembering the turn out from just two weeks ago. "It looks like she's tapped into the mother load of willing helpers."

"Okay, I'll put her in charge of collecting gift money. On their incomes they'd probably appreciate gift certificates to the mall, don't you think? I bet their homes are already filled to the brim with useless teacher mugs that say *#1 music teacher*, or *best teacher in the world* t-shirts, and desk ornaments in the shape of apples," said Chrissie. "I always think it's hilarious when clueless parents give teachers who have a last name of Berg, Stein or Wexsteinberg those lovely silk Christmas ties," she added with a shake of her head. "This year we need to be much more practical, don't you think?"

Indeed, Laurel Somerville *was* up to the task. The day after Chrissie spoke with her about collecting money for holiday teacher gifts, a letter was sent home to the parents of each Kindergarten child.

"Dear Parents,

As you know the Archimedes School teachers give their blood, sweat and tears to educate our children while earning close to nothing. I pretended to apply for a job at Archimedes in order to uncover the annual salary for a typical teacher. Can you imagine living off of less than $40,000 dollars a year, or a month, or *even a week*? Impossible. How do they pay their mortgages, buy groceries, travel to the Caribbean, shop at Neiman's? This holiday season we can open our hearts and our wallets and show the Kindergarten teachers how much we love them. I'm asking that each family voluntarily contribute at least $200 to the teacher gift fund. Imagine, at $200 per family, for three Kindergarten classes with fifteen children in each, we could raise nearly $3,000 for each of our wonderful teachers. Think about it—many of you, our dear Archimedes School parents earn at least $3,000 per day! I know you'll do your part.

Please return your cash contribution in your child's book bag in the envelope provided.

Happy Holidays!

Sincerely,

Laurel Somerville

"At least she meant well," explained an exasperated Chrissie to Jodi over the phone upon receiving the letter that arrived that afternoon in Harrison's book bag. "Jodi, please remember these words; In the future I must review and approve any and all letters written by insensitive, idiotic, bonehead parents. $200 dollars is my entire Santa Claus budget for Harrison," said Chrissie.

"I'll cover you, Chrissie," said Jodi.

"It's not that I don't *want* to donate $200 dollars—these teacher's deserve every penny. It's just that so many of these over-privileged, fucked up, well-to-do people have no idea how the other half lives. There's a bunch of us at Archimedes who are hard working, average Americans, who need a little financial aide to pay that insane $28,000 tuition so we can have the best for our kids. We struggle everyday to make ends meet, shop at Marshall's and second hand consignment stores, write down every goddamn weekly expense in a little notebook, watch our mileage because gas prices are outrageous, buy cheap wine, and squirrel away a couple of bucks here and there for a vacation fund. I'll be lucky to get to Ocean City, Maryland for the day this year."

Chrissie continued her tirade, "Sometimes I get so sick of hearing about these pretentious mothers flying to Europe, St. Barts, or St. *whatever*, hopping around in their fancy pants shoes, buying brand new $60,000 dollar cars once a year, shopping at Barney's in New York...*Oh darling, I just had to buy that $650 dollar white shirt...*IT'S A FUCKING WHITE COTTON SHIRT you could buy at Old Navy for $18 bucks!" Chrissie paused for a moment to collect her thoughts.

"Okay...yeah I know, take a deep breath, I'm done now," Chrissie concluded, realizing little five year old Harrison had overheard her say "fucking" and was running around her kitchen singing the new word with huge enthusiasm. "It's a fucking happy day!" *Great*, wait until Seth comes home.

"Chrissie, I know it's hard for a lot of people. I know you're frustrated. No one suspects that you and Seth are just average Americans," Jodi responded, realizing too late that she had made a poor choice of words.

"Jodi, there's nothing wrong with being *average* Americans! And actually, we're not even average, based on Seth's income we're affluent—if you look at the national data. That blows my mind!"

"Chrissie, you should mail a follow-up letter to every Kindergarten parent explaining that *any* contribution would be appreciated."

"Good idea. Okay, I'll be the spin doctor and fix this political mess before I get kicked off the PTA," Chrissie replied.

"Are you going to Charleigh's house to exercise with the personal trainer this afternoon after school? Her nanny, Miss Elke, agreed to watch all of our kids. It might be a good idea—it could help you blow off some steam," asked Jodi.

"Damn, that's today? I was going to the consignment store to look for a dress—I don't have anything for the Archimedes teacher party."

"I bet Charleigh's got something you can borrow," said Jodi.

"Sure, if I stuff my bra with a small farm animal I could probably fill it out," replied Chrissie, barely containing her perpetually infectious giggle. Jodi loved Chrissie for that. No matter how upset, angry, or hurt Chrissie was, she could never end any conversation in a huff.

"I'll see you there," concluded Jodi, placing the phone in the receiver.

Later that day, sweat dripped from every pore in Jodi's body, drenching her baby blue t-shirt and stretchy Prana capris. She was embarrassed to be anywhere near the young boy-toy, personal trainer, fearing he might catch a whiff of her pungent odor. Plus, moments ago while he assisted Jodi with her lifting technique, a blob of her sweat hit him squarely in the eye. Meanwhile, on the other side of the mirrored exercise room, Charleigh had one teeny tiny bead of glistening perspiration on her brow, despite a twenty minute uphill warm up on the tredmill. Mirrors were placed on every wall in Charleigh's gym—if you were Charleigh you wouldn't mind seeing yourself reflected a thousand times. But, everywhere Jodi turned she saw her thighs looming large and ominous from a myriad of different angles. *Thank God I rarely see my husband in the daylight*, she thought. *This is brutal!*

Chrissie eventually appeared, as did Ayani and Tara. Tara wore a brand new body hugging Puma matching outfit with a top that accentuated her perfect breasts. The poor personal trainer guy had one eye burning from Jodi's blob of sweat and the other eye was distracted by Tara's cleavage—along with Charleigh's stunning good looks. No wonder he inadvertently tripped over a set of hand weights and crashed head first into one of the floor to ceiling mirrors, shattering it.

When the young, firm thing finally left Charleigh's home, he held in one hand a bag of frozen peas to reduce the swelling on his forehead from the collision and in the other hand he held a wad of cash. Charleigh was a big tipper, and the other women chipped in, too, mostly out of guilt.

Charleigh lamented, "Perhaps we better stick to power walking."

"Or better yet, join me at the seminar I'm taking on how to enhance your orgasms with solar yoga!" piped in Ayani. "It's been a breakthrough for me and Derrick."

"I think I'll pass," said Chrissie, cringing at the thought of having sex with Seth while he wore his plastic mouth guard.

"Me too," responded Charleigh and Jodi in unison, both thinking they neither had the time nor the need to do anything to improve their already perfectly satisfying sex life.

"Hummm, when's the class?" asked Tara. "Sign me up, I'll be there!"

———

"The money's missing?" exclaimed Chrissie, yelling into the phone. "What the hell do you mean? Laurel, how did you lose more than $3,000 bucks?"

"I, um, I don't really know," Laurel Somerville began nervously. "One day it was in my purse, the next day it was gone." Laurel hesitated briefly, as if searching for an explanation, "I had my purse on the passenger's seat in my car. I went to the gas station in that scary ethnic neighborhood, you know, where all the *Spanish* people live. The one right next to the liquor store where that old man is always selling wilted bouquets of flowers to people who've stopped at the street light. When I turned my back to fill the tank, a young gangster kid ran past me. I betcha he reached into my car and stole the money," explained Laurel.

"Did you call the police? File a report? Did you hear him open and close your car door?" As Chrissie badgered Laurel with questions she wondered how on earth she would explain this to the PTA board.

"Well no, I figured they'd never find him or the money, so why bother?"

Chrissie took a deep breath and tried unsuccessfully to compose herself.

"Laurel, look…I'm so furious I can't talk to you right now. That money would have been a huge, huge gift for the teachers—they really deserve this more than anyone. Let me get back to you with a plan," Chrissie said, slamming down the phone.

Immediately Chrissie was on the line with Jodi.

"I don't believe her story," said Jodi. "Something's fishy for sure. How could someone silently open and close Laurel's car doors, rummage around in her purse, find the money—and just the money, no wallet, credit cards, or anything else, then quietly run away? And do all of this within one or two seconds while Laurel's back was turned?"

"You're right, I was so mad when she called, I didn't put the whole story together, in fact, it did seem like she was making it up on the fly. Hey, wasn't Laurel also at Astrid's psychic reading party, a week or so ago—when someone stole something like $5,000 cash from her underwear drawer?" asked Chrissie.

"Interesting...let's not jump to conclusions, but I am seeing a pattern here," said Jodi. "It's not uncommon for people with narcoset addictions to fall off the wagon. It's a tough nut to crack."

"What can we do? Is it time for some sort of an intervention?" asked Chrissie.

"Maybe. Let me talk to Laurel's family. I know a private intervention consultant who the Somerville's could afford—she'll arrange the entire event to the tune of about $20,000. It's worth it, she's really good."

"I'll put that in your hands, Jodi, in the meantime, what can we do about the teacher gifts?" asked Chrissie. "It's too late in the evening to call other parents, most of them are probably out on the town or at the yacht club. We'll only reach their nannies at this hour and they'll be in the middle of helping with homework. Damn it, we were scheduled to make the gift presentation tomorrow morning right after Kindergarten drop off."

"I'll call Charleigh, we'll figure it out." Jodi had already donated more than $300 bucks to the teacher gift fund, $200 for herself and another $100 to help Chrissie save face. It wouldn't be a burden to write another check for the same amount, but she felt like she was enabling Laurel's drug addiction and covering for her. But the teachers really did deserve something special this time of year—it wouldn't be fair to only give them a note from Laurel that said "thanks for the percosets."

Two quick phone calls to Charleigh and Ayani and everything was handled. Charleigh had several unused gift certificates to Victoria's Secret, two vouchers for $100 each for the mall, one extra gift certificate to Nordstrom, and a $50 gift for a local garden center.

"Don't you ever use these?" asked Jodi.

"Bud's always tucking them into little presents he gives me and I forget to take them along when I'm doing errands," said Charleigh. "They've been sitting in my jewelry box for months."

"Ayani donated a year of yoga classes for the three teachers plus she cleaned out her pantry and found tons of fancy gourmet food items from Whole Foods. She's putting together three lovely wicker gift baskets. Chrissie whipped up three miniature watercolor paintings and had them framed at the craft store. Along with some cash and assorted gift certificates I think we've got the teachers covered," concluded Jodi. Another crisis averted, problem solved.

Now Jodi had to deal with Laurel Somerville. Jodi placed a call to one of her old buddies from the hospital where she used to work. With a name like Rebecca Friend she was destined to be a people person and thus she aptly chose a career in social work helping others. Seeing the need and a potential career opportunity, Rebecca Friend began her own intervention consulting firm where she was hired by well-to-do families to implement the intervention process. Typically she charged between $10,000 and $20,000 to meet with the addicted individual's family, coordinate the actual intervention, and then arrange to ship them away to one of those touchy-feely, holistically earthy healing spas, where treatments included mineral baths for detoxification, star gazing, spiritual healing, yoga, meditation, acupuncture, and past lives therapy. Not only did most participants rarely experience relapse, they also had an uncontrollable urge to go out and save a whale. All in all, it was a good thing. Jodi provided Rebecca Friend with Laurel's medical background, family contact information, and recent addiction problems, including stealing cash to buy prescription drugs. Jodi was relieved now that Laurel's problem rested squarely on the shoulders of a professional—plus it was out of her hands.

"Chrissie, I have a feeling Laurel won't be at Archimedes for quite a while. Last night I put my former colleague on the job and she's already preparing the intervention," began Jodi. "You should call Astrid and explain that Crystal probably didn't steal the cash that night of her party. I think it's safe to say it was Laurel. When I talked to Laurel's husband about an intervention, he said there was tons of cash hidden in her sock drawer. I'm sure Astrid would love to patch up her friendship with her old buddy."

Indeed, Crystal and Astrid *were* thrilled to renew their friendship and they immediately put any hard feelings aside. When Chrissie, Charleigh and Ayani were presenting the Kindergarten teachers with their holiday thank you gifts, Astrid and Crystal stood in the back of the classroom and whispered conspiratorially about their travel plans that afternoon to New York City. Tara leaned in closely trying to catch every word. Jodi preferred to stay out of the spotlight and chose to sit on the top of an unoccupied miniature desk and listened with one ear tuned to Chrissie's presentation, the other ear caught snatches of Astrid and Crystal's quiet conversation.

"I don't have anything to wear to go shopping," complained Crystal.

"We can pop over to Neiman's this morning," said Astrid. "There was an adorable Burberry coat you would look so hot in, especially with knee high boots." *They're shopping to go shopping,* Jodi chuckled to herself.

"Do you think it would be too 'Paris Hilton' for me to bring Miss Tiffany with us?" asked Crystal. Crystal was also a huge fan of teacup Chihuahua's. "I just bought an adorable couture black croc dog carrier—it's straight from Italy. I can't wait to use it."

"Bring her. She's cute as a button, plus a conversation starter with men. But I doubt you and I need any assistance in that department."

Astrid turned to include Tara. "Tara, we leave at four o'clock today," whispered Astrid. "I've got everything handled. We'll check in at The Ritz, have a cocktail, then our driver will take us out on the town. Dinner reservations are at one of De Niro's restaurants."

Tara quickly jotted down the travel plans with a crayon onto a scrap of paper she found on the classroom floor. Without warning, from inside Tara's purse that rested under one of the student's tiny desks, blasted the lively tune Waltzing Matilda. Tara leapt from her position in the pack of women, grabbed her purse and phone, and bolted out the classroom door, mumbling apologies to Chrissie along the way. Chrissie's presentation to the teachers was briefly interrupted by Tara's quick escape, then, slightly puzzled as she watched Tara literally sprint from the room, Chrissie continued.

"We appreciate everything you do for our children. We know you always go that extra mile, working late at night grading test papers and reports, shopping on the weekends for Preschool physics teaching tools, stocking a supply of back-up safe foods just in case a child accidentally brings in a banned item. We thank you for your dedication to our children," Chrissie said. Then she hugged each of the Kindergarten teachers and handed them their gift baskets.

Jodi looked up to see that the happy caterpillar had been replaced by a snowman which listed all the forbidden substances that were banned from the classroom.

Chrissie's presentation of the holiday gift baskets to each of the Kindergarten teachers was concluded by a round of applause. Jodi predicted that Chrissie would probably be PTA president in a couple of years, if she could handle all of the political bullshit.

As parents filed out of the classroom into the hallway, they passed a thoroughly preoccupied Tara who spoke to the other party with such sweetness in her voice, all the while, twirling her luscious golden hair around one finger.

"Of course, I'd love to see you again. Let me see what I can do," Tara said into her cell. After erasing the incoming call from her phone (no need to have this trail on record), Tara ran to meet up with Astrid and Crystal who were already approaching the Archimedes parking lot. Standing next to Astrid's brand new white 500 series BMW (an early Christmas present from her husband), the three women convened.

"Girls, something's come up. An old friend of mine is in trouble and I, um, need to see, um, *her*," Tara began. Pausing a moment to group her thoughts, she continued, "My husband Randy hates this woman and would absolutely kill me if I ever visited her. So, I was wondering, can you cover for me? Just say I went with you to New York this weekend. Actually, can you do me a favor and not tell anyone—you never know how stuff might get back to him."

"Shit, Tara, we were counting on you. We really hoped you be into our *threesome*," Astrid said beaming a sexy smile. "But, it sounds like your friend really needs you—she must be a fucking awesome friend for you to give up a private jet and The Ritz."

"Yeah, it's a tough choice, and I really appreciate your offer, but I have this overwhelming urge to be there for, um, her. Please understand—don't count me out for the next time," Tara said, turning quickly on her heels, causing her glossy blonde locks to flip from side to side. Over her shoulder she announced, "I've got to run home and pack for a different climate—*she* lives in South Beach." Tara strolled in the direction of her car, sashaying seductively with renewed confidence in her stride buoyed by her upcoming clandestine rendezvous with Ethan.

———————

That Friday night Chrissie looked fabulous and flirty in the dress she had borrowed from Charleigh. For the first time in months, years, maybe, she felt sex oozing from every orifice of her body. The Vera Wang chocolate satin cocktail dress fit perfectly with the help of the silicon bra inserts she bought at Victoria's Secret. They bounced so naturally and added about two cup sizes to her petite shape. Chrissie balked at wearing Charleigh's diamond earrings, fearing she would lose the two carat jewels the minute she left her house. But, Charleigh insisted.

"I know you won't lose them, and anyway, they're insured," said Charleigh. The Archimedes School teacher holiday party began in one hour and Chrissie was giddy with anticipation. But where was Seth? He promised to be home from work in time to take care of Harrison. Just once in a blue moon did Chrissie ask anything of Seth, knowing that any request would be met with grumbles of protest. Seth always made it seem like the slightest favor she asked was on the same level as climbing Mount Everest in flip flops during a blinding blizzard. Last week Seth had reluctantly agreed to allow Chrissie attend the teacher event without him. It was always such a drag to take him to any social event, he'd always park himself in some overstuffed chair and scowl the entire evening, while Chrissie fluttered here and there, chatting and laughing the night away. Such an odd pair.

Chrissie looked down at her newly acquired cleavage and worried that Seth would give her shit about showing too much skin. Then she remembered he hadn't noticed or commented last year when she changed her hair color from brown to red, he never said anything last summer when her ankle was wrapped in bandages from a bad sprain. He never noticed when Chrissie converted from wearing practical cotton underwear to sexy thongs about two years ago. What the hell, he wouldn't say a thing about a little bit of cleavage either!

By eight o'clock Chrissie was simmering with fury. Still no Seth and he didn't answer his cell. Finally, the halogen lights from his SUV flashed in the living room window, indicating his arrival. Chrissie had already done all the hard work with Harrison; she'd fed him, bathed him, dressed him for bed and read him a story. Did Seth thank her for her troubles? *No.* Instead he was pissed, "He's in bed already, damn, I wanted to play with him. I'll just go wake him up."

As Chrissie drove away in her black teacher-like Volvo, she worried that the event would be long over by the time she arrived. She couldn't imagine that the physics, math and science teachers could possibly be up past ten o'clock. *Au contraire.* Nearing the party Chrissie saw that cars were still parked around the block, music blared from the headmaster's waterfront house where the party was being held (at least they paid *him* well, thought Chrissie), teachers and their mates spilled into the streets drinking from crystal wine glasses, a bonfire roared brightly in the manicured back yard where a small crowd clustered for warmth. Snowflakes fluttered from the night sky, creating an occasional sizzle and pop as they landed on the fire. As Chrissie walked toward the front door, she shuttered slightly from a combination of the cold and the anticipation of seeing her English teacher friend again. Chrissie's arrival did not go unnoticed; Nathaniel had been waiting and watching from the vicinity of the bonfire. Silently he stepped onto the front porch and slipped an arm around her shoulders.

"So good to see you, Chrissie," he said warmly. "I was hoping you'd be here."

Chrissie shuttered again, this time it wasn't from the cold. Helping her remove her coat, Nathaniel let out a low whistle, "Man, you look phenomenal. Let's get a drink and walk slowly around this party so I can show you off to the faculty." Then, quietly he said for her ears only, "If only we could sneak away for just one moment." Chrissie was suddenly overwhelmed with a thousand thoughts and emotions coursing through her mind. *How can I feel this way for someone? I can't ruin my family. It's got to stop. I don't want it to stop. Is there anything wrong with being with him just once? Nobody will know. No, I can't, it isn't right.* Confused, conflicted, and tormented, Chrissie wished Ayani was with her, she needed a distraction from this gorgeous, kind, sincere man who was leading her by the hand toward the bar. Male teachers and husbands of female teachers nodded in her direction and smiled appreciatively as she walked by. *This must be what Charleigh feels like everyday,* Chrissie thought to herself. Deep inside her something stirred, she felt a renewed sense of self, her sexuality was revitalized, she felt alive and seductive and *she liked it.*

While Chrissie was a constant presence in the preschool and well known by the staff in that building, many of the middle and upper school teachers did not realize she was an Archimedes School parent and assumed she was simply Nathaniel's date for the evening. Chrissie was soon to be enlightened about the true feelings the Archimedes School faculty had for many of the overly entitled parents. Nathaniel tried to silence them, but Chrissie whispered in his ear, "It's important for me to know this stuff, don't tell them I'm a parent."

"Did you see Hunter Garvey's mother hiding in the bushes during middle school recess?" began the discussion about the Archimedes School parents. "She claims her son's being bullied by Max Sondwell. She wrote a formal complaint to the board of directors saying that none of the teachers are taking care of her kid. She complained he's ruined thousands of dollars worth of clothes because of being accosted on the playground," said one of the middle school social studies teachers.

"Max Sondwell, you mean the sweet, geeky kid who wears his pants pulled up above his waist?" asked another teacher. "He wouldn't hurt a fly—he's probably gay. Actually, *Hunter* is the bully on the playground. All those rips and stains on his clothes are his fault. Hunter's mother is a wacko. Last year she was discovered hiding in a storage closet in the science room because her son said the teacher was always picking on him."

Chrissie listened attentively realizing "wacko" parents weren't limited to just the preschool.

"Did you hear about that kid who came to school with a 103 degree fever last week? He told the school nurse that his mom had an important court case and couldn't stay home with him and that his nanny had been deported," added one of the assistants from the main office.

"How about that dad that knocked up his Brazilian nanny?" interjected another middle school teacher. "She was quite a looker. I used to watch her lying out in the sun at the Archimedes 'beach.' I'd do her in a minute. I heard he paid her tons of hush money and shipped her back to her homeland." This was news to Chrissie, but now that she thought about it, she hadn't seen Jonathan's ever-blossoming nanny since the Thanksgiving play. Well, if the middle school staff knew about it, the hush money hadn't worked very well.

"Oh my gosh! Did you know some of these parents are into swinging? I heard that the Kindergarten potluck ending with some wife swapping." Chrissie gulped hard. *What else did they know?* Nathaniel squeezed her arm gently.

"Yeah, and what about that new southern mom who was showing off her party tricks?" added another male teacher. "I heard she could put her entire fist right inside her mouth."

"Oh baby, what I could do with that," said a physics teacher, spiffy in his holiday tartan red and green plaid pants.

"This is too freaky, Nathaniel. I can't get over the male math teachers with their pocket protectors having sexual thoughts about the moms," Chrissie discretely whispered to Nathaniel behind her upheld hand.

"They're still breathing and they've got a penis, don't they?" responded Nathaniel with a dimpled grin.

The parent bashing continued for several more minutes, deepening Chrissie's understanding of the rift between the have's and the have not's, in this case, the teachers representing the have not's. When Matt Worthington and Berri Franconi joined in the conversation, Chrissie learned more about their financial gripes.

"There's word that a lot of parents want to eliminate tuition remission and they're putting pressure on the administration," said Berri. Teachers who worked at the

Archimedes School did not have to pay the outrageous tuition fees for one of their enrolled children. It was a common practice at many private schools. "If they take that away, they'll need to raise our salaries significantly or else they'll lose lots of great faculty members," she added.

"These parents don't have a clue how hard it is to live in this expensive touristy waterfront town, make ends meet, and be subjected to their snooty affluence day after day," said Matt. "I had one idiot ask me whether I was headed to the ski resorts or the Caribbean for the Christmas break," he added.

"What did you say?" asked another teacher.

"I told him the truth…that I would be spending time at K-Mart shopping for holiday gifts, I might go to the discounted matinee movies a couple of times, and he could find me at Denny's restaurant on Tuesdays when kids eat free," said Matt. The gathered teachers roared in laughter.

"Well, not all of *us* are clueless," said Chrissie, realizing she had probably just blown her cover. Fortunately, no one appeared to notice because at that moment Mr.Greenspring, the owner of the home and the head of school dimmed the lights and told the disc jockey to crank up the dance tunes. Men sporting pocket protectors and bow ties grabbed the closest female and pulled them into the library which now doubled as the disco headquarters. Chrissie watched in awe and amusement as the teachers danced an awkward version of *The Electric Slide*, tripping over each other's shoelaces, sliding right when the person next to them moved left, catching the buttons of their shirts in their partner's long flowing grey hair. In his exuberance, one teacher's wire rimmed bifocals flew across the room and landed at Chrissie's feet. Chrissie carefully retrieved them before they were crushed by a dancer. This was the best party she had been to in years, especially now that Nathaniel's hand was placed gently on the small of her back.

Chrissie observed Matt inconspicuously take Berri's hand and lead her up the stairs to the second floor away from the commotion. Nathaniel pointed in their direction, indicating that he and Chrissie should do the same. Quivering with expectation, steaming with desire, it took everything in Chrissie's being to shake her head "no." She mouthed the words, "I can't." Crestfallen, Nathaniel led Chrissie to the front porch, the only quiet place in the house, away from the music and away from earshot of his colleagues.

Taking a deep breath Chrissie began, "I can't do this Nathaniel. I'm married." Then, searching for words, "I'm so confused. I haven't felt like this...ever."

"I understand. I don't want to pressure you. What should I do? Do you want me to go away?" he asked.

"Yes...*no*...I don't know!" she replied, clearly distressed. "Let me think about it. Nathaniel, I need some time to be alone and just...think. Maybe during the Christmas break I can get my head together." Chrissie took his hand in hers and looked him directly in the eye. "Thank you for making me feel this way. I'm flattered...you're amazing, smart, sexy, and probably my long lost soul mate...it's just that our timing..."

Her words were suddenly cut off when a dilapidated Honda screeched to a halt directly in front of Mr. Greenspring's home. A man and a woman bounded from the car, ran up the front stairs and shoved the door open. Quickly scanning the dance floor, not finding what or who they were searching for, the two harried adults climbed the stairs to the second story. Chrissie and Nathaniel stood in shock as they heard the sound of a bedroom door slamming against a wall. Shouts, screaming, and crying were heard next as Matt and

Berri's spouses discovered and then interrupted the adultery in progress.

"What the fu...," said the surprised Matt.

"I knew it! You filthy slut," said Matt's wife to Berri. "How long have you been screwing my husband?"

"Get the hell off my wife!" yelled Berri's husband to Matt. A loud thump was heard on the floor above. By now the rest of the partygoers had gotten wind of the drama in the bedroom and were clustered at the bottom of the staircase anticipating the next scene. Berri ran from the room with a sheet draped around her body. Matt didn't bother with the formalities of decency and tore from the room and ran down the stairs with both hands covering his privates. Chrissie was impressed that it took *two* hands to shield his parts.

"I'm calling my lawyer," said Matt's wife as she followed on his heels behind him. "I'm getting the house and the kids, you really fucked up this time!"

Berri's husband rudely pushed Chrissie aside as he scrambled to follow his wife out the front door. Nathaniel was positioned to save Chrissie from falling backward into the crowd of teachers.

After their loud and hurried departure, the silence was deafening. The disc jockey tried unsuccessfully to encourage people to return to the dance floor. Somehow the song *Voulez vous couchez avec moi, se soir* didn't seem appropriate considering what had just occurred. Chrissie shrugged and sadly looked at Nathaniel, wordlessly communicating the thought, *"see what could happen to us?"*

Nathaniel nodded in complete understanding, handed Chrissie her coat, and they silently departed down the porch stairs together. Standing by her car, Nathaniel took Chrissie's hand in his. He leaned in to kiss her. At the very last second, mustering all of her will, Chrissie turned her head so that his kiss landed softly on her cheek.

"Merry Christmas, Chrissie. I'll see you when the school break is over." He turned and walked away.

Chrissie sat alone in her car for a long, long time, unable to drive home, emotionally drained, and shivering head to toe from the bitter cold. "What the hell have I gotten myself into?" Chrissie said out loud to herself as she turned the key in the ignition and pointed her car in the direction of home.

———

Two days later the Annapolis area experienced the first significant snowfall of the year. On Sunday night when Tara returned to Maryland's sub-freezing temperatures she faced six inches of fresh fluffy snow on the ground. Tara's re-entry into reality was a shock to her system in many ways. Her departure from Miami International Airport was delayed by several hours while Baltimore's ground crew hurried to clear the first snowfall from the runways. Tara's private driver took nearly two hours to navigate the unplowed roads and bypass the abandoned cars that plagued them on the seventeen mile route from BWI airport to Annapolis. Finally, at midnight the wheels of the Lincoln Town car spun slightly as the driver pulled carefully into Tara's driveway. Tara's summer sandals were no match for the elements and her bare feet were immediately covered by the frozen stuff as she quickly tiptoed, half running, half hopping to her front portico. Her husband Randy was fast asleep on the sofa near the warmth of the gas fire with Clinton asleep in his arms. Reflecting on her weekend of passion, Tara felt pangs of guilt rising in her gut as she looked upon this scene of domestic bliss.

There in front of her was a crackling fire, the Christmas tree twinkling with tiny lights, her husband and child calmly sleeping, gifts wrapped and bowed tucked under the tree, a cup of hot cocoa on the coffee table. It was sweet and lovely.

Abruptly, the storybook image of holiday happiness was thrown into complete disarray. Glancing at her reflection in the hall mirror Tara panicked; she didn't look this tan when she was lying on the beach blending in with all the other bronzed topless bodies. How on earth would she explain these mid-winter New York City shopping spree *tan lines* to Randy, or anyone else for that matter? After all, she was supposed to be on a mid-winter jaunt to a frosty climate. Frantically rummaging through her stash of creams, lotions and gels, she stumbled upon an old tube of self tanning cream. *If I smear this on and streak it everywhere, maybe I can look like I did a bad job of fake and bake*, she thought. When she disrobed to begin the process, she nearly screamed in horror at the image before her. Hickeys! Her breasts, stomach, and butt were covered with tiny red suction marks. Oh my God! That's what Ethan was doing! She was so overcome by the passion and ecstasy of the moment she didn't think to stop him. Then a flash of inspiration came to her. *I've got it! Hives! I got a bad case of hives from the self tanning cream.* Quickly prepping the scene to cover her adulteress crime, Tara put tubes of Neosporin, Calamine lotion, and a bottle of anti-histamines next to the fake and bake cream. Lathering each hickey with gobs of calamine lotion she looked like she had been attacked by a giant deep sea squid. Quietly she slipped beneath the Egyptian cotton sheets on their king sized bed, hoping they wouldn't be stained pink by morning. Her last thoughts before she dozed off to sweet dreams of New Zealand sheep leaping across grassy fields, were, *note to self: don't be so stupid next time, no more tan lines or hickeys on wild sex weekends.*

Life Observations from Vic the Maintenance Guy:
"Life is so much simpler being a worker bee. Hell, if the world only had queen bees, we wouldn't have any honey."

Chapter Nine:
Back to Reality...*Again*

It was a harsh return to reality after a simply magnificent two week December break from the Archimedes School. When they arrived at BWI airport Charleigh was steaming mad. It was rare for her to get this upset over anything. But when the airline forced her to check her Louis Vuitton carry on case because the flight was overbooked and space was limited in the cabin—*even in first class*, she knew in her gut she'd never see it again. Now her luggage, lingerie, and brand new Tiffany necklace, a gift from Bud for Christmas, were somewhere between the island of St. John, Atlanta and Baltimore. After ten minutes on hold with her home owner's insurance company, she was finally put through to an agent.

"No, sir, we didn't have a rider for the necklace. Bud just bought it for me for Christmas," said Charleigh into the phone.

"Sorry, Mrs. Brooks, we can cover the cost of replacing a typical piece of carry on luggage which is between $150 and $250 dollars and we can offer up to $300 for the contents, but that's about it," said the worker bee insurance agent. "Of course, you should also check with the airline for their lost and damaged policy," he added.

"I already did, and they're saying the same thing. But, sir, here's the situation," Charleigh began to explain with all the calm she could muster, "The necklace was worth at least $15,000. The suitcase alone cost $1,800. That's nearly $17,000 and you're only going to give me $500 lousy bucks for my loss!"

"Sorry, ma'm, without that rider on the necklace, that's all we can do for you," the agent concluded.

Frustrated by the answers from the bureaucrats working at both the airline and the insurance company, Charleigh finally lost her temper and slammed down the phone in disgust. This incident put an awful ending on what was probably the most wonderful Caribbean vacation she, Bud and the children had ever experienced. The five bedroom villa they rented over Christmas break was magnificent, perched on a bluff overlooking the crystal clear azure waters of Peter Bay on the island of St. John. Each morning they walked barefoot through the lush gardens and plucked fresh fruit from any of the dozen or so banana, papaya or citrus trees that dotted the property. The main villa was an architectural masterpiece of polished coral stone floors, carved pillars and dramatic archways which led directly from the spacious and airy great room to stone tile terrace outside, making the blend between outside and inside the villa almost indiscernible. On the lower level of the home, the infinity edge heated pool and ten person Jacuzzi served as the main entertainment area for Charleigh and her family. Their vacation day routine began poolside where they frolicked for hours, splashing in the freshwater, then Charleigh and her family migrated down the winding, tree covered path to the pristine white sand beaches, where they spent their midday collecting conch and cowrie shells, only to return to the villa in the late afternoon to enjoy the Jacuzzi that had been readied by the staff. There were warm, fluffy towels placed on the stone edge, and sitting on a serving tray nearby were frosty margaritas for the adults and fresh squeezed lemonade for the kids.

The villa came complete with two very attentive maids and a personal chef who at the snap of two fingers prepared every appetizer, meal, cocktail, sippy cup and chicken nugget her family desired. Normally children under the age of seven weren't allowed in this particular villa, but Charleigh agreed to sign a notarized liability waiver permitting her five year old twins Wilson and Honey and her two year old son Harding to stay there over the ten day break. Charleigh also agreed that a responsible nanny must be in charge of the children at all times, thus Miss Elke was invited to join them on their holiday.

Knowing Bud's middle class upbringing would cause him to balk at the cost, Charleigh took great pains to prevent him from having any direct contact with the rental agent or home owner prior to their trip. Unfortunately, when he stumbled upon a copy of the rental agreement the week before their travel date, Charleigh had to do something she rarely did—she lied. "No, dear, that's not $2,143 dollars per day, it must be a typo, it's $2,143 *per week*," she said to Bud.

Charleigh had been home for less than an hour when her phone rang. Hoping it was the insurance agent now offering huge gobs of cash for her lost luggage and jewelry, *"My mistake, Mrs. Brooks, we'll be sending you a check in the mail today,"* was what Charleigh hoped to hear. She rushed to answer the phone. Seeing caller ID indicate that instead of the insurance company, it was Chrissie was on the line, Charleigh took a deep breath. She missed her dear friend and wanted to talk to her, but she had to tone down any exuberance in her voice and limit the extravagances of the vacation, knowing Chrissie had just spent her entire holiday break at home, here in frozen Annapolis, probably doing mundane chores and errands and being infinitely creative entertaining her son with crafts, puppet shows, and short, educational daytrips to the free local museums. Chrissie was the only one amongst the familiar bunch—and frankly among most of the parents at the Archimedes School who didn't travel during the holiday season—if it required a flight and a hotel stay, Chrissie had to say no. It just wasn't in her budget. Since all of Chrissie's friends and their children were away, play dates for her son Harrison were out of the question; Chrissie was on her own to invent two weeks worth of activities in order to prevent the inevitable, "Mommy, I'm so bored," whine from her son. Ayani and her family always enjoyed a week of skiing in Vail, where Ayani's mother had a ski in, ski out slope side home. Jodi, Rip and their girls vacationed this year at his parent's sprawling beach front home in the Florida Keys, and Tara, Randy and their son Clinton popped down to the exclusive Atlantis resort in the Bahamas. Ayani, Jodi and Charleigh had each at one point in time invited Chrissie and Harrison on their family trips—secretly hoping that Seth was too busy at work to join them. But each and every time, Chrissie had declined, saying she would never impose on her friends and that she had family obligations at home.

"Charleigh, it's so good to hear your voice. Welcome home. Did you have a great time?" asked Chrissie, happy to reconnect after such a long absence.

"Yes, it was wonderful, the weather was great, the kids behaved and didn't break anything in the villa—*thank God*, and Bud treated me like a princess. He wouldn't let me lift a finger the entire trip, plus we were waited on hand and foot by our servants."

"Servants? I bet you just lounged by the pool and the margaritas kept coming your way!" replied Chrissie. "That's *so* awesome," she added.

"Yes, and not to mention our personal chef was some young Italian guy with a great ass. But don't tell Bud I said that. He thinks I never look at other men. How was your Christmas?" asked Charleigh.

"I had a wonderful time with my family. We had about thirty people over at my parent's house for a huge family gathering. And, I got to see my niece's new baby, who's adorable…but…um, Christmas Day was…interesting…I think it was a turning point for my marriage," Chrissie hesitantly began.

"That's wonderful! What did Seth do?"

"Well actually, it wasn't wonderful…and I don't really want to be a downer now, since you just got home and had a great vacation and all," responded Chrissie. "We can talk about it another time."

Sensing her friend's need to talk, despite Chrissie's initial reluctance, Charleigh gently pushed further.

"Sweetheart, I don't care if I just vacationed at a nudist resort and got to play with someone famous like Brad Pitt naked—I'd still want to talk. I'm your friend and I'm here for you," said Charleigh.

"Okay, I'll be brief, though," Chrissie began, not really wanting to reveal her misery, even to one of her best friends. "I'm actually so emotionally drained it's hard to relive," she paused, gathering her courage to continue and groping for words. "On Christmas morning Harrison had just finished opening his Santa presents, I had prepared this great Christmas breakfast—it was keeping warm in the oven for when we were done, Seth had opened each of the presents I had carefully picked out for him, and then I just sat there, waiting. Nothing happened. Seth didn't give me any presents—I noticed that nothing was under the tree for me, but all week long I thought something, *anything*, must be hidden in the house."

Charleigh was confused, "I don't understand, what do you mean? He didn't give you a gift?"

"Nope. Nothing. I kept waiting for him to give me a present and at this point, I would have been happy with a trinket from the Dollar Store…stupid reindeer socks or one of those emergency plastic ponchos, even. But, then he looked at me and said with this evil grimace, *"I didn't get you anything this year."*

Charleigh's breath caught in her throat and she sat there stunned, staring at the phone in her hand. How could anyone be this cruel to our little Chrissie? Chrissie was the kindest, most giving person, a great mom, a super volunteer, her house was always clean as a whistle, every meal was always ready on time, she anticipated Harrison's every need. How could anyone do this to her?

"I tried to hide my tears from Harrison—I didn't want to spoil *his* Christmas, too. I was completely numb. Not just from Seth's vindictive action, but from my mind spinning with thoughts of stuff like; Where will I live when I leave him? Will I have to go back to work? Will Harrison have to be in after-care at Archimedes? How will I possibly afford that school now? Charleigh, I think I'm done with Seth. The marriage is over. I just need to wait for the right time to move on."

"Have you considered marriage counseling?" asked Charleigh. "I know that's not what you want to hear right now, but you should look into it."

"We did some counseling right after we got married when I was already worried about some of his negative personality traits that were interfering in our relationship. It wasn't until that first year of marriage when he became so controlling and, well, just *mean*. Something happened when he said "I do" that seemed to give him permission to act like primal man—you know, *"I'm man, you're woman, do what I say, and do it now."* I guess we could try again....but not until I recover a little and cool down some. I'm angry, scared, hurt, confused—how could Seth treat me like this? *Why* would he treat me like this?"

"Chrissie, you're right, it's some sort of control thing—*again*. He's got so much anger stewing in him and it comes out sideways at you. This is not about you...it's about his problem with anger management. You two need some counseling. Give it one more shot, then you'll know if the marriage truly is over."

"Thanks for listening, Charleigh. I'm done talking about it. Really. Don't tell the others, at least not yet. I don't want to be the friend everyone tries to avoid because she's got another sob story to tell!" said Chrissie with a tiny giggle. "We have this one relative like that in my family, he's a total hypochondriac. On Christmas Day he had me cornered on my mom's sofa talking about his *hemorrhoid operation*. Then he whipped out the before and after photos the doctor had taken! Normally I do a good job avoiding him; it helps not to have eye contact and to never, ever ask the question "how are you?" But I made one fatal mistake—I gave him a Merry Christmas hug—then he said, *careful, the sutures are still fresh*, I was captured from that moment on." *There she goes again*, thought Charleigh as Chrissie relayed her story, *trying to cover her pain with a laugh.*

"Let's get together tomorrow morning for coffee. In fact, let's get all the girls together tomorrow. I think everyone will be home from their travels by this afternoon. Better yet, we could do Sunday brunch at the Mariner House," said Charleigh.

"That would be great. Since I don't have any unpacking to do, I'll make the phone calls to Jodi, Ayani and Tara and make reservations for 11:00 am," said Chrissie. "Charleigh, see you tomorrow, and thanks again for being there. Love ya."

Charleigh set the phone in the receiver and took a mental inventory of all the blessings in her life, she had a wonderful caring husband, three beautiful children, a home that could easily be featured in Southern Living magazine, and enough money in the bank to retire on right now...and still live the lifestyle of the Annapolis rich and famous...not exactly on mega rich standards, but comfortably enough. Life's inequities weren't fair at all. Chrissie was too good of a person to suffer like this. Charleigh's thoughts wandered to "why do bad things happen to good people?" Chrissie deserved only the best and yet she was stuck with this creepo, control freak, evil spouse who didn't appreciate that she always waiting for him each night with homemade meals (not cold delivery pizza or limp wontons), their house was spotless, their child was bright, happy and well cared for, and all of Seth's errands were done by her during the day according to his precise list and in the proper order. Charleigh figured the thought never crossed his mind to say, "Chrissie, you do too much for me!"

The next morning proved to be a classic crisp, cold and clear January day, with the brilliant blue sky reflected on the icy water that lay just beyond the expansive windows of the Annapolis Mariner House. Inside the restaurant it was warm and inviting. The lounge was filled with people drinking their Mimosas or Bloody Mary's as they sat comfortably in the overstuffed chairs positioned next to the crackling fires burning in the two huge stone fireplaces at either end of the restaurant. When Charleigh entered the lounge to meet up with her four women friends, she was greeted kindly by people she vaguely knew just from doing her errands and business about town—Annapolis is a small, friendly city, where everyone you meet is somehow connected to someone else you know. It was a good practice never to say anything bad about anyone in this town!. At a cocktail party Charleigh once made the mistake of telling a casual acquaintance "that idiot actually tried to feel my breasts when the sail boat keeled into the wind." Charleigh's comment was met with the terse response, "that *idiot* was my brother-in-law." In this town, it's best to remember that tried and true rule; if you can't say something nice about someone, don't say anything at all.

Tara, who was standing near one of the fireplaces, was holding court with three extremely attractive men who stared at her attentively and were either enthralled by the deep intellectual conversation they were having or the deep cleavage between her breasts. It was hard to tell. Nearby Chrissie, Ayani and Jodi sat closely together, knees to knees, heads nearly touching, whispering conspiratorially as they discreetly pointed to a few of the restaurant patrons, then laughed in unison—the fashion faux pas game again. One of the targeted women definitely deserved to be on the back pages of Glamour Magazine with the black strip covering her face to mask her identity. She was a middle aged woman, perhaps in her early sixties, dressed as a bad imitation of Joni

Mitchell from her hippie heyday. She had long, untamed, frizzy grey hair, huge wire rimmed sunglasses with pink lenses, and a tie-dyed peasant dress that fell to her ankles, almost covering her purple leggings and black buckle earth shoes.

"Ouch," Chrissie said, "hope that doesn't happen to us one day. Girls, please do me a huge favor, if I ever look like that when I leave the house, please call the fashion police and have them haul me away!" Their laughter was interrupted by the waiter who came to announce that their table was ready. Walking to their table, this impressive group of five lovely women turned heads from everyone in the restaurant. Men stopped chewing their muffins to blatantly gawk, women scowled in their direction, probably wondering how much "work" these unnatural beauties had invested in.

Once their brunch order was taken, Tara promptly announced, "The only bad part about going away on vacation is facing that massive stack of mail and bills when you return. I still haven't opened everything."

"Wilson and Honey are so excited about Truman's pirate themed birthday party next week. Wasn't that invitation amazing?" said Charleigh.

"What invitation? We didn't get one." asked Ayani, "Isn't Truman that Kindergartner who won the best animal costume at the Halloween party?"

"The one and the same," said Tara. "Truman and Carver are in the same class."

"Oh, Carver's invitation probably hasn't arrived yet. I wouldn't worry. It came in a cardboard box decorated to look like a pirate's chest. It was filled with sand, fake gold coins, and included a treasure map for the actual invitation," said Charleigh. As Charleigh was talking, Chrissie looked slightly concerned. Since she was in town over break, she knew the invitation had arrived nearly ten days ago. Was Ayani's son being snubbed? It was a very, uncool political move if that was the case. It was a cardinal rule at the Archimedes School—at least in the preschool—that *every* child in the classroom was required to be invited to any birthday party, regardless of friendship ties.

Chrissie looked around the room and seized the opportunity to quickly change the topic, "Look who's here, it's good old Deborah Brown with her husband. Oh, and apparently she brought her new dog along. Check out that pet purse," said Chrissie. On the floor at her feet was a tan leather Versace purse with a little black nose poking from a gap left unzipped. Not surprisingly, Deborah's waiter began to sniffle and sneeze, apologetically and unknowingly blaming the sudden onslaught of his "cold" on a previous customer.

Annapolis was a small town, where recognizable faces popped up everywhere. Seated at a table not far from Deborah and her husband (and dog) were the omnipresent botox blondes who stared at their cheese omelettes with that familiar frozen look of astonishment plastered on their faces. Looking at these artificially preserved women, Charleigh hoped someday, she too wouldn't yield to temptation and intervene with the natural aging process (although most of the women in the restaurant already thought that Charleigh was the poster child for one of Annapolis' leading plastic surgeons).

After they completed their meal and had gathered their coats to leave, Chrissie tapped Charleigh on the shoulder.

"*Psssst*," she whispered in Charleigh's ear. "I need to tell you something very important. In private." Charleigh feared Chrissie had more bad news to share about her marriage.

After the five women said their goodbyes and gave each other air kisses while lingering within the warmth of the restaurant's foyer, Chrissie then followed Charleigh to her car.

"I think Ayani's son is being dissed." Chrissie began. "Those party invitations were mailed nearly two weeks ago—Ayani would have received it by now."

"Do you think Truman's mom only invited a few kids?" asked Charleigh.

"Doubtful. She loves to flaunt her wealth to everyone she knows. I fully expect this birthday party to be *the primo kid event* of the year. But, I'll check around tomorrow at school. I'll ask a few random moms what they think Truman would like for a gift, that'll give me a good idea if Carver's not on the A-list."

"Hard to believe we have to go back to Archimedes tomorrow. I hate the harsh re-entry to reality," said Charleigh.

"Actually, it's good for me. I'd rather leave my reality at home," Chrissie concluded.

The next morning at the Archimedes School, a steady stream of tanned, shivering children ran from the warmth of their European sedans through a blast of freezing outside air and headed toward the Kindergarten classrooms. Their metabolic systems were still in shock after leaving 85 degree sunny temperatures less than twenty-four hours ago and returning to this frozen wasteland at latitude 38.9N above the equator. Most of the girls sported hair meticulously braided for a fee by island women who wove the soft and silky little girl locks into corn rows with plastic colorful beads attached—this was probably the only source of income these island women had during the busy Christmas tourist season. The braids on these girls jingled slightly as they scurried to their classrooms. Outside the preschool building a clutch of women who were bundled against the cold chatted conspiratorially. Agape's mom Sheryl Waters was amongst the group, as was Truth's mom, Michelle Baker. Occasionally a word or two of their conversation could be heard above the noise of the whistling January wind.

"…out of control…"

"…bad influence…"

"…needs meds…"

"…she's having nightmares…"

"…diversity requirement…"

When Chrissie and her son Harrison briskly walked past (Chrissie and her friends refused to do the drop and run like so many of the other parents), she caught bits and pieces of their dialogue. *I wonder what's up?* She thought to herself. Then, as Ayani and her son Carver approached the gathering of women, one of the schemers turned, saw the mother and child draw near, and sounded the alarm, "*SHHHHHHHHH!*"

Their eyes shot daggers at Ayani and her child, following them along every step of the way. Once Carver and his mother were safely behind the closed Kindergarten door, the women resumed their tete-a-tete, speaking with greater intensity and heated anger this time. Nodding their heads in agreement to something that was said, they marched determinedly as a unified force directly to Mrs. Marsh's office, the division head of the preschool.

Inside the classroom, Mrs. Casper greeted Carver with a big, warm and genuine hug.

"Welcome back, little man, I missed you," she said.

"Hi, Mrs. Casper, I missed you, too!" Carver replied with his infectious wide grin. Looking around the room at all the bronzed children, Ayani noted that for the first time Carver blended in with his classmates. Normally his light chocolate brown body, the product of merging Native American with African American heritage, stood out like a sore thumb amongst this group of lily white children.

"Mrs. Casper, Carver's still extremely tired from our long flight home on Saturday. I'm worried he might not make it through the day," said Ayani.

"No problem, dear. I'll call you if he starts to fall asleep at his desk," responded Mrs. Casper.

Chrissie was waiting outside the classroom for her friend Ayani.

"Let's head to the coffee shop. It's too cold to walk. I already called Charleigh and Jodi and they'll meet us there. Tara's on her way, too."

"Did you notice those moms standing by the door?" asked Ayani. "I felt a very bad vibe coming from them. Maybe it's just my psychic paranoia, but I felt like they were talking about me."

"Who knows? I wouldn't worry. Those women always have way too much time on their hands and spend their days slamming others with their gossip. Damn it, Ayani, if we had a personal assistant, personal trainer, personal shopper, personal housekeeper, and personal butt wiper, we'd have nothing better to do than stand around gossiping, too."

"You're right Chrissie, but my gut says they're up to no good."

Just as Ayani and Chrissie sat down in the restaurant's vinyl covered booth with coffee mugs in hand, Ayani's cell phone rang. It had been less than ten minutes since Ayani had passed the gossiping gaggle of women. On the phone was Mrs. Casper, the Kindergarten teacher.

"Has he fallen asleep already?" Ayani asked, surprised.

"No, something else has come up and Mrs. Marsh and I need to see you in her office *immediately*," Mrs. Casper emphasized.

"Girls, I gotta go," said Ayani, reaching for her wallet to pay the tip. "I knew something was up. They want me in the head of preschool's office ASAP."

"Should one of us go with you?" asked Charleigh.

"Thanks, but no thanks. I worried it's about Carver's score on that damn calculus test. Next time I'm hiring a tutor, as jappy as that sounds."

As Ayani hurriedly left the coffee shop, Chrissie whispered to Charleigh, "I'm afraid this is much bigger than Carver's test scores." Ultimately, Chrissie's intuition was correct. The problem was much, much bigger.

It was over the Christmas break when the trouble began to brew. Innocently enough one phone call from one mom to another mom started it all. By the end of the winter break, that little snowball of trouble had grown to become a huge, unstoppable avalanche rolling out of control.

"Truth has been having nightmares about some dark, scary person at school," said Michelle Baker who called Sheryl Waters at her vacation home in Palm Springs, California. Michelle and her family were vacationing about two hours away in a $1,000 dollar a night premier ocean front suite at the Hotel Del Coronado in San Diego.

"That's funny. Just last week, Agape said there was an evil person in her Kindergarten class. He threw a chair at her, then spit on some other child," replied Sheryl.

"On the airplane ride here, Truth colored a picture of a black kid, then added a bomb dropping on his head," said

Michelle. "That's when she started screaming at the top of her lungs—loud enough for people in the last row of the plane to hear, "bad, bad black boy...bad, bad black boy." Michelle added, "I had to slip her a tiny piece of one of my valiums to get her to stop."

That same day, Agape's mom then called Patience's mom who called Truman's mom just as she was about to put the pirate themed birthday party invitations in the mail. By now, the alleged Kindergarten culprit had been identified. Ayani's son Carver, the only person of color in that class, was then blacklisted by this powerful clique of some of the wealthiest, most entitled moms at the Archimedes School. Sadly, at any private school, the voice of money speaks loudly and with a very big stick. Carver's longevity at the Archimedes School was in serious jeopardy.

Upon receiving Mrs. Casper's phone call, Ayani had returned to the school grounds in record time and sat obediently on one of the expensive leather chairs in the head of preschool's office. Mrs. Marsh sat behind her imposing oak desk and looked sternly over her bifocals at Ayani. As Ayani entered the office and took a chair, Mrs. Casper carefully avoided eye contact by intentionally looking down at her own skirt while picking at some non-existent lint. Ayani sat and quietly composed herself using all of her yoga techniques—deep breathing, relaxing thoughts, repetitive mantras, and imaging of still, calm waters. Ayani waited patiently for Mrs. Marsh to pull out Carver's test scores, but was blindsided by what happened next.

"Ayani, it has been brought to our attention that several children in Mrs. Casper's class have complained about your son, Carver. They say he has bullied them, spit on them, choked them, and threatened them. One parent claimed he said "I'll scalp you if you don't give me that crayon!"

Several of these children are now having nightmares and stomach aches, fearing to return to school," announced Mrs. Marsh.

Stunned to the core, Ayani could barely squeak out a response. "But...but...no one has said anything to me about a problem." Ayani turned to Carver's teacher and said, "Mrs. Casper, your most recent progress report indicated that Carver was a dream child."

"Indeed, Carver does *not* have disciplinary issues," responded Mrs. Casper, carefully saying her words. "He is a model child in my classroom. The faculty and administration share your confusion and we plan to get to the bottom of this." After years of teaching at Archimedes, Mrs. Casper knew she had to walk the fine line of appeasing both groups; the mob of angry parents and this women before her who was a huge financial donor to the school *along* with being an alum of Archimedes.

"We'd like to dispel some of the parent hostilities before they augment into a feeding frenzy. We were hoping you could take a few weeks to home school Carver until we have the situation under control," said Mrs. Marsh.

"What? Home school?" asked an astonished Ayani.

"Yes, these women are on a warpath—oh, sorry, Ayani, bad choice of words," said Mrs. Marsh. She continued, "We think it is the only way to calm these evil bitc..., oops, I mean—*women*—down." At least Mrs. Marsh's slip had revealed the faculty's' true opinions of the situation.

"We'll send you all the curriculum materials and we'll provide a tutor free of charge," added Mrs. Casper. "Ayani, I'm so sorry about this. You know how much I love your son."

"I…just…don't understand…he's a good little boy, why are they picking on my child?" stammered Ayani, the tears now welling in her eyes.

"We promise to investigate this situation fully and expect a complete resolution in the next few weeks," said Mrs. Marsh, using politically correct administrative speak. "If you wouldn't mind gathering your son's things, you may begin home schooling today."

Wordlessly, Ayani left the office and brushed tears from her checks. Mrs. Casper escorted Ayani to the classroom where she scooped up her confused child.

"Mom, why are we leaving? I want to stay and play," Carver complained. Ayani and her son then headed to her car, arms loaded down with a month's worth of school supplies, work books and text books.

"This is an outrage," Charleigh shouted to Ayani over her cell phone as she drove her car down a dip in the Route 50 highway where cell coverage was spotty. "Carver can't be railroaded out of Archimedes because of some overly entitled rich and bitchy snobs who think they can control the school with their check book!"

"Ayani, you donated more money last year than most of those women combined," Charleigh added. "I don't care if Truman's mom is an alumni of Archimedes, she shouldn't have this much power. After all Ayani, you're an alum, too!"

"Charleigh, there's more. Michelle Baker's lawyer contacted Derrick's law firm and they're threatening to sue us for damages, claiming her daughter Truth has suffered psychological pain from being assaulted by a black child. Michelle said Truth continues to scream out the car window "bad, bad black boy," whenever they pass the liquor store on their route to school."

"*Oh…*so now we're getting to the heart of the matter. It's not about an alleged disciplinary problem, it's about the color of Carver's skin," concluded Charleigh.

"Yes, it's a very touchy and potentially explosive situation," said Ayani. "We're stepping into deep routed racial fears and stereotypes. In their myopic world, it's always the black and Hispanic kids who disrupt the classroom, right?"

"Ayani, ultimately this might boil down to money. How much more cash are you willing to donate to the school to get the administration back on your side?"

"*No…*please tell me I don't have to resort to that," begged Ayani.

"Sweetheart, if you want to resolve this problem quickly and get your child back into the classroom—your money has the power to move mountains."

The next morning Derrick and Ayani met secretly for several hours behind closed doors with Mr. Greenspring, the Archimedes Head of School, Mrs. Marsh, the head of preschool, the three Kindergarten teachers, and the school psychologist. All it took was Derrick and Ayani's endowment check to the Archimedes School for $50,000, along with a commitment from the school's administration to create a *Child Sensitivity Program to People of Color*, and voila, within days Carver was reinstated into the Kindergarten classroom.

As part of the 'sensitivity program' the Archimedes School's music instructors were directed to write several happy tunes touting the benefits of living in a diversified world. Within days of Carver's return to school, he had learned each song by heart. He sang his favorite ditty at the top of his lungs every day on the ride home from school:

"Black, white, yellow, brown and purple, too,
Everyone loves you through and through.
It's a great big world with many faces,
People of color from different places.
One big hug, and smiles all around,
Make this place a happy, happy town."

Life Observations from Vic the Maintenance Man:
"Don't you hate it when you get a song stuck in your head? I woke up today with that George Thorogood song, Bad to the Bone, as my theme song for the day. It's been haunting me during all my chores at school— it ain't going nowhere."

Chapter Ten:
When in Rome...

By early February the Archimedes School's four week program on "Child Sensitivity to People of Color" was completed and no further classroom crises had erupted, although Ayani continued to be snubbed by the women who instigated the uprising over her son, Carver. For the Kindergarten children, the school year was again proceeding smoothly with their typical days filled with K-Calculus, K-Latin, Language Arts, Computer Labs, and French lessons. Time on the playground was limited—their expensive designer coats just didn't stand up well to the bitter cold. Instead of running and squealing, they often huddled together en masse, shivering and stamping their feet, their backs turned away from the wind gusts, like male penguins in Antarctica awaiting the return of their mates.

Meanwhile, the winter doldrums were used as an excuse for several of the Archimedes School moms to volunteer as a host of Astrid's *special* in-home parties. Now, what was once a simple excuse for female bonding over cocktails at Astrid's home was slowly blossoming into a potentially huge business opportunity attracting the likes of several entrepreneurs, investors and franchise firms, all wanting to become involved in lucrative sex toy and lingerie sales, along with how to unleash your sexual prowess and improve your marriage therapy sessions. Astrid had enlisted the creative services of her close friend Crystal, a former marketing director for a local advertising agency, to develop logos, slogans, and a media kit for her new company. But, first they had to come up with a company name. Days of brainstorming yielded unsatisfactory results, which led Astrid to the idea of a sponsoring a naming contest for her new business. The winner would receive an all expense paid four day weekend trip for two on a cruise ship bound for the Bahamas, joining Astrid and Crystal on the ship, of course. The cruise was scheduled for that upcoming President's Day weekend.

"What the heck, I'll work on some business names," said Chrissie after Tara told her about the contest. "I could use a weekend away." In her mind, Chrissie could already see herself leaning across the railing of the cruise ship as the bow cut through the turquoise sea; a pod of dolphins leaped joyfully alongside. She could almost taste the salty air. This contest was Chrissie's best shot at ever getting a true vacation, at least one that didn't involve taking the D.C. Metro to the Natural History Museum.

After dropping off their children at Archimedes one morning, Tara and Chrissie met for coffee and batted around a few ideas. They ended up with a list of a dozen or so possibilities. Not able to choose among them, they decided to submit them all.

Ladies of Lust	Hot 'n Spicy Moms
Goddesses of Love	Keep It Up, Inc.
No Down Time	Libido Lifters

Fabulous Flirtations	Luscious Ladies
Cock-a-Doodle	Lace & Leather
Booty Boutique	Babe-A-Luscious
PlayDate After Hours	M.I.L.F., Inc.
Mom-A-Luscious	Let Me Entertain You

"If we win, we'll share the trip, okay?" asked Tara.

"Of course! Astrid told me they booked it for President's Day weekend. Believe it or not, Seth actually took off from work for that Monday, so he *could* watch Harrison all weekend long."

"Randy said I could go if I let him have a golfing weekend with some of his buddies in Hilton Head next month," said Tara.

The competition for the Bahamas trip was stiff, hundreds of names were sent in by Archimedes moms anxious to get away from it all. Visions of Strawberry Daiquiris and tan, firm cabana boys, void of love handles and beer bellies, ran through their heads. "Oh *cabana boy*, another Pina Colada please. By the way, dear, I think I missed a spot on my upper thigh, would you be so kind?" While images of lounging in a hammock under the swaying branches of palm trees captivated her, Chrissie still couldn't imagine having a weekend without her son Harrison, and the guilt pangs were already coursing through her body. *I haven't even won and I'm already a mess*, she thought. Conversely, Tara was already planning her travel wardrobe. One day after school at the afternoon Kindergarten pick-up, Tara asked Chrissie for an honest opinion. Tara was wearing exceptionally revealing tight jeans, almost to the point of showing the old "camel toe" at the crotch.

"Chrissie, look at my butt. Any cottage cheese back there?" Tara asked. "I want to wear the thong bikini, but I haven't worked out in weeks."

Chrissie leaned down to take a closer look, causing some of the nerdy male math teachers passing by to do a double take.

"Looks good from here," Chrissie replied. "Even if I had the nerve, I don't think I could get away with a thong bikini bottom."

"If you do wear a thong bikini, don't forget to get a Brazilian waxing," said Tara.

"What's a Brazilian waxing?" asked Chrissie, somewhat bewildered, imagining ripping the tiny, nearly indiscernible hairs from her rear. "I wax my own eyebrows with one of those kits from CVS, but I've never needed to wax my butt."

Catching the tail end of their conversation, Astrid walked by with her child in tow and then interjected, "Chrissie, dear, it's when these sweet little Asian girls wax every little hair from your privates—I mean front, under, and sides. You are as bare as a pre-pubescent babe. Men love it—and trust me, you will, too! It opens up a whole new world of tantalizing sensations."

Astrid started to walk away, when she suddenly remembered something. "Oh, once you get that Brazilian waxing and the thong bikini—try this: Find some unsuspecting good looking man lounging in a beach chair, then stand in front of him…*with your back to him*, of course. Take a moment to bend over from the waist, ever so slowly, to adjust your toe ring. It's a real hoot to watch their reactions. He'll be licking his lips for sure!"

"Oh my *God*," Chrissie whispered to Tara. "Do women really do this?"

"Obviously some of us do," responded Tara. "I wouldn't have the nerve, at least not in public. Maybe I'd finally get Randy's attention if I did." Right on cue, Tara's cell phone rang with the happy Down Under tune of Waltzing Matilda.

"Chrissie, 'cuse me for a minute," Tara said, then spoke a buttery smooth "hello" into her phone. Chrissie unintentionally overheard bits and pieces of Tara's conversation with the unknown caller.

"You're in town....you left a gift on my car?" Tara said into her phone. She literally skipped in the direction of her car, dragging her son Clinton by the hand. Curious at Tara's sudden and exuberant departure, Chrissie encouraged Harrison to hurry toward the Archimedes School parking lot. Watching carefully from the distance of several car lengths away, Chrissie saw Tara retrieve a small blue Tiffany box that was placed on her windshield. Opening the gift box, Tara gently unfolded a stunning platinum necklace graced with a huge solitaire diamond that sparkled and danced with the light. Clasping the necklace to her chest, Tara's eyes scanned her surroundings for a glimpse of the gift giver. Pressing redial, Tara swooned words of "thank you," and "you shouldn't have," into her phone. Chrissie was touched by what she assumed was Randy's romantic gesture. *I guess Randy's just returned from another business trip. It's good to see Tara and her husband working on their marriage,* she thought to herself. Chrissie turned and walked with her son Harrison in the opposite direction toward her Volvo. From halfway across the parking lot she spied something oddly out of place on her car, too. Something red had landed on her windshield. "It's just a piece of trash blown by these brutal February winds," she thought to herself. Quizzically she studied the odd red thing, until she got closer and it became clear—it was a rose, a single red rose tucked under her windshield wiper.

Attached to the rose was a tiny envelope with her name handwritten on the outside. The handwriting was familiar but it wasn't Seth's. Inside was a simple, succinct note;

Dearest Chrissie,
Valentine's Day is this Saturday and you'll be in my thoughts.
I cherish our friendship and miss you with all my heart.
Your special friend,
Nathaniel

A warm, soulful tingle spread through her body as she touched the petals of the rose to her cheek. Ever since the Archimedes teacher Christmas party Chrissie had been unsuccessfully trying to get Nathaniel out of her thoughts. Now all of her feelings and sensations came flooding back with a force that nearly knocked her off her feet. When her son began asking questions about the mysterious gift, her reverie was broken.

"Mommy, where did the flower come from?" Chrissie realized this story would be repeated later that night to her husband, so she quickly contrived an explanation.

"It's from Miss Ayani, isn't she the sweetest?"

"Why'd she give you a flower, Mommy?" Harrison continued.

"Oh, friends do nice things for friends," Chrissie replied, hoping the questions would end soon.

"Did she write you a letter?"

"No dear, nothing special…just a note to say she was thinking about me."

"Mommy, why did you hug the flower?" Chrissie hoped the interrogation was over because she was running out of excuses.

"Sweetheart, I just smelled it for a moment."

"Mommy, does Daddy ever give you flowers?" asked Harrison.

"Well…sure…sometimes…" she lied. The last time Seth bought her flowers was the day Harrison was born. His simple "everyday" bouquet from the grocery store was overshadowed by the artistic masterpieces sent by family and friends from the local florist. Finally, after a brief pause Harrison got distracted by a book he had left unattended on the back seat and the questions ceased. Leaving the Archimedes School parking lot Chrissie had to screech her ancient Volvo to a halt to avoid rear ending a behemoth SUV that nearly rammed her as it was backing out. Apparently, use of rear view mirrors was unnecessary for some SUV owners. Her friend Vic from maintenance, who was busy at work tossing salt onto the icy parking lot, saw the incident and just shook his head in disgust. Chrissie watched Vic as he stopped his work briefly to chat amicably with one of the teachers who had finished a long day at school and was leaving for home with a briefcase bulging with more work to be done later that night. The teacher's back was to Chrissie's car and he was unidentifiable due to being bundled against the cold in a heavy wool coat with a scarf wrapped nearly to his nose. When Vic nodded in her direction, Chrissie waved and smiled at her friend. The unknown teacher turned and looked at Chrissie through the car's windows. She then instantly recognized Nathaniel's face which lit up in a smile so broad and endearing it sent shockwaves through her. Chrissie's smile met his as she mouthed the words "thank you" to him. Driving past Vic and Nathaniel, Chrissie again touched the silky petals of the rose to her cheek. *"Why is life so damn complicated?"* she asked herself.

"Today's the day Astrid picks the company name," Tara reminded Chrissie as they stood in the school parking lot the next morning after Kindergarten drop off. "Are you going to her house for the big event?"

"Of course, I'm heading there now," said Chrissie. "Keep your fingers crossed, I think you and I've got a great chance to win," she said with a giggle, and began jogging to her car when she stopped abruptly. "Hey, shouldn't we be eco-friendly and share a ride?" Tara glanced at Chrissie's ancient Volvo, a car she wouldn't be caught dead in, and quickly replied, "Oh, thanks honey, but I've got errands to run right afterward."

Astrid was hosting a brunch for anyone and everyone who had contributed a name to the contest and was preparing to announce the winner in grandiose style. White linen cloths draped the buffet tables where the caterer had placed warming trays filled with Eggs Benedict, crepes and bagels. Mimosas were the signature drink of this event. The powerful scent of dozens of lilies strategically placed around the room fragranced the air. A female reporter from the local newspaper was called in to cover the story, *"Hometown Mom Makes Thousands of Husbands Happy"* the headline might read later that day in the evening edition. This was big news in this small town.

Flute glasses bubbling with champagne and orange juice were handed to each arriving guest. The crowd of twenty or so women, and one token male, mingled and chatted politely about their children, politics, money, and any recent major purchases they had made. When Astrid stood at the front of her living room and raised a glass to make a toast, the gathering of Archimedes School parents was silenced.

"Thank you for coming this morning and thank you for all your wonderful ideas and contributions," Astrid began. From the side of the room, Crystal looked on fondly at her friend. "After carefully reviewing all of the entries, we have decided on the brand new name for this exciting company. We know that very, very soon people across the country will be hosting parties with this as the company name." Everyone in the room held their breath.

"The winner is "Hanky Panky" submitted by our *dear* Tara!" announced Astrid with a flourish. Chrissie stood there stunned, every fiber in her body was aflame, her mouth gaped open in a huge "O." Hanky Panky was one of the names she and Tara had originally thought of together, and then rejected, or at least she thought so.

"What the fu…" Chrissie said. Her words cut off by the smattering of applause from the rest of the disappointed contest contributors. "You and I came up with that idea together, how could you?" was all Chrissie could mutter as Tara weaseled her way past her and bounded to the center of the room, beaming with pride. Burning with fury, hurt by her friend's deception, Chrissie scooped up her coat and purse from the entryway and stormed from Astrid's home with tears streaming down her cheeks. She slammed the massive front door behind her.

"That evil bitch, she's got more money than God and could buy ten trips on that cruise ship and not even flinch," complained Chrissie to Ayani over the phone. Chrissie was so mad that she really wanted to use the "c" word, but that obscenity had actually never crossed her lips—it was just too vile, even in her incensed state. "That was my idea first and we *both* rejected it."

"Chrissie, let it go. It's just gonna eat you alive if you keep thinking about it," said Ayani. "Come over today and I'll give you a private, cleansing yoga session."

"No offense, Ayani, I don't want to do yoga...I don't want to meditate...I don't want to cleanse...I want...a.... freaking VACATION!" Chrissie exclaimed loudly into the phone receiver.

"Okay, here's the deal. Let's do a spa weekend with you, me, Jodi and Charleigh. I'll book it. There's a wonderful resort in the Catskills that boasts a raw food diet, sun yoga, Reiki work, and hot stone massage. One of my yoga students raves about it," said Ayani.

"Fine, but I really wanted the warmth of Caribbean sunshine, lots of starchy over-cooked food, and my personal boy toy waiting on me hand and foot refreshing my cocktail every half hour. I didn't want some touchy-feely sun fucking yoga and a raw carrot...no offense Ayani. I'm sorry. I'm so God damn pissed! But, at this point I'll take anything I can get." Chrissie took a deep breath, "Ayani, I'm sorry, I don't mean to sound unappreciative."

"No offense taken," said Ayani in her calm, reassuring tone of voice. "But, you do need to let go of that anger at Tara. Try to think that the *universe* meant for her to go on the cruise and not you—and that this was out of everyone's control."

"Great, then I'm pissed at the entire freaking universe, now," Chrissie said with a chuckle, already softening.

Ayani booked the retreat at the exclusive Crunchy Radish Spa Resort for that upcoming President's Day weekend—the same weekend Astrid, Crystal, Tara and her husband Randy would be floating in the azure waters of the Caribbean. It had been two years since Chrissie, Charleigh,

Jodi and Ayani had escaped together without children or husbands and the women were giddy with anticipation and excitement. One of the Baltimore television stations had recently done a piece on several of the trendiest spas on the east coast and Crunchy Radish resort was at the top of the list. Wealthy women from Virginia to Maine were packing the place in droves willing to cough up mega bucks to endure a 500 calorie a day starvation diet, skin peeling high pressure pulsating showers, Vera the 200 pound masseuse with the brick layer's hands, and 5 a.m. wake up calls to ascend snow covered mountains on three hour hikes with the body fueled on just green tea and raw seaweed crackers. At Kindergarten pick-up the four women connected to review their travel plans.

"Ayani, I'm packing granola bars and croissants. I'll die without a few carbs," worried Chrissie. "You know I'm used to eating healthy, like my veggie lasagnas and stir fried concoctions, but this raw food meal plan has got me concerned."

"Hide your carbs well so they won't confiscate them. You know they check every bag for contraband," replied Ayani.

"I'm bringing two bottles of pinot noir in my snow boots," said Charleigh. "I don't mind a little hunger, but I can't live without my one little vice."

"Charleigh, I promise not to rat you out if you let me have some, too!" said Chrissie. "I'll even share my chocolate croissants."

"Oh girls, please don't tell Derrick, but I'm bringing Orme," said Ayani.

"Who's Orme?" asked Charleigh, disappointed that Ayani might be introducing one of her earthy yoga students into their entourage.

"It's not a who, but a what," replied Ayani. "It's this amazing substance that all my astrology friends are using. The ancients knew about it 4,000 years ago. Some people think that aliens from other planets have been harvesting this stuff on earth for over 100,000 years."

"Ayani, *what the hell* are you talking about?" asked Jodi, always ready to criticize any new hippie-esque trend that was sweeping the nation. "Is this stuff safe? Do you smoke it, inhale it or eat it?"

"You *drink* it, and yes it's safe. It's basically a precious metal—the powder of white gold—mixed with water. People are doing Ormus parties everywhere. I got invited to one in Dupont Circle in D.C. last week. That's where I got this," Ayani explained as she held up a small glass vial containing a pearly white liquid that jiggled and floated with the same qualities as the goo in a lava lamp. Somehow the liquid seemed alive.

"I'm really, really confused, Ayani. Does this stuff get you high or what?" asked Chrissie, who appeared to be intrigued yet cautious.

"Here's what they claim Orme will do. If you use it every day for a month or so it will raise your consciousness to a new level. You're supposed to become telepathic, you can heal people by the laying on of hands, you should be able to levitate yourself and possibly objects around you, plus you'll be able to identify good versus evil if it walks in the room. They say the Egyptians used the white powder of gold to help them levitate those huge stones when they made the pyramids."

"That's insane, Ayani, what will these people think of next?" replied Jodi, dismissing Ayani's claims. "I'll be the designated driver if you girls plan to try it."

"Hey, Seth's got Harrison for the weekend, we'll be in a safe place at the spa, and we'll stick together. What the heck. I'll try it. It's not like we're dropping LSD," said Chrissie. "As long as you're sure it's safe."

"I'm in, too," said Charleigh with a smile. "If Ayani's drinking this stuff it can't be bad for your body. After all, look at her, she's the picture of health!"

"That's great! Bring something comfy to wear, just in case we start to levitate!" exclaimed Ayani. "This should be fun."

Meanwhile, Tara was desperately trying to secure a babysitter to stay with her son Clinton for the President's Day holiday weekend. Tara had convinced her husband Randy to join her on the cruise and was hoping that her new Brazilian thong bikini would help save their marriage and finally catch his attention. Despite recent liaisons with her special New Zealand friend, Tara ultimately wanted to fix her marriage—*why the hell can't I get Randy to look at me?* Sure Ethan was fun, sexy and rich, but this was just an 'innocent' fling, after all. She read in Cosmopolitan magazine that at least 60% of married people had some sort of extra-marital affair, she was just contributing to the national normative data. She didn't expect her extra curricular activities to last much longer and Tara really didn't want to go through the hell of divorce.

She had it all planned. On the cruise she'd parade around their suite in front of Randy in her new Prada high heel sandals, a gold ankle bracelet would sparkle on her left leg, and the black mesh thong would leave nothing to the imagination. *If this doesn't turn him on, nothing will,* Tara thought. After making at least twenty phone calls, sadly, all of the nannies in town were already booked for the holiday weekend—when half of the parents in town ditched their kids in favor of schussing down the slopes or soaking up the sun. Three days of intoxicated behavior was preferred over watching Disney videos at home with their five year olds.

"Randy, it's hopeless. I've called every nanny service, contacted every Upper Schooler at Archimedes, and even called a few churches looking for granny-types willing to make some extra cash—no luck!" said Tara. "I guess we're not going." She plopped onto their living room sofa with a thud, disappointment and frustration clearly displayed on her face.

"Tara, you won the trip fair and square," said Randy, unaware that originally Chrissie had thought of the name. "You should go without me. I'll take care of Clinton." Tara thought she detected some relief in the tone of Randy's words, as if he was hoping for the opportunity not to go.

"Oh honey, I was hoping we could spend quality time together and have wild sex like we did before Clinton was born." Tara watched as Randy unconsciously grimaced at her words. It looked like he had just sucked on a lemon. That one grimace was all the incentive she needed. Her tone changed instantly. "Fine, then, I'll go without you." Tara jumped off the sofa and turned on her heels to leave the room.

The following Friday afternoon the black stretch limo pulled into the driveway of Chrissie's Eastport home just before 4:00. Jodi, Ayani and Charleigh were already on board with champagne flutes in hand. The driver greeted Chrissie at her door and witnessed the touching moment of mother and son saying goodbye. Harrison was glued so tightly to Chrissie's leg that she had to drag him along with each step. She reached down to peel him away and held his tiny body tightly in her arms. Tears streamed down both of their faces.

"It's just until Monday night, honey. Daddy will take good care of you. I'll call you everyday," said Chrissie in between sobs. A confused mélange of emotions filled her heart. She was excited to embark with her girlfriends on her first real get-away in years, yet overwhelmed with sadness about leaving her only child. On top of that, she was extremely worried that Seth wasn't up to the task of taking care of their son. Just a few months ago, when Chrissie volunteered for a few hours to help plant drought tolerant earth friendly perennials in their community park, Seth was assigned the extremely taxing responsibility of feeding Harrison breakfast. Unfortunately, Harrison wanted pancakes that morning and Seth felt it was the pivotal time to get their five year old to "man up" and learn to fix his own—no matter the fact that Harrison couldn't fully read the instructions on back of the Bisquick box. A power play ensued with Harrison having a six hour melt down, "Daddy, I'm soooo hungry, please, please feed me." While Seth replied, "Figure it out, if you can't make pancakes, get something else to eat." Seth's parenting skills teetered on the fine line of "sink or swim" and child abuse. Chrissie returned home just after lunch time to find her child eating a year old frozen bagel that he found in the back of the freezer. Harrison's face was swollen and red from hours of crying, Seth's face was swollen and red from hours of enforcing his man up policy. Needless to say, Chrissie was extremely anxious about leaving Harrison alone with Seth for a few hours, let alone for a few days. Post-it-notes were now plastered all over the house with instructions on the care and feeding of their child:

"Don't forget—midnight snack is at *8:00 p.m.*"

"Saturday breakfast is always oatmeal, Sunday is pancakes (she had already made mini-pancakes and frozen them to avoid another incident), Monday is Cinnamon toast with cereal"

"He only takes a bath at night—bath toys are in the hall closet"

"Don't forget math homework—K-Physics test on Monday!"

"Please read 2-3 books per night"

"Don't talk about clowns at night—causes nightmares"

"Vitamins! Fluoride treatment!"

Seth appeared relieved when Chrissie reached for the doorknob after giving Harrison a final hug goodbye. She actually saw Seth smile, what a concept!

As she collapsed on the plush leather sofa that wrapped around the interior of the limo, Charleigh handed her a glass of chilled champagne.

"Thanks, but do you have a valium, instead? That was the hardest thing I've ever done. I've never left my baby for more than one night," said Chrissie.

"It's good for him and Seth. They need to get acquainted and do some father and son bonding," said Jodi.

"I guess. I just hope he doesn't get on another one of his kicks to teach Harrison how to be independent," Chrissie said, reflecting on the pancake crisis. "Shoot, just last Saturday when I ran to the grocery store to get a carton of fresh milk, I came home to find Harrison writhing on the floor, complaining that he couldn't go outside and play because Daddy wouldn't tie his shoes for him. Meanwhile, Seth had told him the famous line "figure it out yourself, you're five now."

Charleigh muttered under her breath to herself, "What an idiot."

"I heard that. Yeah. I agree. Seth had printed out some diagrams illustrating how to tie shoe laces and thought Harrison could master it on his own with the help of those visual aids," said Chrissie."

While sipping the champagne, Chrissie lounged comfortably on the overstuffed limousine sofa and became absorbed in her surroundings. Chrissie noted that her friends were striking, each unique from the other. Ayani was sinewy, dark and mystical, Jodi was determined, tall and curvaceous, Charleigh was sultry and sensuous with classic movie star facial features and could be Michelle Pfeiffer's double. They were good, reputable women, who put family first. It was where Chrissie belonged even though she felt like an imposter at times. Their Prada, Michael Kors, and Gucci bags were at their feet, while Chrissie's knock-off Coach bag rested by her side.

Ayani intuitively sensed Chrissie's insecurity and said, "Chrissie, you look like a million bucks, never have I seen you so totally together and sexy."

"Thanks Ayani, it's not easy keeping up with you gorgeous, young things." Chrissie raised her glass to propose a toast. "Let's toast to us. Um...I think I remember this old Irish proverb my grandfather used to say...May the hinges of our friendship never grow rusty." The women clinked their glasses together and echoed the words "Cheers" in return. Just at the moment their glasses touched, a slip of paper emerged from Chrissie's coat pocket and fell to the floor of the limo.

"What's this?" asked Jodi as she reached to retrieve the folded paper. Jodi's eyes unintentionally scanned the brief note. It only took one quick glance at the handwritten words to absorb the importance of what she had found. It was the note Nathaniel had left on Chrissie's car.

"*Nathaniel? The teacher?*" she said, raising her eyebrow in Chrissie's direction. "What's going on, Chrissie?" asked Jodi, her question mixed with tone of worry and criticism.

"Let *me* see," said Charleigh, as she reached for the scrap of paper. Chrissie tried unsuccessfully to steal it away.

"We're just friends, really. Nothing's happened. *Really.*" Chrissie replied while glancing in Ayani's direction. Ayani was the only one of the women who had any inkling about Chrissie and Nathaniel's romantic entanglement. "He's got a crush on me and I'm trying to do everything in my power to stay away from him—or else something may happen for real."

Charleigh and Jodi leaned in closer toward Chrissie. Jodi gently touched Chrissie's knee then began a minor tirade.

"Chrissie, your husband Seth is the biggest asshole this side of the Mississippi. He treats you like shit and is a complete social moron. We hate it whenever he comes to any of our get-togethers," began Jodi. With that comment Charleigh's elbow dug into Jodi's side, "Shhhhh, tone it down a little," she whispered.

"Well it's true! He's a jerk who's always so goddamn condescending—the stuff he says about you makes my skin crawl," Jodi said. "I think you deserve better. This Nathaniel dude seems to be a sweet, sensitive guy. But…Chrissie, you've got to be very, *very* careful. If one peep of this falls on Seth's ears, he might go postal. He's the type who's got so much anger buried inside he might blow sideways and the next thing you know, he's holding you hostage in the Archimedes School astronomy tower while wielding a machine gun pointed randomly at any unsuspecting teacher."

"Really, Jodi, *nothing* has happened!" said Chrissie. "I admit that I'm enjoying Nathaniel's attention. He makes me feel sexy and appreciated—something I've been missing for years—something you girls get everyday. Geez, look at the Valentine's Day gifts your husbands bought you! You got diamonds, lingerie, trinkets galore. I got a 99 cent card. I know to be careful about my timing. I have a little confession to make. I went to Dolly the psychic a few months ago and she told me all about my, um, future rendezvous with Nathaniel and she warned me about all the potential consequences if I didn't handle this exactly right."

"Good. Enough said. I know you're not stupid. Think about Harrison and how this might impact him at the Archimedes School. Parents dating teachers is totally forbidden—there's this unspoken rule of separation of 'church and state.' Parents aren't supposed to know too much about teachers and their private lives and God forbid teachers should know anything about the private lives of these wacko parents."

"I hate to break the news to you, Jodi, but the teachers already know way too much about us—all of us—from wife swapping to sex toy parties to young studs for hire on shopping splurges to New York City. I found that out at the teacher holiday party in December."

"Great. Now *you'll* be an informant to the Archimedes faculty," Jodi said. Chrissie appeared wounded by Jodi's seemingly heartless remark. "Don't worry sweetie, I'm just kidding."

Charleigh looked over at Ayani and said, "You've known about Nathaniel for a while, haven't you? Confess! You've got a guilty little smile on your face."

Ayani simply nodded in agreement. "At least now you know your secrets are safe with me," Ayani replied. "There is a Cherokee prayer that I use as a guideline for living, it goes like this: O' Great Spirit, help me always to speak the truth quietly, to listen with an open mind when others speak, and to remember the peace that may be found in *silence*."

Ayani's words of wisdom had an almost hypnotic affect on the four women. Wordlessly and silently they rode the rest of the way to the airport, absorbed by their innermost private thoughts, each not wanting to intrude on another's quiet time or personal space.

As Charleigh, Ayani, Chrissie and Jodi flew across the northern night sky en route to the Crunchy Radish Spa, Tara was trying to track down Astrid and Crystal at the Miami International Airport. Tara finally hooked up with her two voluptuous friends at one of the raucous, smoke filled bars in the terminal. They weren't able to coordinate being on the same flight together, but they did make plans to meet upon arrival in the Sunshine state. Astrid and Crystal were preoccupied with entertaining an assortment of weary business travelers who tried in vain to look tropical by removing their smart corporate ties and loosening their collars and cuffs. Astrid was doing a fabulous job of teasing these poor, unsuspecting "boys grown tall" by bending down seductively to tie the laces of her espadrilles around her calves, while presenting ample cleavage for their viewing pleasure. Crystal sauntered up to one fifty-ish businessman, intentionally brushing her breast against his arm as she stepped up to the bar to order another "Sex On The Beach" cocktail. When Tara hurriedly strolled in, pulling her luggage behind her, one of the three men commented, "Hot shit, now there's one for each of us!"

Tara completely ignored his comment and grabbed the arm of one of her friends.

"Astrid, Crystal! My flight arrived late. We've got to hurry. Are you aware that we need to be at the cruise ship port in fifteen minutes, or we'll miss the boat?" Tara said with her sensuous southern accent.

"Oh, and she's a little southern thang, too!" responded the businessman.

"Yeah, buddy, and I bet your little 'thang' is always *hanging* south, too!" Tara retorted. Everyone within earshot of Tara's comment burst into laughter. Astrid, Tara, and Crystal snatched up their luggage and briskly ran—as fast as their high heel sandals would let them—to the taxi depot. Men everywhere along their path, stopped to watch them pass through the airport. Even the federal security agents were briefly distracted, making one supervisor worry that bouncing and jiggling breasts might be a possible terrorist strategy.

By five o'clock that evening the three women had settled into their adjoining staterooms and had already received at least five separate invitations from several handsome European and American gentlemen to join them for dinner at the second meal seating on the cruise ship. By five thirty the three women had stripped down to bathing suits, sarongs and sandals, and were dancing to reggae music by the pool at the cruise ship's huge bon voyage festivities. By six o'clock several men were playing pool side adult games and were using their teeth to pull ripe and juicy cherries stuffed into any visible crevice in Tara's bathing suit and passed the fruit to Astrid and then Crystal—which continued down a long row of beautiful bathing suit clad babes. By six thirty Crystal was leading a conga line around the perimeter of the pool with about one hundred inebriated people in tow. At seven o'clock Astrid was hoisted up by four young college bucks who entered her into the impromptu wet t-shirt contest taking place on the small stage set between the hot tub and the pool bar—she had to borrow a white t-shirt from one of the 'boys.' By seven fifteen Astrid's breasts were dripping wet and visible through the t-shirt. The crowd cheered her on when she shimmied them in a mock belly dancing move. By eight o'clock their dinner plans were forgotten as the three women floated topless in the bubbling hot tub, joined by hirsute, drunken and bleary eyed men who spoke with thick Italian accents. And finally, by eight fifteen Tara, Astrid and Crystal had ditched the Italians and moved the continuing party to their adjoining suites. Their suite was packed to the hilt with scantily clad twenty to thirty something men and women, along with a handful of folks over the age of fifty, who assumed the roles of voyeurs, preferring to stand by the small bar and watch the activities. By nine o'clock Tara's party tricks were once again a huge hit and she was introduced to a few new tricks by the younger women.

"I can remove my bikini bottom over my head!" said one nubile young thing. "I've got you beat," said another, "I can put on my bikini top using only my teeth." The gauntlet was thrown down and the men in the room thoroughly enjoyed the show.

"Enough with the party tricks. Let's do party *games,* now." announced Astrid. She had conveniently brought along some of the accessories from her sex toy parties. "I've got a deck of flashcards that I'll give to the men. They pick a woman, and ask them to do what the card says."

The first card to be drawn from the deck read 'Spank Me....Please.' Followed by 'I'm Rich, Kiss Me' which was followed by 'Flash Me Your Boobs.' Each targeted women kindly obliged, stirring hoots and hollers from everyone. By midnight two burly men from the ship's staff had arrived with the arduous task of breaking up the partygoers and sending them away from the sleeping decks down to the public areas which included the disco and casino. Tara, Astrid and Crystal chose instead to stay in their suites to privately—and as they promised the ship's crew, *quietly* entertain a few of the choicest selections of men.

Sadly, Tara's phone was ringing constantly throughout the evening but couldn't be heard over the noise of the music and boisterous party crowd. Little did Tara know that her sweet child Clinton was frantically calling his mom to tell her he how much he loved her and missed her.

Meanwhile that same night, yet more than a thousand miles away, Jodi supervised her three friends as they put five or so drops of the pearly white liquid powder of gold under their tongues. The Ormus party had begun.

"It just tastes like salt," said Chrissie, who was slightly nervous that this strange substance would generate hallucinations of floating pigs or whatever.

"Trust me, this batch was made organically by a trusted alchemist who lives in Takoma Park, Maryland. I wouldn't give you anything that could harm your body," promised Ayani. A sudden knock at the door caused the women to quickly stash the vial of Ormus under a pillow.

"Room service," the waiter announced through the door. The menu on the first night was fresh carrot juice, green tea, and an assortment of raw vegetables including a special snow pea, sprouts and shredded cabbage salad with olive oil drizzled on top. For protein, each person was issued 15 unsalted almonds. The "meal" was delivered by a hot, young Johnny Depp look-alike. Each of the four women couldn't help but to check out his ass when he left their room, holding Charleigh's fifty dollar tip in his hand.

"Fifty bucks? Isn't that too much?" asked Ayani.

"Not if we want to see his cute butt again. I guarantee he'll be scrambling to deliver each and every one of our meals."

"Oooh, Yummy," Chrissie said sarcastically when she peered under the silver covers protecting their dinners. She reached into her suitcase to pass around granola bars. Charleigh opened a bottle of pinot noir, pouring a little into each of the paper cups provided by the spa. Printed on the cups was the claim that they were corn based, biodegradable and compost friendly. Charleigh hoped that the pinot noir wouldn't cause the cups to instantly dissolve.

"Hey, is the Ormus doing anything yet?" asked Chrissie.

"I think I'm starting to feel something," said Ayani. "My body feels lighter than air. Oh heavens, I forgot something." She opened her suitcase and pulled out at least ten votive candles, her ipod loaded with nature sounds, a few sticks of incense and an old copper incense holder. "Mood enhancement," she replied as she turned off the electric lights, placed the candles around the room and popped the ipod into the player. The soothing sounds of mating whales filled the room.

"Ayani, you're right, I'm feeling lightheaded, too. The Ormus must be working," said Chrissie.

"It's from the hunger," Charleigh said, as her stomach rumbled. Chrissie opened her mouth to respond, then stopped suddenly and squealed.

"Look! The cashew, it jumped right from the salad onto the table. I think I made it levitate!" she said.

"Eeek! No, Chrissie, look. I think there was a cricket under that cashew," said Jodi as she burst into laughter. Even without the influence of Ormus, Jodi was able to enjoy her role as voyeur.

"Yuck, damn organic vegetables. What's wrong with just a little pesticide? I was hoping the Ormus was kicking in," Chrissie moaned, lifting the cabbage and snow peas to inspect her salad, then she too starting giggling uncontrollably. Charleigh and Ayani joined in, laughing to the point where tears were pouring down their cheeks. By now the whale mating calls on the ipod were replaced with the sounds of a babbling brook and chirping birds.

Barely able to catch her breath between fits of laughter, Charleigh said, "Can someone please stop that watery music, I think I'm about to pee my pants!" By now the four women were rolling on the shag carpet, holding their sides, laughing so hard their stomach muscles hurt.

"I...think...the Ormus...is working!" Ayani managed to say between the hysterics. At least ten minutes passed while the women alternated between laughing, trying to catch their breath, brief moments of silence, interrupted by another laughing spell. Finally, they managed to pull it together.

"That was the best! I've never laughed so hard in my life," said Chrissie, holding her side. "I think I pulled my spleen."

"Well, the Ormus definitely worked. The last Ormus party I went to ended the same way. We were all on the floor giggling our brains out."

"As you know, laughter releases all those healthy endorphins. If this is the typical result, I wouldn't mind trying it tomorrow night," said Jodi.

"Hey, you didn't need to use it and you still laughed harder than we did," said Charleigh. "It must be the group dynamics." Reaching for the bottle of pinot noir, she asked, "More wine, girls?"

After three days of decadence, Tara awoke on Sunday morning in a foggy haze confused about her unfamiliar surroundings. This wasn't her deluxe suite on the cruise ship, it was a small windowless cabin, probably on one of the cheaper decks below hers. In the bed next to her was a gentleman she had never seen before, or at least she thought. The floor was littered with an assortment of empty wine bottles and plastic drink cups emblazoned with the cruise ship's logo. Pieces of limes and lemons were scattered about.

Quietly Tara slipped out of the bed so as not to awaken the unknown passenger next to her. She had apparently fallen asleep fully dressed. Everything was intact. Except, the brand new champagne hued Versace cocktail dress which she bought specifically for the cruise had a huge sticky stain on the front. *Please don't let this be anything biological*, she prayed to herself. Somehow this triggered vague memories of a blue dress from The Gap and something to do with Bill Clinton. Her Prada sandals and purse stuffed with $1,000 dollars in crisp new $100 dollar bills were sitting on the tiny bureau in the cabin! Thank God! As she was preparing to leave the claustrophobic cabin, a huge hairy hand reached out from the bed and grabbed her by the wrist. Tara noticed that his other arm was plastered with a full sleeve of tattoos that ran from his shoulder to his wrist. One of the tattoos was of a woman with her head buried in the crotch of a man. "Explain that to your grandchildren when you're eighty," thought Tara.

"Don't leave *girlfriend.* I'm sorry about last night. I guess I had too much to drink. Let's try again tonight," the ape man pleaded.

"Thanks, but no thanks," replied Tara, self consciously touching the stain on her dress.

"I understand. I'll see you top deck, then, girlfriend. By the way, your phone was ringing all night long, some stupid Waltzing Matilda tune—it drove me crazy," the tattooed stranger said.

Tara quickly left the cabin and checked the call history on her cell phone. The tattooed ape man was right. She had missed eight calls from Ethan during the night. *But, no messages from my husband, Randy!* At least Ethan left a message.

"Tara, sweetheart, I'm headed to New Zealand on Monday—*tomorrow.* My mum is sick. I was hoping I could see you one more time before I leave. I'll be at BWI this Monday evening for the 6 p.m. overnight flight. Call me." Ethan's sexy accent made Tara quiver with desire. *Yes, Ethan, I'll be arriving at BWI airport just in time,* Tara thought as she absently touched the diamond solitaire around her neck which he had delivered to her just weeks before.

"Oh my God, it's 1:00!" Tara said with alarm when she glanced at the time on her cell. "What the fuck happened last night?" she muttered to herself as she stepped into one of the cruise ship's elevator to ascend to the higher echelons of the upper decks.

"Tara! How the hell are you?" said one middle aged beer bellied stranger wearing a New York Mets team tank top with jersey shorts. *Ohhh baby, there's nothing sexier than a man wearing a wife beater tank top to show off all that underarm hair!* Tara thought.

"Hey good looking, thanks for showing me those dance moves last night!" said another equally repulsive man who's deodorant had stopped working at least ten hours ago.

Standing quietly in the back of the elevator was a freshly scrubbed young couple, probably newlyweds, Tara thought. The groom tapped Tara on the shoulder and whispered in her ear, "Thanks for telling me about that special move in bed—Betsy loved it!"

Tara had no recollection of ever meeting these people in her entire life. As she walked through the maze of vendors and boutiques on the ship's main deck, she was greeted with smiles and waves of recognition from nearly every person she passed. "*What the hell happened last night?*" she again asked herself, this time with more urgency.

Standing in the lunch buffet line, Tara donned her dark sunglasses and prayed for anonymity. Suddenly a chorus of "TARA, TARA, TARA," rang clear from a herd of tan and muscular young twenty-somethings drinking Margaritas at a table nearby. She was just about to muster courage and ask these "boys" what happened last night, when she was tapped on the shoulder from behind. Astrid and Crystal, who were both sporting large floppy hats and dark sunglasses, flashed their perfectly white teeth in huge smiles as they greeted their comrade. Just above their sarongs, their belly button jewelry sparkled in the light.

"Great show last night, Tara," said Crystal, grinning ear to ear.

"I'm so impressed you got up on stage—and in front of the entire ship!" said Astrid. "When did you learn to dance so well?"

"Dance? Stage? What the hell did I do last night?" stammered a completely bewildered Tara, her southern drawl thick with worry.

"Honey, don't you remember? At the Cabaret show last night they asked if anyone in the audience wanted to join the professional dance team up on stage. You raised your hand and that bunch of guys sitting over there hoisted you right up. Not only did you dance the Can-Can, but you also taught the audience how to pole dance!" said Crystal.

"Oh my God!" was all Tara could say. "If Randy finds out, he'll divorce me for sure. Please, *please* keep this quiet."

"What's with the stain on your dress?" asked Crystal.

"Don't even go there. All I know was that nothing happened. At least that's what he said. So, I'm sticking with that story." For the rest of that Sunday, the last full day on the ship, Tara laid low. She booked a hot stone massage, had her nails done, read a book in the library, played monopoly with a seventy year old woman, ordered all of her meals as room service, and sipped gallons of diet coke hoping to douse her headache and re-hydrate her body after her bout of binge drinking to the point of oblivion. Basically, her plan was to avoid anyone and everyone who had witnessed the events from the previous night and for the remainder of the cruise keep a million miles away from the limelight.

All during the flight home the next afternoon, Tara remained quiet and contemplative while Astrid and Crystal continued to party at 30,000 feet. The minute the fasten seat belt sign wasn't illuminated, Astrid hopped out of her seat in first class and plopped into empty seat next to the handsome man sitting across the aisle. She had been batting her eyes at him since they boarded, and he was thrilled to have her breasts pressed up against him. One of her hands rested on his leg, the other gently touched his forearm. Within minutes they were both glancing in the direction of the tiny first class rest room, hoping to sneak past the flight attendants and find the opportunity to join the 'mile high club.' Crystal focused her attentions on a silver haired, well appointed fellow wearing an Armani suit. By the time they arrived in Baltimore, she had convinced this distinguished chap to join her in a downtown Annapolis bar for an "after-flight" cocktail.

Tara wanted no part of it, she was too immersed in thought. She was feeling guilty about whatever shenanigans she had done on the cruise—most of which was clouded in a tequila fog. She wanted to rescue her marriage to Randy, but couldn't stop thinking about her New Zealand boat dealer friend Ethan. At least *he* paid attention to her. Tara's mind swirled in confusion the entire length of the flight. *Randy. Ethan. Randy. Ethan. Save my marriage—what the hell, have some fun.*

When they landed in Baltimore, Tara politely air-kissed Astrid and Crystal and thanked them for a "fantabulous" time. Tara paused a moment at the end of the jet way to watch the two women sashay toward baggage pick-up, their two new male friends in tow.

"Don't worry, I'll catch up," Tara said as they walked away. Secretly she wanted to be alone just in case Ethan kept his promise to greet her in the terminal. Stepping from the jet way tunnel into the vast space of the terminal, her eyes quickly surveyed the scene. No Ethan. She was almost relieved—while on the plane she decided if Ethan was a no-show, all of her efforts from that moment forward would be dedicated to saving her marriage to Randy. She'd go to counseling, attend those touchy-feely weekend marriage workshops—where you're required to fall backwards, blindfolded, trustingly into your husband's arms, she'd even hire a professional coach to observe them interact in their home—whatever it took, she'd do it.

Her high heels clicked on the tiled center aisle of the terminal as she confidently walked toward baggage pick-up. She caught the attention of both male and female arriving and departing passengers with her tan and firm body that glistened from the sparkly moisturizer she used—part of the Hanky Panky line of products. From behind her she thought she heard the sound of running footsteps, so she naturally stepped aside to let the tardy traveler pass. As she did, Ethan was finally able to catch up to her, slightly breathless from his jog.

"You're the fastest Sheila I've ever met. And the most beautiful one, too!"

"Ethan! You're here!" was all she could say, realizing the master plan to preserve her marriage was now crumbling apart. Ethan put both of his hands on her shoulders and kissed her deep and long. After a moment, Tara remembered the public nature of this venue and she pulled away.

"I cracked a fat one nearly the entire drive to BWI just thinking about you," Ethan said. Tara looked baffled at his remark. Ethan clarified, "Sorry dear, that's Down Under slang for a sporting a woodie." Tara blushed at his words. At least for now, her fate was sealed. Saving her marriage to Randy could wait—perhaps for a month or two, she thought to herself. *What's wrong with getting a little attention once in a while?*

"When can we be alone again? I can't be with you here," Tara asked breathlessly as she scanned the terminal, praying there was no one nearby who she recognized.

"Soon, very, very soon," replied Ethan, the glint in his eyes combined with his sexy smile made Tara quiver down to her toes. "I'll call you when I get back in the states."

Ethan then gave her a tiny squeeze on the forearm and sent her on her way.

Life Observations from Vic the Maintenance Man:
"My goal is to always keep flying under the radar. Don't want anyone knowing my business and I don't want to know theirs. Just keep your head low and don't make trouble—that's my motto."

Chapter Eleven:
"In like a lion…out like a lamb"

Chrissie awoke with a start. She glanced at the alarm clock on the nightstand. Three o'clock a.m. *Damn. I'll never get back to sleep now,* she thought. The dream was so vivid and lifelike she was afraid Nathaniel was actually in the bed with her now. Guiltily, she checked to confirm that she was still properly positioned on *her side of the bed* and that Seth was sleeping soundly nearby, mouth guard and earplugs firmly in place. When they first married, Seth drew an imaginary 'line' down the middle of the mattress and told Chrissie "that's your side, this is mine, don't cross over."

Chrissie could almost taste Nathaniel's kiss on her lips. She had been having 'sex dreams' for weeks now. Despite the inconvenience of the sleep disruption, she hoped that this meant her hormones were getting a healthy jump start after being suppressed for so long.

"This is insane. I've got to get him off of my mind," she thought to herself. Sleep was impossible; she was still flushed and drenched in sweat from all the excitement she had just experienced in wide screen full Technicolor. She shook her

head in amazement—her dream even had a music track—
"Julia" a Beatles tune from the White Album. Slipping out
of bed, she silently crept downstairs and signed onto the
computer in the kitchen. The email she wrote to Nathaniel
was simple and discrete—it had to be since she knew Seth
monitored every move she made on the computer.

> *Nathaniel,*
> *I hope you get this message this morning. I need to talk to*
> *you about another project at Archimedes. Can you meet*
> *me at the Whorl after drop off?*
> *Thanks,*
> *Chrissie*

At four thirty a.m. she turned off the computer and
began quietly cleaning her house. Sleep was hopeless now.
Her decision was made. She had to talk to Nathaniel and
move on with her life.

Since returning from the girl's spa weekend back in
February, Chrissie had spent most of her waking hours
doing everything she could to avoid thinking about him
or bumping into him on the Archimedes school campus.
The payback was a steady stream of clandestine nighttime
'meetings' she continued to have in her sleep.

Chrissie confided her worries to Ayani, "How will I get
this man off my mind?" she asked her friend one morning
when they were alone at the local coffee shop.

"There's nothing wrong with sex dreams, Chrissie,
especially if you're not getting any at home," said Ayani.
"They are as normal as brushing your teeth or putting on
your shoes each day."

"These are different. They're deep and passionate and
filled with emotions, not just pure, raw sex," said Chrissie.

"Last night's dream was amazing...," Chrissie began, then drifted off as she recalled the vivid details in her mind.

"Go ahead, tell me," encouraged Ayani.

"All right. We were on our honeymoon in this adorable post and beam creek front cabin in Sedona Arizona," Chrissie began. "I've never been there, but somewhere in the back recesses of my unconscious mind I must know this would be a fabulous place to visit."

"Actually, that's a great place for a honeymoon. Was the cabin near the male and female vortexes? You might have gotten pregnant with all that earth energy swirling through you," Ayani said.

Sometimes Ayani's words went right over the tops of the heads of people, and this was no exception. "Um, I don't really know," said Chrissie, "It was near a place called the Enchantment Resort, I think." Ayani just smiled with the profound understanding that Chrissie was getting powerful messages from beyond. Yes, the Enchantment Resort was right next to the male and female energy vortexes located in Sedona and unbeknownst to Chrissie, this would have been the perfect spot for a honeymoon.

"Nathaniel and I were lying naked on the huge, oak four post bed, it was in the fall, I think, since there was a fire in the little wood burning stove. He was gently running his fingers over every part of my body---no sex yet, just touching. It was better than sex. Kind of like the "old people sex" that I read about in some magazine. You know, people in their 70's consider "sex" to be anything with simple skin to skin contact," Chrissie said. Ayani gave her a little smile, and then motioned with her hands to continue.

"Yeah, yeah, sorry. Then Nathaniel slowly kissed me all over—like *everywhere*. Every inch of my body felt his kisses. They were tender and sweet and loving. It was agonizingly awesome and left me begging for more! Then a stupid car alarm in the neighborhood went off and forced me to wake up. I was nearly dying for completion," Chrissie said. "I can't take it anymore. These dreams follow me around all day long!" Then she hit upon an idea.

"Hey, Ayani, if he's dating someone else, I'll be forced to forget about him. That's it—I'll find him someone to take my place."

Now, after another night's sleep interrupted by phenomenal sex dreams, Chrissie pushed the "send" button to email the simple letter to Nathaniel. She then surfed the internet for several dating websites and wrote down the more palatable options, those she thought would appeal to Nathaniel's discriminating taste in women. ShakespeareLovers.com and TeacherplusTeacher.com were at the top of her list. She was amazed when she saw the dating website that appealed to the finite sect of the population of "tie dyed guitar playing veggie dead heads." *Maybe there's something for me called "women in their forties with one child who have joy sucking husbands,"* she thought. At four thirty a.m. she turned off the computer and began quietly cleaning her house. Sleep was hopeless now. Her decision was made. She had to talk to Nathaniel, give him a list of these websites and move on with her life.

―――――

A few hours later that same morning at preschool drop off, Tara had just parked her Chevy Suburban in the Archimedes School lot when her phone jingled signaling a call from Ethan. She hoped it meant he had finally returned to the states after spending weeks in New Zealand tending to his ailing mother. Tara looked over her shoulder and motioned to her son Clinton to remain quiet. He was still strapped into his booster seat and was squirming to bolt out of the car.

"She died? Oh my gosh! I'm so sorry Ethan," Tara said. "I was hoping you were back and your mother was healthy and well," she almost purred. Tara's southern accent always became buttery smooth when she spoke with Ethan.

"Yes, it's been a tough month for all of us—but I think Mum was ready. After all she was 92 years old. Tara, sweetheart, I'll be back in the states in a few weeks. It shouldn't take too long to settle her affairs and divide her estate with my brothers. We all get along quite well."

"Let me know your plans. The minute you learn when you'll return, I'll make special arrangements for my son. Ethan, *I need to see you.* I know you've got other things on your mind, but nothing's changed between me and Randy. I've been trying forever to fix our marriage, but it's no use. He hasn't touched me in years, he ignores every advance I make, he sleeps on the living room sofa, he stays out late, travels all the time, and *I think he's having an affair*! Ethan, I'm done with him."

"Darlin' you're on my mind all the time. Especially now. You know how it is when you lose someone you love, you don't want to take anything—or *anyone* for granted. I'll call you when I book my flight."

Tara hung up her cell and remembered with horror that Clinton had overheard her entire conversation. He had stopped wiggling in the booster seat and, of course, listened intently to every word. On any other day but this one, he would have been distracted by his toys, books, or snacks and not heard a word! "What did he understand?" Tara worried. "Will he tell his Dad what he heard?"

Tara's fears were confirmed as Clinton leaped through the entrance to the Kindergarten classroom and boldly announced to Mrs. Casper—along with all the other moms who were still standing in the classroom, "Mornin'! Guess what? Mommy said Daddy's having an affair. Mrs. Casper, what's an *affair*?"

Mrs. Casper looked sympathetically over at Tara, who stood by the door, her hands covering her eyes, completely mortified as the other moms gasped in surprise. Chrissie and her son Harrison arrived at just that precise moment, missing the announcement about Tara's affair, but witnessed the reaction of the adults gathered in the room. She was still furious with Tara for "winning" the Caribbean trip, but tried to keep her anger in check, as per Ayani's coaching. Nevertheless, she still slipped and said in passing to Tara, "Guess you were showing another one of your party tricks this morning. Don't you think these kids are a little young?" Tara pretended to ignore Chrissie's comment and fled the room.

After depositing her son in the Kindergarten classroom, Chrissie knew she had a painful mission to complete that morning. Chrissie walked across the vast lawn of the Archimedes School campus, headed toward the central gathering point of the campus known affectionately as the "whorl" where all the sidewalks connected in a spiral pattern to represent the nautilus shell—the school's symbol. The weather was unseasonably warm this March morning and Chrissie wasn't surprised at all to see a clutch of Brazilian nannies shivering in their micro shorts and tube tops as they tried to ward off their winter blues by catching a few rays of sun. Their group had grown in numbers over the winter. Now four of them sat comfortably in folding lawn chairs at the Archimedes "beach"—la playa. Chrissie remembered

Jonathan's special nanny who was probably six or seven months pregnant by now, and was hopefully enjoying the $100,000 payoff he gave her to return to her homeland. Chrissie caught a word or two of their conversation.

"Ele emocionado my mama como eu foi cambiante os nens cueiro," said one of the young, firm things. Chrissie loosely translated the nannies words as something about a man touching her breast when she was changing a babies' diaper.

"Ele esta uma gordura porcalhona," responded the other lovely young thing. Chrissie thought she deservedly called him a fat pig. *"Sounds like the dads are at it again with their young concubines,"* Chrissie thought to herself, disgusted with the perpetual cycle.

Rounding the side of the physics building, Chrissie paused momentarily to summon her courage. Then, all her strength dissipated when she saw Nathaniel, looking handsome and dapper as usual, wearing a tweed jacket with patches at the elbows and slightly faded blue jeans. He was sitting patiently on one of the marble benches positioned around the whorl. She smiled at him and lifted her hand in a feeble wave. Even from this distance she could see his eyes sparkle and his dimple appear when he smiled. *"Damn, why won't Seth just choke on his mouth guard and quietly die in his sleep?"* she wished.

Nathaniel jumped to his feet and gently touched Chrissie on her forearm. She saw that he had a sealed envelope in one hand. She hoped it wasn't for her, but she knew otherwise.

"Hi, it's great to see you," he began. "I feel like you've been avoiding me lately."

"Actually, that's partly true…Nathaniel, I'm a mess. I'm so confused, I…," her words trailed off. He reached again to touch her arm, but she pulled back, conscious of their public meeting place.

She continued, "I think about you all day long, I dream about you all night."

Nathaniel's interest was peaked, "You dream about me? What kind of dreams?"

"You're *really* good in bed, that's all I know," she said with a slight smile. In typical Chrissie fashion, always trying to make light of a tough situation, she added, "I love that special thing you do with your foot," she giggled.

"My *foot*?" now Nathaniel was laughing, too. Sensing that the tension was eased and the ice was broken, Chrissie continued more confidently now.

"I care about you. I know you're my soul mate. I think we'd be great together...but I can't do it. Not *now*. I've got my son. I've got my house. And I've got my miserable husband. Nathaniel, you need to move on. Find someone. Be happy."

Crestfallen, the wind knocked out of him by her words, she could see his demeanor immediately change as his shoulders slumped and the smile vanished from his face. He discretely tucked the envelope in the pocket of his blazer. Chrissie guessed she'd never discover the contents.

"Okay, if that's what you want." He stood to leave.

"Wait, I have something for you." She handed him the slip of paper with the names of the dating websites written down. He grimaced when he realized what these .com sites were.

"Um...thanks," was all he said. Then he turned and walked away. Head down, crushed, Chrissie thought that Nathaniel looked like an innocent lamb forced to march to the slaughterhouse.

"*Oh God*, what have I done?" Chrissie said to herself as she watched Nathaniel slowly walk out of her life.

Life Observations from Vic the Maintenance Man:
"All this texting and sexting is getting our kids in big trouble. Before they push that send button, they better think about all the consequences. Kids can get hurt. Really hurt. It used to be you could pass a simple note, or send a letter, and not be afraid it would end up on YouTube the next day."

Chapter Twelve:
Back in the Saddle Again

Back in March the four women had once again resumed their power walks around the Archimedes School neighborhood. The arrival of warmer weather not only enticed the daffodil bulbs to show themselves outside in public, but also a few humans, too. Jodi was thrilled. Over the winter she had gained so much weight she looked like a swollen sausage stuffed into her $200 dollar jeans. Hardly anything in her closet fit properly anymore, but she refused to buy up to the next dress size. Instead she rummaged around in the dark, dusty corners of her wardrobe and found a few pairs of those loose, elastic waist linen pants—the same kind you'd find on middle aged, neatly coiffed women who dabbled in selling real estate for a hobby. If she couldn't get the weight off, Jodi was worried that soon she'd be sporting boxy, over-sized linen jackets layered over a shirt imprinted with tiny watering cans or gardening tools. So much for wearing Manola's with form fitting jeans!

The weather on this first day of April—April Fool's Day, was almost balmy. A warm breeze drifted up from the south, giving people the opportunity to shed a few layers of tired winter clothing. Everyone, including the Archimedes School preschoolers, wanted to take advantage of the warmer weather. Trying to get the children into their Kindergarten classrooms was akin to herding cats—they kept running this way and that way, sniffing the air, batting at whatever, and chasing each other. After finally securing their children in the classroom, Chrissie, Jodi, Charleigh and Ayani convened at the familiar picnic table outside of the preschool building and warmed up for their morning walk by performing a brief stretching routine—reminiscent of that first day of school when Tara joined them on their walk. Yet on this day, Tara was no where to be found.

Vic, the maintenance guy, sauntered casually by, presumably on his way to work on a repair project somewhere on the school's campus. Not knowing he was approaching from the rear, Jodi almost kicked him in the groin when she lifted her leg behind her to stretch her hamstring muscles.

"Ooops, so sorry Vic," she said. "I almost made you a soprano." At that moment, Jodi noticed that an unusual number of the Archimedes male staff members appeared from nowhere to suddenly pop by to observe their stretching techniques. Even a creaky, old and gray physics professor strolled by and sucked in his gut while winking at the four women.

"Hey girls, let's get outta here before Charleigh's body makes all of these teachers late to class while they wait for their hard-ons to settle," said Jodi.

"Hey—don't blame me! All of you look awesome—even edible," replied Charleigh with a laugh. Chrissie, who was normally right in the midst of any banter, remained silent and contemplative.

"What's up with you these days, Chrissie?" asked Jodi, as they began their morning power walk. "I've never seen you so down."

"It's just the reality of my miserable life sinking in," she replied. "Remember back in February when you all found that note Nathaniel Anderson had written to me? Jodi, you told me to be very, *very* careful even though you think Seth is a complete asshole."

"Yes…so?" asked Jodi.

"Well, I was totally obsessing about him—to the point where I was having amazing orgasms in my dreams—oh, *sorry*, over sharing," Chrissie giggled slightly, then continued. "I had to move on, or else I knew my marriage was over. So, I told him to find someone else using one of those internet dating services."

"He must have been royally pissed," interjected Charleigh.

"No, *crushed* would be a better word for it. But, last night when I was shopping at the mall, I saw him at the bookstore's café with another woman. I hid in one of the aisles, pretended to read a book, and tried to casually spy on them. That's when I noticed I was in the Women's Sexuality aisle and had absently grabbed a book on *positions preferred by lesbian lovers*. With my luck, I figured Astrid and Crystal would be there just at that moment to witness my reading preferences!" Jodi was pleased to see that Chrissie's sense of humor had returned.

"Anyway…they were having coffee and they may have simply been old friends—or then again, he may have actually met someone on that *damn* TeacherplusTeacher. com website," Chrissie said.

"Chrissie, it's better this way, dear. You need to let it go, or rather let *him* go. You didn't want to get involved with a *teacher*, anyway. Too much of a financial struggle. Plus, Seth would go ballistic," Jodi said abruptly. Jodi had a way of cutting to the chase quickly.

"Yeah, you're right, if I'm stupid enough to have an affair, I should at least pick one of the Archimedes School millionaires—maybe I'd finally get a pair of Jimmy Choos out of the deal," Chrissie concluded with a giggle.

"Speaking of millionaires, did you get the invitation to the Archimedes School fund raising auction?" asked Charleigh. "Mine came in the mail yesterday."

"I got mine, too," added Jodi. "If you two girls haven't seen it yet, just wait 'til you read it—you'll flip," Jodi said as she pointed to Chrissie and Ayani. "I'm not going to give any details, this is something you've got to see first hand."

Chrissie groaned, then oozed with sarcasm, "Oh goody, another opportunity to remind half of the parents just how rich the other half is."

Life Observations from Vic the Maintenance Guy:
"Hey, almost getting kicked in the nuts is worth a close up look at these fine looking MILFs. God, I love my job!"

Chapter Thirteen:
The Archimedes School Fundraising Auction—"It's A Small, Small World"

Ayani was beside herself. *"How on earth did this invitation get approved by the Archimedes School administration?"* she wondered. She had just received the formal gold embossed invitation in the mail that day. Ayani read the invitation for the second time to be absolutely certain of the inappropriateness of the language:

The Archimedes School Annual Auction
"It's A Small, Small World"
A night of exotic foods, unique music, and
colorful costumes,
Designed to celebrate the diversity of humankind
Please dress as your favorite ethnic group
$150 per person
Baltimore Aster Hotel
Saturday April 25th, 7:00 pm
Prizes awarded for the best costumes

It was the part about 'dressing as your favorite ethnic group' that stunned Ayani the most.

"Which clueless, lame-brained, wacko parent created this theme?" Ayani asked Chrissie over the phone. Ayani was so unusually agitated, Chrissie's ears perked up at when she heard her tone of voice. *"Wow,"* she thought to herself, *"I've never heard Ayani this upset."* Chrissie proceeded cautiously, not wanting to make the situation worse.

"I bet you can guess. It was Leona Lowe, of course. She's always trying to demonstrate how politically correct she is. Remember her Native American sign language fiasco from the Kindergarten play? She's trying to redeem herself," replied Chrissie.

"But, how did the invitation get past the school's administration?" asked Ayani, still incredulous at the faux pas.

"Rumor has it that this was her first draft. It got rejected by the Head of School, Mr. Greenspring. Unfortunately, the first version was mistakenly sent to the printer and mailed to the parents before the error was caught. Mr. Greenspring had eliminated the line about the dress requirements for the auction," Chrissie explained. Since she was on the PTA she was often a good source for the inside scoop.

"I guess it's too late to do anything now," Ayani said. Now Chrissie heard frustration mixed with sadness in her voice, Ayani's anger was already dissipating. Chrissie could also hear Ayani inhaling and exhaling deeply, using the same calming techniques she taught her yoga students.

"Somehow I doubt there will be a lot of white people dressed as migrant workers from Mexico—or, worse yet, smeared in black make-up wearing tap dance shoes. It's hard to show off your Donna Karan outfit if you've got a burlap sack of beans on your back.

"I guess you're right, Chrissie, we'll just have to see."

━━━━━━━━

Ultimately Chrissie was right. During the weeks preceding the auction the buzz around school, in the coffee shops, and at the nail salons was, "how will I wear that new dress by *so and so* and still have a chance at winning one of the prizes?" Ayani noted a unique sociological pattern that no matter how rich or entitled, people still wanted to win something for free.

Since Annapolis is a relatively small town—at least compared to D.C. or Baltimore, with a limited number of resources, the Archimedes School parents knew they had to schedule and book any special personal services well in advance. The minute the invitations arrived in the mail, hundreds of phone calls were placed for limos, hair dressers, masseuses, facials, appointments with private shoppers, baby sitters, jewelers, *and* their plastic surgeons—after all, two weeks was surely enough time to let any swelling and bruising subside—especially for those quick touch-ups with injections of collagen or botox. This year the competition was especially tight for arranging these special services since another private school in town had scheduled their auction on the exact same night. Because of this scheduling conflict, it was not unusual for parents from both private schools to offer promises of huge tips and bonuses to anyone in Annapolis who serviced the public in one way or another. One high-in-demand dermatologist received an all expense paid trip to Las Vegas. Another popular and very handsome gay 'hair designer' was promised a walk on role in a local movie producer's upcoming film. It was rumored that one mom even offered a special 'oral' treat to the first physician who would do a mini liposuction on her abdomen—to prevent the 'cottage cheese' from showing through her body clinging dress.

On the morning of the auction, Ayani still didn't know what she was going to wear. Derrick was set. The dry cleaners had delivered his freshly pressed tuxedo the afternoon before. She pushed the button that automatically rotated the racks of clothing in her expansive closet. Armani, Vera Wang, D&G, Diane von Furstenberg, Laundry, Escada, whirled by—an entire section of her collection was devoted to formal wear. The name brands didn't impress her, but as the wife of a partner who worked for a prominent law firm, she had to play the role. Then she remembered a lovely dress she had purchased on a visit to Taos, New Mexico, handmade by an up and coming Native American designer.

"Perfect! It sure beats wearing my fringe moccasin boots and deerskin dress," she said to her husband who sat on the edge of the bed and sipped his morning coffee, watching her every move.

"You know, honey, that's a great idea. Instead of dressing like 'our favorite ethnic group' we should support the talents of all the people of color," replied Derrick. "I wish I had a FUBU tuxedo."

"There's still time, I'll see what I can find," said Ayani.

Later that night when the limo arrived, Charleigh, Chrissie, Jodi and their husbands were already inside, martini glasses in hand. Ayani noted that Seth sat a few feet away from Chrissie, looking miserable and stiff as usual—as if this evening's event had somehow completely interrupted something much more important in his life. Ayani thought to herself, *"Maybe some yoga lessons or massage therapy might help that poor, angry man."* Then uncharacteristically, her next thought was, *"No, that stick is too far up his butt to ever budge, not even yoga could loosen him up."*

Derrick looked handsome and dapper in his new tux and Ayani was drop dead gorgeous in the handmade silk screened evening dress—the colors and pattern were reminiscent of a southwestern dessert at sunset. In fact, everyone—including Seth—could have graced the cover of the monthly Annapolitan magazine that kept locals informed of the latest news, parties and society events.

"Hey, what gives? None of you are dressed like the invitation required," asked Ayani.

"Last night Chrissie had an idea. She made each of us hats," said Jodi as she reached into a large Nordstrom shopping bag. Inside were four identical straw cowboy hats with about twenty miniature flags glued in place on the top, each flag representing a different country.

"I went a little crazy with the glue gun," she giggled. "I think that between the four of us, we've got most of the population of the world covered."

"Chrissie, this is great!" exclaimed Ayani. "So politically correct of you!"

"We only have to wear them during the contest judging," Chrissie added.

"I can't wait to see what the rest of Archimedes will be wearing," said Ayani, a hint of sarcasm in her voice.

As the limo approached Baltimore, they could see the rotating search lights from miles away signaling their destination. When they arrived ten minutes later, they saw that the front entrance to the hotel looked like something from Oscar night in Hollywood; a long red carpet was cordoned off by velvet ropes; potted palm trees decorated with sparkling white lights lined the pathway. A steady stream of limos unloaded their passengers at the entrance, greeted by two white gloved bellhops who politely opened the limo doors for the partygoers.

A seven piece Mariachi band played cheerfully as Ayani's group of friends and spouses passed by. Inside the hotel's lobby the theme song for the evening was piped in. Disney's "It's a Small World," was heard by every arriving guest. The massive banquet hall, with seating for at least 700 people, was breathtaking. Leona Lowe and her troupe of volunteers had done a superb job decorating the hotel's giant hall. It resembled a Moroccan marketplace, with stalls and tapestry covered tents lining the perimeter of the room, each tent or stall representing a different flavor of international foods or a different theme of alcoholic beverages from several countries. The variety of food and beverages was impressive and designed to appeal to everyone's unique palate. At the Italian booth the signature drink was a Bellini—puree of white peaches and champagne. Of course Ouzo and Retsina could be found at the Greek booth, while vodka martinis were properly represented at the Russian tent. The Irish booth featured the "Kiltlifter" cocktail, a blend of Scotch, Drambuie and lime juice. And the Hasidic bartenders at Israel's tent served up sweet, kosher Manischewitz wine.

Ayani and her friends arrived early enough to be able to avoid the long lines at the registration table (where everyone's credit card number was obtained and an auction number assigned). They quickly retrieved their first round of appetizers and cocktails, and promptly sat at their table so they could casually observe the evening's most entertaining event—watching the parents arrive in politically incorrect costumes.

"*Oh my God!* Look at Sheryl Waters and her husband," exclaimed Chrissie. Sheryl and Dave were dressed in the outfits worn by their household staff—Sheryl in the short black dress and apron worn by her maid and Dave was in the butler's get-up.

"Since when is 'hired help' an ethnic group?" asked Ayani, shaking her head.

Next to arrive were the two women known affectionately as the 'botox blondes' who were dressed in lovely, form fitting evening gowns while balancing large Styrofoam headdresses on their heads. One was shaped into a two foot tall Eiffel Tower and other was formed into the Arc de Triomphe. Ayani nudged Chrissie when she noticed that 'boob lift' had been added to their body treatment regiment—both of the women had breasts so perky one man mistakenly attempted to set his cocktail on one set of them.

Deborah Brown entered the room wearing a boldly printed African Caftan, draped casually over a sparkling designer dress. Perched on top of her head was a large water jug that she carefully held in place with one hand. Charleigh and Ayani whispered to each other as she passed nearby, certain that they had heard the whimper of a small dog echoing from deep inside the jug.

Astrid and Crystal had selected stunning Geisha girl costumes and shuffled into the room with their large American feet stuffed into tiny wooden platform sandals. Their eyes batted seductively from behind Japanese fans at every man that crossed their path. Appreciative whistles came from many husbands in the crowd.

Tara and Randy's arrival caused quite a stir amongst the gathered parents. With her flawless body presented in a Samba Dancer costume, the men in the room enjoyed an eyeful of skin as Tara paraded by. The crop top with puffy sleeves barely contained her perfect breasts and the slit in the ruffled skirt was so high up her thigh it left little to the imagination. Randy looked like a singer from the Village

People, stuffed into a Matador costume, the body fitting pants accentuated his 'package' so well that every woman (and even a few men) found themselves staring at his crotch. Seeing the four beautiful women at the table, Tara nodded in their direction and gave them an awkward smile, then squealed and ran to air kiss Astrid and Crystal, who were sitting at an adjacent table. *Where were their spouses? Don't they ever come to any function? Ayani wondered.* Also at their table were older couples Ayani didn't recognize. *Must be parents of upper-school students,* Ayani thought to herself. Ayani knew nearly every parent in the preschool, lower school and middle school, thanks to having her daughter Sara who was had been there for years.

While Ayani was busy pondering the identity of the two older couples, Chrissie gasped audibly when she saw the next group to arrive. A clutch of twenty or so Archimedes school teachers entered the banquet hall en masse. Their individual $150 dollar entry fee was waived by the PTA so that they could attend. Positioned safely in the middle of the group of teachers was Chrissie's friend Nathaniel, who entered the room walking hand in hand with the new, spunky red headed Librarian the school had recently hired. Ayani grabbed Chrissie and gently massaged her arm, whispering in her ear so Seth wouldn't hear, "It's okay, dear, it's okay." Chrissie immediately excused herself and ran quickly to the women's room presumably to pull herself together.

Finally, the last to arrive was a mysterious woman, who looked vaguely familiar to many in the banquet hall, yet was massive beyond belief. Easily exceeding 350 pounds, her swollen body was packed into a red floral Hawaiian MuuMuu, probably chosen because it was the only clothing that could possibly fit her impressive size.

Grabbing Chrissie as she exited the women's powder room, the colossal woman said, "Chrissie, how the heck are you?" Chrissie looked puzzled for a brief moment, then identified the voice.

"Oh my goodness! *Laurel Somerville*! You're back!" Chrissie exclaimed. Overhearing Chrissie's words, parents politely began to applaud as Laurel Somerville proudly thundered by, each of her steps reverberating throughout the room.

"Looks like she found a replacement for Percoset," said Jodi with a chuckle. "I told you narcoset addictions were brutal to beat."

The applause for Laurel was interrupted as the recessed lights in the banquet hall dimmed and a bright spotlight illuminated 'center stage' in front of the room. Leona Lowe stepped purposefully into the spotlight to begin her welcoming speech. Ayani was so stunned by Leona's choice of costume—that she couldn't focus on a word she said.

"Blah, blah, blah, *welcome everyone*, blah, blah, *hope to raise $700,000*, blah, blah, blah, *exceed last year's total*, blah, blah, *everyone reach deep into your wallets*, blah, blah, *isn't everyone excited?* blah, blah," Leona said.

Leona Lowe had layered a torn and filthy, almost toxic, plaid flannel shirt over the top of her beaded Versace evening gown. In her hand was a dirty brown paper bag containing a bottle of some sort of hard liquor. Parents seated near the makeshift stage area immediately put their hands to their noses to mask the smell that swirled around her. Apparently Leona had 'borrowed' the shirt from a homeless man sitting outside one of the Washington, D.C. Metro subway stops. Leona dramatically waved her hands high in the air to silence the crowd. Then she resumed her monologue. When Leona started to explain her rationale for the costume she had chosen, Ayani decided to pay closer attention to her speech. *This is going to be good*, Ayani thought to herself.

"You may be wondering why I've chosen a 'monetarily challenged person' as my favorite ethnic group," Leona began.

Ayani whispered in Chrissie's ear, "She means *broke*."

"These 'outdoor urban dwellers' sometimes intentionally choose this existence and they enjoy the nomadic lifestyle. But typically their state of 'mental exploration' makes it difficult for them to fit properly into our society," Leona continued.

Ayani continued the translation, while Chrissie began to giggle uncontrollably, "She means they are *completely insane* and *can't find a place to live*."

"We may be envious of these 'mortgage free living' conditions—imagine not having to pay that $7,000 payment to the bank each month," (many parents in the room nodded their heads in agreement). "However, many of these residentially flexible persons might simply be living on the streets due to some sort of uncontrollable addictive behavior."

Ayani leaned over to Chrissie to say, "*meaning that they're wasted out of their minds!*" Chrissie's hysterical outburst caused heads to turn her way. Scowling faces looked at her with disdain at her 'rudeness.'

"I implore you, the next time you see someone with 'special living conditions' please reach deeply into your pockets and drop them a ten dollar bill, or a twenty, *or if you have it handy*, a crisp one hundred dollar bill." Several heads around the room nodded in agreement. Ayani was surprised. These Archimedes School parents must be caught up in the spirit of giving on this special fundraising evening.

"With that in mind, LET THE AUCTION BEGIN!" Leona announced. Cued by Leona's words, the professional auctioneer emerged from a side door in the banquet hall and stepped into the spot light. The mariachi band trumpeted the auctioneer's arrival.

A huge recessed screen sank down from a slot in the ceiling of the hotel. The first auction item of the evening was projected onto it in a full thirty foot high Technicolor display. Ayani sucked in her breath as the giant image of an adorable Cairnoodle filled the screen. *"It's a sweet, little puppy, not an **auction item**,"* Ayani thought to herself. Ayani recognized this puppy to be a designer mixture of Cairn Terrier and Miniature Poodle. The expected sound of 'oohs' and 'aahs' filled the room as Archimedes School parents melted at the sight of this white, fluffy puppy that will *bring complete and total happiness to your home*—as the auctioneer positioned. Cardboard auction numbers began to wave wildly in the air. The bidding began at $500 dollars and within seconds had increased to over $2,000 dollars. The auctioneer interjected, "Who could possible deny their child this wonderful pet?" The bidding frenzy continued until it reached the ridiculous sum of $5,550 dollars. When the auctioneer proclaimed "SOLD, the Cairnoodle puppy for $5,550 dollars to Debra Conroy," the parents in the room burst into applause, those sitting near Debra reached out to give her a warm, appreciative hug. The tone of joy and giving had been established for the evening.

At their table, Ayani, Charleigh, Jodi and Chrissie monitored the auction items and their purchase price— Ayani had brought along a tiny pad of paper and pencil to keep track of the Archimedes parent's buying power for the evening. Thus far, none of the auction items appealed to any of the women at the table. Plus, Chrissie knew that nothing was in her price range. All she could afford would be to 'go in on something' with the other women.

The auction item list and tally totals were already quite impressive:

Walk on role in hot new crime television series, shot in Baltimore--$4,300

Private jet trip for ten people to anywhere this side of the Mississippi--$45,000 *(Complete with in-flight personal chef, masseuse, nanny and gift baskets)*

Seven night stay at an Archimedes parent's villa in Tuscany (for up to 18 people!)--$22,000

One private guitar lesson by famed guitarist Jimmy Page of Led Zeppelin--$7,500

The toilet seat from Bob Dylan's house--$5,100

Cognac and cigars with Bill Clinton (offered by a Archimedes School parent who had a key position on Bill's campaign team)—Astrid's winning bid of $25,800 was met with squeals of delight by several Moms who begged to join her.

A 4 ct diamond from a recently divorced Archimedes school mom--$99,000 (Ayani noted that several Archimedes Dads commented that the winning bidder got a great deal)

A foreclosed house in the Annapolis neighborhood of Eastport, sight unseen--$200,000 (the auctioneer described it as needing lots of tender, loving care, i.e. *dilapidated shack*)

Used five year old 500 series Mercedes, donated by the Archimedes parent who owned the local dealership--$41,000

Accompanying local sportscaster and former Orioles pitcher, Bud Brooks, on an Orioles road trip, hang out with team in dugout and locker room--$11,200

Tastefully done nude photo session for your wife with a world renowned photographer—the winning $18,000 dollar bid came from Jonathan Smyth for his loving and dedicated wife Ellyn (she had yet to discover the true story behind the sudden departure of their Brazilian nanny, but he continued to compensate for past guilt).

Seated nearby at an adjacent table was Tara who nearly missed seeing the next item projected on the gigantic screen. She was just about to slip off to the ladies' room before the bidding began on the Archimedes School class gifts—the ones made by the students, (she was determined to lay claim to the Kindergarten quilt)when an image of a sleek Italian mega yacht appeared on the screen. From the corner of her eye she saw a familiar figure standing on the main deck, smiling that beautiful dimpled grin while leaning casually on the polished teak railing.

The auctioneer began, "The next item for your entertainment pleasure is a three night weekend cruise on this magnificent 115 foot yacht, where your captain will take you anywhere you like, a gourmet chef will prepare every meal, your personal assistant will attend to every need, and an assortment of watercraft toys will be at your fingertips. By the way, before the bidding begins, the captain would like you to know that this fabulous Italian yacht, just two years young, is available for sale to a discriminating buyer, such as yourself."

Tara immediately sat down. Stunned, her mind whirled with a thousand thoughts. *"Ethan is home! Why didn't he tell me? What the hell was Ethan doing? Why did he choose the*

Archimedes School auction as a donation for using his boat? Was Ethan trying to send her a message? Did he want her to bid on the weekend cruise? Or, perhaps this was simply a marketing strategy and he wanted to find a boat buyer with this captive audience of affluent buyers?" It only took Tara a split second to respond.

She leaned into her husband and announced with determination in her voice, "I'm bidding on this trip."

"Over my dead body!" Randy responded. "I have no interest in stepping foot on that yacht to spend an entire weekend with you and some of your crazy female friends."

"No problem, *dear*, you don't have to go anywhere with me, as *usual*," was Tara's terse reply. The bidding began in earnest, with the starting bid placed at $9,000 dollars. Tara immediately countered with a $10,000 bid. The auctioneer nodded in the direction of an anonymous bidder in the back of the banquet hall and asked, "Do I hear $11,000?" Tara tried to see who she was bidding against, but the lighting was too dim in the far reaches of the room. She could vaguely make out a shadowy figure of a man who continued to counter her amount with a subtle waive of his hand. Back and forth the bidding went, higher and higher. The tension in the room was building just as high as the monetary count. When the number hit $77,000, Randy stood up to protest and left the table in disgust.

"You're not spending my money on that friggin' boat," he shouted as he stormed out of the room. As Randy left, he brushed past the anonymous bidder in the back of the room. Hearing his outburst, several people seated nearby gasped in dismay. This was getting nasty.

Astrid leaned over to Tara and quickly suggested, "Perhaps you should throw in the towel—that or you'll lose your husband over this." Conflicted, Tara didn't have time to hesitate. The bidding was nearly over.

"Going once, going twice…" the auctioneer said, pausing momentarily to give Tara a chance to counter the final bid. Reluctantly, Tara shook her head from side to side. "SOLD for $77,000 dollars, the weekend yacht cruise goes to bidder number 857—the gentleman in the back of the room."

The Archimedes School parents burst into frenzied applause. Nearly every head turned to acknowledge the winning bidder, who had silently and mysteriously slipped from the room. He was nowhere in sight, causing speculation amongst the gathered parents.

"Who was that?"

"Did you recognize him?"

"I couldn't see the guy from here."

"Do you think he was that rock star parent?"

Tara was filled with a mix of sadness, frustration, and confusion at the missed opportunity of seeing her New Zealand friend again, when her phone suddenly rang from her tiny sequined purse placed in the center of the table. She was about to ignore the call, when she realized it was singing that happy familiar tune.

"*ETHAN*!" she exclaimed out loud causing Astrid and Crystal to smile quizzically and stare at her with curiosity, "What a coincidence, I was just bidding on the cruise you donated. I'm so sorry, *I lost*!"

"No you didn't, dear girl. *I* was the winning bidder. It's my little gift to the Archimedes School," replied Ethan in his smooth Aussie accent.

"Oh my God! That was you! You're home? You were *here* at the auction?"

"I thought I would surprise you. It worked, didn't it? I got here in Annapolis yesterday, saw the announcement about the auction in the local paper, and made a quick decision to offer up the boat. When will you be ready to join me on our little trip around the Chesapeake?" he asked eagerly.

"How about next weekend?" was her breathless response.

"Done. I'll have the ship ready and waiting at city dock by Friday night," Ethan said. Tara clicked her cell phone off and gathered her things in preparation to leave. Ethan had completely changed her focus. She didn't care that she wasn't going to bid on the prized Kindergarten quilt. She didn't care that Randy was missing from the banquet hall. She had had enough excitement for one evening. Tara just wanted to go home. She'd wait in the lobby until the auction was over and then get a ride home with Astrid and Crystal—or perhaps hitch a ride with Chrissie and the other girls in their limo—perhaps they would take pity on her sitting dejected in the lobby. Just as she began to push back her chair, she was gently tapped on the shoulder from behind. Jonathan and Ellyn Smyth were standing behind her. Jonathan opened his mouth to say something, but stammered gibberish instead.

"Tara, um, um, I think I just, um, saw your husband, oh...*never mind*," Jonathan began, but was too embarrassed to finish.

"Honey, move aside, let me talk to Tara," said his wife Ellyn. Ellyn leaned closer to whisper directly into Tara's ear, "I hate to break the news to you, but Jonathan just caught your husband in the men's room fooling around with another guy. Here's the best part—it was with one of the firm, young bellhops from the hotel!"

"It's true, Tara. From under the bathroom stall, I saw *four* feet in there and their pants were down around their legs," added Jonathan. "Apparently they had just finished and didn't hear me enter the restroom. When Randy stepped out, he tried to cover his face when he saw me."

"Oh yeah, Tara, I'm pretty sure your husband left the building. I saw him heading to the exit," said Ellyn.

Enjoying the scoop, Ellyn and Jonathan returned to their assigned table and apparently continued to spread the word, since their table mates promptly turned to look in Tara's direction.

For twice in one night, Tara sat there stunned. *That explains everything*, she thought to herself. *He's gay.* Numbed to the core, Tara remained frozen in her seat throughout the rest of the auction and tried to avoid the barrage of curious stares shot her way from the other Archimedes parents in the room. News this juicy traveled like lightning.

Meanwhile, Ayani calculated that the Archimedes School had already raised more than $500,000 and the night was still young! The next items for auction were meant to show the parent's loyalty and commitment to the school—*how much would you actually pay to be Headmaster for a day?* $2,000 dollars was the final bid. The bidding got really ugly when it came to acquiring your personal parking space at Archimedes School for the year. In the end, the Cadillac Escalade owner outbid the Land Rover owner for the $7,500 privilege of always knowing where to park in the perpetually congested lot.

The much anticipated final auction item was the beloved Kindergarten quilt. Each patch, handmade by the five year old students, represented some sort of mathematical symbol, simple equation, or formula. Creation of the quilt was a long standing annual tradition at the Archimedes School and typically generated more than $50,000 in donations. Also, the family that bid the winning amount always enjoyed bragging rights in future years. "*They're the family that bought last year's quilt!"* one mom would announce jealously to another mom. This simple statement was enough to immediately establish their financial prowess within the parent community.

The auctioneer asked for two volunteers to bring the famed Kindergarten quilt into the room. The two math teachers and former lovers Berri Franconi and Matt Worthington quickly shot their hands into the air, exchanging knowing looks as they scampered from the room to retrieve the quilt.

"I wonder if they're at it again?" Ayani asked Chrissie.

"Hey, I'm out of the loop now. How would I know?" Chrissie replied, while surreptitiously glancing over at Nathaniel and his date.

A chorus of "ooohs" and "aaahs" filled the room as Matt and Berri brought the colorful and charming hand made quilt to center stage.

The bidding began in earnest, with the first bid cast at $25,000 dollars. Steadily the number grew, each parent outbidding the next. At the $35,000 dollar mark, several parents dropped out of the contest saying the number was 'too rich' for them. The final two bidders remained in the contest, each determined to get that quilt. "$49,000… $49,500…$50,000…$50,500…," the auctioneer continued to play the parents back and forth. Unexpectedly, one of the bidding dads announced, "Screw this, how about $65,000 dollars." The auctioneer jumped on the opportunity, "$65,000 dollars going once, going twice….SOLD to Sheryl and Dave Waters for $65,000 dollars—the highest price ever paid for the Archimedes School Kindergarten quilt." Shrieks, squeals and thunderous applause filled the room. Once the applause had died down, Leona Lowe resumed her position in center stage.

"Thank you for coming....blah, blah, blah...most successful auction ever....blah, blah...," Ayani was again able to effectively tune out Leona's mindless dribble.

Suddenly an irritated female voice from the back of the room yelled out, "What about the prize for best costume?"

"Oh my goodness, I completely forgot," was Leona's reply. Reaching into her pocket Leona retrieved a tiny, velvety jewelry box—that by now had presumably absorbed the smell of Leona's costume. Popping open the box, Leona revealed a stunning diamond encrusted nautilus pendant, representing the Archimedes School's symbol. "The PTA committee had an extremely difficult time deciding which Archimedes School parent should receive this prize for their creativity. But, at Mr. Greenspring's *insistence*, we decided the most politically correct costume was Chrissie Thompson's international hats which she designed for herself and three of her friends. Chrissie, would you please join me up here?"

Charleigh, Jodi and Ayani jumped simultaneously to hug their dear friend as she left the table to receive her prize.

"Thank you, this is *really* lovely," said Chrissie as Leona placed the pendant around her neck. The spotlight made the tiny diamonds sparkle and dance. Walking back to her table, an Upper School parent felt the need to touch Chrissie's hand to inform her that the necklace was worth at least $10,000. Chrissie wasn't concerned about its monetary value, she was just proud to wear something that represented the school she cared so much about. Once seated, her friends reached out to hug Chrissie again.

Ayani completed her tally of the night's donations and let out a long, "whewwwww," when she arrived at the final number.

"$635,000 dollars!" Ayani announced. "That's a record breaker, for sure."

"Not bad for a night's work," said Charleigh. As the other women gathered their things and prepared to leave, Chrissie sat quietly and appeared to be deep in thought. From the corner of her eye she watched as Nathaniel left the banquet hall with his librarian date.

"I gotta say," Chrissie began, "I'm really conflicted. I loved getting this beautiful necklace and it's great that so much money was raised for the school, especially since a good portion goes toward financial aide. But, it's so hard to observe this conspicuous display of wealth. It gets me every time...Maybe I won't go to next year's auction."

"Oh, sweetheart, I think you forgot. You signed up to be in charge of next year's auction!" said Jodi. "You're the *committee chairperson*."

"*Damn!* Next time I raise my hand to volunteer again, I need one of you to grab my arm and tie it behind my back," Chrissie groaned. She scooped up her purse and linked arms with Charleigh, Jodi and Ayani as the four women led their husbands out of the nearly empty banquet hall and headed down the red carpet to their awaiting limousine.

Life Observations from Vic the Maintenance Guy:
"You know what the guys on the maintenance crew say—the bigger the boat, the smaller the penis. Ha! I've got a thirteen foot Boston Whaler. Think that might impress some of these folks around here?"

Chapter Fourteen:
Preparing to Launch

The travel arrangements for the upcoming weekend were all made. Tara's son Clinton would fly south to spend a three day weekend with his grandmother who still lived in Texas. Tara booked his flight despite his Kindergarten teacher's concerns that Clinton would miss the end of year K-Calculus final that was scheduled for that Friday. These test scores were critically examined when placing the child in the appropriate math curriculum for first grade. A make-up test was scheduled for the following week and Clinton's K-Calculus workbooks would be sent in his luggage to Texas. Tara hoped her 75 year old mother would be up to the task of tutoring her child.

Randy's weekend 'business trip' had been scheduled months ago, so he was unable to watch their son while Tara 'busied' herself over the next three days. He was headed to Myrtle Beach, South Carolina to play golf with a gentleman who was the founding partner and owner of a successful paper manufacturing company. Serious talk of a merger and acquisition was being bantered about with the paper manufacturing company being a perfect compliment to Randy's toilet paper import and export business.

In the meantime, tensions between Randy and Tara had reached a fevered pitch. Randy was furious with Tara for two reasons. Number one, she told him that she, Astrid and Crystal were taking the PJ (*private jet*) to L.A. for a weekend of star gazing and shopping on Rodeo Drive. This of course was a lie to cover Tara's weekend rendezvous with Ethan on his yacht. Tara wasn't worried about being discovered. Randy had never checked up on Tara before, why would he start now? Randy's response was, "First you try to spend my money on that stupid yacht trip at the auction, and now you'll be spending thousands of dollars while shopping in California on some skimpy, overly revealing, slutty outfit." And number two, Tara had caught Randy surfing an online gay chat room. He scrambled to cover and was livid that she had been snooping. He claimed he accidentally stumbled on the site when he mistakenly typed in the word 'gay' for 'bay'—he said he wanted to check the 'fishing conditions' on the Chesapeake Bay and said he hoped to chat with some local watermen. Tara scoffed at his excuse, reminding Randy that he had never fished a day in his life, and the local, salty crabbers probably didn't spend a lot of time chatting on the internet. Tara had yet to mention that she was well aware of the incident in the men's bathroom during the Archimedes School auction, thanks to the ever so helpful disclosure by Jonathan. But, by catching him on the internet, her suspicions were confirmed. *"Now I know why he hasn't touched me in years. At least it wasn't anything I did do or didn't do to screw up this marriage,"* she comforted herself with the thought.

Randy was scheduled to pick up their son at the airport on Sunday night, since his plane from Myrtle Beach would be arriving at approximately the same time as Clinton's flight from Dallas. Tara wouldn't return until mid-morning on Monday, leaving Randy with the job of getting Clinton ready for school. It would be the first time Randy had ever performed this parental responsibility. He was always so consumed with work and business travel he never been faced with the opportunity to immerse himself in the daily parenting activities.

All Tara had to do was pack a few warm weather outfits for the upcoming weekend with Ethan. The weather forecaster on the local Baltimore news channel predicted 'unseasonably hot' temperatures this early in May. Tara had just the right thong bikini for the forecast.

Now, everything was set. Nothing could go wrong now.

Life Observations from Vic the Maintenance Guy:
"I like my simple life. I go home at night, forgot about work, crack open a beer, and grill some burgers for me and my son. Most teenagers won't give their parents the time of day. At least my kid still likes to talk to his old man—even though he does call me a fossil sometimes. Hey, is it my fault I can't see the letters on the damn cell phone to send him a text?"

Chapter Fifteen:
A Parent's Worst Nightmare

When Tara arrived at school the next Monday afternoon to retrieve her son Clinton, her entire body was still quivering from the weekend of intense lovemaking she had just experienced with Ethan. Evidence of their passion could be found in every nook and cranny of that massive yacht. A private investigator would have had a field day documenting the chronological order of events. "This stain is the oldest—hummm—smells like red wine, yup, it all started right here in this lounge chair on main deck." Then, following the path of undergarments down to the stateroom, he would add as he picked up something in his hand, safely protected by a latex glove, "You can tell by the crushed, and, uh yuck, *damp* magazine on the floor that they never made it onto the bed." The PI would have further discovered an assortment of unusual objects, from feather ticklers to partially eaten edible underwear, strewn about the boat. "Yup, no doubt about it, these two people had *way* too much fun to be married to each other."

On Sunday afternoon, during one crazed and slightly tipsy moment of dancing to Bob Marley blasting from the speakers on the top deck, Tara unknowingly knocked her iPhone overboard. Unfortunately, just as her phone slowly sank from sight into the murky water of the Chesapeake Bay, Randy was trying to inform Tara that the merger deal with the paper manufacturer was being struck that night and he wouldn't arrive in Baltimore until Monday morning. The last words of his message were, "I'm sure you or maybe one of your *dear* friends can pick up Clinton at the airport tonight. Handle it. This deal is too important to miss."

That Monday afternoon at Kindergarten pick-up, Tara had an unmistakable glow about her. Her short and flirty, cleavage revealing halter sun dress, coupled with the pheromones that emitted from every pore in her body were attracting men like moths to a night light. One distracted physics teacher buzzed about her so much that he forgot he had neglected several 9th graders who were scheduled for tutoring that afternoon. Later, when he came to his senses and remembered his responsibilities, the physics teacher walked into his classroom now filled with entangled and partially disrobed teenagers who had decided to study *human biology* instead. Vic and the entire maintenance crew quickly decided that *now* was the perfect time to finally fix that lock on the Head of Preschool's door. Why it took five men to perform a simple repair was anyone's guess?

It was Mrs. Casper's surprised look—which immediately morphed to a look of fear and concern, that caught Tara off guard.

"Clinton's not here. He never showed and we didn't get a phone call. The preschool office has been trying to contact you all day," said a breathless Mrs. Casper.

"*What!* Where is he? Where's Randy? He was supposed to pick Clinton up at the airport last night!" exclaimed Tara. The hot, burning sensation of raw panic was now rising to her shoulders.

"We've called your home, your cell, no response. We didn't have any contact information for your husband."

"*OH MY GOD!*" was all Tara could say. A cluster of Archimedes School moms had now gathered around her, bonded together by the primal and overwhelming fear of a parent's worst nightmare—a missing child. Chrissie immediately grabbed Tara by both forearms and flew into action, the months of subtle and simmering hostility between two women instantly abated.

"Let's get to your house, maybe someone's been trying to call you there. I'll drive," said Chrissie. By now Tara was shaking so uncontrollably her car keys had fallen from her hand and dropped to the sidewalk. Scooping up the keys, and then taking Tara by the arm, Jodi said with authority in her voice, "I'm coming, too." Charleigh and Ayani jumped quickly into action and assumed the responsibility of watching Chrissie's son Harrison and Jodi's daughter Faith.

"*Go!* Don't worry. We've got your kids. We'll be at Charleigh's house with your children," said Ayani to the other women who were already sprinting toward the parking lot while half carrying, half pulling Tara along.

"Please call us the minute you hear something," added Charleigh as she held Chrissie's son by the hand.

The five minute drive from the Archimedes School in downtown Annapolis to Tara's house in the Murray Hill neighborhood seemed like it took an eternity. Tara's hysterical tears caused her black mascara to drip in rivulets down her checks. Chrissie pushed her ancient Volvo to the fastest speed she dared to go on Annapolis' narrow streets, while Jodi called 911.

"I need to report a missing child," Jodi began. The horror of her words caused Tara to wail even louder. "*SHHHHH*, they can't hear me," said Jodi, attempting to quiet Tara momentarily.

"He's five years old, blond hair, blue eyes, about forty pounds. He may have been lost at the airport last night," Jodi described. "Tara, any birthmarks?" Tara nodded and tried to form the words, "A mole on his right shoulder—shaped like a tiny dollar sign." Overhearing this, Chrissie simply shook her head. Jodi wrapped up her report and snapped her phone shut.

"They're sending the police right away. They'll meet us at your house," announced Jodi.

The brakes on Chrissie's Volvo screeched to a halt in Tara's driveway. Tara's hands were still shaking so badly that her attempt to use the key to open the front door was futile. Frustrated at the delay, Jodi grabbed the keys from her hand and gently, but authoritatively pushed Tara aside.

Once inside the foyer, Tara immediately noticed that fifteen messages were on her answering machine. Deleting past the mundane, "Your prescription is ready at the pharmacy," and "Tara, let's do girl's night at Pacific Rim on Saturday," from Crystal, Tara finally hit pay dirt with the message, "Mr. and Mrs. Hunter, this is Detective Peterson from the Anne Arundel county police. We have your child in protective custody here in the Annapolis headquarters. He was found abandoned at the BWI airport on Sunday night at 8:15 p.m. We've been trying to contact you and your husband since last night."

Relieved beyond belief, Tara collapsed onto the antique Persian carpet gracing her hallway. Coincidentally, at that precise moment, Randy's car pulled up behind Chrissie's Volvo in the driveway. Oblivious to the drama that had just unfolded, Randy waltzed into the house, golf clubs in one hand, carry on luggage in the other, and proclaimed, "I'm home. I got the deal. As of last night we now own the largest…" Seeing Tara's crumpled body on the floor, he stopped in mid-sentence.

"What the hell's going on?" he demanded. "Were you out drinking with your wacko female friends again?" Then, looking at his watch, he added, "And, it's only three thirty in the afternoon!"

Jodi seized the moment to explain, "Randy, she fainted. She was in a blind panic about your child. Apparently Clinton was left alone at the airport last night and he's now in protective custody with the Anne Arundel county police. I don't know what happened, and *maybe I don't want to know*. But, the police will be here in a minute to explain."

Randy opened his mouth to speak, but was interrupted by a firm knock on the door.

"Mr. and Mrs. Hunter, I'm Detective Peterson. I was just about to issue a court summons for you when the dispatcher handed me this 911 call. We have your son in protective custody after he was found abandoned at BWI airport last night. Your son is safe and in good hands."

Tara jumped to her feet and attempted to hug the Detective. "Thank you, officer…" He held up his hand to cut her off.

"I'm here on official business ma'm. In accordance with provision 37-1-606 of Maryland law, I must inform you that you and your husband are required to attend the next regularly scheduled weekday session of juvenile court, which will be tomorrow at 9:00 a.m., where a hearing will be conducted to review this civil child protective case. Your son will remain in protective custody until that time." The detective handed Randy an official document imprinted with the Maryland state seal.

"What the *hell* happened with airport personnel? Aren't they required to monitor children flying alone?" Randy angrily asked. His face was flushed with rage.

"Sir, that's a separate issue we are already addressing with airport management. It appears your child started to walk off with someone he thought was his father—some guy in a business suit," replied the Detective. "Fortunately, he brought your child to Airport Authorities. Neither one of you were anywhere to be found."

Hearing this, Jodi whispered with her hand cupped to Chrissie's ear, "If Randy were around more, maybe his child would recognize him."

This is ridiculous! We want our son back NOW!" Randy demanded. "We haven't neglected him or abused him— it was a simple miscommunication between me and this *woman.* She should have been at the airport." Randy pointed to Tara, apparently too angry to call her his 'wife.'

Tara began to wail again, "*I want.... my....baby.*" She pulled on the detective's sleeve, "Can I *please* see him?" she begged.

"No, ma'm, you'll be in court tomorrow morning. By law, we cannot hold your child in protective custody for more than 72 hours without a hearing. You'll be able to see your child then. I suggest you contact an attorney as soon as possible." The detective turned smartly on his heels and marched deliberately down the front sidewalk to the awaiting dark blue sedan parallel parked on the street. Throughout this entire exchange with the detective, Jodi and Chrissie attempted to melt into the plaster walls of the house. They wanted to be anywhere but here. This was too much of an intrusion on Randy and Tara's private affairs. At least they knew that little Clinton was safe. When the detective walked to his car, Jodi and Chrissie followed stealthily behind.

"Don't tell anyone about this," Jodi said to Chrissie.

"I won't have to, someone else will do it for me," Chrissie said, as she nodded in the direction of another Archimedes School mom, who was standing by the road scooping up the miniature poop from her miniature pincer, slack jawed with the news she had just overheard.

"At least the boy is safe," were Jodi's final words as they drove away.

Life Observations from Vic the Maintenance Guy:
"I figure I've always got to be the best Dad to my kid. After all, he's the one who will choose my nursing home someday."

Chapter Sixteen:
Paying Penance

The white brick façade of the Juvenile court house building was austere and imposing, triggering Tara's knees to tremble and shake as she approached. She lost her footing momentarily on the cobble stone pathway leading up to the entrance, causing the three inch heel of her Pradas to nearly break. *"A broken heel on that damn boot is what got me here in the first place,"* she thought to herself, remembering the first time she met Ethan. She had spent a sleepless night wracked with guilt over her rendezvous on the yacht with Ethan this past weekend which was ultimately the cause for her being in court this morning. And, she was also consumed with worry that the master in charge of the CINA hearing (Child In Need Of Assistance) would recommend that their five year old child be sent to foster care, or worse yet, a group home, due to their negligence at the airport on Sunday night.

Randy and Tara had retained the best attorney in town and had already spent nearly six hours preparing for this hearing the night before. In those hours Tara had become intimately familiar with every section of Maryland law for the protection of juveniles and she had learned the terminology that would be bantered about during the court hearing process, (CINA, adjudicatory hearing, congregate care—group home, Section 5-706, parental treatment plan, etc…) At $350 dollars an hour, Tara and Randy felt their money had been well spent on their attorney and they were confident they were in good hands. Their lawyer was also quite pleased that his brand new clients had already provided him with enough money to put a down payment on that $23,000 eighteen foot jet boat for his fifteen year old son.

Their hearing was the first scheduled on the court docket and immediately upon arriving the bailiff called out their names.

"Randy and Tara Hunter, you are to appear in court room 2C, with master Johansson." Taking a deep breath, Tara attempted to muster all of her courage, keeping her head held high as she followed the bailiff into the court room. She had chosen the most conservative outfit she owned for this somber day. Somewhere in the dark reaches of her closet was a simple chocolate brown colored Valentino business suit—the one she typically wore for funerals. Normally she wore it without a blouse underneath, just a bustier, but today she selected a crisp white shirt that had recently been delivered from Neiman's.

Today, for the first time in her life, Tara set foot in a real live court room. It wasn't like those impressive and wood paneled court rooms she had seen on television which had a jury box and rows upon rows of seating benches for the public and press. Instead, court room 2C looked like a typical office building conference room with a ten foot long, Formica covered table positioned squarely in the middle, surrounded by eight swivel chairs, and at the head of the table was a special elevated area where the master or judge would preside. The room was illuminated by harsh fluorescent lights which served to emphasize the dark circles under Tara's eyes as a result of her restless night. Tara nervously tapped her perfectly manicured fingernails on the table, while Randy's knees jumped rhythmically under his chair. Anticipating the worst possible outcome, the two parents were a mess. Finally, after seeming to wait for an eternity, but which was actually just ten minutes, the master entered the court room. He was attended by the court reporter whose job it was to document every word spoken within the four walls of that room. The master was a squirrelly little man, mid-fifties, with oversized and outdated aviator glasses perched on his beak-like nose. He appeared to be more nervous than either Tara or Randy, but when he spoke his voice was rich and full and the words he said carried power and authority which sunk deeply into Tara's soul.

"Mr. and Mrs. Hunter, I have reviewed your case and I believe that while this was a serious infraction—leaving your five year old son alone in the airport while you were too preoccupied with your own lives to insure his safety and well being—this was a *single* incident. I see no record of prior incidents and your child appears to be well cared for and loved. While I'm not certain that your child takes priority in your lives, I cannot find you guilty of the failure to provide adequate care for your child. Therefore this investigation is concluded and the charge of neglect is unsubstantiated."

Tara began to speak, but with a wave of his hand she was quickly silenced by her attorney. From behind his hand his whispered to Tara, "Whatever you do, don't say a word. This is going well."

"However, I will recommend that both of you participate in a treatment plan designed for educating parents in the hopes that this type of incident will never be repeated. Mrs.

Hunter, would you please stand? Tara willingly obliged, pushing the chair from the table to stand which subsequently give the master an eye full of her lovely thigh that slipped from behind the six inch slit in her skirt. Distracted for a millisecond, the master began, "I have assigned you to spend twenty hours as a volunteer houseparent in a congregate care facility for children which is located conveniently right here in Annapolis." Remembering the terminology she had just learned last night, she recalled that 'congregate care' meant 'group home.' While Tara's face remained stoic, inwardly she was revolted at the prospect of working with sticky, dirty, rambunctious, street urchins who were forced to live in a group residence. She promptly sat down, furious at the master for assigning her such a disgusting penance. Her lawyer leaned close to whisper his comment, "You were very, very lucky."

Next came Randy's assignment. "Sir, would you now stand?" asked the master. "Mr. Hunter, I am ordering you to work in the Social Services Administration offices on May 20th and May 21st to assist the staff with any child protective cases that arise on those two days."

Randy began to object and started by saying, "Your Honor, I have meetings…" Their attorney yanked on the sleeve of Randy's suit, silencing him quickly.

"Your Honor, we may have another suggestion for how Mr. Hunter can benefit the child protective system. If we may meet in your chambers, I think you will find the solution most agreeable."

"Fine. See me immediately in my chambers." Then rising to leave, the master added, "I hope to never see you in this court room again. Do you understand?"

Both Tara and Randy nodded sheepishly, avoiding the master's gaze by looking deliberately at the Formica table top. In the master's chambers Randy and Tara's attorney presented the alternative proposal.

"$25,000 dollars *would* go a long way toward helping 'Caring Sisters' with the much needed roof repairs and getting the playground equipment up to safety code. But, will Mr. Hunter adequately learn his lesson by simply donating his money toward this congregate care facility?" asked master Johansson.

"I assure you he will," responded their attorney. Randy obediently reached into his suit jacket and quickly wrote the check for the $25,000 dollar donation, anxious to be done with the legal process.

Once they were dismissed and out of ear shot from the master, Tara started to whine, "This is not fair, you write a check and I have to be exposed to all those nasty, low life children," she said with a sneer, her southern accent no longer sweet and inviting.

"Tara, money talks, you know how the world works," was Randy's terse response. "Anyway, you have more time on your hands—God knows what you do all day while Clinton is in school."

"I bet it's a lot more productive than what you're doing on the computer with those 'Chesapeake Bay' chat rooms all night long," Tara replied, with bitterness and sarcasm spilling out from every pore. Randy didn't bother to respond, but Tara could see the muscles tighten in his jaw as he hurriedly walked ahead.

Leaving Tara to negotiate the bumpy cobblestone path on her own, he announced over his shoulder, "Why don't you hike up your skirt a few more inches? Maybe you'll entice one of these nice young lawyers to help you?"

"No thanks," she retorted, "Perhaps *you'd* like to try walking on these damn stones wearing my shoes next time.

Who knows? Maybe cross-dressing is another passion of yours," Tara said with a sly smile. Randy just shook his head. As they approached Randy's car, Tara's newly purchased iPhone rang—to replace the one that was mired somewhere on the bottom of the Chesapeake—a gift this morning from the ever-efficient Jodi who had arranged with an Apple salesperson at the mall for a new phone to be programmed and delivered to Tara. It was their lawyer. He had remained back in the court house to wrap up a few details of their hearing.

"Sorry to bother you, but the master was wondering *when* you'd like to pick up your child," he said, "I need you back here."

"Oh *dang*! I forgot," said Tara, suddenly aware of her oversight. "My poor dear baby," she said as she immediately turned around to retrace her steps and head in the direction of the Juvenile Court.

Life Observations from Vic the Maintenance Guy:
"What's all this crap about karma? Though, I'm pretty sure I've already paid my dues from past lives. Hey, wouldn't it be funny if some of these parents end up as maintenance workers for some private school in their next life?

Chapter Seventeen:
Row, Row, Row Your Boat

At the sight of seeing his mother for the first time in days, Clinton's initial reaction surprised and hurt Tara. Expecting the typical after school greeting of him running joyfully to leap into her arms, Tara was rebuffed by her five year old as he grimaced, clasped his arms together across his chest and turned his back to her. Tara's lawyer stood outside in the hallway and watched the scene unfold; it reminded him of something akin to a Hallmark special on television. Tara cautiously placed her hands gently on her son's tiny shoulders.

"Honey, I'm so sorry. Mommy loves you more than anything in the whole world."

"Why'd you forget me?" was his pitiful reply. His words were barely audible.

"We didn't forget you, baby. Your Daddy thought I was picking you up at the airport, and I thought your Daddy was there," she said. "It was a horrible, horrible mistake." Clinton began to well up and cry; his little shoulders shook with each sob. Distracted by his tears, Tara was finally able to coax him to turn so she could enfold him gently in her arms. They held each other with the intensity that can only come from that profound mother-son bond, both were sobbing now. Not wanting to break the physical bond, Tara picked up her son and carried him from the county court offices. Clinton willingly wrapped his arms around her and clung in a tight death grip.

Later that night, Clinton was securely tucked into his brand new trundle bed which had been ordered weeks ago and, of course, was delivered to their home right smack during the turmoil from the last 48 hours—somewhere in between the Anne Arundel county police officer visiting their home and the meeting in their living room with the $350 dollar an hour lawyer. Tara and Randy wordlessly watched their sleeping child, their relief and love for this little boy palpable in the air between them. They knew a fundamental shift was about to occur in their relationship with each other—it had to.

"Randy, now what?" asked Tara, after they had gently closed the bedroom door and sat across from each other at the dining room table, the dinner plates were still there with half eaten remnants of their comfort meal of macaroni and cheese and hot dogs.

"I know I'm not leaving our son. I don't want to be one of those part time dads who only sees his child every other weekend and on Wednesdays," Randy stated.

"Clinton will probably be our only child—since you'd rather not have sex with *me*," said Tara, not wanting to go into the details of Randy's entanglement with the 'opposite team.'

"Perhaps we can figure something out and keep Clinton's life as normal as possible," Randy said. Tara put her head down and nodded in agreement. With that, Randy and

Tara began to hash out the revised rules of living their life together, *yet separate*, under the same roof for the sake of being with their son.

The next day, Tara thought the nightmare from the past forty eight hours was finally behind her. She was very, very wrong.

The events that unfolded that morning on the Archimedes School campus were analogous to a wild life documentary on Animal Planet where the victim is stalked, encircled, and then pounced upon by a voracious feeding frenzy of hungry prey. Tara needed assistance and she needed it fast if she was to survive:

8:00 a.m.—Tara and her son Clinton warily approached the clutch of angry preschool moms assembled near the entrance to the Kindergarten classroom. Rumors of Tara's brush with the law had spread faster than a wild fire fed by ferocious winds. However, the accuracy of those rumors was in question based on the high pitched level of hatred emanating from these normally sweet, maternal creatures.

"How dare you lock your child in a closet for two days?" said one mom.

"I heard you burned Clinton with cigarettes. How *could* you?" said a furious mom.

"What kind of drug did you give him?" hissed another.

"*Slut*," was all another mom could utter.

"Go back to Texas, we don't want your in-bred, redneck kind in these parts," said one woman with her thick New Jersey accent.

8:03 a.m.—Tara and her son managed to navigate past the first angry mob, only to be assaulted inside the classroom with snide remarks mumbled under the breath of the other moms who lingered a little longer on this eventful morning, in anticipation of confronting the accused.

8:05 a.m.—Tara rushed from the classroom, tears streaming down her face, and bolted in the direction of her Chevy Suburban. The pack of hungry prey hurriedly followed.

8:05 a.m., three seconds later—Chrissie, Jodi, Charleigh and Ayani, who were preparing to leave on their morning walk, quickly intervened, physically blocking the prey from consuming their latest victim. Jodi, the bravest of the four, stood firm, one arm outstretched, and shouted, "STOP!" Obediently the voracious mob of angry moms halted in their tracks.

"Whatever you've heard is not true. I was there at the scene on Monday night—at Tara's house," said Jodi.

"Me, too!" said Chrissie firmly, "Tara's innocent. It was a simple miscommunication with her husband. You know how hard it is to contact the male species, especially when they're traveling on business. He didn't check his messages…it wasn't her fault…the child pick-up plans had changed!" Several heads nodded, somewhat reluctantly, in understanding.

Watching her friends come to her defense, Tara was filled with a mixture of gratitude and guilt. These women would never learn the real truth about the liaison with her New Zealand lover the night her son was left abandoned at the airport. Of course it was a miscommunication with Randy, but at the exact moment that poor little Clinton was sobbing in the terminal, Tara was certain she was fully engrossed in some sort of deviant sexual act with her paramour.

Jodi continued, "Her child is safe, he wasn't hurt. I think you owe Tara an apology."

Several women simultaneously mumbled the word "sorry" as the crowd halfheartedly dispersed. With the crisis averted, Tara could not contain her thankfulness.

"Why did you come to my rescue? That was so amazingly kind of you," she said sweetly, her Texan accent coming through loud and clear.

"Look, you've done some stupid stuff this year, but it doesn't mean you're a bad person," said Jodi. "We know you love your child. We also know these women were ready to taste blood."

"That's right, Jodi. These women may be preoccupied with getting their nails done and hair highlighted, shopping all day, and driving their Mercedes, but when it comes to protecting their children, the primal instinct kicks in," clarified Chrissie.

It was Ayani's turn to add her two cents, "Tara, look—it's a beautiful day. Why don't we try to put this insanity behind us and enjoy a healthy release of endorphins? A good, sweaty power walk will help reduce your stress."

Tara beamed at the four women and opened her mouth to speak, but was too overcome with emotion to continue. She could feel the tears pooling in her eyes. She joined them as they marched on silently across the Archimedes School whorl.

Finding her voice, Tara announced with the quiver of emotions still audible, "I can only walk for a short while because I have to report to Caring Sisters this morning. Its court ordered," she said with embarrassment, looking down at her feet.

"Tara, don't be surprised if this becomes a life changing moment for you," interjected Ayani. "I know a woman who volunteered to teach just one week of art classes for the children in that same group home. That was two years ago and she's still teaching there now. These poor children make your heart ache. You may never want to leave."

Tara didn't respond out loud but internally dismissed Ayani's remark. *There's no way I would ever intentionally expose myself to a house full of germ-ridden, poverty level kids,* she thought to herself. Little did Tara know the truth of Ayani's prediction.

———————

By 10:30 a.m., sweat trickled between Ayani's breasts and her tie-dyed yoga pants and jogging bra were moist with perspiration—the result of their fast paced power walk with Tara on this hot and humid morning in May. People were already complaining about Maryland's chronic problem with humidity, 'you can cut the air with a knife,' or 'it's not the heat but the humidity' but Ayani didn't mind at all. She had spent her whole life in this Mason Dixon line state and the summer wouldn't be complete without it.

Upon arriving home, Ayani decided it was time to finally face yesterday's mail which was still unopened on the counter. As usual there were more bills, more solicitations for donations to several worthy causes, an invitation to attend a special black tie event at the Smithsonian's Native American Museum in Washington, D.C. (Ayani and Derrick were major gift givers to this institution), a spring sale catalog from LL Bean, and a letter from the Archimedes School. Opening it, Ayani discovered that the letter was actually a questionnaire written by Laurel Somerville, who after returning from rehab, immediately immersed herself back into volunteer work at the school. *Good for her*, thought Ayani, until she began to read the contents of the questionnaire. Although the questionnaire was written with good intentions, somehow these over-privileged moms continued to miss the mark. The questionnaire was designed to ascertain two things, 1) the type of end of school year gift the parents would present to the Kindergarten teachers and 2) the venue for the Kindergarten class party. The questionnaire began:

1. Which gift would you choose for our beloved Kindergarten teachers?
   A donation in their name to the ivy league college of their choice
   A bird bath for the whorl, with their name on a gold plaque
   A tree planted in their honor, with their name on a gold plaque
   A bench placed in the whorl, with their name on a gold plaque

"What about a gift certificate to the mall?" Ayani said out loud to her empty kitchen. "These poor teachers hardly earn enough to feed their families, what do they want with a silly bench?" Ayani read the next two questions:

2. Where should the Kindergarten class picnic take place?
   The Downtown Yacht Club
   A Day Trip to Rehoboth Beach
   A 'Day on the Bay' on the 110 foot cruise ship, The Lady Maryland

Private tour of the Governor's mansion and picnic
on the grounds
A Day Trip to New York City, with tickets to a
Broadway Show

3. In order to cover the expenses of the teacher gift
    and Kindergarten picnic, we need to determine
    your gift-giving comfort level. How much would
    you be willing to pay?
    $50 dollars
    $75 dollars
    $100 dollars or more
    The sky is the limit

Blaze, the service dog, sauntered into the kitchen and
flopped down at her feet. He was originally scheduled to be
delivered to a soldier who lost his sight in the Iraqi war, but
an infection in his right paw sidelined the assignment at least
for now. Ayani didn't mind, she loved the dog's company.
Setting the questionnaire on the granite countertop, Ayani
muttered to Blaze, "Looks like Chrissie's got her hands full
again. But, she'll have this straight in no time."

Ultimately Ayani was right. By the next morning
Chrissie had successfully intervened and had contacted
every Kindergarten parent, or left messages with their
household staff or personal assistants, to inform them that 1)
the Kindergarten teachers would receive a sizable monetary
gift certificate to the local mall, 2) the Kindergarten class
'picnic' would be held on the 110 foot cruise ship (which
was actually owned by a Archimedes School parent whom
Chrissie convinced to donate the trip free of charge), and 3)
parents could make a *voluntary contribution* to the gift fund
in any amount that is comfortable to them. Chrissie also

requested a five dollar donation from every Kindergarten family to cover the cost of a buffet lunch on the ship for the children. By the end of the week, Chrissie had collected enough money to purchase a $500 dollar gift certificate for each teacher and she had helped the Kindergarten children create charming thumb print designs on ceramic flower pots as their personal gift to the teachers.

The morning of the Kindergarten picnic proved to be warm, but blustery and overcast. Ayani interpreted it as an ominous sign and she was worried from the moment she woke up.

"Not the best day for a cruise on the bay," she said to Chrissie, who was in the parking lot assisting with loading the children onto the yellow Archimedes School bus.

"Yep, the weather channel reported that there would be waves of three to five feet," replied Chrissie with concern in her voice. "Even a one hundred foot yacht will feel that chop."

As the bus drove away on the five minute jaunt to the Annapolis city dock, Ayani said, "Let's hope the children will be too preoccupied with playing to notice the swaying."

Each child was issued a day-glow orange life jacket as they stepped from the bus. The teachers then instructed the five year olds to line up in single file on the pier. The parents arrived separately by car since there was limited room on the bus. Nearly every child had some sort of adult to accompany them on this trip. Of course *moms* far outnumbered any other adult category, with a sprinkling of dads, nannies, housekeepers, and grandparents comprising the rest. Nearly every adult had a small cooler in tow or Gatorade bottle in hand, quite probably with the original contents drained and then replaced by some concoction of alcoholic beverage. Chrissie just shook her head in disgust and whispered to

Ayani, "What the heck, I guess its cocktail hour *someplace* in the world right now, isn't it?"

The captain of the boat stood on the bow to welcome the assembled crowd of children and adults. Scanning the collection of beautiful women standing below him on the pier, he mumbled under his breath, "Ooh baby, I'm the luckiest man alive." The twenty year old Brazilian nannies wore their usual summer uniform of body clinging micro shorts and tank tops. Several of the moms (Astrid and Crystal included) who *wished* they were still twenty years old were displaying well toned artificially tanned legs under short skirts. Their large American breasts jiggled slightly underneath tiny silk camisole tops. Not surprisingly, Tara was trying to remain under the radar, fearing an outbreak of any additional wrath directed her way by the mob of angry moms. Her outfit of choice was decidedly inconspicuous—loose tan Capri pants, a demure button up plaid shirt, and flat sensible shoes—she could almost pass for one of the moms from the private Presbyterian school in town. When the captain caught sight of Charleigh, the welcoming words he was about to say to the gathered crowd caught momentarily in his throat. Everything about her was white, blonde or gold—from her long, golden locks, to the body clinging off white Donna Karan wrap dress, to the gold shimmering espadrilles highlighting her perfectly polished sparkling toes, to the diamond encrusted bracelets she donned on her wrists. She literally had a halo glowing around her. The captain kept his focus in check, along with other parts of his body, by briefly shifting his thoughts to a memory of his seventy year old mother-in-law in a bathing suit. That usually did the trick. Then he began his speech.

"Welcome to the Lady Baltimore," he started. "I am required by Maryland law to review the safety regulations.

First, life vests must be worn by everyone under the age of twelve. The adult life vests are located under the seats in the main salon...." He continued to drone on for several more minutes, oblivious to the restlessness of the children jumping excitedly on the dock. Sensing her inability to contain the children any longer, and fearing some of the unruly boys would begin pushing each other into the water, Mrs. Casper waved her arms at the captain, interrupting his soliloquy.

"Excuse me sir, may we *please* board now?" she begged. The captain begrudgingly stepped aside to let the passengers cross the loading plank. Even though the ship was tied up securely at the dock, the yacht was rocked by the wind and waves.

"This is gonna be fun," said Chrissie sarcastically, already feeling slightly queasy. Seeing Chrissie's discomfort, Ayani quickly demonstrated the acupressure point for nausea.

"If you're feeling sick, just hold your wrist right here between your thumb and forefinger. It's just like those bands we wore for morning sickness when we were pregnant."

"Thanks, Ayani. I'll tell the kids, too. It looks like some of them are already turning green," replied Chrissie.

When the ship was untied and pulled away from the dock, the wave action could be more clearly felt. The bow rocked up and down over each four foot wave, causing the Kindergarteners to either squeal with excitement or scream in terror, based on their boating orientation. Those accustomed to weekend sailing trips with their parents were enraptured by the ships' roller coaster movement, those not so privileged cowered in fear with every wave.

Once the coolers were opened and the Gatorade bottles unscrewed, the adult party began in earnest up on the top observation deck. The sun had poked out from behind the clouds, warming the air enough to encourage the Brazilian nannies to remove their tank tops to reveal bikini bra tops underneath. Not surprisingly, the handful of dads on the yacht decided that *now* was the perfect time to climb to the top level to observe the 'natural floral and fauna' of the Chesapeake Bay. For some inexplicable reason, their interest in the bay's wildlife was suddenly peaked. Over the next half hour, the yacht continued on its perilous journey down the bay, pitching violently over every wave—which by now had grown to five foot swells thanks to a sudden squall that had blown in from the west. Meanwhile, down in the main salon, Mrs. Casper and the other Kindergarten teachers were trying to distract the nervous children by singing songs, however, their twist of lyrics may have been poorly chosen:

The bow on the boat goes up and down, up and down, up and down,

The bow on the boat goes up and down, all along the Bay.

The captain on the boat says 'the ship won't sink, the ship won't sink, the ship won't sink,

The captain on the boat says 'the ship won't sink', all along the Bay.

Unexpectedly, Chrissie's son Harrison bolted from the singing circle and ran to his mother's arms, screaming, "Mommy, the ship's gonna sink, the ship's gonna sink!"

"No dear, you misunderstood the song. It said 'the ship *won't* sink,' we'll be okay—everything is fine." Chrissie said, trying to reassure her child, not believing her own words.

Tara and her son Clinton, who had spent most of their Texan summers boating on the unpredictable Gulf of

Mexico, were well accustomed to the power of the seas. For once, Tara went to Chrissie's rescue.

"Sweetie, look out the porthole and focus on the shore, that will take away the feeling of motion," Tara explained to Harrison. "See, we're not far from land," she added. "Let's count the sea gulls." Both Harrison and Clinton enjoyed the counting game. After a few moments, Harrison settled down.

"*Thank you*, Tara," Chrissie said.

Seeing that there was still intense fear on the faces of other children, Mrs. Casper tried another distraction tactic. "Children, I think it's time for lunch!" she announced.

Mrs. Casper led the flock of hungry kids to the wheat free, dairy free, nut free buffet. Staring at the politically correct slabs of broiled chicken breasts, baked tofu, steamed cauliflower and mashed potatoes, there was no discernable difference in color from one food item to the next. Everything was a pale shade of creamy beige. Ayani and Chrissie dove into action and aided the teachers by piling the whitish substances onto each child's plate. The hungry children streamed by and forlornly accepted their plates of food with no sign of enthusiasm.

Chrissie leaned over to Ayani to remark, "Thank goodness I packed a peanut butter and jelly sandwich for the ride home."

Ayani added, "Carver's got one waiting for him, too."

Just as the last child was served, Charleigh's son Wilson began to have trouble breathing. Jodi, who was attempting to cut the rubbery chicken breast for her daughter Faith, saw Wilson struggle for air.

"Charleigh, is Wilson allergic to anything here?" Jodi barked while sprinting to the boy's side, her medical background immediately kicking back in.

"No, he doesn't have food allergies. Just a problem with latex," replied Charleigh who was trying to remain calm. She stroked her son's hair, while continuing to utter a steady stream of comforting words. Wilson's breathing became more labored and he was beginning to show signs of panic on his face. "Don't worry, everything's okay, mommy's here."

"Latex, huh," Jodi paused deep in thought for the briefest moment, and then jumped into action, "Quick! Let's get this damn PFD off his body." When they removed the life jacket they could see the early stages of hives spreading from his chest and down his forearms. Angry red welts were beginning to rise across his little body. Wilson's fraternal twin sister Honey stood nearby and began to sob with worry over her brother's condition. Charleigh's attention shifted from Wilson to Honey, then back to Wilson again.

Jodi shouted out to Mrs. Casper, "Get the epinephrine." Mrs. Casper stood still and looked slightly confused. "Get the *God damn* EpiPen, stat!" bellowed Jodi, unconcerned that the Kindergartners had heard her curse. Mrs. Casper rushed to retrieve the black leather Archimedes School pouch that contained a stash of EpiPens, band aids and assorted medicine, along with a print out of emergency contact information on every child. Jodi grabbed the bag from her hands and expertly and swiftly administered the dose of adrenaline directly into little Wilson's thigh. Within seconds the medicine began to counter the effects of the anaphylactic shock. By now Leona Lowe and her allergy prone five year old daughter were also by Wilson's side.

"See, dear, this is what would happen if you ever ate a peanut," Leona explained to her child as if they were watching a Discovery Channel documentary together.

"Look how swollen his lips are. Do you notice how difficult it is for him to breathe?"

"Leona—butt out. Your educational experience will have to wait. I'm dealing with an emergency here," instructed Jodi. Fortunately, the effect of the medicine was immediate. Within seconds the swelling around his mouth had reduced and the child's breathing pattern had returned to normal.

"He's stabilizing now. Adrenaline works quickly on the cardiovascular and respiratory systems. Plus it relaxes the muscles and lets the lungs do their job," explained Jodi. "But, we still need to get him to the emergency room for evaluation."

Charleigh, who remained relatively calm throughout her son's emergency, burst into tears, relieved that his life was no longer in jeopardy.

"*Thank you*, Jodi, thank you," Charleigh sobbed while hugging her friend.

"Mrs. Casper, get this boat turned around. We've got to get this child to the hospital," said Jodi who was calm and cool now that the crisis was averted.

Mrs. Casper obediently followed Jodi's orders—as did the captain of the ship, who promptly pointed the bow back in the direction of the Severn River, headed up the Chesapeake Bay to their Annapolis port.

The adults on the top deck, who were oblivious to the life and death drama that had just transpired in the main salon, began to shout their complaints.

"It can't be over already!" slurred one inebriated dad, his arm draped around Crystal.

"We were just about to do a conga line," said one of the Brazilian nannies.

"Party poopers," said another mom, who was precariously perched on the top deck's railing.

Overhearing their complaints, Jodi angrily climbed the ladder two steps at a time to give the partying adults a piece of her mind. Charleigh tried to stop her, saying, "Ignore them. They're wasted out of their minds." Jodi paused momentarily on the top rung of the ladder with the realization that any attempt to enlighten the intoxicated crowd was probably futile.

"You're right, Charleigh," Jodi began. "Why bother? They're too busy trying to cop a feel to care that we've got a seriously ill child down here, food so bland that prisoners would revolt, a thirty mile an hour squall that's kicking up white caps and four foot waves, and a captain too enthralled with all the exposed skin that he almost ran into the Thomas Point Lighthouse."

Jodi climbed back down the ladder to rejoin the other worried parents and panicked children huddled in the salon. One parent began a feeble attempt to sing 'Kumbaya,' but the combination of the roar of the wind outside and the heavy drone of the ship's engines cranked up to full throttle drowned out the words. Ayani and Chrissie continued to demonstrate how to counter sea-sickness using the acupressure point on the wrist. It worked for a few, while others heaved remnants of their beige lunch into the empty coolers left behind by the parents up on the top deck. Chrissie started to intervene, and then reconsidered.

"Serves them right," she said to Ayani who nodded in agreement.

The change in tone of the yacht's engines as they were powered down and the veer of the bow to a new direction signaled that the ship was approaching city dock. Parents and children who were hunkered down below in the main salon let out a simultaneous cheer that their life threatening picnic adventure would soon be over. Parents and nannies on the top deck let out a simultaneous moan.

Tara glanced out the porthole once again to get her bearings only to observe them pass within fifty feet of Ethan's immense yacht. It had been nearly three weeks since their weekend of passionate lovemaking on Ethan's ship, and the subsequent 'oversight' of leaving her child alone and abandoned at BWI airport, which, of course, resulted in the penalty sentencing by the Master. Tara had intentionally avoided answering any cell calls from Ethan, fervently closing the door on the prospects of continuing their relationship. She had learned her lesson. As far as Tara knew, Ethan was oblivious to the drama that had resulted from that weekend. Randy's penance of paying money to repair the roof on the children's home had also served the dual purpose of keeping the incident and their names out of the local newspaper. Fortunately their reputations within the Annapolis community were not tainted and their 'crimes' were not known beyond the tiny circle of preschool moms at the Archimedes School.

Tara gasped as she caught a glimpse of Ethan's handsome face. He was on the bow of his boat, preoccupied with securing the canvas deck chairs that had been blown around by the powerful wind gusts and only did a fleeting look at the Archimedes School picnic yacht as it meandered slowly by. He had no idea that his former paramour was within fifty feet of him. She knew she had fallen in love with Ethan and just three short weeks ago she would have been content to spend her entire life in his arms. But, her brush with the county court system was life-shifting for Tara. Now, the fear of having her baby placed in a group home usurped any desire for another rendezvous with Ethan—albeit the reality of having her child taken away was probably far fetched—

after all, if there was a future mishap, their financial prowess had almost limitless power to persuade.

For a fleeting moment, though, her passion once again overcame logic. Remembering the feel of his firm body on top of hers, and the warmth and fervor of his kisses, her loins began to quiver. She regained her composure and quieted her desire by inwardly repeating her new mantra for living:

"Keep Clinton, Stay married, Avoid Ethan"
"Keep Clinton, Stay married, Avoid Ethan"
"Keep Clinton, Stay married, Avoid Ethan"

The mantra had an almost hypnotic effect, reminding her of her priorities in life. Her loins ceased to quiver, her excitement was abated and she tried to ignore the moisture she felt between her legs. Once the ship docked she smoothed the wrinkles from her conservative tan Capri pants and re-fastened the top button of her plaid shirt that had come undone during the turbulent journey home, and inconspicuously departed the ship hand in hand with her son. Her focus was straight ahead as she refused any temptation to look back in the direction of Ethan's boat.

Life Observations from Vic the Maintenance Guy:
"I believe in the old rule of "lead us not into temptation"—then again, some of the people I see have their GPS permanently set on finding it."

Chapter Eighteen:
The Final Days

"For the most part it's been a good year here at the Archimedes School. You know, me and the maintenance crew have seen the usual stuff with only a few surprises," Vic began. "We've especially enjoyed some of the new MILFs who came to school this year. Hanging out by the preschool at drop off and pick up time is our favorite 'extra curricular' activity. *Man*, if I could only give the Admissions Department a hand with screening new student applicants—"Mom is a babe" would surely be high on my criteria."

"I'm glad my son Rob only has two years left at this school. Yeah, he's getting a great education, but the peer pressure from these overly entitled, upper-class kids is wearing him down—and my wallet, too. On my salary I just can't keep up with the others who are compensating for being absent parents by divvying out $100 dollar weekly allowances, setting up debit cards for their offspring, and wisking them off to Europe or the Caribbean for any school break. At least I'm here for my kid everyday, and not leaving my teenage son at home alone—while the wife is off doing *who knows what* and the husband is in some Board of Director's meeting in New York. I get the inside word on the goings-on with these Upper Schoolers, and it's pretty scary."

"There were at least five girls that got pregnant this year—and then 'un-pregnant,' one girl got busted for shop lifting despite the fact she had at least $500 dollars cash on her, and one guy is in rehab for a heroin addiction—yes, *heroin*! Apparently that's the new drug of choice for rich folks. Not to mention all the 'robo-tripping'—you know slugging down vats of cough medicine to get a buzz. That just turns my stomach!"

"But the best story yet is the one about the forty-eight year old, and *very*, very hot, Upper School mom who treated her son and ten of his friends to a *wine tasting party*. Then, when the young studs were properly inebriated, she asked the teenage boys to show their stuff. You know, whip it out! My son Rob wasn't there, but several of his friends were. At least that mom restrained herself and didn't touch the boys—or she'd be busted. But, the weirdest trend these days is all this lesbian love that's going around. I don't get it. When did fifty percent of the human population suddenly turn gay? Not that there's anything wrong with it, but of the forty or so young ladies at Archimedes who are graduating seniors, I've seen at least half of them making out with each other behind the school physics building. Maybe it's just a phase."

"My friend Chrissie updates me with the latest scoop in the preschool. They've certainly had their share of insanity, too. But with the younger grades, the children are normal, it's the parents who've lost their minds. Yeah, I've heard about the 'key parties,' the sex toy parties, the parent school pot lucks gone wild, and the outrageously over-the-top birthday and holiday parties for the kids. There's nothing new there. I've seen it all over the last ten years."

"There's only two weeks left in the school year and I've got my hands full with getting the grounds ready for all the different graduation events. Let's see, we've got the huge, did I say, HUGE, senior graduation ceremony. Then the fourth graders have a graduation event that marks the end of their lower school education. And, those cute little Kindergartners have their graduation tomorrow in the 'whorl.' I hope it doesn't rain like last year. We had forty wet little puppies scurrying for cover while their moms were too busy protecting their latest hair-do. I'm off to meet with Chrissie to finalize the details now," Vic concluded, as he headed in the direction of the preschool to meet his friend.

When Vic caught sight of Chrissie, she was standing alone near the preschool building and trying to be inconspicuous by wearing a baseball cap pulled down low over her face and she sported dark sunglasses, which was unusual for this overcast morning. Once he got closer and saw her face, swollen and red from crying, he knew something was horribly wrong.

"Vic, please no questions right now, buddy," Chrissie began. "I just need to focus and get this stupid Kindergarten graduation event planned."

———

Charleigh, Jodi, Ayani and Tara were still reeling from the story Chrissie had just revealed. Chrissie stayed back at the Archimedes School to meet with Vic and finalize the schedule for the Kindergarten graduation ceremony, so the other four women made plans to grab a quick breakfast. They convened in the coffee shop down the street to discuss the shocking news Chrissie had shared. They knew in their hearts that Seth was full of anger and hostility, but they never suspected he would actually become physically violent and hurt their dear friend. You could literally see the bruises made by each of Seth's fingers when he grabbed Chrissie's arms and pushed her against their bedroom wall. What inspired the violence? Chrissie wasn't exactly sure. She replayed the events of last night over and over in her head. Seth was as condescending as usual, questioning every action, again putting Chrissie on the witness stand as he interrogated her about the errands of the day.

All Chrissie said was, "Seth, I did everything you told me to do. Please, *please* stop all the questions! I can't take it anymore," she pleaded. That's when he grabbed her and slammed her against the wall.

"Don't you tell me what to do, you lazy bitch," he sneered with teeth clenched, three inches from her face. Chrissie was too scared to respond and simply collapsed in a heap to the floor when he left the room. Quietly and deliberately she moved all of her belongings from their bedroom into the guest room down the hall.

"I will never sleep with that evil son-of-a bitch again," she said to herself that night. The same sentence was later repeated to her friends the next morning. Charleigh insisted on running to her car to fetch her digital camera.

"If you ever go through an ugly divorce, you'll need these photos," Charleigh said as she quickly snapped front and back shots of her friend's arms.

Jodi said, "Honey, if this ever happens again, you've got to call the police, remove your child from the premises and get yourself to a safe house. Any one of us will do—you know we're here for you. Just the get the hell out of there."

Ayani and Tara chimed in, "Jodi's right," they said in unison.

"Girls, I'm still in shock and I don't know what to do," Chrissie began. "I know the marriage is over, but how, where and when will I go?"

"If you think he's going to be violent again, you've got to get out now. But, if you think you can wait a while, it's time to start squirreling stuff away," said Tara, her voice filled with care and concern. "My old friends in Texas starting buying dinnerware, utensils, linens, bedding, cookware and all the normal household necessities. They stored everything at my house and they hid money at my house, too. When they had enough items to live on, they moved out."

"Chrissie, let's go to Target today," Charleigh said. "I've got plenty of storage room in my basement. Bud won't know because he never goes down there."

Chrissie lowered her head down and silently nodded in agreement. Tears streamed down her face and fell to the ground. Her dear friends surrounded her with nurturing hugs and rested their hands gently on her shoulders and back—each woman wanting to touch her and comfort her in any way.

"Just let me get through this *God damned* Kindergarten graduation. Then I can move on," Chrissie said reluctantly, wishing her final PTA responsibility was already completed. She had much bigger changes and life altering events that lay ahead.

Chapter Nineteen:
Pomp and Circumstance

Vic and the maintenance crew had indeed done a superb job preparing the Archimedes School grounds for the graduation ceremonies scheduled for that week. New and fragrant mulch was neatly compacted into the recently weeded flower beds. Huge ceramic containers with freshly planted flowers graced the intersections of every pathway and were also placed in front of the entryways to each school building. The expansive lawn was patched and repaired from the wear and tear caused by nine months of children's feet scurrying this way and that. The Kindergarten graduation was the first of the three ceremonies scheduled for that dreadfully hot and humid June day. By 8:00 a.m., the temperature in downtown Annapolis had already risen to 85 degrees. The weathermen were predicting unusually hot summer weather for the area with temperatures in the 90's and a chance of severe afternoon thunderstorms.

Long white collapsible metal benches were set in a semi-circle around the 'whorl' and a temporary elevated stage was erected directly on the center swirl of the spiral pathway.

Chrissie watched as the maintenance crew struggled with installing the p.a. equipment and microphone stand which would be later used by the Kindergarten teaching team leader, Mrs. Casper, and the head of school, Mr. Greenspring. Two potted palm trees had been placed at both ends of the stage and swayed slightly in the steamy breeze. Once Chrissie personally saw to it that all preparations had been readied, she felt comfortable enough to head home to shower and change into something dressier than exercise shorts—hopefully she had a summer dress which wouldn't display the bruises on her arms. After a few days, the bruises were now faded to dull shades of brown, but were still clearly visible.

By 10:00 a.m. the Archimedes School Kindergarten parents had begun to arrive and were chatting while standing in the shade of the trees that dotted the perimeter of the whorl. As Chrissie walked to a particular willow tree to meet her clutch of friends, she overheard snatches of conversation from the assembled parents.

"Oh, Agape's going to simply love the new Yorkiepoo we bought her for graduation," swooned Sheryl Waters. "We got a great deal and only spent $3,000 dollars, including this fabulous Coach carrying bag! We really needed a new pet since the last one dove into the South River in April and never returned." Chrissie silently hoped her son Harrison would be happy with the $25 dollar gift certificate she got him from *Stuff Your Pup*, that store where you paid money to create your own stuffed animals.

"My husband and I bought our child that sports car in the Neiman catalog—you know, the smart red electric convertible," said one overly dressed mom, wearing her lavender Valentino sleeveless shift and matching high heeled sandals.

"We've been saving this adorable Hello Kitty diamond necklace we bought from that same catalog. Yes, it was a little pricey at $4,000 dollars, but our daughter Truth deserves the best," responded another fashionably dressed mom in her Burberry outfit. Sadly the heels of her brand new shoes were already coated in mud apparently as a result of sinking into the freshly watered sod patches.

Chrissie made a mental note to check the preschool playground today after the graduation festivities to look for the soon-to-be lost necklace. *"I could hit the pawn shop and sell it to get some divorce lawyer cash,"* she thought to herself, knowing she'd never really do such a thing.

"Are you going to the graduation party at *so and so's?*" Chrissie couldn't hear the name of the family, but knew that neither she nor her son Harrison had been invited.

"No, we're going straight to the airport after this. We gave Truman a gift to Disneyworld for his graduation," replied one mom.

Chrissie picked up her pace, anxious to be connected with Charleigh, Jodi, Ayani and Tara. The four friends beamed at Chrissie as she approached. Chrissie felt the intensity of their warmth and affection from twenty feet away. Each of the women had huge, genuine smiles on their faces, showing their perfectly white teeth. Tara was almost giddy with pent up energy.

"What's up, guys?" Chrissie inquired quizzically. "It looks like you all ate the canary."

"Chrissie, we know you've had one hell of a year," began Jodi in her usual matter of fact tone of speaking. "We wanted to get you something special as a thank you for all your volunteer work here at Archimedes."

Chrissie was intrigued, but already felt guilty that her friends had done something special for her. She was in the habit of doing for others.

"Sweetheart...Guess what? You're going to Jamaica!" interjected Tara, too excited to contain the news. Instantly, Chrissie was filled with conflict, but tried not to show it. *Oh Wow...*a vacation, but did this mean she had to travel with Seth? She'd rather poke her eye out with a fork! Would she have to leave her son at home? She'd rather cut off her arm.

"The best part is that we're going, too!" added Charleigh, giving Chrissie a big hug.

"No, the really *best* part is that the trip is just for us moms and our children," announced Ayani. *Now* Chrissie could really celebrate. She was headed to the islands with her best friends and the most important little person in her life, her son Harrison.

"The only caveat is that we have to wait three weeks until I'm done with my probation sentence at Caring Sisters," said Tara. "But, the minute we get back, I'm signing on for more volunteer work there," she said with enthusiasm. Charleigh, Jodi, and Chrissie stared at Tara, stunned. Ayani didn't flinch.

"I hate to say 'I told you so,' but I'm not surprised," Ayani said. "The foster children at Caring Sisters have a way of capturing your heart." Tara nodded in agreement. Charleigh looked up to see her husband Bud arrive with Ayani's husband Derrick and Jodi's husband Rip who followed closely behind. Tara and Chrissie exchanged knowing looks, both realizing that neither of their husbands would be at the graduation that morning to share this special moment with their children. Tara simply dismissed the thought with a shrug of her shoulders. Chrissie did the same. Oh well, they'd capture the moment with their digital cameras.

Without warning the instrumental tune of Pomp and Circumstances began to blare over the p.a. system, signaling the start of the graduation proceedings. The parents scurried to their seats. Mr. Greenspring and Mrs. Casper appeared to be caught off guard and quickly made their way to the podium. The Kindergarten children had been sequestered in an adjacent building where they had gathered to dress for the event. They had each donned crisp tiny white gowns and white caps with a fringe tassel attached. They looked like innocent little angels as they floated across the whorl and walked carefully up the stairs, lifting their gowns so as not to stumble, and across the stage to receive their 'diplomas.' Mascara began to drip down the cheeks of several of the emotional moms who cried as their babies graduated one by one from the Preschool to the Lower School. Even one of the "botox blondes" with her perpetual frozen look of astonishment shed a silent tear that glided from the corner of her eye. When the last child crossed the stage, the parents burst into simultaneous applause, literally leaping from their seats with joy. Mrs. Casper tried in vain to squelch the outburst, repeatedly making the bunny ears sign over her head, gesturing for silence. She was completely ignored. As the parents were readying to leave, Mr. Greenspring shouted into the microphone.

"We still have to present the awards, please, *please* take your seats," he bellowed. The boisterous crowd obediently obeyed. Anticipation filled the whorl. Who would receive the prestigious Kindergarten awards this year?

"We are so proud of each and every one of our students this year. They truly were an outstanding group of young people," began Mrs. Casper. "It was extremely hard to choose any child above another. But, it is tradition, and so we must proceed," she said somewhat reluctantly, aware of the ramifications when children are excluded from receiving prizes.

"The award for the highest score on the K-Calculus test goes to....Carver Jenkins," announced Mr. Greenspring. Carver bolted from his seat to receive his trophy—a six inch high gold nautilus statue perched on a wooden base. Derrick squeezed Ayani's arm and whispered, "He got that part of his brain from you, dear."

"The award for best fingerpaint artist goes to Agape Waters," Mr. Greenspring announced as he held up a sample of her artwork. The crowd responded with the appropriate "ooohs" and "aahs."

"The award for best penmanship goes to...Clinton Hunter," Mrs. Casper said as she handed the child his trophy. In the absence of her husband, Chrissie reached out to give Tara a tender hug.

"Finally, as you all know, the student who wins the award for best all around Kindergartner receives a full scholarship next year to the Archimedes School," said Mr. Greenspring. A low whistle emanated from the crowd as they acknowledged the sizable scholarship contribution of at least $25,000 for first grade. A hush fell over the assembled parents as Mrs. Casper took the microphone.

"We review each child's performance in the categories of citizenship, analytical ability, overall behavior, language arts proficiency, and artful expression. After careful and tedious consideration, the award for best all around Kindergarten student at the Archimedes school is.... *Harrison Thompson!*" announced Mrs. Casper, grinning from ear to ear. Chrissie, who could hardly contain her elation, jumped to her feet and squealed in delight. Her son Harrison literally skipped to the podium to accept his nautilus statue and tuition check. Jodi, Charleigh, Ayani and Tara simultaneously swarmed around Chrissie and gave her an affectionate group hug. As they hugged her, a familiar face on the bleachers caught Chrissie's eye, then made her breath catch in her throat.

"Nathaniel! Why is he here?" Chrissie wondered. It was rare for any of the Upper School teachers to attend a Kindergarten event. But seeing him so near, she realized how much she longed for him and missed him after so many months of deliberately avoiding any contact. Over the past few months, she had intentionally stayed far away from any Archimedes School building where he might be teaching, parked what seemed like miles from the teacher cars in the parking lot, and circumvented the whorl at lunchtime where teachers often took their breaks. Now, seeing him sitting on the bleachers, she realized her efforts to avoid him were in vain, she knew in her heart that this man was her destiny and only he could fill the empty void in her life. Nathaniel smiled broadly at her and waved slightly in her direction. Chrissie's heart skipped a beat. *"He still wants me,"* she knew. *"Did he just wipe away a tear?"* Chrissie wasn't sure, but he stopped applauding for her son Harrison just momentarily in order to wipe a red bandana (which he always kept in a pocket) over his eyes.

Ayani tracked the object of Chrissie's gaze and whispered in her ear, "It's okay now, your marriage is over. You may follow your heart *if you desire.*"

Life Observations from Vic the Maintenance Guy: "Getting an award or trophy used to really mean something—you know, like winning the baseball championship for the county. Nowadays, kids get a trophy just for showing up with the shoelaces on their cleats tied. Everything has to be so politically correct with no one getting their feelings hurt!"

Chapter Twenty:

New Beginnings

The weekend boat excursion with Ethan could have been a distant memory, at least Tara wanted it to be that way, if it hadn't been for the incessant ringing of her iPhone. Tara had resorted to setting it on 'manner mode' in order to avoid hearing that damn Waltzing Mathilda song one more time. As the weeks progressed, Ethan's messages were becoming more and more desperate. "Tara, where are you? I miss you, what in God's name did I do?" was one of the most recent messages. She realized it was unfair to Ethan to leave him in the dark—after all, she had never officially closed the door on their relationship. Four weeks had passed since that weekend and she still hadn't told him about the consequences of their passionate lovemaking on his boat, or her child being abandoned at the airport, or her subsequent sentencing and probation, nor the fact that her life was almost shattered. Yes, she knew her husband Randy was gay. Who cared? At least that explained why he had avoided touching her for years—and why he was so darned tidy and loved Donna Summer's disco music! She also knew he was now actively involved with one of the Archimedes School dads he had met at the auction. She didn't care. Well, at least he's not sleazing around doing it in bathroom stalls with bellboys, she thought. She and Randy had come to an arrangement where they would maintain their sexless marriage, enjoy their combined wealth, share their child, and remain under the same roof—like 50% of the other 'happily married' couples in the world! No questions asked. Nevertheless, she didn't want to expose herself to *any* possibility of accusations by the courts or other Archimedes School parents of being a 'bad mother' and risk losing her child to the system. That's why she had to terminate her affair with Ethan. On the other hand, Randy could do as he wished—she didn't care if he had hundreds of lovers, as long as he didn't bring them to their home. Tara preferred her new world where khaki capris, conservative sweater sets, and sensible flats defined the essence of her being. It was time to let go of Ethan. On the last vibration of her phone, she finally answered his call. The brief conversation that ensued was one of the saddest moments of Tara's life—she thanked Ethan for making her feel physically alive and desirable once again and that she would never forget him. She was resigned to leading her new life where her priorities were set on responsible motherhood and where her son came first.

"Thank God, darlin', I've been worried sick about you. Where have you been? I've been trying to call for weeks," Ethan blurted out.

"Ethan, I'm so sorry, we've got to talk…Yes, I've been avoiding you…*boy* do we have to talk," Tara said, her voice barely above a whisper. She proceeded to fill in the blanks from the past four weeks and explained the importance of why she had to follow the straight and narrow. Sadly and reluctantly her last words to Ethan were, "Maybe someday, Ethan, but not now....I'll miss you...."

Chrissie stared at her phone for what seemed like an eternity. During yesterday's Kindergarten graduation ceremony she had experienced complete and final clarity about the course of her life. Seeing Nathaniel for that brief moment was all it took for her to realize she had truly found her soul mate. It was time to move on. She and Seth would separate, she would survive on her own—*somehow*, and her son would continue to be the primary focus of her energies and affection. But it was also time for her to grow as a woman, develop a nurturing and supportive relationship with Nathaniel and *thrive*. Conveniently, Ayani's son Carver had been begging for a play date with Harrison and Chrissie decided to take her up on the offer. For the first time ever, Chrissie dropped off Harrison and *left*—typically she preferred to stay and visit with the play date's mother. With hours on her hands, and no errands to run, nothing to do, she continued to gape at the phone. Her decision made, she began to dial his number.

"Nathaniel, may I come over?" asked Chrissie nervously, knowing the consequences of this simple question would be pivotal and life changing.

"Oh Chrissie, I've been waiting what seems like forever for this phone call," was all Nathaniel said. Chrissie locked her front door and got in her car. Her new life was about to begin.

Life Observations from Vic the Maintenance Guy:
"It's funny how life changes. But, then again, what's the alternative? Without change, there isn't life."

Photo courtesy of Laura LaRosa Photography

About the Author

In her former life, Julie Heath wore obligatory conservative business suits and deftly climbed the broadcasting corporate ladder for twenty years. She was the founding partner of a successful national radio consulting firm, where eighty hour work weeks seriously impacted any contact with people beyond broadcasters. She has published two previous books (nothing that would interest anyone outside the radio) and she was a frequent contributor to several industry trade publications.

In her current life, Julie lives in Annapolis with her son and is fulfilling the job of being a private school mom— carefully balancing a life of meaningful simplicity while striving to create the *illusion* of being a "hot mom."

Breinigsville, PA USA
03 September 2009
223473BV00001B/1/P